The Lost Priest

by

Karl Boyd

The contents of this book regarding the accuracy of events, people, and places depicted; permissions to use all previously published materials; and opinions expressed; are the sole responsibility of the author, who assumes all liability for the contents of this book and indemnifies the publisher against any claims stemming from the publication of this book.

International Standard Book Number 13: 978-1-60452-044-6
International Standard Book Number 10: 1-60452-044-2

Library of Congress Control Number: 2010933695

BluewaterPress LLC
52 Tuscan Way Ste 202-309
Saint Augustine Florida 32092-1850
http://www.bluewaterpress.com

This book may be purchased online at -

http://bluewaterpress.com/priest

The Lost Priest

Prologue

For years after this fateful day, Jocquin "Jock" Becker would wonder; *"Was the tragic event that haunts me night and day another mystery connected with the Bermuda Triangle? Or, was fate was working overtime. Could it have been bad luck?"*

Perhaps Jock's overpowering misery and grief was a combination of all three. *("But, as a mere mortal and storyteller, who am I to say?")*

Jock's quest for an answer would trouble his dreams and turn them into nightmares. In grief and desperation, he turned to alcohol to dull his senses for a few restless hours and chase the ghosts of the past away while allowing the liquor to ease his tortured soul.

When Jock was "in his cups", (an act which recurred ever more frequently), he often blamed God for his loss as retribution for some forgotten youthful transgression; (although he couldn't remember one so vile to call for this terrible reprisal). Then Jock would remember God was benevolent, not vengeful – such rancorous behavior was the Devil's business.

So Jock's pent-up anger and booze-muddled mind caused him to curse Satan as the culprit. But when Jock was sober, deep in his heart he knew the true fault was his and his alone. As a result, sorrow and heartache would continue to rule Jock's life for years to come.

Then one day, an angel of mercy came to visit. (*From of all places, the city of Peoria, Illinois - not exactly where I would have looked for assistance, had I been in Jock's shoes*).

Again, I interrupt my narrative to ask: *"Who am I to question God's response to one of His troubled servants?"*

But, perhaps I have already gone too far. Let me begin on that fateful day, to tell Jock's tale - the powerful story of his family, friends and lovers, and how they all intertwined with a lost priest, a lost soul and a lost spirit.

So, join me, my friends, and let's begin. It's a journey you will remember for years to come, just as Jock does each and every day.

Book I

"The Lost Soul"

Chapter 1

There; there it was again. Two miles off the coast of Belem, Brazil, when the great white shark first felt the tiny vibrations on the pores of its skin, the wily predator also heard the same sounds with its highly sensitive ears.

Although its eyes are the shark's greatest asset, (they see well in the dimmest light), the beast's lateral line, (a sensory system of fluid filled canals running down both sides of its body), enables the predator to easily detect these minute electrical fields of smaller fish and larger prey.

Over the past seven years, the beast had grown increasingly aware of such tiny signals as those it now detected. They signaled a prey easily killed and one that provided a filling meal. The shark turned its massive body and swam slowly in the direction from where the vibrations originated.

Always moving, never sleeping, the beast's voracious appetite drove it on, day and night. This year, due to changes in the world's temperature, the great white was early in its rounds off the coast of Brazil.

There; the shark felt the vibrations again. Only this time the hunter was nearer to its prey. It recognized the sensations in the water as the steady paddling of oars, and swam more slowly. Many times in the past, the great white had heard this sound and knew the pattern.

Finally the beast located the source. As it anticipated the final outcome of its hunt, the shark could almost taste the sweet treat above. It increased its speed and opened a huge mouth to reveal row upon row of razor sharp teeth.

Seven years ago, this beast of the deep killed and ate its first man, and thereby discovered human beings were indeed a wonderful source of nourishing food. Since then, this one white shark successfully attacked and devoured an astounding total of thirty-seven victims.

Most of the missing and dead were not counted as having been eaten by a single, lone, giant predator. Each random attack that made the five o'clock news was usually considered a random act of several different rogue sharks.

Most of all, no one connected this particular beast with all the reported deaths. Certainly, no one knew the total victims the shark successfully ambushed and made its meal for the day.

Only twice was the great white seen by a witness – once in Bermuda and again off the coast of Brazil. Both these attacks were so random and far apart no one made a connection. The media called each incident a one in a million occurrence, and they were soon forgotten by the public.

Most of this shark's victims were native fishermen plying their trade off the shores of South America, which was the hunter's usual haunt during the winter months. The weather in this climate is so changeable it is not uncommon for fishermen or other water voyageurs to disappear. If they were able, survivors of the victims searched for their loved ones; but the government didn't go out of its way to assist in a hunt for a tiny canoe on such a great expanse of ocean.

If the shark could somehow compute its conquests, lone fishermen in small boats or canoes would total twenty-three of its victims. The others were spread across a wide expanse of the Atlantic Ocean. In the waters surrounding Bermuda alone, the great white shark took seven people into its stomach.

Now the beast was approaching another canoe with a single occupant. As usual, the stealthy hunter ignored the three lines with small fish attached that hung beneath the narrow boat.

From past experience, the shark knew what was contained within the bait. A number of small to large hooks were imbedded in the gristle of its gums. Although they were no longer painful, the barbs were an irritant.

From deep beneath, the wily predator silently approached the canoe. Then, as it attacked, it swam upward, gained momentum, increased its speed and propelled itself like a projectile. The beast struck the canoe solidly and split the fragile craft in two.

The occupant, a fisherman from Belem, Brazil named Felix Sanchez didn't stand a chance. The force of the attack threw Felix into the air and he landed on his back in the warm, blue water.

Felix struggled to regain his senses and attempted to grab onto a portion of the wreckage, but the shark attacked his legs and pulled him underwater. Felix screamed in pain, but as his mouth filled with water, his terrified cries soon became a gurgle of bubbles.

The shark dragged its victim deeper. The wounds its teeth made caused rivulets of blood to spread in a circle around Felix's body. Soon, a path of crimson led downward into the depths.

Deep underwater, the shark released its hold on Felix. Although Felix's legs were horribly mangled, he made a feeble attempt to swim upward, but his limbs refused to cooperate. His lungs were already partially full of sea water. Before he could reach the surface, Felix knew he would surely drown.

In horror, Felix watched as the shark turned and swam swiftly toward him. With his eyes wide open in silent terror, the last thing

Felix saw was the massive maw of the voracious carnivore. The final sensation Felix felt was a horrible, crushing blow as the powerful razor edges of the shark's teeth cut his body in half.

Above the shark and its thirty-eighth victim, the two broken halves of the hollowed-out log canoe continued to float and bob silently on light waves. Several small metal fishing lures that once belonged to the dead fisherman slipped from the seat of the ruined craft. As they slowly twisted and turned on their last voyage to the bottom of the ocean, these artificial baits reflected the sunlight and sparkled brightly.

The two halves of Felix's body rotated in bloody circles and seemed to dance in the slow-moving current. These small crimson patches expanded until they became one large red spot that marked the shark's latest killing field.

Felix's dead eyes stared into the sunlight, but they reflected nothing.

In a feeding frenzy, the shark tore at each portion of the body, ripped large chunks from what was once Felix and swallowed them whole.

Other creatures of the deep joined the feast and fed on what small pieces of Felix the shark left floating in the water. As the beast added them to its menu, several latecomers paid the supreme price.

Soon, its hunger dissipated and the silent hunter of the deep slowed its feeding and ate almost delicately of what remained. When it was finished with its meal, in a never ending quest for food, the great white shark swam slowly onward.

Chapter 2

In Hamilton, Bermuda, the day that would haunt Jock's dreams for years to come began peacefully. There was no forewarning of danger lurking in the near future.

Jock and his new bride, Lori, (short for Lorelei), were enjoying the tenth day of their honeymoon in the Bermudian Isles. So far, this amazing adventure was everything the local Chamber of Commerce claimed it would be in several brochures that were lying scattered atop the bedroom dresser.

This tropical climate was decidedly different from their native land of Germany, where twenty-four-year-old Jock was the son of a wealthy industrialist. Two years younger, Lori was the daughter of a rich landowner and homebuilder. A year ago, the young couple met while skiing in the Swiss Alps. From that moment on, their life together resembled a fairytale come true.

Just four inches shorter than her husband, Lori was a slim, buxom, statuesque blonde. Her turquoise Nordic eyes reminded Jock of the color of the lakes on both sides of Interlaken, Switzerland. Lori exercised daily to keep her curvaceous body toned and as a result, she often drew lusty glances of envy from the male population.

Six feet two inches tall, with long blond locks, Jock was a large, heavily-muscled man. His black eyes sparkled when he was happy, but turned steely when riled. One look at Lori's companion told any would-be suitors to mind their step and seek love elsewhere.

After a six month courtship and another six spent living together, Jock and Lori were married in a small chapel in Bavaria. Jock's father, Dieter gave them this fantastic trip as a wedding gift.

The day after their marriage vows were exchanged, Jock and Lori flew to Bermuda.

For the first week, Jock and Lori traveled to all the main tourist venues and were fascinated by each new strange and exciting adventure. But, alas, Bermuda is only twenty-one square miles of islands. After seven days, there was little new remaining for them to explore. Either they must find something to fill their time, or, other than their nights, the next week would be boring.

Then just three days ago while they were eating lunch, Jock and Lori overheard other visitors touting the fabulous diving trips they had taken to visit sunken ships on the coral reefs that surround the islands.

Lori's interest was piqued, and although she and Jock had never tried the sport before, Lori said, "I want to go scuba diving. Come on, Jock, let's do it."

Jock was never one to deny his wife anything she desired, and as he felt the thrill of a new adventure, he replied, "Why not? It should be fun."

That afternoon, Jock inquired about a guide on the nearby docks. Eventually he hired a reputable boat captain named Leroy Jones, who provided them with the latest and best equipment.

After two days of instructions in proper diving procedures, Leroy felt Jock and Lori were ready to go out and try diving on their own.

This morning, as the sun broke over the far-off horizon, its rays chased away the night and illuminated the Beckers' luxurious suite on the sixth floor of the Palms hotel.

Jock awoke slowly, rolled on his side and reached out for his wife, but Lori wasn't in their bed. Puzzled, he turned on his elbow and gazed around the room.

Lori stood on the threshold between their room and the small balcony outside the French doors, watching the glorious sunrise. The sunlight filtered through her flimsy nightgown and made it appear almost transparent.

Firm, unfettered breasts strained against the thin material. As Lori turned to catch Jock's eyes with hers, he could see the faint darkness of her golden point of passion.

"Ah, my caveman awakens," Lori said. "Today is the day we go diving. Will we find any gold or jewels?"

"I've found all the treasure I want in you," Jock said and motioned for her to rejoin him in their bed.

When Lori returned to his arms, Jock held her close and asked, "What time is it?"

"Nearly seven a.m. We must get up. Leroy expects us at nine sharp."

After she kissed him deeply, Lori jumped out of bed, leaned back down and kissed him again, this time lightly on the lips. "Aren't you excited? I am. Come on, sleepy head. You can shave while I shower."

Lori's joy was infectious. Jock couldn't help but smile at her antics. "I wish you awakened me an hour ago," he said and winked.

"You're a wicked old man, but I love you."

When Jock went to her and tried to pick her up to carry her back to their bed, Lori pushed him away firmly, but with a smile. "No, Jock, we don't have time. Wait until tonight and I'll make it up to you."

"Promises, promises," Jock said and reluctantly let her go.

After a hurried breakfast, Jock and Lori walked briskly down the quay until they found Leroy's forty-two foot boat, "The Tern". As they approached, Leroy waved hello from the rail. The weather-beaten

Tern wasn't much to look at, but Leroy and several other captains Jock asked had guaranteed the seaworthiness of the vessel.

Over the noise of several gulls calling out for scraps of bread from a nearby boat owner, Lori shouted, "Hi, Leroy."

"Are you ready to find some treasure?" he asked.

"Let's get with it," she said and waved Jock ahead.

For this unique experience in their lives, Leroy selected an old wreck of a square-rigged sailing vessel. Lying in less than seventy-five feet of water, the ship sank in a storm so long ago the date was no longer remembered. Over the years, the wreckage was explored many times, but no treasure was ever recovered.

Most skippers of the many boats serving the tourist trade forgot about this old relic. Leroy wasn't about to tell his customers there were more recent discoveries and other interesting wrecks nearby. He lied convincingly. "This is a great place to try your luck."

Small in stature, Leroy possessed a body that was slowly turning to fat from inactivity. As he and his customers motored to their destination, Leroy attempted to keep his attention on steering the boat and not on his beautiful female passenger. He didn't want to upset Jock.

After they arrived at the site and a few last minute instructions, Leroy tied a small wire basket to the anchor line, let it slip beneath the water, slide down the anchor rope and settle on the sandy bottom.

Then he told Jock and Lori the same fairy tale he laid on most of his customers. "Who knows? You might discover pirate treasure or gold bars down below. If you do, use the basket and we'll haul it up after your dive."

Although there were a few very rare instances where someone found an overlooked gold coin or other valuable relic that had been uncovered by the varying currents, Leroy knew those events were not common. *"Still, a little white lie never hurt anyone."*

He also knew the unrealistic notion of their finding anything valuable gave his customers a good feeling and put them in the mood to enjoy their diving experience. *"I'd say anything to earn a bigger tip."*

Leroy could use the money. He and his live-in girlfriend, a stewardess named Sherry Lee enjoyed smoking pot and the price of their pleasure had gone up recently.

After helping Jock and Lori strap individual air tanks on their backs, Leroy made a final check of the equipment and escorted them to the side of his boat. "Remember you have only sixty minutes of air. Pay strict attention to your diving watches and stay down no longer than thirty minutes. Then use the anchor rope to make your way to the surface. Enjoy your dive."

Jock and Lori smiled through their masks and climbed down the ladder into the water. Then with a splash, they disappeared beneath small waves.

Leroy walked to the depth finder, where he watched the explorers' images in black and white as they made their way to the end of the anchor line and then swam over to the wreck.

Everything appeared normal. Bubbles from their air tanks rose slowly to the surface, where they broke and the oxygen dispersed while making a slight gurgling sound.

Leroy busied himself with other tasks, but still took time periodically to check the progress of the divers. He watched them enter the hold of the ship through an opening in the side of the wreck.

From previous dives of his own, Leroy knew there were only scraps of old, rusted and barnacled machines remaining in the hold. After all these years there couldn't be anything of value.

Jock and Lori were inside the hold approximately fifteen minutes. Their time on the bottom was quickly expiring. After checking his watch again, Leroy knew that within another ten minutes they should begin their ascent. Then he saw them finally emerge from the hold.

Jock was walking crab style and appeared to be carrying

something.   When they reached the anchor rope, Jock placed whatever he had in the basket. Then he pointed to the rope and with a few hand signals, indicated Lori should start swimming upward.

Then to Leroy's amazement, Jock turned and swam back into the hold.

"What is he doing?"

As Jock entered the wreck again, Leroy noticed a large shadow appear on his depth finder. Whatever it was, it was huge – at least twenty feet long.

Hand over hand, Lori continued to slowly ascend. Suddenly, as if something startled her, she moved her head to look over her shoulder. Then the huge image rocketed toward her.

Instantly, Leroy recognized the shape and size of the silhouette. He shouted to the heavens, "It's a great white shark."

As the monster raced toward Lori, Leroy stared in disbelief and watched in horror. Moving faster than Leroy thought possible, the shark reached Lori's position. With ease of practice, the beast caught her legs in its open mouth and dragged Lori from the rope as if she was a gnat on a spider's web.

When a large, dark spot filled the screen, Leroy knew it was Lori's blood staining the water. The scene was horrible, but he couldn't do a thing to help her. In a blood-curdling instant, the shark and Lori were gone.

Leroy turned his attention to Jock, who was just emerging from the hold. Again, the diver appeared to be carrying a heavy load.

After placing another object in the basket, and since he had no idea of the danger, Jock began to follow the anchor rope to the surface.

Although Leroy knew it was a terrible thought, he prayed the shark would be eating its fill of Lori and allow Jock to return to the boat safely. He staggered to the rail and watched as Jock's shadow and the bubbles from his air tank drew closer to the surface.

When Jock surfaced, he glanced up at Leroy.

Leroy was going into shock. Although Jock didn't notice, fear was reflected in Leroy's eyes.

As if in slow motion, Jock climbed the ladder with a smile on his face. After he glanced around the boat and didn't see Lori, his happiness was replaced with a frown.

Jock's face was tight with anger as he asked, "Where's Lori?"

Still in shock, Leroy couldn't answer.

Jock shouted, "What happened to her?"

When Leroy didn't respond, Jock slapped him across the face. The shock of the blow brought Leroy to his senses.

Jock asked again, "My God, what happened?"

Leroy's eyes welled up with tears. "I was watching on the depth finder and saw your wife on the rope. I was surprised when you went back to the ship. Then it happened."

Terror filled Jock's voice as he asked, "What? Tell me."

"A great white shark attacked her. One minute everything was fine and the next moment it swam into the picture. I doubt Lori saw it. The shark grabbed her and carried her off. It's a wonder the beast didn't get you on the way up."

Jock cursed and grabbed his long blond hair with both hands as if he wanted to tear it out by the roots. "If I stayed with Lori, maybe we both would have made it back."

Leroy shook his head. "You wouldn't have stood a chance. If you were together, the shark would have eaten you too"

Grasping at straws in a hurricane, Jock asked, "Are you sure Lori didn't get away? Maybe it wasn't as bad as you thought."

Leroy continued to shake his head in disbelief and horror. "I've never seen anything like it. The shark wouldn't let her go, and she couldn't have withstood its attack. There was blood in the water."

They remained in place for another hour while Leroy attempted to calm Jock down. Jock continued to curse himself for Lori's disappearance. Finally he collapsed on deck and lay there sobbing for his lost love.

As Leroy prepared to leave, he turned his attention to the anchor rope. When he began to haul in the wire basket, he discovered it was extremely heavy and difficult to bring to the surface. The container broke water and sunlight glinted from two golden bars. Leroy couldn't believe his eyes. *"Is it really gold?"*

He grabbed a bar, looked closely and noted it bore an imprint of a Spanish name. Then he asked, "Is this what you found, Jock? Is that why you went back to the wreck?"

Jock looked at the treasure in disgust and cried out, "Yes it is."

"What should I do with them?"

Jock hid his eyes from the treasure. "I don't want them. If you're brave enough to challenge the shark, there's even more on board the ship. Either take them or throw the bars back into the sea. If I hadn't wasted time getting the treasure, Lori would have been on board before the shark arrived."

"Not me," Leroy exclaimed. "I wouldn't dive on the wreck now – not for all the gold in the world."

Leroy threw out a marker buoy to indicate where Lori disappeared and said, "It's getting dark. We have to leave. I've marked the spot. Now we have to report the disappearance of your wife to the authorities and let them know a great white shark is on the prowl."

When they returned to the dock, Leroy notified the police of the accident. An Inspector named David Smythe took Leroy and Jock's statements.

For a few days, the newspapers and local television stations followed the story, but pressure from the local Chamber of Commerce soon put a stop to any further publicity. The shark attack was written off as a one in a million occurrence and quickly forgotten.

While Inspector Smythe was interviewing the two survivors, Leroy waited for Jock to mention the gold. When Jock said nothing of the treasure, Leroy breathed a sigh of relief.

In his grief, Jock fell into a bottle and never came up for air. Slowly, over the next two years, he became the town drunk and laughing stock of the entire island. Now, in his liquor induced stupor, if Jock remembered the gold, Leroy would be surprised.

After waiting until the uproar over the shark attack died away, Leroy brought the bars home. When he showed them to Sherry, she was enthralled.

Although he now possessed the gold, Leroy was unsure of how to cash in on his discovery. Since the government of Bermuda claims ownership of any treasure salvaged within a fifteen mile radius of the islands, Leroy knew if he turned the bars into the authorities, he would receive only a small finder's fee. Compared to what the gold was worth on the open market, the reward would be peanuts.

In an attempt to solve his problem, Sherry suggested she should smuggle the bars into New York on her next flight. "The flight crews sail through customs. Usually all the crewmembers take home are the rations of booze we buy duty free in Bermuda. The inspectors are used to our coming and going and take little notice. I can waltz past them with the gold in my bag.

"There are a number of people in New York City who will buy the gold and never ask questions about the source. There's no other way to cash in on your luck."

Leroy decided to give Sherry's plan a try. After wrapping one of the bars in a heavy sweater and placing it in the bottom of Sherry's bag, he purchased a ticket on her next scheduled flight.

Everything went as slick as grease on a railroad track. As she did so many times in the past, Sherry rolled her small carry-on case through Customs with a smile and a wave of her hand. While he checked out her well-endowed body, the guard on duty returned Sherry's smile and passed her through.

They spent the next week in New York City at Sherry's small apartment in the Bronx. Sherry knew some people, who knew a reliable but shady individual. Finally they made connections with a "fence" who handled stolen or otherwise "hot" merchandise.

Since Leroy had previously checked the weight of the bars, he knew each weighed just over fifteen pounds. With sixteen ounces to the pound, each bar contained at least two hundred and forty ounces. At the going rate of five hundred dollars plus per ounce, each bar was worth in the neighborhood of one hundred and twenty thousand dollars.

That was a very nice neighborhood for Leroy and Sherry.

But they both knew, *"Because the fence needs to make a profit, we can't expect to get top dollar."*

When Leroy was offered three hundred dollars an ounce, he decided to sell. Seventy-two thousand wasn't a bad neighborhood either, especially when you didn't have to pay taxes on the cash received. Sherry smuggled the money into Bermuda the same way she took their precious cargo to New York City.

Two months later, they repeated the trip and received an equal reward. With over one hundred and forty thousand dollars hidden in a closet, Leroy and Sherry felt they were rich.

Although they attempted to watch what they spent carefully, Leroy and Sherry were into pot, which soon led to cocaine. Before they knew where the money went – it was gone. Leroy wasn't too surprised. *"With Sherry, I'm amazed the cash lasted two years."*

Now desperate for funds to support their habit, when Leroy mentioned the possibility of more gold bars to be found on the old wreck, Sherry was anxious to acquire them.

Leroy attempted to put her off, but Sherry was not to be denied. Her craving for a greater "high" made her ignore the supposed danger and drove her onward.

So today, against his will, Leroy would see that Sherry got her way. The sun shone brightly overhead, while a light breeze created ripples on the azure blue water of Hamilton Bay.

Aboard his boat, Leroy stood at the weathered rail, rubbing the two-day-old stubble on his chin and watching a fat brown pelican dive for bait fish nearby.

An aroma of food was lingering on a freshening southwest breeze, which told Leroy someone was grilling breakfast on one of the high-priced yachts anchored nearby.

Wearing a tiny yellow bikini, that exposed most of her dark flesh to the bright sun overhead, Sherry was standing next to Leroy. As usual, she was complaining. Her black eyes glowed with greed while she harped on her favorite subject – a way to get more gold to buy drugs.

Since he knew Sherry was strung out and badly in need of a hit of coke, Leroy attempted to ignore her. But she wouldn't be denied. Her shrill voice broke through his musing. "Well, great captain of the sea, are we going or not?"

Leroy hated Sherry's overbearing attitude and smart mouth, but he said, "I don't know, Sherry, you weren't there last time. You don't know how bad it was."

The thought of diving where the shark attacked Lori two years ago still frightened him. Sherry thought Leroy was too cautious. Her shrill voice cut like a dull knife. "There hasn't been another case of a shark attack in two years. Your fears are groundless. I thought I was living with a man, not a coward."

Still afraid, but resigned to his fate, Leroy said, "Okay, Sherry. I give up – we'll go. Help me load the supplies and I'll take you to the wreck."

On the way, Leroy was worried. *"I hope no one else got to the gold first."*

During the past two years, he spread the word the area was jinxed. So far, there had been no rumors of anyone finding any gold bars. *"Of course, if they did, I wouldn't have known. I'm not the only one in these islands who can keep a secret."*

As they approached the site of the wreck, Leroy watched the

sun break out of a few low hanging clouds and bathe the sea with a golden glow. He crossed himself and silently prayed, *"Let it be an omen of good luck."*

Leroy viewed the site with trepidation. After two years, the picture of the shark grabbing Lori and dragging her off to eat was still fresh in his mind. While he buckled on his weight belt, Leroy's hands shook.

Sherry finished strapping an air tank onto her back over her skimpy bikini and spat into her mask to clear the faceplate. Then she said, "Let's get with it."

Leroy dropped the anchor into the sea and tugged on the line to make sure it was securely fastened to the sandy bottom. They would be diving together and leaving no one aboard. He didn't want the boat to drift away. *"If you didn't have a boat when you surfaced, what good would all the gold in the world do?"*

In a rush, Sherry said, "Let's go; there's gold waiting."

Through lips that had suddenly gone dry, Leroy replied, "Okay, Babe."

His hands were still shaking, but Sherry didn't notice. She was too caught up in the excitement of the moment.

This time, Leroy lowered a new and stronger wire basket fastened to a thick steel cable. It was capable of lifting a great amount of weight. Since he didn't know how many bars of gold remained in the wreck, his greed knew no boundaries.

As they made their way slowly to the anchor rope, the sky was clear and sunny. They could see for miles.

They swam down the anchor rope and then over to the wreck, where Leroy led the way into the hold. Immediately he spotted a broken box and several gold bars lying on the deck. One bar glinted in the defused sunlight, while the others were still wrapped in oilskin.

He gave an involuntary gasp.

Behind her mask, Sherry smiled greedily and gave Leroy the

thumbs up sign. They each lifted a bar, only to find the gold was heavier than they had expected.

Leroy had hoped to carry at least two while Sherry hauled one. Now he knew they would be lucky to handle one apiece. *"I hope Sherry is strong enough to handle a bar alone."*

If she weren't, Sherry suddenly found strength from the greed deep in her heart. So, with Leroy leading the way, they began the trek to the anchor rope.

Leroy checked his diving watch and noted only fifteen minutes of their time underwater had elapsed. *"If we hurry, we might be able to salvage all the gold in one dive."*

The excitement of their find, combined with his fear, filled Leroy's body with adrenalin. He raced on ahead while motioning to Sherry to move to the basket as quickly as possible.

Leroy reached the container first and attempted to place the gold in the basket. But in his haste, the bar slipped from his hands and fell to the ocean floor. While uttering a silent curse, he reached down to retrieve his treasure. At the same time, he glanced at Sherry to see how she was doing.

To his amazement, she was standing stock still thirty feet from the basket with a look of fear in her eyes. She was staring in horror at something over Leroy's left shoulder.

Shivers of fear ran up his spine as Leroy turned slowly to see the same dark shadow from two years ago. Instantly he recognized the shape for what it was. *"I can't believe it; the shark is back."*

Leroy panicked and displayed his true nature. He completely ignored Sherry's perilous situation. If he could, it was time to save his own skin. He dropped the gold bar into the water and never saw it sink out of sight into the sand. As he attempted to release his weight belt, for a moment his shaking hands betrayed him, but finally he succeeded in loosening the buckle. The heavy metal weights fell to the ocean floor.

Then, for a split second, Leroy thought he should remove his air tank, but he knew there wasn't enough time. *"I won't need air to rise seventy-five feet in a hurry, but the tank might provide some protection from the shark."*

He grabbed the anchor rope and swam upward, watching in silent horror as the great white shark attacked Sherry, who appeared to be anchored to the ocean floor. She dropped her gold bar and stood as still as death, staring at her attacker. Her arms were outstretched as if she could fend off the beast with her bare hands.

The shark attacked swiftly, bit into her body and then shook its head. While Sherry thrashed around with her arms and legs flailing, her blood filled the water. Suddenly, her air tank exploded in a surge of bubbles.

As Leroy continued to climb and swim upward, for a moment, he actually believed he would escape. But it was not to be.

Since the great white knew its prey was dead and it could return to its meal at leisure, the shark abandoned Sherry's lifeless form. The beast shook her body from its mouth and left her remains adrift in a pool of crimson. Then it turned its attention to the other fleeing "fish", and the predator rocketed upward.

From the start, the contest was unfair. Leroy attempted to outrace the shark to his boat, but he didn't stand a chance. The beast grabbed Leroy's legs, pulled him deeper underwater and shook his body as a dog would worry a favorite chew toy.

The water around Leroy turned blood red. He was alive, but just barely. Seawater filled his lungs and death was only a ragged breath away. Suddenly the beast released its hold on Leroy's legs and swam off a short distance before it circled around and attacked once again.

Then, the great white made a final run and sank its ivory teeth into the upper torso of its latest victim. The last thing Leroy saw was the open mouth of the great white shark. With a snap no one heard, Leroy's head was severed from his body.

The dive to hell was over.

Two days later, a passing fisherman, Sidney Perkins noted the anchored boat and called out, "Hello, the Tern."

When he received no answer, Sidney pulled his craft alongside the other boat only to discover no one aboard. He thought perhaps the occupants were diving on the wreck below, so he waited an hour for them to surface.

But when his depth finder displayed no action near the wreck, Sidney was puzzled. He left the empty boat in place and returned to Hamilton Harbor to report the abandoned craft to the authorities.

The Coast Guard dispatched a rescue ship. But they discovered no survivors or bodies, so they towed the boat to the harbor. A close inspection by the port authorities revealed no clues as to the whereabouts of the occupants.

Eventually, the disappearance was another mystery that reached the desk of Inspector David Smythe.

A small article in the local newspaper told of the missing entrepreneur, Leroy Jones and his lovely girlfriend, stewardess Sherry Lee. No bodies were ever found, and to this day their disappearance remains a mystery.

Three years later, while reviewing other mysterious disappearances, only Inspector Smythe took note of the fact two of his seven missing person reports occurred in close proximity to each other. Nevertheless, David was still mystified by the connection.

After writing a yearly report to his supervisor stating there were no new leads, David stacked the files neatly in his desk drawer. Then he closed it tightly and leaned back to light his pipe.

"Someday, somehow, I hope I can solve all the cases."

Chapter 3

Near Santa Maria, Brazil

Two hours after sunset, deep in the uncharted jungle of Brazil, in a clearing near a branch of the mighty Amazon River, a forty-two-year-old priest, Father Tom Fitch, sat searching his soul at a smoky campfire outside the primitive thatched hut in which he was imprisoned.

While asking for forgiveness from the Big Guy up above, Tom looked deep into his heart and knew he had screwed up royally. As a result of his own stupidity, Tom's life was on the line. In a nearly defeated mood, he raised his hands toward heaven and called upon his maker. "I'm sorry if my actions have offended You, Lord. Let Thy will be done."

As Tom prayed, darkness descended slowly but surely around the village. The night seemed to cover the jungle like chocolate on a hot fudge sundae. With daylight gone, the spooky sounds from the thicket surrounding the village did not diminish.

To the contrary, the noise increased in volume, and the animals making those blood-curdling calls appeared to be moving closer. In a contradiction of terms, and to use an old cliché, Tom thought, *"It's enough to scare the Devil out of me."*

The silent pun made Tom smile through his misery, but so far, that was the one bright spot of his entire day. He heard a mosquito buzz in his ear and made a half-hearted attempt to swat the pest away, but he knew his effort was in vain. In a few seconds, it or another of its blood-sucking family would return with a host of others and begin to feast.

Slowly, Tom inspected his body to find insect bites covering most of his face, arms and legs. He shook his head at the sight of his tortured torso and limbs, and knew the bloodsuckers must have drained away at least a pint of life-giving fluid. Hoping that his actions might keep the bugs away long enough for him to fall asleep and be oblivious to their attack, Tom shuffled closer to the fire. Then he tucked his legs under his mud-splattered, used-to-be-white, Chasuble.

The smell of rotting vegetation and the scent produced by the villagers defecating wherever they pleased was overpowering. A strong odor of urine invaded Tom's nostrils. He wrinkled his nose in distaste, ran his fingers through his long blond hair, felt sand on his scalp and grimaced. With his arm upraised, he caught a whiff from his armpit and was disgusted by his body odor.

A swirling rogue wind blew around Tom's head, causing smoke from the fire to blow into his blue eyes until they watered. Tears of shame ran down his cheeks to cut thin trails and wash away some of the dust and dirt from his sturdy, handsome face.

The only halfway clean water available for washing was collected from a small stream a few meters away. Since he owned no soap, Tom knew he was a mess. *"If my mother could see me now, what would she think?"*

When Tom arrived at the village, he was accompanied by his guide, Miguel, and two paddlers, Felipe and Pedro. For the first three days after the "incident", his captor, the medicine man of the tribe, Narro, kept Tom and his three companions tied to the center pole of the communal hut with leather thongs.

Finally realizing there was nowhere for his captives to go, Narro allowed them the freedom of the village. Their surroundings consisted of twelve small primitive huts spaced out unevenly around a large circular, open-sided, thatch covered communal tribal hall setting in the center of the clearing.

Several thin, hard-packed trails led off into the jungle to who knew where. Tom watched as the fast-growing vegetation threatened to overtake those narrow aisles. With the wide variety of flesh-eating animals in the undergrowth, Tom knew if he attempted to escape overland he would be taking his life in his own hands.

The only other area open to the sky was where the village set on the edge of the muddy, fast-moving Amazon River.

Miguel said, "If we attempt to get away by water, we'll need a boat."

Their canoe and a few water craft possessed by the villagers were stacked to one side of the clearing. The captives knew during daylight hours it would be impossible to steal a boat without being detected. It was even more foolhardy to attempt the same thing after dark.

"We wouldn't stand a chance at night," Miguel said. "If we hit a log, we'd drown."

After the sun went down, the villagers kept to their huts, either conversing in quiet tones or retiring for the night. Early the next morning, they arose again to continue their fight for existence against the overpowering jungle surrounding them.

Before it grew too dark to see, Tom managed to gather a pile of small twigs and limbs for firewood. The flickering glow from his fire didn't reveal more than a few miserable feet of mud-packed earth around him.

Although the ragged, dirty huts of the villagers and his chief inquisitor were within a stone's throw, Tom felt as if he was the only living soul on earth.

Thoughts of remorse ran through his head and the fear of imminent death filled Tom's heart with dread. *"If only I had listened to Father Mendez and did as he asked, none of this would have happened. God help me, I can't even remember the verse where He says pride goes before a big fall. If they find my body after Narro gets done with me, I guess they can put that on my tombstone."*

As if reading Tom's mind, Narro walked up silently and threw a wooden plate filled with monkey stew on the ground near Tom's feet. Startled, Tom attempted unsuccessfully to stop the soupy mixture from slopping onto his vestment. Gravy with the texture of three-day-old grease oozed off the edge and dribbled onto his black Alb.

Narro was short and thin, but muscular. He possessed a face that resembled an ape-like creature. Tom thought Narro looked like King Kong in his heyday, when the big ape was a real swinger in New York City. Numerous scars dotted Narro's body – possibly scabbed over bites from some unknown insect.

Twigs were tied in Narro's long stringy hair and a necklace of bones hung around his neck. The only other item Narro wore was a short thong made from the skin of some animal that was held up by a thin leather strap. White circles were painted around his eyes and jagged streaks of yellow ran down his legs from thigh to ankle.

Narro smiled wickedly while displaying a mouth full of teeth filed to points. Then he continued to jabber away in his native tongue.

Although Tom didn't understand a word Narro said, the tone of Narro's high-pitched voice and implied threats still got through to Tom. *"If only Miguel were here, he could translate."*

Unexpectedly, three days ago, Narro allowed Miguel and the other two Spaniards to leave in their dugout canoe. Now, Tom could only imagine what Narro was saying, but the chill of fear filled his heart until it felt like a cold hard stone was locked in ice in the middle of his chest.

When things looked dismal and Tom questioned his calling; the one small ray of hope in the darkness of Tom's present situation was Miguel.

Tom prayed the bond he and Miguel had formed over the past month while visiting native tribes would help. He trusted his guide and new friend would want to save him. Just how, Tom didn't know, but the thought was something to hold on to and pray for.

A shooting star blazed across the heavens, drawing Tom's attention to the sky. He wished with all his heart it was a sign from God to say He understood and was watching.

Narro noticed his captive glance upward, did the same, also saw the comet and took the sight as a sign from his own Idol.

With his right hand, he removed a razor-sharp machete from his ragged belt and swung it in a vicious circle above his head. Then, while gesturing with his left as if he was about to slit someone's throat, Narro pointed the deadly weapon at the three-quarter moon high in the dark sky overhead, and then again at Tom's neck.

Narro's uglier-than-sin face turned into an evil, open-mouthed leer. The dying flames from the campfire reflected from his teeth and his evil black eyes made him appear to be an apparition from the bowels of hell.

Tom needed no interpreter. He knew in seven more days, when the moon was full, he would be sacrificed to the God of Narro. Soon, Tom would be deader than the monkey whose leg dangled from the slop on his dinner plate.

Chapter 4

Above the Amazon River near Prainha, Brazil

As a sleek white helicopter trimmed with green stripes flitted back and forth across the wide expanse of the mighty but murky Amazon River, it resembled a dragon fly searching for food.

Out of a clear, azure-blue sky, the hot sun blazed down on the occupants as if it was attempting to fry their brains. Almost unbearable heat beat unmercifully against the clear Plexiglas windscreen.

Huge black trees wrapped with green vines towered on both riverbanks. They seemed to form a tunnel for passage of the aircraft. The tangled foliage was as dark and forbidding as a childhood nightmare. Sunlight glinted off wide, slick leaves and several small streams meandering through the undergrowth to join the fast-flowing river.

For a few fleeting moments, the sun's rays reflected off the mist of the morning dew and formed miniature multi-colored rainbows in the air. Then in a heartbeat, these apparitions disappeared so swiftly viewers were left to wonder if they were truly mirages or figments of their imagination.

Even at this height, the smell of rotting jungle growth and dead fish penetrated the interior of the helo.

As the pilot flew the craft close to the trees, huge flocks of frightened multicolored birds rose majestically from the limbs on which they rested. Climbing into the sky, they beat their wide wings against the hot morning air. Then, when the helo passed by, they settled once again onto the tree tops like falling snow.

Inside the aircraft were two men. The passenger, Tim Fitch was a building contractor from Fort Worth, Texas. The pilot, Jose Hernandez had retired recently from the Brazilian Army as a Major, and within a month of retirement he began his charter ferry service.

A handsome forty-two-year-old man, Tim wore his brown hair cut close to his scalp. His rugged face was clean shaven and tanned dark brown from exposure to the sun. He wore a pair of faded tan shorts and a white T-shirt stained dark with perspiration.

Although Tim and Jose wore headsets and a microphone was dangling in front of their mouths, there wasn't much idle conversation. Silently, their individual thoughts unspoken, they searched both riverbanks for a sign of Tim's twin brother, Tom.

Down there somewhere, Tom, a missionary for the Catholic Church was either alive or dead. Since Tim didn't consider the second choice valid, (call it intuition or brotherly love), somehow, he knew Tom was alive.

Tim looked away from the shoreline for a moment and glanced at Jose. When examining Jose closely, Tim could see a faint resemblance to Mohammed Ali when the fighter was a younger man.

Jose's eyes were black. His dark-skinned face was handsome in a rugged way and proudly displayed several scars from previous battles.

Of course, Jose was a few pounds heavier than Ali at any point in the fighter's career. Today he wore his usual, casual flying outfit – ragged Levi cutoff jeans and a hideous, flowered Hawaiian shirt. A well-rounded stomach protruded ponderously above Jose's tightly cinched belt, which made the buttons on his shirt strain to retain his bulk.

As he held the aircraft in a steady, slow-moving hover exactly fifty feet above the river, Jose's large, callused hands were relaxed. Without thinking, he made necessary, repeated and minute adjustments to the controls.

Tim's thoughts returned to Tom and his troubles.

Six weeks ago, Tom began a journey in a dugout canoe on a mission of faith. He left the small river town of Prainha behind while attempting to bring Christianity to the native tribes deep in the jungles of Brazil. The last time Tom checked in by radio was four weeks ago. Nothing was heard from him since. Now Tom was more than a month overdue.

Squinting against the glare, Tim swore silently and strained to remain focused on his search. Although he wore dark sunglasses, they didn't do much good against the brilliant reflection of the sun glinting off the Amazon below. The light added the pain of an eye ache to a brutal headache Tim had endured for the past fifteen minutes.

The hot temperature didn't seem to affect Jose. He sat stoically beside Tim, carefully, but silently scanning the muddy riverbanks and impenetrable foliage lining the shore.

Tim's memories flashed across the ocean and his mind pictured his parent's home in the beautiful tropical paradise of Bermuda. *"It's early October and the temperatures there are comfortable, with a low of sixty-five degrees and a high of seventy-five. I can see myself asleep with the windows open, listening to the rolling surf crash on the rocky coral and white sand beach below."*

As Jose swung the helo closer to the bank, the glare from the sun struck Tim's glasses and brought his thoughts back to the present.

Sweat from his head and the back of his neck trickled slowly down his spine. During the flight, the perspiration had turned his T-shirt and shorts into damp rags, which were now wringing wet with sweat. Even his leather sandals were sweat-stained.

Tim shook his head to clear the cobwebs in his mind and thought,

"The sun and heat have made me lightheaded. Get your act together, Tim. Don't screw up and miss something."

As Jose turned the helo up a wide tributary, he said, "Here's a new stream we haven't checked."

While continuing to scan the shore for any sign of life, they followed the meager flow of water upstream. The thickly packed undergrowth was seemingly unbroken and unending.

The fuel capacity of this small helicopter seriously limited the range of their search. They had been flying for an hour and a half. In another hour they would be forced to return to Prainha to refuel.

Tim's mind wandered and he forgot about the microphone dangling in front of his mouth as he whispered aloud, "Where are you, Tom?"

The metallic voice of Jose crackled and echoed in Tim's earphones. "What?"

Reaching up, Tim attempted to steady the microphone that was bouncing in front of his face. The instrument was keeping time with the slight vibrations of the helicopter.

"I'm sorry, Jose. I was daydreaming again and thinking about my brother."

"I understand. Keep your hopes up. Today may be the day we find him."

"I hope so."

The monetary charge for this search was costing Tim's parents a small fortune. At four hundred and fifty dollars an hour rental on this helicopter, the price tag for Tom's foolishness was adding up quickly. *"In the end, when we find Tom, it'll be a bargain."*

In Tim's mind, there was no doubt about the final outcome, but as the days continued to end with no good news, he tended to pray a lot.

Breaking into Tim's thoughts, Jose said, "There's a village ahead."

After slowing the aircraft to a hover, Jose moved the helo closer to the riverbank.

Tim removed his sunglasses and placed a powerful pair of binoculars to his eyes to conduct a complete search of the small village.

As Tim scanned the pitiful thatched huts, he noted the ragged, dirty cloth coverings of the doorways were rolled to let in what little air was stirring. Jose swung the helicopter to face the village, while Tim looked into the interior of each hut. But he saw nothing but dark skinned natives.

Naked as the day they were born, three young dark-skinned boys came running from the river. The noise from the helicopter and its sudden appearance in the sky must have frightened them.

Pointing excitedly at the aircraft, the youngsters called to several adults, who ran from the huts. It appeared they were seeing a whirlybird for the first time. One native found his courage. He waved and smiled at the two aviators.

Tim said, "I doubt they see many helicopters."

"This is probably their first," Jose replied. "They seem surprised."

Although Jose already knew the answer, he asked, "Did you see anyone resembling Tom?"

Disappointed again, Tim replied, "No, he's not here and there's no boat similar to his. Let's move on."

Jose turned the aircraft to the right, allowed the helo to drop slightly and then flared it up over the middle of the small stream. Without thinking, he brought it into a hover at exactly fifty feet.

As they flew on, Tim glanced over his shoulder and watched the three boys run along the beach to follow the helicopter as far as they could.

He replaced his dark sunglasses on his nose, slid the binoculars into a leather carrying case, stared at the jungle and silently repeated, *"Where are you, Tom?"*

The sun continued to dull Tim's senses and his thoughts turned to better days of the past.

Born forty-two years ago, he and Tom were twins. Amazingly, other than a resemblance in their facial features, most people didn't realize the two brothers were paternal twins.

Tim was tall and rangy, large boned and heavily muscled. He weighed in at two hundred fifteen pounds and loved to eat, so he worked out regularly, watched his diet and struggled to maintain his weight.

Although as tall as his brother, Tom was slight of build and never weighed more than one hundred and sixty pounds. Tom could eat a cow a day and never gain a pound.

Early in his life, Tom set his goals high when he decided to become a priest.

Tim chose to follow in his father's footsteps and made medicine his field of expertise.

Their parents, George and Pearl, allowed the boys to choose their own vocations and supported each in their individual desires.

The boys spent long hours studying and eventually prevailed in their ambitions. As a result, Tom and Tim earned scholarships to two Texas colleges.

While attending the University of Texas (UT) in Austin, Tim met a girl named Cheryl and shortly thereafter, they married.

Soon, Cheryl became pregnant, but before the baby was a year old, Tim was drafted and sent to Viet Nam.

Tom completed his dream and spent four years studying for the ministry at Texas Christian University, (TCU), in Fort Worth. He graduated a few days before Tim and was also drafted. A few months later he went to Viet Nam as a Chaplin.

When they completed their tours of duty, both returned home to Bermuda.

Tim served as a helicopter pilot and faced death every day. Although wounded in action three times, he returned to Bermuda with his body, spirit and mind intact.

After viewing the inhumanity of war, Tom's faith was severely tested. He came back from overseas in a state of depression.

Tim completed his residency and became a general practitioner for several years. Then impulsively, he chucked it all to follow another dream of becoming a successful contractor. He knew his change of vocation didn't make sense to his friends and family, but Tim had finally found his niche in life and was extremely happy.

On the other hand, while attempting to find his true calling, Tom struggled through depression and guilt. He spent several years in various ministries, where bad luck seemed to dog his every move. Although suffering a series of setbacks that would have made most men throw up their hands in despair; Tom's determination to succeed kept his hopes alive.

When he received a chance to become a missionary in Brazil, Tom made up his mind to go to South America to save souls.

As he came to the end of his reminiscing, Tim shook his head and thought, *"Although we all attempted to talk him out of accepting the challenge, Tom came down here. Now look where it got him – lost and nowhere to be found."*

Jose's voice broke into Tim's reverie, making him aware his mind was drifting from the chore at hand. "It's time to head back to home base, boss. I'll check another tributary on our way. Keep a sharp lookout."

Tim put his daydreams behind and returned to the business at hand. He continued to search the length and breadth of the new stream they followed to their home base in Prainha.

Along the way, they found several small, isolated clusters of huts or villages they hadn't visited before. Where landing space was available they stopped and conducted a careful search of each. At others too small, Jose held the helo in a controlled hover while Tim searched with his binoculars. None of the villages revealed a thing to determine Tom's whereabouts.

On previous flights, they discovered Tom's group had visited two villages, Juruti and Faro several weeks ago. After Tom and his companions left the villages, no one knew where they were headed next.

The search was becoming discouraging. Tim knew he couldn't continue to spend money indefinitely on a fruitless air search. Tom departed Prainha via canoe, and, if by the end of the week Tim hadn't found his brother by searching with the helo; he would be forced to use the same type of conveyance.

When they arrived in Prainha, Jose flared the helo over the landing strip for a moment; then he brought the aircraft to a controlled hover a few feet above the ground.

When Tim glanced through the windscreen, he saw the local priest, Father Mendez waiting next to the landing pad.

Small and thin, the priest wore his usual long, flowing black Chasuble over a mud-splattered, white Alb. His feet were bare and covered with dirt. A tiny hat perched atop his head resembled the "pill box" style made famous by Jackie Kennedy.

Tim asked, "How can he wear those heavy clothes in this heat?"

Via the intercom, Jose replied, "I don't know. As thin as the Father is, maybe I should start wearing similar clothes. I might lose this spare tire."

Tim chuckled and said, "There's no way, Jose. You love your tamales too much."

After setting the helicopter down smoothly on the pad, Jose threw a switch to cut the flow of fuel to the engine. As the sound of the motor slowly died, Tim removed his headset and hung it on a hook behind his seat.

Then he unfastened his seat belt, climbed down from the copter and attempted to stand upright. The blades kept spinning slowly, so he leaned over unnecessarily until he was several feet away. His headache was still beating the anvil chorus behind his skull and his shoulders were stiff as boards. Tim stomped his feet to regain circulation while glancing at his seat in the copter. A small puddle of sweat was rolling back and forth and keeping time with the swaying motion of the helicopter blades.

Tim thought, *"God, it's even hotter here on the ground."*

Father Mendez waited patiently on the side of the landing pad until Tim finally got all the kinks out. Then he asked, "No luck again today?"

Although Tim didn't mean to be so abrupt with the priest, he replied with a terse, "No."

Tim wasn't truly upset with the priest, but the fact remained, he placed part of the blame for Tom's disappearance on Father Mendez' back. *"If the padre hadn't filled Tom's head with this nonsense of bringing Christianity to the native tribes of Brazil, perhaps Tom wouldn't have traveled to South America on his own."*

Although both Tim and his father, George were against Tom's decision to move to Brazil to fulfill his goal in life, there was no way to talk Tom out of going.

George cautioned, "I'm not sure the natives will take too kindly to a white priest who is attempting to change the way of life they've known for as long as they can remember. From what I've read, the natives are very superstitious. Make one wrong move, Tom, and you might wind up dead."

Still with his head in the clouds, Tom said, "Don't worry about me, Dad. The Lord will look after me."

Tom was as bullheaded as they come. George knew when his son's mind was made up; there was no way to change it. But before he gave up, George offered some advice of his own. "If you're going and I can't stop you, at least be careful. Listen to your elders down there. I'm sure they have more experience in the jungle than you."

Father Mendez took no offense at Tim's one-word response to his question. He knew how Tim felt toward him for encouraging his brother. While he waited for Tim to unwind, the priest remembered the fateful day when he allowed Tom leave on his own.

"I blame myself for allowing someone so inexperienced to go into the jungle alone. I should have insisted Tom wait until a seasoned priest arrived to accompany him."

Since they possessed a small two-way radio, for the first three weeks, Tom stayed in contact off and on. When he failed to report within the next two weeks, Father Mendez figured Tom's radio had probably given up the ghost, so he waited another seven days. When Tom still didn't return, the priest notified the boy's father, George Fitch in Bermuda. George called Tim in turn, and here Tim was, searching for his brother.

Silently Father Mendez admonished himself. *"I should have stopped Tom somehow. If anything happens to such a fine, young man, I'll never forgive myself."*

Finally, Tim asked, "Is there anything new?"

The priest nodded. "I may have some good news. I don't know how reliable it is. You know how it is – one man sees something, he tells another, who in turn, tells another etcetera."

Tim hoped some of his prayers might have been answered, so he said, "I hope its good news. The Lord knows I could use some."

Father Mendez smiled and said, "There's been a report of a 'white church man' up river near Santa Maria. Supposedly this man found himself in trouble with a medicine man of a primitive tribe nearby. That's all Sister Kate could tell me in her radio report."

Still lightheaded, when Tim heard the name "Kate", he thought, *"Kate? Did he say Kate? I've been so wrapped up in this search I haven't taken time to think of her or Cheryl either."*

Both women lived in Austin, Texas. Kate was his sixteen-year-old daughter. Cheryl was her mother and Tim's ex-wife.

Tim's subconscious heard Father Mendez' report concerning the possible sighting of his brother, but his mind was suddenly filled with memories of Cheryl and Kate, which drowned out the priest's words.

With his mind drifting back in time, Tim thought, *"I can't believe Kate is sixteen years old. I wonder how she is."*

When they were both in their senior year at UT, Tim met Cheryl in Austin at a "mixer". He had seen her around the campus and thought they might have shared a couple classes.

After noticing she was drinking Shiner beer, Tim bought a bottle from the bartender, carried it to her table and said, "Hi there. You look like you could use another beer. Is this seat taken, or are you waiting for someone?"

As she pushed a chair out from under the table with her booted foot, Cheryl said, "Thanks; sit down and take a load off. I'm here by myself – a couple sorority sisters talked me into coming. Haven't I seen you in class?"

"I thought I knew you from somewhere," Tim replied. "Last year, we took Biology together."

Cheryl frowned. "Ugh, I hate to cut up frogs and bugs."

"I didn't enjoy it either. What are you studying to be, a doctor or a nurse?"

There seemed to be a hidden message when she replied, "I hope to receive an all-around education." She clasped his hand in hers and held on a moment longer than necessary as she said, "My name is Cheryl."

While they listened to the band play an old country favorite, Tim studied her for a few moments. He noted Cheryl's light brown hair was stylish and attractively cut. When she laughed, her grey eyes sparkled.

Cheryl wore a two-piece western outfit with a short top, and Tim could see her navel. When she leaned across the table for a pretzel, he noticed a tattoo of a rose on her lower back.

"To top it all off, she's shapely and well endowed."

He stood up and asked, "Would you like to dance?"

"Yeah, I would. It appears my sisters have abandoned me for greener pastures. Come on; let's dance. I love this song."

She slipped easily into his arms and moved closer. Tim could feel the pressure of her warm breasts against his chest.

Cheryl was light on her feet, a good dancer and felt good in his arms. When she ran her finger around the tip of his ear as they danced, Tim had never felt anything as erotic.

"A penny for your thoughts," she said.

"I was thinking how pretty you are."

She leaned back in his arms and smiled up at him. "Flattery will get you everywhere."

A few more drinks and an evening of pleasant conversation later, Tim decided Cheryl was the girl of his dreams. Later in life, he wasn't sure if the feeling was a result of the booze or simply infatuation.

The evening ended with a few passionate kisses at her door, where Cheryl invited him in. "Can you come up for a nightcap?"

For the first time in his life, Tim passed up a sure thing. "Can I take a rain check? I drank too much and feel a little drunk. One more and I'll fall down."

Although she didn't mean it, Cheryl said, "I understand, but I'm disappointed. Call me."

She wrote her phone number on the inside of a match book cover and pushed the pack into his shirt pocket. Then she kissed him again, opened the door to her dorm and walked inside.

The next morning, when Tim awoke with a hangover and took time to think about the events of the previous evening, he was as surprised as Cheryl. He realized he could have ended up in her bed on their first date and felt stupid. Tim was amazed he hadn't taken the initiative.

But love was in his heart and on his mind. He wrote the previous evening off to his being a gentleman while he naively believed Cheryl wasn't "that kind of woman".

Later, Tim called and made a date for the following evening. He took her to a fancy restaurant on Sixth Street – the "In" place to eat in Austin.

While they dined, they consumed a bottle of wine and afterward in a local bar, several mixed drinks. The next morning, when he awoke naked in Cheryl's bed, Tim wasn't too surprised to find her sleeping nude and lying on his numb arm.

He sat up slowly on the edge of the bed and watched Cheryl's well-endowed chest rise and fall with her steady breathing. He glanced at her face. She winked and then moved to Tim's side, slid her hands up his back, gently massaged his neck and said, "Last night was wonderful."

She beckoned him to return to the bed, where they spent the rest of the day talking and making love. Without having to be told, Cheryl knew Tim was hooked.

This began their life together. Cheryl loved to party, was fun to be with and enjoyed sex. At this point in Tim's life, three of his major requirements in a woman were met. Naively, he continued to believe Cheryl was the woman for him.

Two months before graduation, when Tim walked into their apartment one afternoon after class, Cheryl hit him with the news. "I'm pregnant."

Tim was surprised and asked, "Are you sure?"

"Yes; do you want me to keep the baby or get rid of it?"

Tim's face grew stern. "Don't talk such nonsense. There's no way you'll abort our baby. I can't believe you would think of something so stupid."

Cheryl realized she had pushed him too far. "I'm sorry, Honey. You know I'd do anything for you. I want to keep the baby too, but I wasn't sure you would want to marry me."

Tim's tone of voice told her he was more than a little upset. "I'm not the kind of guy who screws around and leaves a pregnant girl with a baby."

Trying to pour oil on troubled waters, Cheryl said, "I know, Honey, but I don't want anyone to think I trapped you into marrying me. You know I love you."

Tim wasn't absolutely sure of his decision, but wanting to be a man, he said, "Sure, Babe. We'll get married right away. You'll be a wonderful mother and I'll do my best to be a great father."

They didn't have much time to explore their marriage bonds. Three days after walking across the stage at his commencement and being handed his diploma, Tim also received his draft notice.

As American citizens, Tim and Tom were required to register. Although he was married with a pregnant wife, Tim wasn't exempt from duty to his country.

After taking a complete physical and receiving his immunizations, Tim was sworn into the U.S. Army as a Second Lieutenant.

Upon completion of his aptitude tests, a Staff Sergeant named Morgan said, "Lucky you, Lieutenant Fitch. The test results determined you have a natural ability to learn to fly. You're on your way to Fort Rucker in Alabama for helicopter training."

Waiting for Tim's return in Texas, Cheryl was three months pregnant and growing bigger every day. When she learned Tim was about to become a pilot, she was upset. "What am I supposed to do while you run around with your buddies and learn to fly? You got me pregnant. Now you're leaving me alone to have your child."

Tim attempted to calm her down. "There's not a thing I can do about the situation, Babe. I'm in the Army now, and they call the shots. I'll send you all the money I can afford. You have friends here and you'll be so busy with the baby, it won't seem long. Time will fly by."

Cheryl continued to stew. "Big deal - while I'm in this apartment getting fatter each day, you'll be with your Army buddies, having a wonderful time."

"I wouldn't call my time in Georgia 'wonderful'. I probably won't have any off duty time. They need pilots in Viet Nam."

Cheryl cried out, "What am I supposed to do for a year while you're overseas playing soldier?"

"I won't be playing. I'll be lucky if I don't get blown away. Have you thought of that possibility?"

"Yeah, I have," Cheryl snarled. "It would be great to be a widow at twenty-five with a squalling brat. Who would want me then?"

They went to bed angry. In the morning, when Tim attempted to make love, Cheryl pushed him away. A week later when he left for flight training, Cheryl was still fuming.

But when Tim received Cheryl's first letter, he thought she had changed her mind. She signed her letter with love and kisses, and said she was sorry about the fight.

They agreed on the name of Kate for a girl and Robert for a boy. Although Tim wanted a son, he would be happy with whichever the good Lord provided.

While Tim was in the final phases of flight training, Kate was born. Cheryl wanted him to come home, but it was impossible to get leave. As a result, it was only after graduating from flight school that Tim finally met his new daughter.

His first thoughts were, *"God; she's like a little doll."*

He whispered in her ear, "I love you, Kate. Daddy will be gone for a while, but I promise to come home and make up for all the times I miss."

When they didn't go out dancing or partying every night, Cheryl griped and complained. "You've been with the kid all day. Why can't we go dancing tonight? What about me? I spent eight months practically locked in this lousy apartment."

"Good Lord, Cheryl, I have only ten days of leave. When I return from Viet Nam, we can go dancing. Let me spend as much time at home as I can with you and the baby."

As she ran into the bedroom and slammed the door, Cheryl cried out, "Go to hell."

During the next few days, things went from bad to worse. Tim knew his marriage was falling to pieces. Cheryl wouldn't allow him access to her bedroom and they hardly spoke.

Then, all too soon, Tim's furlough was over. As he left their apartment in a taxi bound for the airport and then on to Viet

Nam, Tim shed tears for himself, his daughter and his wife. He knew his marriage was over, but the thought of failing was a difficult pill to swallow.

After Tim left for Viet Nam, Cheryl sat down to take stock of her situation. Tim was her meal ticket to the future. Now with her complaining, she was afraid she had screwed up all of her well-made plans.

Although Tim wasn't aware, Cheryl had worked and schemed to get his attention. Finally she screwed him into marrying her, (literally and figuratively). Now he was running off to play war.

When Cheryl's parents were killed in an automobile accident shortly after she graduated from high school, they left her thirty-five thousand dollars from an insurance policy. She decided to take her mother's advice and get a good education.

College was the first stop on Cheryl's agenda. Her grade point average was sufficiently high to insure her admittance to the college of her choice. Now as a bonus, she possessed the money to ease her way.

In the fall semester, she enrolled at the University of Texas. There she spent her first year learning the playing field and setting goals for a husband. In order to maintain her residency in a student's dormitory, Cheryl took the minimum number of classes required. She partied hearty whenever possible and learned a lot about men.

During her second year, Cheryl reduced the amount of her social life and studied harder, (mostly the men around her). A few times, she thought she had struck pay dirt and carried on several short affairs, but soon found them all to be duds.

Cheryl learned to enjoy sex, but always did it on her terms. Upon completing her sophomore year, she was no closer to catching her rich husband. With her money in the bank now half of what she began with, Cheryl knew she must work harder.

At a dance during her junior year, she spotted tall and handsome

Tim Fitch. When she asked one of his friends about him, the guy told her Tim came from a wealthy family in Bermuda. Tim was studying to be a doctor, the profession of both his parents.

Tim was currently involved with another girl, but Cheryl thought, *"This is the man for me."*

Setting her sights high, Cheryl schemed her way into his sight and finally met Tim. They dated; Cheryl let him in her pants and then trapped him into marriage.

But that was then. This is now.

As she came to the end of her reminiscing, Cheryl thought, *"Tim is just like any other man. They're all no good. Well, to hell with him. I'm not about to sit here 'pining away'. I'm going to have fun, but he'll never know. I'll keep Tim on the string until he comes home. Then I'll tell him to go fly a kite."*

Cheryl didn't have Tim's address yet, but she sat down and wrote him a long, loving letter, telling him how sorry she was she treated him so bad. She continued to write every day about Kate, plus what she and the baby did. She also took pictures of their daughter and enclosed them in her letters.

"When I get Tim's address, I'll mail all my letters.

In the first response from Tim, Cheryl discovered he listed her as his beneficiary of a fifteen thousand dollar life insurance policy.

"Now there's something to look forward to. If Tim gets killed, at least I'll receive some money plus whatever benefits I might have coming as the 'grieving widow of a brave helicopter pilot who lost his life in Viet Nam'."

After dispatching all her pre-written letters immediately, Cheryl continued to write daily. Then she took a chance and asked Tim for money for Kate's needs.

She laughed when he sent all he could afford. *"God, for a college graduate, Tim is so stupid!*

"Things have worked out well. Maybe my original plans didn't pan out, but I'm smart. I can adjust to changes. Now, it's time to party."

Chapter 5

Father Mendez asked, "Tim, did you hear what I said?"

The priest's words finally broke through Tim's musings. "No, Padre, I'm sorry, I didn't. Lately I've been doing some serious thinking about my family. When I do, I tend to block out everything else."

"I understand," the priest said.

"I apologize again, Father. Would you repeat what you said?"

The priest nodded. "Sister Kate is checking for more information. Later today, if she finds anything new she'll contact us. When I asked her about Tom's interpreter, Miguel and his native helpers, she didn't have any news. Let's pray she learns something to help us locate Tom."

"I'll leave the prayers to you, Padre, but I will do some serious hoping. This isn't much to go on, is it?"

"No, Tim, it isn't. But it's the first time we heard any mention of a white church man. So please, have faith."

Tim attempted to sound contrite. "Okay, Padre, if you say so. You must excuse me. I'm worn out from sitting too long, day after day and staring at the jungle. I know you're as concerned about Tom as I."

"Thank you, my son. Tonight I'll say a prayer for you both."

As Tim made his way across the cluttered ramp and into the patched-up shack Jose used as his headquarters, he continued to stretch his legs and arms. He knew he was tired, out-of-sorts and may have sounded sarcastic, but he hoped he hadn't upset the priest. *"All I need is another black mark on my big, bulging scrapbook in the sky."*

Jose's two helicopters were setting on a ramp nearby. Both looked like a pair of vultures silently waiting for road kill. One was the small bird they used every day. It seemed like a mosquito beside a large cargo helo that was capable of hauling ten men or a heavy load.

The second aircraft was entirely black. Jose had painted two white eyeballs with black pupils at the bottom of the windscreen in front, one on each side.

Tim thought, *"It looks like a big, bad bird"*

Jose greeted Tim with a wave of his hand. "Come in, boss."

After he told Jose of the report from Sister Kate and her promise, Tim said, "You might want to lay out a flight plan to Obidos tomorrow, Jose. We haven't searched the area, so the news is encouraging."

"I'll be refueled and ready to fly at first light, boss. I hope you receive some good news from Sister Kate. She's quite a woman."

"Okay, Jose. I'll be here at 0600 hours. As for Sister Kate, I've never met her."

Jose smiled knowingly. "You'll like her. When we get to Obidos, I'll land and introduce you. She really isn't a Nun, you know. The padre gave her the nickname and it stuck."

"This place gets more interesting every day. Now we have a Sister who isn't a nun. What's next?"

"I'll see you bright and early tomorrow," Jose said. "It looks like clear skies here in Prainha, but I can't promise a thing about the weather in Obidos."

While making his way back to his small room at the Remington Hotel, Tim tried to avoid stepping into any of the mud and water-filled holes in the dirt road the locals called Main Street. The first day here, he tripped, fell into one and ruined a nice pair of Dockers.

After he successfully navigated the treacherous passage from Jose's shack to the front porch of his hotel, Tim saw he had accumulated an inch of mud on his boots.

Tim knew if he dragged any dirt inside, he might catch the devil from the proprietress, Miss Lela, so he used the foot scraper to clean his feet. Then he scuffed his boots thoroughly across the surface of a deep, rough-woven mat that was lying in front of the door.

Everyone in Obidos knew "Miss Lela". She was a crusty, very opinionated lady of eighty-eight years, who owned a sharp tongue and supposedly angered easily.

Soon after he met Lela, Tim discovered his landlady's bark was worse than her bite. Once you got to know her, Lela was a sweetheart. She was also a great cook. Her once brown hair was now nearly snow white. When she laughed, her grey eyes still sparkled with energy.

Every evening when Tim returned from his search, he made it a habit to eat supper with her. His first night at her table, Tim asked, "How did you come to be in such an out of the way place?"

Lela smiled at the recollection. "Jesse, my late husband and I came down here from Louisiana so long ago I forget the year. He worked in the oil fields and I used the money we saved to open a small café. We did all right until Jesse went and got himself killed about fifteen years ago.

"He was working on a rig when it blew up. I don't think Jesse knew what hit him. They didn't find much to bury."

Tim reached out and took her hand. "I'm sorry; Jesse sounds like quite a guy."

"Yes, he was. I loved him and he loved me. That's all you really need in this world."

Tim asked, "Why did you stay here?"

"I couldn't leave Jesse down here all alone. He's buried in the churchyard down the street. At least I can be close by. I don't have too many more years left and I couldn't see going back to Louisiana."

He nodded and said, "You're probably right."

"I know I am," Lela said. "Jesse carried life insurance and the oil company gave me a nice settlement, so I had this hotel and restaurant built. It keeps me busy and I make enough money to provide what little I need."

Tonight, Lela was behind the counter waiting for Tim. She wore a light blue dress, which highlighted her hair and eyes. "I heard the good news. I hope it's your brother."

"So do I. Early tomorrow, Jose and I will fly up to Obidos. But tonight I'm hungry. What's for supper?"

"I made spaghetti and meatballs. Go upstairs and get cleaned up."

Tim took a long, lukewarm shower and then turned the handle to cold, but it barely made a difference in the water temperature. Then he enjoyed two mixed drinks to unwind. *"I think I earned them today."*

When he returned to the lobby, Tim found Lela had changed into a very pretty chartreuse dress.

He said, "You look lovely, sweetheart."

"Thank you, Tim. Sit down and eat. Then you can go see Father Mendez."

After supper, Tim made his way down Main Street and approached the church. A cool breeze was blowing out of the north and it had lowered the temperature a few degrees, but the evening was still very warm. An aroma of fresh baked bread in the air made Tim's mouth water.

With the exception of a few flickering candles someone lit while they prayed, the chapel was empty. As Tim approached the priest's living quarters, for a moment he was startled by a woman's voice. "I'm signing off for tonight, Father. Good luck to your young man."

Then Tim realized he was listening to Sister Kate on her two-way radio. He smiled at his mistake and knocked on the door.

When Father Mendez saw who his visitor was, he said, "Ah, Tim, come in. I was about to send for you."

"I decided to take a stroll to see if you heard anything more from Sister Kate. Was it she I heard on your radio?"

"Yes, it was. The good news is Miguel and his two men have returned."

Ever the pessimist, Tim asked, "And the bad?"

"I'm afraid your brother wasn't with them. From Sister Kate's report, Tom has been detained by a medicine man in a village about thirty miles upriver from Urucara."

Angrily, Tim asked, "Detained? Is that a nice way to say Tom's a prisoner somewhere?"

The priest shook his head, "I'm not sure. When you land in Obidos tomorrow, Sister Kate will fill you in on the details."

His momentary angst gone, Tim said, "At least we know Tom's alive. After all this time it's good news."

The padre put his hands together as if in prayer. "Three days ago, when Miguel and his men were allowed to leave the village, Tom was alive. I pray whatever problem he experienced isn't serious. You've heard how superstitious these natives are. If Tom broke one of their taboos, he could be in real trouble."

"How serious is 'real trouble' Padre? You're beginning to frighten me."

"I don't mean to, Tim, but it could be a matter of Tom's life and death. After they inadvertently offended a native ritual, people have been killed or simply disappeared."

Tim wasn't happy. "Do you have any other good news to share?"

"Only the old adage; 'no news is good news'. I'm sorry I can't be more upbeat, but you did say you wanted to know how bad Tom's situation could be."

"Yeah, Padre, you're right again. I'm sorry. I didn't mean to get on your case. I'm a little shook up, thinking my brother could end up being killed by the same people he came all this way to save. Please don't take my comments personally."

"I don't, my son. I know how devoted you are to your brother. Tonight I'll say a prayer for his deliverance."

"Thanks, Padre. It won't hurt to have the Man Upstairs on our side. While you are at it, say a prayer for continued good weather. I have to fly to Obidos, and I don't want any rain tomorrow."

"The weather is always in the hands of our Savior, but I'll ask Him to provide fair weather for a few days."

Tim retraced his steps back to the hotel, where Lela was waiting, and gave her the good/bad news scenario.

"I'll keep my fingers crossed your brother is alive and well," she said. "It's a good sign they allowed Miguel and the others to leave the village. If they meant to kill Tom, the natives wouldn't have released any witnesses. They would be afraid his companions might tell what they knew. Think positive.

"Now drink this wine I poured and try to get some sleep tonight. Tomorrow may be a long day."

Chapter 6

Narro's village, deep in the jungles of Brazil

Across a hard-packed clearing, a young girl of twenty named Tila was watching the white man Narro held captive. Tila was the sister of Saire, one of the women who lost their sons to a mysterious illness.

As Saire grieved for her lost child, she kept repeating, "The white devil will pay for Nali's death."

Tila asked, "Are you sure the white church man is to blame for Nali dying?"

"Our medicine man says it is so," Saire said. "Why do you question Narro?"

"Perhaps Narro was embarrassed by the white man's magic box. Several of us were given pictures. If the box killed Nali, why haven't we all perished?"

"I don't know," Saire said. "Why don't you ask the chief?"

"I may."

Tila left Saire and made her way slowly across the community circle, where she approached Tom warily.

Tom noticed her interest, but kept his head down as he read his Bible.

Still a little frightened, Tila sat down gingerly across the dead fireplace from Tom. When Tom raised his head, she looked into his eyes.

"The stranger has nice eyes, soft and caring. Those aren't the eyes, and his is not the face of a murderer. Narro is wrong."

Tila stood up slowly without speaking to Tom and walked to her hut, where Saire was cooking a large fish on a slab of rock. The aroma wafted around Tila's head. Tila turned and saw the white man glance her way and lick his lips.

"Give me some fish," she said. "The white man is tired of monkey stew."

Saire asked, "Why should I feed the murderer of my son?"

"I looked into the stranger's eyes. He's not the type to kill. He can have my share of the fish."

"You're crazy," Saire said. But she used a thin board to cut a portion of the fish, placed the food on a large, flat green leaf and said, "Take the fish to him if you must."

"Thank you, Saire."

Carrying the food carefully, Tila approached Tom slowly and laid her offering at his feet. Then she made a motion with her fingers toward her mouth and said, "Eat."

Tom picked a large piece of fish from the leaf and placed it in his mouth. "Thank you."

A respite from his steady diet of monkey stew, the fish was delicious. He nodded and said, "The food is very good."

Tila didn't understand him any more than Tom did her, but they both smiled.

He handed her a piece of fish. "Here, join me."

She took the fish and ate it while savoring the herbs Saire used as seasoning.

Suddenly from behind, Narro bellowed, "Who said you could feed my prisoner? Get away from him!"

"You don't frighten me, Narro," Tila said. "This man could no more murder children than I."

"Leave before you try my patience," Narro commanded. "Go, or I'll cast a spell on your family and you'll all die."

"I'll leave, but feed this man more than monkey stew. You wouldn't treat a dog this way."

"A mongrel deserves more," Narro said.

Narro stared after Tila as she walked slowly away. *"She's a troublemaker – not what I need right now."*

Turning back to his prisoner, Narro saw Tom quickly gobble down the remainder of the fish.

Narro sneered and said, "Eat well. In a few days you'll feel my power. Nothing can save you now."

Although he didn't understand a word Narro said, Tom smiled to let his tormentor know he wasn't afraid.

Chapter 7

As Tim attempted to sleep, he was jittery at the thought of the wonderful possibility he might find his brother. Finally he dropped off to sleep, where his dreams were filled with thoughts of Viet Nam, Cheryl and Kate. When the alarm clock rang at five a.m., he awoke with a start.

The damp, tangled sheets made Tim realize he spent most of the night dreaming of his wartime experiences. After all these years, it was strange how clear those memories could be. But there was no time to reflect on them this morning.

He shaved quickly, pulled on a clean pair of shorts and light weight t-shirt for the trip upriver and laced his boots tight. He didn't know how long he might have to remain in Obidos, so he packed three changes of clothes and an extra pair of sandals in a backpack.

As the night slipped away with the morning sun, Tim saw Jose's weather forecast was accurate. The sky was mostly clear, with a few scattered and broken clouds. Small patches of ground fog hovered near the shoreline and moved with the wind. The mist appeared to be wispy ghosts chasing each other through the dark trees.

Drops of water from the morning dew fell from the eaves of the hotel and splattered noisily onto a muddy street below. Steam rose from the tops of trees as the sun attempted to dry the dampness from a tangle of vines that struggled to encompass the town.

Miss Lela's senses must include keen hearing. As Tim walked down the stairs and into the kitchen area, she was seated at the kitchen counter and waiting to pour him a cup of coffee. The aroma of freshly baked pastries wafted from a platter of doughnuts on the table.

"You're spoiling me, Mom," Tim said.

In tune with Tim's jovial mood, Lela replied, "Sit down, Son. I'll scramble a few eggs and fry some bacon for breakfast."

Tim started to object, but Lela was adamant. "Don't tell me there isn't time to eat. Jose will wait. This may be a long day. You'll need your strength for whatever you find in Obidos."

Tim raised his hands in surrender. "Okay, Mom, you're the boss."

He was sopping up the remains of a few small pieces of egg with his toast, when without knocking, Father Mendez walked into the kitchen.

"Sister Kate radioed," he said. "There is nothing new from Obidos, Tim. I stopped by to wish you good luck and God speed."

"Thank you, Padre. I have to get to the airport."

As he walked by Lela's chair, Tim paused and kissed her cheek. She smiled and reached up to touch his face. "Be careful, Tim."

Tim kept his upbeat mood intact and navigated Main Street with no problem. He arrived at the ramp in front of Jose's shack/office to find him seated in the pilot's seat of his helo with a map spread across his generous lap.

Tim asked, "How's it going, Jose?"

"I feel good. Today we find Mister Tom."

"I hope you're right," Tim said. "I'm ready when you are. Go ahead and fire up the bird."

After scaring a flock of black and white gulls from the landing pad in Obidos, Jose set his helo down safely on a clear patch of ground near the outskirts of town. Then he locked the helo to prevent theft and said, "We'll walk into town to find Sister Kate."

Above him, the raucous birds cried out their displeasure at being disturbed. As they continued to cry out, Jose looked up, gave them the finger and laughed.

The dirt road that led to town was pitted with mud holes almost as bad as the ones in Prainha. Tim followed Jose to a schoolhouse located near a bank of the Amazon River. He noted there was a playground behind the building with a high fence between it and the river. There was the usual assortment of swings, teeter-totters and a small sliding board - all of which appeared to be rusted and worn.

When they got closer to the school, they heard the "singsong" voices of small children reciting the English alphabet.

Jose said, "School's in session, so Sister Kate will be in the classroom. She won't mind if we interrupt their day. I know she wants to meet you."

"If you say so," Tim said. "I have no desire to start off on the wrong foot with the old gal."

Jose laughed at Tim's comment, opened the door and ushered Tim in ahead. Then Tim discovered why Jose was so amused.

The "old gal" was a very pretty young woman approximately thirty-five years old. Her light brown hair was cut short and she wore a lightweight, yellow dress with a series of small embroidered flowers surrounding the neckline. A pair of old, semi-white tennis shoes were on her feet.

As she smiled first at Jose and then at Tim, Sister Kate's green eyes sparkled. Tim felt his heart flutter and was surprised. Since Cheryl, no woman had affected him in this way.

She said, "I heard your helicopter arrive and thought you might be here about now." Then she turned to a group of children gathered in a circle on the floor and said, "Thanks to Jose and his friend, you'll be dismissed early today. Mary and Cloe, please make sure the younger ones get home safely. I'll see you all again early tomorrow morning."

Sister Kate waited patiently before she spoke again. When the last child marched obediently out the door, she extended her hand to Tim and said, "You must be Mister Fitch. Father Mendez told me of your search for your brother."

Her hand was warm to the touch. "Please call me Tim, Sister."

She laughed. "I will, if you'll call me either plain Kate or Catherine. Father Mendez calls me Sister Kate, but I'm not a nun. I'm a schoolteacher."

Tim allowed his eyes to roam over her body and thought, *"She's anything but plain."*

He returned her smile and said, "I'll call you Catherine. I have a daughter named Kate, so two women with the same name might be too confusing."

Her smile disappeared. "Oh, you're married?"

"Divorced," Tim said, and her smile returned.

Then he asked, "Has there been any news of my brother?"

"No, I'm sorry to say. Miguel will be here shortly and tell you everything he knows. He will have heard your helicopter arrive. Let's adjourn to my house and we'll wait for him."

Catherine's home was an old, but well-maintained one bedroom structure built of wood and adjacent to the brick schoolhouse. The living room featured a couch against one wall, plus three comfortable recliners and a small coffee table. Off to the right was a well-stocked kitchen with modern appliances, plus a breakfast area with a table and six chairs.

Catherine led them inside and motioned for them to take seats around the table. Then she asked, "Would you like a cup of coffee? I can make some in a few minutes."

Tim and Jose both accepted her offering. They watched as she scooped coffee into an automatic coffeemaker, added the correct amount of water and then flipped on a switch to activate the heating element. Within a few minutes, the tantalizing aroma of fresh coffee filled the kitchen/dining area.

Five minutes later, as she was pouring them a cup, Miguel arrived at the door. Although small in stature, he was darkly tanned and the muscles of his arms and upper body were well defined. He wore a faded, blue shirt tucked into a pair of brown shorts, and appeared nervous to meet the brother of a man he left behind.

While he shook Miguel's hand, Tim attempted to ease his discomfort. "Hello, Miguel, I'm pleased to meet you. Don't worry – I don't blame you for my brother's problems. Tell us what happened."

Miguel choked back a lump in his throat, smiled for the first time and said, "Mister Tom wanted to stop at every village and talk to the villagers, so it took a long time to travel.

"We paddled up and down several streams to meet new tribes, and Mister Tom attempted to convert everyone. I think they admired the trinkets he gave as gifts more than his words. The natives will say anything to receive something shiny. Mister Tom, he didn't mind. He thought he was saving their souls.

"We were on the river for four weeks, and I was ready to return to Prainha, when Mister Tom heard of a new tribe thirty miles or so up river. He wanted to visit the village and spread the word of Jesus."

Tim broke into Miguel's story and asked, "Can you pinpoint the location of the village on a map?"

"Sure, Mister Tim - when they let us go, I located landmarks to help me find it again."

"Good," Tim said. Then he asked, "For the last few days of your trip, why weren't you in radio contact?"

Miguel's eyes grew wide as he explained. "One night while we were unloading, Mister Tom accidentally dropped our radio in the water. Afterward, the radio didn't work; but Mister Tom didn't care. He said we would return to Obidos in a few days, so we didn't need one."

Tim shook his head at Tom's stubbornness. "That explains the mystery of no contact. Go ahead with your story, Miguel."

"I told Mister Tom it was dangerous to approach a tribe so far from civilization. Especially one who had never seen a white man before, but he wouldn't listen."

"Yeah, that sounds like Tom. He's bullheaded."

Miguel continued, "The current was very strong against us, and it took three days to reach the village. The place is very small. There are only twelve huts, plus a large lodge in the middle of a clearing. There were perhaps thirty-five people there – maybe twenty adults and several children."

Tim interrupted Miguel to ask, "Father Mendez said Tom experienced trouble with the medicine man of the village. What kind of trouble?"

Sweat broke out on Miguel's brow as he remembered. "It began when Mister Tom took photographs of the villagers. He brought along an old Polaroid camera that made pictures as they watched. The natives were amazed when he gave them a blank piece of paper and it changed to reveal their faces. To them, it was big magic.

"The camera also made the medicine man angry. It was better than anything in his bag of tricks.

"The day after we arrived, one villager Mister Tom took a picture of went fishing in his canoe and never returned. Later the same day, the others found his overturned canoe downriver. They think he drowned, but didn't find his body.

"The next day, two children became ill with a strange fever. The medicine man, Narro used all his spells and potions, but the boys died.

"Narro blamed Mister Tom and his camera. He said Mister Tom stole the spirits of the villagers and hid them inside his evil box. The villagers are very superstitious, so they believed Narro. With three of their tribe dead in such a short time after we arrived, what else could they think? The chief sided with Narro, so they tied us up for several days and later put us in a hut."

Tim asked, "Why did they release you and the others?"

Miguel wiped his brow and replied, "The medicine man said we weren't to blame. Only the 'white devil' must pay. Narro told us to leave, but never to bring another white man into their village."

Although Tim didn't want to hear the answer to his question, he asked, "What do you think Narro will do with Tom?"

Miguel's arm muscles shook in fear under his shirt. "One villager told me the medicine man would sacrifice Mister Tom to appease their God at the next full moon. It's only a week away."

Jose spoke for the first time. "We have to get Tom out of the hands of this stupid witch doctor. We don't have much time."

Tim agreed. "The medicine man probably feels he lost face to Tom. Tom made him look mediocre and now Narro needs to even the score."

Catherine gave Tim an idea when she said, "I believe you need to 'out-medicine' this jay bird, Tim. If you can convince the chief you're more powerful than Narro, perhaps your medicine can save Tom's life."

"I see what you mean, Catherine. In Viet Nam, we flew Phys-Ops missions and attempted to frighten the natives enough so they would surrender instead of fight. Sometimes we were successful."

She asked, "Would something like that work here?"

"If the natives are as superstitious as you say, maybe it will."

After thinking about the problem for a few minutes, a plan began to take shape in Tim's mind, so he asked, "Jose, what are the chances these particular natives have seen a helicopter up close and personal? And, what about fireworks? I mean the big, loud booming type and star bursts that light up the sky. Would they have seen any of those?"

Jose shook his head. "They may have seen a helicopter from a distance. But I doubt this particular tribe ever saw one land in their backyard. Is that what you have in mind?"

"Possibly," Tim said. "I wonder what we might do to make some big medicine, but I don't have any firm plans yet."

Jose laughed. "If they saw a big black bird drop from the sky, it might be called big medicine. If I was a poor, primitive native, I know it would impress me.

"As for the fireworks, there's no way the natives would have been exposed to those. When they hear or see pyrotechnics for the first time; it will have a serious effect on their minds."

"Can we find a source for fireworks and starburst shells within a week?" Tim asked. "We wouldn't need many, perhaps a dozen each. They need to be loud and light up the sky at night."

"I'm catching on," Jose said. "Are you going to challenge the medicine man to a duel?"

"That's exactly what I have in mind. If we can find the fireworks and someone to set them off at the right time, we may be able to pull off a small miracle of our own."

Miguel interrupted their thoughts by asking, "Why don't you just fly in and rescue Mister Tom?"

"We'll only do that as a last resort," Tim replied. "For one thing, we can't be positive where they're holding Tom captive. Narro may think Tom called in a magic bird to eat the villagers. Before we could get to Tom, Narro might kill my brother to appease the bad spirits."

"You're right, boss," Jose said. "Let me radio Macapa and call in a few favors."

As he left to use the more powerful radio on his helo, Jose waddled off in a hurry toward the landing strip. If he couldn't find the fireworks, they would come up with another plan.

While they waited, Tim, Catherine and Miguel talked over Tim's initial idea and attempted to formulate a viable plan to rescue Tom.

Fifteen minutes later, Jose came in the door out of breath.

Between gulps of air, he said, "We're in luck. I spoke with a buddy of mine at Macapa. He knows a store where we can buy fireworks and a guy who will set them off.

"He volunteered to fly into Santare'm tomorrow to pick up your fireworks and the explosives expert. Then he'll fly this guy and his playthings to Prainha to meet me."

"You'll need to change helicopters, Jose," Tim said. "With

the fireworks expert, you, me, Miguel and Tom, we will need the bigger aircraft."

"No problem. I'll fly home tonight, pick up the other helo tomorrow and bring everybody and everything here the next day."

Tim handed Jose a list. "I made up an inventory of equipment we need. Miguel can buy a two-man canoe here in Obidos. Take a look at the items and tell me if you can find them all."

After quickly scanning the page, Jose looked up and said, "No problem."

"Okay, Jose. You're off and flying. If I think of anything else, I'll contact Father Mendez, and he can give you my message. We have three days to get our act together. While you're gone, we'll refine the plan. Then we can go over it again when you return."

After Jose left, Tim said, "We're done for today. Where can I hang my hat, Catherine?"

"We're not as fancy as Prainha and don't have a nice hotel like Miss Lela's. When visitors drop in, they usually stay with friends. Since you're my new friend, you'll bunk at my house."

"Thanks, friend – I accept."

"I'll be on my way home," Miguel said. I'll see you in the morning."

"If you want a drink, the ice is in the freezer," Catherine said. "Whiskey is in the cabinet over the refrigerator and glasses are in the hutch to your right."

Tim inspected the neatly arranged items setting on wide shelves in the kitchen and said, "You have all the comforts of home. Between Miss Lela and you, I may stay here forever."

There seemed to be a hidden message in her reply when Catherine said, "First, you have to find and rescue your brother. Then you can stay for a while so we can get to know each other."

As they sipped their drinks and talked, Tim helped Catherine prepare a mixed salad and three juicy cheeseburgers with all the trimmings. They ate at a picnic table on the veranda overlooking the Amazon.

Catherine opened a bottle of beer for Tim and poured a glass of wine for her. Then she lit a small coiled item that glowed softly and produced a small column of smoke supposedly guaranteed to keep mosquitoes away. The scented smoke curled around their heads and hung heavy in the night air.

In spite of their good intentions to retire early and sleep all night, Tim and Catherine stayed up late to talk. She was fascinating. Tim couldn't imagine how a beautiful young girl found her way into the interior of the jungle of Brazil.

"To quote an old cliché: 'What's a girl like you doing in a place like this'?"

"My father was a teacher all his life and I always dreamed of becoming one. Since I was born and raised in the small town of Des Moines, Iowa, making my wish come true seemed the logical thing to do.

"To make a long story short, I attained my goal and taught fifth grade in a public school in Des Moines, which made my father very proud.

"I quickly became disillusioned by today's youth. In their minds, all they need to know is how to operate a computer or watch TV. As if they're Gods to be worshipped, they stare at those two screens until their brains are fried.

"Nowadays, if students need an answer to a question, they get it from the internet. They can't comprehend utilizing their brains for a definite purpose. There's no such thing as common sense.

"If you're able to use spell check on the computer, then who needs to learn to spell or use a dictionary?

"With a calculator, they figure 'to hell with taking math'.

"Today's parents are too busy with their careers to worry about any children they bring into the world. They throw money at their youngsters and tell them to get lost. Then the teenagers become so self-centered they are impossible to approach on any level.

"Sex education? The kids today know more about it by the fourth grade than I did as a senior in high school.

"Sure there are a few children who have the desire to learn, but classes are too big – too many students and not enough time.

"And when I attempted to fail a student who wasn't performing adequately? Forget it. If Junior didn't learn anything, the teacher must be at fault.

"Finally, I'd had it. I wanted to teach children who weren't exposed to our modern marvels. That's when the Brazilian government entered my life.

"They were tired of paying 'gringos' to come here to work in their oil fields and wanted more local people to learn the trade. Then the country could reduce unemployment and lower their overhead with locals who would do the same job for less pay.

"The oil companies stepped in and created a great instructional program. Today I teach English to the children and some adults who already live in the jungle and haven't seen the big cities. This life is the only one they know. If they earn a good wage in Obidos, then here is where they'll stay.

"The program pays more than I earned in Des Moines, and I'm making a contribution to the future of these children and their parents. End of story."

"I admire what you're doing," Tim said.

Catherine covered a yawn with her hand and said, "Now let's hear your tale,"

"Not tonight; it's long and boring. Today has been exciting, but it's time to hit the sack."

Chapter 8

"On a Hill", White Sands Road, Paget Parrish, Bermuda

As she addressed her husband of forty-nine years, Pearl Fitch asked, "George, have you heard anything new from Tim?"

"Not since his last report. He hasn't found any sign of Tom."

"Keep praying Tim finds him," Pearl said. "Prayer is the only thing we have to turn to now."

Before she spoke again, Pearl paused to wring her hands worriedly. "On another subject, I wonder if Tim knows Cheryl has finally allowed our granddaughter to visit Bermuda."

"I doubt it," George replied. "Since their divorce, Cheryl and Tim haven't spoken a hundred words."

"I hate to be judgmental of anyone," Pearl said. "But it's a sin the way Cheryl has prevented Tim from seeing his daughter all these years. Think what he and Kate have missed."

"I know, dear," George said. "I'm sick of paying Cheryl to allow us to see Kate two or three times a year and then having to travel to Austin to visit her on neutral ground.

"Tim probably has no idea I pay Cheryl two hundred dollars a month for the privilege of visiting my own flesh and blood. Cheryl is a conniver."

"Now George, watch your blood pressure. I don't care for her either, but Cheryl finally relented and Kate will be here for Thanksgiving. Give the woman a little Christian charity."

"Charity begins at home," George said. "I love my granddaughter, but she's the only good thing to come from Tim's marriage to the conniving witch."

Ever the optimist, Pearl said, "Perhaps Cheryl's seen the errors of her ways and turned over a new leaf."

George snorted and said, "Yeah, and pigs can fly."

Chapter 9

It may have been the beer with dinner, plus the wine they consumed while they talked. But no matter the cause, Tim's nervousness at the thought that he might possibly rescue his brother departed with the sun. He fell asleep easily and slept soundly.

At six a.m., Catherine called out, "Wake up sleepy head. It's a beautiful day out. I have ham and eggs and hot coffee to offer."

Tim yawned and said, "Give me time to shave."

They were almost finished with breakfast when Miguel came by with good news. "I found a small canoe to buy. A friend of mine says he wants to build a new one, so he'll make us a deal on the old one. It looks pretty sturdy and should be okay. He wants fifty dollars. What do you think?"

"You're the expert, Miguel. I know nothing about boats, except how to fall out of one."

"Then we'll buy it," Miguel said. "Felipe will help me carry the canoe to the riverbank. Later today we can take a trial run."

"Thanks," Tim said. "That's one more worry off my mind."

The trio reviewed Tim's plan again and attempted to find fault with his ideas.

Catherine shrugged and said, "There's nothing wrong with your idea."

Miguel agreed. "It's a winner."

Tim thanked them both with a smile. "At least we don't need any additional supplies. Let's wait until Jose returns. Then we'll make sure everyone knows the part they'll play."

"It's too bad we can't hold a dress rehearsal," Miguel said.

"I'll cancel school for the next few days," Catherine said. "I'll be busy enough without my having to worry about the children. I'd like to help as much as I can."

"Thanks," Tim said. "I appreciate everything you're doing."

"If it's okay, Mister Tim, I'll go home and spend some time with my family and help Felipe move the canoe," Miguel said. "When I hear Jose arrive, I'll meet you at the landing strip."

"Sure, Miguel, there's nothing to do around here until then."

After Miguel departed, Catherine turned to Tim and asked, "Do we have time to hear your story now?"

"My tale is not as meaningful as yours, but I'll give it a shot."

Tim settled back on the couch to begin his story.

"Forty-two years ago, Tom and I were born in Bermuda. My mother, Pearl is a doctor from the United States who fell in love with my father, George, who is also a physician from Bermuda.

"Since the day they were married, they have lived in Bermuda. But when Tom and I were about to be born, our mother returned to the states so we would be U.S. citizens.

"We grew up, went to school in Bermuda and then on to college in Texas. I wanted to be a doctor, and Tom decided to become a priest. I attended the University of Texas while he went to Texas Christian University. When I was a senior, I met my wife, Cheryl and we were married shortly before graduation.

"She became pregnant and our daughter, Kate was born. Then Tom and I were sent to Viet Nam where I flew helicopters and Tom was a Chaplain. We both survived our tours and came home to Bermuda.

"While I was gone, Cheryl ran around and experimented with drugs. When I returned, we had a big fight. She filed for divorce and received custody of Kate. Under one pretense or another, Cheryl's prevented me from seeing my daughter for fifteen years.

"I was a doctor for several years, but grew tired of working with sick people every day and decided to try something new.

"I hired two sub-contractors to help me build a new house and they liked my style of work, so we became partners. I do the paperwork and rustle up new customers, while Ken and Bill do the actual work. We're a very successful team.

"When Tom came up missing, Father Mendez called my father and he phoned me. I flew to Brazil to find Tom and now here I am, spending my time with a very lovely woman. End of story."

Catherine applauded softly. "Thanks for the compliment. I only have one comment; you and your daughter need to form some kind of a relationship. At this time in her life, Kate needs a father. Your ex-wife is crazy to keep you two apart."

Tim nodded his agreement to her statement. "Since Cheryl began doing drugs, she hasn't been the same. According to her, Cheryl's life was well planned and I ruined it. She can't see she's caused her own problems."

"I hope you two can work something out so you can see your daughter," Catherine said. "The next time you're home, contact Kate."

"You're probably right. You know, it's strange, but I feel I can tell you anything about my life and you'll understand."

Catherine blushed momentarily. "I'm pleased you think of me in such a way. Let's see what we can rustle up for dinner. What about another salad and a bowl of soup?"

In Austin, Texas, Kate's mind was focused on her parents and their strange, almost non-relationship.

As a youngster, Kate grew up knowing her parents were divorced.

It wasn't as if she was alone in the ruined marriage department. Half the kids in her class were from a one parent family.

When Kate innocently asked about the size of her father's family, due to all the "uncles" who slept in her mother's bed, Cheryl stopped allowing her latest flame to stay overnight.

As she grew older, Kate learned about drugs in grammar school. Before long, after seeing all the symptoms in her mother, Kate knew Cheryl was experimenting with drugs. More than once, Kate found strange-looking pills in her mother's medicine cabinet and residue of a white powder on the coffee table.

Kate kept her knowledge a secret and never told her mother. She was frightened and worried the police might learn of the drugs and arrest her mother. *"What would happen to me then?"*

Finally one morning, after finding Cheryl stoned and out of it, Kate knew she must say something. When confronted by her daughter, Cheryl swore she would quit drugs. For a while, she kept her promise, but Kate always knew when her mother slipped back into her old habits.

She also knew when Cheryl stayed out nights with a new boyfriend. Kate wasn't dumb enough to buy Cheryl's story of, "I had to work late."

"I'm not a kid anymore. I know the facts of life, about sex and all that icky stuff, but I don't know what to think about mom anymore. When mom's high, she gets so upset with dad. Why does she hate him so?

"I'm caught in the middle. I wish dad would call and talk to me. I wonder why he doesn't. Grandma and Grandpa Fitch tell me he loves me. Why don't you call, Pops? I would love to tell you I've maintained an A average in school and talk things over with you. I've never heard your side of the story."

Recently, things had changed for the better. For the past two years, since her mother got a job at the First National Bank in Austin, their life together was better. The salary Cheryl made allowed them to live well. Kate noticed a definite and positive change in Cheryl's moods and knew her mother's attitude was upbeat. She even smiled more.

Then suddenly, a few weeks ago, Cheryl became ill.

As Kate stood by her bed, Cheryl said, "I don't feel very well. I think I'll stay home from work today."

Kate felt her mother's forehead and said, "You're running a temperature and need to see a Doctor. I'll call and make an appointment."

Cheryl shook her head. "I'm just dizzy and a little rundown. I'll be okay in a while."

Kate insisted. "You're going to see a doctor,"

"Okay, I give up. Go ahead, call the doc."

A week later, after a follow-up visit to the doctor, Cheryl said, "It's time you visited your grandparents in Bermuda, Kate. You're sixteen and old enough to travel by yourself. You can fly down, spend Thanksgiving and stay a week. Maybe this will get them off my back for not allowing you to visit in Bermuda before."

"Super, Mom, but will you be all right by yourself?"

"I'll be fine," Cheryl lied. "I'm tired of listening to your grandparents complain about not having you visit. I'll phone and let them know."

The next day, Cheryl kept her promise. When Pearl answered, she was surprised to hear who was calling. She was even more amazed at Cheryl's proposal to allow Kate to visit.

"Of course, we'll be thrilled to have Kate visit us," Pearl said. "If you like, we'll pay her fare."

A little stiffly, Cheryl said, "No, thank you; I'll buy her ticket. She'll arrive in Bermuda on Wednesday, the day before Thanksgiving and can stay until the following Tuesday. Kate will miss a day or two of school. When she returns, I'll write an excuse for her absence."

"You're very gracious," Pearl said. "We hope you'll come to visit us some day."

"Perhaps in the near future," Cheryl lied, while she thought, *"I have no intentions of ever going to Bermuda. While Kate's gone, I have other plans."*

"We'll be at the airport to meet her plane," Pearl said.

"When I have her flight number, I'll phone again," Cheryl said. She hung up without waiting for Pearl's reply.

Kate put her arms around her mother's shoulders, kissed her on the cheek and said, "You're super, Mom. You know I always wanted to go to Bermuda and see the islands. Thanks; I love you."

"I love you too, Honey. I hope you like Bermuda and enjoy your visit. Send me a post card."

"I'll be home before it would get here," Kate said. "I'll buy a pack of pictures. When I get back, we'll look through them together."

With a pained look in her eyes, Cheryl said, "That's nice."

Alarmed, Kate asked, "Are you okay, Mom?"

"I'm fine," Cheryl lied. "Don't worry about me. Just go and have a good time."

Kate hugged her mother again. "I will. You're the greatest."

The next afternoon, Catherine's radio crackled to life.

"I'm about five minutes out," Jose said. "I have everything Tim ordered and the fireworks specialist, Frank Moses is aboard."

"Great," Catherine said. "Tim and I will meet you at the landing strip."

Without knocking, Miguel walked in the door. "I heard Jose coming up the river."

"Yeah," Tim said. "He just called in. Come on; let's go meet him."

After setting his big black helicopter down on the pad outside of town, Jose and another large man climbed out.

Jose pointed to his companion. "Tim, this is Frank Moses, the expert on explosives."

Frank was six feet tall, with blonde hair and blue eyes. He weighed no more than two hundred pounds, but the muscles on his arms were well defined, which said Frank was no slouch when it came to hard work. Frank's darkly tanned and clean shaven face was handsome and unmarked.

While Tim shook hands with the newcomer, he said, "It's nice to meet you, Frank. This is Catherine, our hostess and local schoolmarm, and my brother's guide, Miguel."

Frank nodded knowingly. "Jose told me about your problem upriver. I hope I can help. I brought along a good selection and assortment of fireworks. I believe they're what you have in mind."

"I'll leave the explosives to you, Frank. Let's adjourn to Catherine's home and I'll explain our plan."

"I got everything you asked for, boss," Jose said. "Do you want to check the items over?"

"Sure, Jose; let's see what you have."

"I got three AR-15s from the local armory. I also borrowed six revolvers – four .38 caliber and two .45s, plus ammunition for all. The guy who sold me six Walkie-talkies says they have a range of more than fifty miles. I hope he's right.

"He only had twelve extra batteries, but that's probably enough to do the job. I found a bunch of key ring chains I can hook together so you can hang the radio around your neck.

"The trinkets you asked for are in the back seat. There aren't many left in the local five-and-dime store in Prainha."

"Everything looks good," Tim said. "What about the search light, tape recorder and speakers?"

"The searchlight is a hand-held type and will light up the entire village. Two speakers are already mounted, one on each side of the bird. On the way upriver, I played a CD and you should have seen the birds fly out of the jungle."

Tim patted Jose on the back and said, "Good work, Jose. I believe we're ready for Narro."

"You'll love it when you get the bill. Remember, you said cost wasn't a factor."

"I learned a long time ago not to sweat the small things, Jose. If we get Tom back, I really don't care what it costs."

Miguel interrupted to ask, "While we're here, Mister Tim, do you want to see the canoe?"

"Why not? Let's take a look."

After the group walked to the shore of the murky river, they found a small wooden canoe bobbing with the current and tied to a stained, creosoted piling. Cut from a long log and then hollowed out, the homemade craft seemed small.

At first glance, Tim expressed second thoughts about the size. "It doesn't appear the canoe will hold us both and all our equipment."

"You'll be surprised," Miguel said. "Do you want a test ride to see how it handles?"

Tim put his hands up in surrender. "We have to find out sometime."

"Don't worry, Mister Tim. You'll do fine."

While Miguel held the canoe steady, Tim climbed in cautiously. He was surprised when the sturdy little craft didn't sink lower. "I thought my weight would have taken it to the bottom."

"It's stronger than you might believe," Miguel said.

Without a warning, Miguel jumped into the rear and the canoe rocked gently.

Tim grabbed the sides of the craft and held on for dear life. "Whoa, Miguel, don't do that again."

Miguel's reply didn't sound sincere. "I'm sorry, Mister Tim. Let's paddle it out on the river."

Tim was astounded to find he had a natural ability with the paddle. "This is easy. It handles like a dream."

After they paddled a few hundred yards down the bank, they turned to return to the landing site. Tim found going against the current was more difficult; but with a few minutes of hard work, they were back where they started.

As Jose reached down to hold the canoe in place, he asked, "What do you think?"

Tim rubbed his sore shoulders and replied, "We shouldn't have any problems. We'll be headed downstream on the way to the village. Let's tie it on your helo and go to Catherine's."

When they were gathered around the kitchen table, Tim said, "Okay, Frank, I'll go over the gist of the plan for you and Jose. The rest of our team has reviewed it and so far they can't find anything wrong. If you see something you feel won't work, don't be afraid to let us know. I'm open to any suggestions. God knows I'm no expert."

Tim spent the next hour informing the newcomers of his plan. When Tim was sure everyone knew their parts, he asked, "Do you see any problem with us using your helo as planned, Jose?"

"None at all. If everything goes well, we can pull this off and get Tom out of harm's way."

Miguel broke in to say, "I'm worried about Narro after he told me not to bring any more white devils into their village. How will you handle him?"

"We'll play it by ear," Tim said. "We'll both carry a revolver under our shirts and I'll leave my radio on so everyone can hear what happens. If we run into trouble and have to fire our weapons, you'll have to come to the rescue, Jose."

Jose assured them, "I'll be there."

"Everything hinges on timing," Tim said. "If we stick to the basics and adjust as we have to, we should be able to get Tom away from Narro."

Tim turned to Frank and asked, "What about you, Frank?"

"I'm ready. You tell me when to set off the fireworks and where to put them. If you want, I'll drop them down the shorts of this medicine man."

Tim grinned. "There's nothing like having confidence in your abilities. I hope you're as good as you say you are."

Frank didn't say anything more, but somehow, Tim knew he was even better.

"When you make your getaway, don't forget me," Frank said. "I don't want to be out in the jungle alone any longer than necessary. I'm afraid of those big, fat, hungry crocs."

"Don't worry," Jose said. "I'll pick you up as planned. I doubt you'll be bothered by any animals, but you'll have a rifle to protect yourself. All I can say is; be careful of logs with teeth."

When Jose laughed at his own comment, Frank flipped him the bird and said, "I'll be extremely careful."

Jose laughed louder.

"There's one more thing in our favor, "Tim said. "We'll leave all our gear and the canoe behind as gifts for the chief."

Jose frowned. "I'm worried about you and Miguel staying overnight in the village, Tim. You know Narro will be after your hide."

"I know, but we'll take turns sleeping, with at least one of us on guard. Maybe I can talk the chief into allowing us to spend the night in the hut where Tom is being held.

"The biggest break we have in our favor is the fact the natives don't understand English. I can talk to Tom right in front of them and explain things so he can react well when he needs to. If they let us sleep in his hut, I'll fill him in on the entire plan."

As he concluded the discussion, Tim said, "I know there are a lot of variables that may go against or work for us. We'll have to hope our big medicine does the trick."

Catherine got up from the table and said, "The hardest part may be making it into the village without finding an arrow through your heart, Tim."

"I think the chief will control his people – I'm counting on it. No one other than Narro is angry at Tom or wants him sacrificed. The villagers have to go along with their leaders. The natives will be curious enough to listen to me, and Miguel's presence will help. He made friends with several members of the tribe.

"You have your radios. If things go south and you hear shooting, make like John Wayne and come to our rescue."

"Let's hope you don't become involved in something you can't handle," Catherine said. "Your plan is sound. All we need now is a large supply of luck."

Chapter 10

Tila knew something was wrong with the white man. His face was flushed and he appeared to be talking to himself. Sweat ran down his arms and dripped onto the dust. In her native tongue, she asked, "What's wrong?"

Tom continued to speak gibberish and didn't appear to know Tila was by his side. After feeling his brow, Tila saw he was shaking with fever. She motioned toward Tom's hut. "You're sick. Come inside, out of the sun."

She helped Tom to his feet and he leaned heavily on her shoulder. After leading him into the filthy hut, Tila laid him on a ratty mat, where Tom collapsed into a stupor. There was no other cover available, so after raising her long flowing robe, she pulled it over her head to reveal her nude body.

Tila lay down at Tom's side, covered them both with her wrap and hugged him close. It was the only way she knew to break his fever.

Tom was oblivious to her ministering. His mind was lost in the past as he dreamed of his failures as a priest. He was experiencing more second thoughts of his vocation, and the fever he contracted only brought his feelings to the surface more vividly.

The first time Tom experienced anxiety pains was shortly after he was ordained. From the time he was seventeen, Tom knew he wanted to be a priest, but to be honest, he couldn't explain why he chose the path to be a man of God.

When first questioning his calling, Tom knew the feeling was mostly nerves. He prayed to God for an answer or a sign, but when nothing was forthcoming, he went on with his life.

If God wanted me to speak to Him personally; I imagine He first would have appointed me Pope."

When Tom graduated from college, he was drafted into the Army and sent to Fort Campbell, Kentucky, where he received his indoctrination into the Chaplain's corps. A few weeks later, he was sent to Viet Nam.

His experiences there were not pleasant memories. While viewing so much inhumanity to others, Tom was horrified at the number of young men whose lives were cut short. When Tom returned to his parents' home in Bermuda, he was in a depressed state.

When George saw the "thousand yard stare" in Tom's eyes, common to those who have experienced warfare up close and personal, he contacted Ted Garcia. Ted was a good friend of the family and a psychiatrist. He soon helped Tom overcome the demons that seemed to haunt him.

Finally, after recovering his senses, Tom decided to join the peace movement that was sweeping the nation. Although battle scarred in body and mind, he was still a young man seeking answers.

While spending the next year serving as spiritual leader to a California commune filled with the dregs of society called "Hippies", Tom soon discovered the members of the group were searching for truth themselves, while proclaiming loudly that they already knew the answers.

The time was one of confusion for Tom. Finally, he saw no future with his companions and lost count of the questions in his mind. *"Why did I come here? What have I accomplished? What is my purpose in life?"*

Once more, Tom returned to Bermuda and the bosom of his family. While he was away, he failed to keep his parents informed of his state of mind. When they saw Tom's physical condition, they were appalled. From his sunken eyes and apathetic demeanor, George and Pearl knew their son was close to a mental breakdown.

With home cooking, love from his parents and talks with Ted, Tom soon returned to his old self. Within a year, he was ready to return to his chosen vocation and felt there would be no other second thoughts.

When Tom received an appointment as a priest for a congregation in Chicago, Illinois, he was exuberant. He soon found he was happy with his new surroundings, the church and his parishioners.

During his tenure, rumors began to circulate of child molestation by priests in the city and nation. Tom couldn't believe any man of the cloth could be involved in such behavior. But before the scandal was hushed, several of Tom's fellow priests were named in lawsuits by those they abused.

After he resigned his position as a form of protest, Tom left Chicago bitter and disappointed. As before, he sought solace and returned to Bermuda. He remained there for another year, while he attempted to bring peace to his mind.

Tom served as an assistant pastor in his local Catholic Church, but soon he grew restless and weary of the same repetitious routine. Then to his surprise, an offer came to serve as a missionary in Brazil. *"Perhaps this type of work might be what I've been looking for. I think I'll apply."*

To Tom's amazement, his application was accepted. After he prayed for guidance, he decided to serve with Father Mendez in Prainha, Brazil.

His father and brother attempted to persuade Tom not to go, but his mind was made up.

As he lay in the filthy hut, Tom's tortured dreams of failure continued to haunt him. *"I wouldn't listen and look where it got me. Everyone tried to tell me, even Father Mendez. When will I learn? Please, Lord, give me another chance. Dying in the jungle at the hands of an insane medicine man can't be the reason You called me to Your side."*

When Tom regained consciousness, he was startled to find Tila lying nude by his side. His sudden movements awakened her from a troubled slumber.

After Tom pulled her robe from beneath his body, he handed it to her. But Tila pushed it aside and attempted to cuddle closer. It was obvious there was more on her mind than curing his fever – the look in her eyes told Tom all he needed to know.

Tom held up his hands and said firmly, "No; thank you for your help, but you have the wrong idea."

Tila was surprised and disappointed at his reactions to her advances. Sex wasn't a big thing in the tribe. If you felt like lying with another, as long as he wasn't married, no one objected.

She stood up abruptly, pulled her robe over her head and covered her body.

Tom smiled and said, "Thank you."

From his tone of voice, Tila knew what Tom meant. She returned Tom's smile, leaned down to feel his brow and said, "You're better." Then she made motions of eating and drinking. "I'll bring you something."

Chapter 11

E arly this morning, after everyone ate a good breakfast, Tim looked into the pantry and remarked, "When we finish this rescue mission, we'll have to go on a restocking trip in the copter. Your larder is almost empty."

"I'll hold you to your promise," Catherine said. "I'll make up a list of things to buy in Prainha."

Jose interrupted their conversation. "It's time to get on the road, boss."

"I'll walk to the airfield with you," Catherine said.

When they were positive all their equipment was on board, Jose lifted off without any fanfare. Tim was sure everyone knew their jobs. Now all they needed was to have luck on their side.

To be sure the big black bird wasn't seen or heard; Jose flew a roundabout route and landed near the riverbank five miles upstream of the village.

Jose dropped an anchor to hold them in place while Tim and Miguel untied the canoe from the floats. Once the helo was made fast, they put the tiny craft in the water and tied it to a strut. Then they transferred their supplies from the helo as Tim checked each item off a master list.

Jose laughed and said, "You're one organized dude, boss."

"It's my military training kicking in. Laugh if you will, but I learned a long time ago that it's better to have too much than too little."

When Tim was satisfied everything was where it should be, he shook Jose's hand. "At 1200 hours, listen for my signal. If you can't hear me, take off and fly upriver. I'll call every five minutes until you receive my message."

"As far as the radios are concerned, boss, we shouldn't have a thing to worry about. I'll stand by at noon. Think positive."

Tim and Miguel used their machetes to cut a small trail from the riverbank to a nearby grove of trees, where they set up camp.

"This will do," Miguel said. "I'll fix a lean-to to keep out the sun and rain."

The jungle was thick with vines and the dead vegetation under their feet was spongy, but the ground was drier then Tim had anticipated.

At noon, after saying a silent prayer Jose would hear him the first time; Tim switched on his walkie-talkie and called, "Hello home base."

Jose responded immediately, "I read you loud and clear, boss."

Tim reported, "Camp is set up and we'll stay here overnight as planned. Tomorrow morning when we paddle to the village, I'll signal before we arrive. Beginning at 0700 hours, listen for my call."

Jose's voice sounded metallic. "Ten-four; Sister Kate says to wish you luck. I think she likes you."

Although Jose couldn't see, Tim smiled. "Tell her the feeling is mutual."

After he unpacked the lunch Catherine prepared, Miguel gave Tim a ham sandwich and potato chips. As birds chirped merrily from limbs overhead and an occasional scream from a monkey or parrot was heard, the surroundings made lunchtime seem almost like a picnic in paradise.

They brought along netting for protection from mosquitoes and other biting bugs, but Tim spent a restless night. It wasn't the insects that kept him awake – his mind was busy with thoughts of this new woman in his life. Tim realized he wanted to get through tomorrow and the remaining day safely – not just for Tom's sake, but his own.

"So Catherine likes me. That's nice to know. I like her too. I'm surprised how the short time we spent together has affected me. I haven't felt anything for any woman in a long time. Now, Catherine is interrupting my sleep."

Tim missed his daughter and was tired of being single. Since he came from a loving family, he longed to have his own.

"What does Cheryl tell Kate about her father? Did she ever mention I phoned? I doubt it. Her hatred for me goes deep to her soul."

The strange thing was; Cheryl allowed Tim's parents to maintain a relationship with their granddaughter. As a result, George and Pearl knew more about Kate than Tim did.

Pearl told him Kate was doing well in school, with nearly a straight A average. "Each time we visit, Kate's always well dressed and neat."

Then this problem with Tom came along and here he was, deep in the Amazon jungle. Bill and Ken both had brothers, so they were sympathetic to Tim's situation and took care of the business while he attempted to find Tom.

And now by luck or God's will; Catherine came into his life. *"Maybe things were meant to be and something good will come out of this Brazilian adventure."*

But Tim would have to wait for a few days to see how things would work out. Before dawn broke over the Amazon River basin, his mind drifted to thoughts other than Catherine, and he managed to catch a few hours sleep.

At six a.m., the sun shone down through a double canopy of tall trees and bathed their small clearing with rays of filtered light. Miguel used dry wood that didn't create smoke to brew two cups of coffee over a small fire to add to a cold breakfast of day old rolls and grape jelly.

Tim referred to the tan shorts and oversized shirts they wore to conceal their weapons. "We'll wear the same clothes as yesterday. Give me your revolver and I'll check it for rust."

Before Tim and Miguel left Obidos, Frank mixed a small amount of gun powder with a bottle of glitter from school supplies. Then after putting the mixture in four small plastic bags, he handed them to Tim. "If you get in a fix, throw one into a fire. The results should dazzle the natives."

As a precaution, before leaving the campsite, Tim took one of the plastic bags and put it in the pocket of his shorts.

They loaded their canoe and set off downriver just as the sun broke through a low hanging morning fog. As slowly and quietly as possible, they alternated drifting with the current or paddling until they heard voices from the village.

Then Tim stopped the canoe and whispered, "Hold it here, Miguel, while I call Jose."

Fumbling nervously under his shirt, with a shaking hand, Tim turned on his radio and clicked the send button twice.

Immediately, Jose replied, "I read you loud and clear."

With Miguel setting the pace, they continued downstream until they sighted the village. Then Miguel pointed the canoe so they would land on the muddy riverbank near the middle of the settlement.

When they saw a white man approaching, two youngsters who had been pulling in a net cried out in alarm. As a peace sign, and to show he didn't possess any weapons, Miguel held his hands in front of his body with his arms bent upward at the elbow and his palms outward. Speaking gently to the children, he attempted to calm their fears, but their eyes were wide with fright.

Several men, who had been alerted to Tim and Miguel's presence by the youngster's cries, gathered in a half-circle near the shore. They were armed with spears or machetes, but appeared uncertain as to what to do.

Suddenly, the chief of the village arrived, dressed to the

nines. He made a grand entry with a flourish worthy of one of the three musketeers.

A once fancy feather headdress made of bird feathers that were now stained with mold and drooping in the heat and rather ratty from use and abuse set atop a crop of long, stringy black hair. But Tim figured his accouterments were probably considered appropriately frightening for a person of the chief's high rank and bearing.

To complete his ensemble, the chief wore a ring of equally moldy feathers around his neck over a dirty brown shirt, and a filthy skirt of brown material held up by a rope belt.

The chief recognized Miguel and gave the peace sign, which Miguel returned. Then Miguel spoke in the natives' tongue and asked permission to come ashore.

The chief appeared uncertain if he should grant their request. He frowned and asked, "After our medicine man told you not to; why do you bring another white devil into our village?"

Miguel spread his arms wide and then indicated Tim with a pointed finger. "My companion is a medicine man from the same tribe as the man you hold captive. He has come to bargain for the life of the white church man. Do not anger him, for his medicine is very powerful."

Hoping Tom would hear his voice, Tim shouted, "We come in peace. Tell him Miguel. Make the chief understand we don't mean any harm to his people."

As Miguel was translating his words, Tim reached into his backpack, removed a handful of trinkets and held them high in the air.

Just as Tim had hoped, the chief's eyes glinted with greed.

Tim knew he had made a good first impression. As if in submission to the chief's authority, Tim bowed in the direction of the chief and continued to speak through Miguel's translation. "I bring many gifts for this great chief from my tribe. Allow us to land so we may present our offerings."

His comments and the sight of so many gifts brought fast results. The chief quickly motioned them to come ashore.

Tim stepped from the canoe, bent low with his hands full of trinkets and said, "These gifts and many others are yours. We come as friends."

After the chief picked out a mirror, he looked at his reflection for a few moments. Then he smiled at his image and asked, "What do you want and why have you come so far?"

Feeling the truth in his words, Tim said, "I come to ask forgiveness for my brother, who has been falsely accused."

Before Tim could continue, Narro arrived on the scene. From his demeanor, it looked like he has just awakened from a deep sleep. At first, he appeared flustered at the arrival of these newcomers.

Tim took the time to check out his opponent. Narro wore only a loincloth made from a dark material and a pair of dirty leather sandals. Tied around each arm were strips of leather with fractured bones and weather-beaten feathers attached.

Narro's teeth were filed to points and his long, dirty, shaggy hair didn't appear to have been washed in a year. Beyond a doubt, Narro was one of the ugliest individuals Tim had ever seen.

Ignoring Tim, Narro ran up to Miguel and screamed in his face. As Narro rattled on, Tim made out the words, "white devil", and knew Narro was referring to him.

Miguel told Narro the same story he had related to the chief. At first, after hearing that Tim was also a medicine man, Narro appeared frightened; but then he swelled up in a big bluster and shouted, "The white church man must pay for his crimes."

While Miguel translated as quickly as he could, Narro continued in a loud voice, "The white devil has locked the spirits of our villagers in his evil box. Only his death will stop the bad magic and appease our God."

Narro's ranting began to grate on Tim's nerves. Suddenly he shouted, "Bring forth the evil box and I will destroy it to show you nothing will happen to anyone in the village."

Pointing toward Narro as if he owned him, Tim demanded, "Go, Narro, bring me the box. I will place my spirit inside and it will not harm me. You will see; my medicine is more powerful than yours."

As Miguel was translating, the chief continued to listen to the exchange without saying a word. Although the chief was obviously intimidated by his medicine man, Tim knew the tribal leader was also frightened by this newcomer and his unknown medicine. Now the chief must make a choice.

When Tim ordered Narro to bring the camera, the chief suddenly made up his mind. With authority in his voice, he said, "Go, Narro, bring forth the evil box. Let this white man do what he says he can."

With his eyes dark with hatred, Narro slunk away and made his way to a nearby hut. He disappeared inside for a moment, and then returned with the Polaroid camera in his hands. Narro threw it at Tim, who caught it in mid air. In anger, Narro sneered, "Do your magic. But do not think it will make a difference to the white devil's fate."

Tim put on a good show for his audience. First he carefully examined the camera while noting it still contained a film pack. Then he crossed his fingers and hoped the sun hadn't damaged the film. Finally, with great flare, Tim handed the camera to Miguel and struck a pose of ferocious concentration as he stared into the lens. "Here, Miguel; take my photograph and give the negative to the chief."

Miguel took Tim's photo, pulled the blank, white piece of thin paper from the camera and handed it to the chief.

It grew deathly quiet as Tim watched the chief staring at the paper. When Tim's image appeared like magic, the chief's eyes grow larger in fright. Then Tim spread his arms wide to encompass the entire village. "Tell everyone who has a picture to bring them to me."

Several villagers still retained their photographs. When the chief gave the order, they hurried to surrender their images. From a pocket of his filthy shirt, the chief removed his and handed it to Tim.

Tim held the pictures high in the air and turned in a circle so all could see. Then he faced the chief and said, "I shall burn these and see if we go up in smoke. Mine will be the first. If something evil happens to any of your people, I will meet the same fate.

The chief nodded his approval.

From the corner of his eye, Tim saw Narro glaring at him, but he paid no attention to the medicine man. Tim walked to a nearby fire pit and placed the photographs onto the hot coals, one at a time.

As each photograph curled, smoked, burned and turned to ash, Tim sang a verse of "Old Mac Donald Had a Farm". It was the only song he could think of that sounded like a chant, with the refrain of e, i, e, i, o.

It took all Miguel's inner strength not to laugh out loud.

When the photographs were reduced to ash, Tim scattered the remains to the four winds and continued to chant. Then he took the camera and smashed it against a rock until the Polaroid broke into several pieces.

Tim picked up each piece and placed them on the fire, where they lay smoldering and refused to burn until he added more wood. Tim created a good-sized blaze, and finally the pieces slowly melted and disappeared into the ashes.

Throughout all Tim's nonsense, Narro stood watching with hatred in his eyes while mentally measuring the power of his opponent. Tim knew he was now as much an enemy to Narro as Tom.

Tim whispered, "I hope Tom heard all this mumbo-jumbo and knows what's going on."

Two clicks sounded from his radio, telling Tim the others at home base heard his remarks.

Since no one was injured by Tim's display, the chief was duly impressed. After checking the wellbeing of the villagers who had given their photos to Tim, the chief stared into Tim's face for several long moments before he spoke.

As he waited, Tim put his hand in his pocket and broke the thin string on the bag that held the explosive powder. Then he turned the bag upside down in his pocket and collected a handful of mix in his closed fist.

The chief asked, "Are the spirits free once more?"

Tim withdrew his hand from his pocket, threw the powder into the fire and replied, "Yes, my God and my medicine are powerful."

The resulting small explosion and sparkling bits flying through the air made his words even more powerful. The chief actually ducked away from several that were blown his way.

Although for a moment Narro was taken aback by the fiery display, he quickly regained his courage and screamed out, "Tomorrow night when the moon is full, the sacrifice of the white devil will take place."

To Tim's surprise, the chief didn't voice any objection.

While pointing at Narro again and waving his index finger in a circle, Tim shouted his reply, "I challenge you for the life of the white church man. Let my God guide my hand against your medicine. If my magic is not stronger than yours, you can have my brother. If my God is more powerful, you will give up your claim."

Then Tim put his hand inside his shirt, grasped the handle of his revolver and continued to shout. "Accept my challenge now or my God will strike you dead where you stand."

Narro was frightened by the sudden shift in authority, and appeared to have been struck dumb. He knew the villagers were watching every move to see what would happen.

Through his dark glasses, Tim stared Narro down while waiting for his reply.

Boxed in by Tim's dare, Narro thought, *"I can't avoid the challenge of this new white devil and remain the spiritual leader of the tribe. If I don't accept, and the new white man's God possesses the power he claims, I'm still a dead man."*

Either way, there wasn't much choice, so Narro called out, "White devil, I accept your challenge. When my God defeats yours, you and the other white man will answer to me."

When Miguel's translating was complete, Tim said, "Very well. The contest shall take place tomorrow night under the full moon of your God and mine."

Turning his back on the gathering, Narro stalked away toward his hut. Tim knew the wheels were spinning in his opponent's head. Narro needed to come up with a plan to combat Tim soon or he was out of business.

When Tim heard two short clicks again, he knew his team was aware the events were going according to plan.

"Miguel, ask the chief if we can see Tom."

After Miguel translated Tim's request, the chief led them to a nearby hut. When they walked in, Tim knew his brother must have heard the exchange, because Tom played it cool.

Tom bowed at Tim's feet and said, "Welcome, great one. I'm sorry to have caused you to come so far to work your magic on my behalf."

When Tim saw the chief was impressed with Miguel's translation, he said, "Leave us."

Without a word, the chief departed. He appeared glad to be rid of his unwanted visitors for a short time.

Tom grabbed Tim's hands in his. "I'm sorry about this, Tim. Now I know you and dad were right. I shouldn't have come to Brazil."

"Yeah, but we'll worry about that later. In case Narro makes the chief change his mind about allowing us to stay here tonight, I'll tell you what we have in mind."

As Tom listened while Tim explained their plan of action, he was impressed with the way Tim and his group of helpers was able to put the plan together in just a few days. Then he turned to Miguel and said, "I'm glad you made it back to civilization, Miguel. I owe you."

"First, let's get you out of here. Then you can buy me the coldest beer in Brazil."

Tim pointed toward the entrance. "Miguel, you need to go out and speak with the villagers. Tell them Narro is evil. Ask them whether anyone saw him when the fisherman died, or if Narro was near the children when they came down with a fever."

Miguel nodded in agreement. "I'll be back before it gets dark. We'll have to be on our toes tonight."

"One other thing," Tim said. "Tell the villagers to stay together tonight and tomorrow. Don't let Narro have a chance to kill another person and blame the death on me."

After Miguel departed, Tom attempted to joke about his situation, but his humor didn't go over well. "I'm tired of bananas, fish and fried monkey. The natives don't have a wide variety on their menu. Miguel left me most of our food, but it didn't last long."

Tim slapped his brother on the back and said, "With a little bit of luck, the day after tomorrow you'll eat steak and potatoes. One way or the other, we're going to get you out of here, Tom."

Tom's face grew serious. "I don't want you to use force to rescue me – I feel strongly about that. God wouldn't want you to kill more innocent natives to save me from a situation I created through my own stupidity.

"If you can get me out of here with no further damage to these wonderful people, then it's God's will. If not, I'll take whatever He has in mind."

"I told the team I'd use force only as a last resort," Tim said. "I don't want to cause these people any more trouble, but I won't let them kill you for no reason other than a crazy medicine man's ego."

When Tom looked forlorn, Tim said, "I'll try it your way and see what happens. The only one I'm worrying about is Narro. If necessary, I have no qualms about taking him out."

In Narro's hut, the medicine man knew he was in serious trouble. So far, his primitive magic tricks had kept the villagers and chief in line. But now, Narro's trickery was no match for the newest arrival. If Narro couldn't find something to defeat this white man, he would lose his prestigious position.

When first viewing the magic of the evil box, Narro saw a way to disgrace the white church man. Somehow, Narro knew the photographs posed no problem to the villagers; but at the same time he saw a chance to increase his power over them.

Early in the morning the day after Tom's arrival, Santiago the fisherman left the village, and Narro followed. While Santiago was busy with his nets, Narro stole up behind him and hit Santiago in the head with a rock, killing him instantly.

After tying some heavy stones to the legs of the body, Narro slipped the corpse into the river and watched as it sank quickly. He knew the Piranha would make short work of the evidence and he smiled evilly.

Narro paddled Santiago's canoe for a short distance downstream. There, he overturned the craft near a pile of brush, where later other villagers would find it.

The day after Santiago's death, Narro put a clear liquid poison on a stalk of bananas and offered them to two children. The boys ate the fruit and soon developed a high fever accompanied by vomiting and diarrhea.

When the parents called Narro for help, they watched as he went through a long ritual of chants and rubbed potions onto the boys' arms and legs. They both perished shortly afterward and Narro blamed the three deaths on Tom. The superstitious natives accepted Narro's claim.

Now with the arrival of the white medicine man, all Narro's well-laid plans were in jeopardy.

As he looked out the entrance of his hut, Narro saw the newcomers' canoe. The bedrolls lying in the boat gave him an idea.

"After the new white devil allowed his picture to be taken by the evil box, if I can cause him to die, it will reinforce my hold on the villagers."

At the rear of his hut, Narro kept a special cage containing a green snake – a deadly pit viper called a bushmaster. When it was small, Narro captured the reptile and often used its venom for his potions.

Over the years, Narro became adept at handling the snake, so with the ability of past experiences, he quickly caught the serpent behind its head. Then he dropped it tail first into a small pouch and quickly closed the neck with a drawstring. When it was quiet outside, he left his hut and strolled to the riverbank near the canoe of the newcomers.

After checking to make sure no one was looking, Narro moved to the canoe and pulled back the top flap of one of the sleeping bags. Of the two, he chose the largest, believing correctly that it belonged to the tall white man.

He untied the pouch, shook out the snake, allowed the reptile to fall into the folds of the sleeping bag and chuckled in glee as he saw the snake creep deeper into the darkness, away from the heat of the sun. Then after looking around the clearing to be sure he hadn't been observed, Narro walked slowly away and returned to his hut.

While making his rounds of the village and speaking to the villagers he knew, Miguel also met some new friends.

Santiago's widow told Miguel her husband could swim like a fish. "There is no way Santiago could have fallen from his canoe and drowned so close to the village."

"Did you see Narro on the day Santiago went fishing?"

"No, our medicine man wasn't here until late in the morning. When Narro heard Santiago was missing, it was he who suggested we hunt downstream where we found the overturned canoe. Who will feed my children now?"

When Miguel spoke with the parents of the two dead children, one mother said, "I saw the boys eating bananas and sharing them with their pet monkey. Later, after they became sick, I found the monkey dead. No, I don't know where the children got the bananas."

As Miguel was speaking with this woman, he was crouched down on his haunches behind a net she was repairing. When he noticed movement near his canoe, Miguel hid behind a nearby dugout and watched Narro approach the craft.

Narro looked around the clearing and Miguel ducked down out of sight, but he was watching when Narro placed something in Tim's sleeping bag.

Miguel remained motionless and waited until Narro returned to his shelter. Then he stood up and walked to Tom's hut, where he reported what he saw. "Narro is out to get you, Mister Tim. I don't know what he put in your sleeping bag, but when we bring them inside, we need to be careful."

"Narro may have put a snake or a tarantula in our bags, Miguel. Borrow a machete from one of the villagers. Then make a big production of dragging the sleeping bags inside by the drawstrings."

"I hope Narro is watching," Miguel said. "It'll make his day if he thinks he has us. Hopefully he won't try anything else and we can sleep tonight."

"In the morning, he's in for a big surprise," Tim said.

Miguel returned shortly with a long-handled, very sharp machete. Then he helped Tim move everything from the center of the hut, leaving a large, empty space to work in.

As Miguel dragged the sleeping bags toward their hut, he stopped for a moment to rest in front of Narro's as if the load was too much. Then he pulled the bags into the tent and quickly let go of the drawstrings.

"How do you want to handle this, Mister Tim?"

"Look in your bag first, Miguel. I think Narro is after me. If yours doesn't contain anything, we'll have more room to work on mine. Use the machete to cut the drawstring. Then take the point of the knife and unroll the bag. If you see anything, kill it as quickly and quietly as possible."

Slowly and carefully Miguel unrolled his bag, but found nothing on the outside. Then he hooked the point of the machete into the zipper, undid it and used the knife to spread the bag out. After inspecting the bag thoroughly, again, Miguel said, "There's nothing here."

"Okay," Tim said. "Roll it up and put it in the rear of the hut."

Miguel cut the drawstring to Tim's sleeping bag and then unrolled it. "Whatever Narro put in here, it's not on the outside."

"Then it has to be inside," Tim said. "Be ready for anything.

Tim turned to his brother. "Tom, move to the rear of the hut – I don't want you in the line of fire."

As quietly as possible, Miguel slowly undid the zipper, hooked his knife into one side of the sleeping bag and threw it open. Inside he found a small green snake asleep in one of the folds.

With one swift swing of the machete, Miguel cut off the reptile's head. "I got him," he said and smiled.

"Good work, Miguel."

"I cut all the way through your sleeping bag."

"Do you think I care? Thanks, my friend. I owe you my life. After seeing the snake, I don't really want to use the sleeping bag. It's a good thing you kept your eyes open, Miguel. You earned a big bonus."

"I didn't do this for money," Miguel said. "The creep made me mad. Killing his own people to increase his power over them is unbelievable."

Attempting to make light of the incident, Tim said, "I wish there was some way to save the snake. I'd love to drop it down Narro's shorts tomorrow."

Tim's statement broke the tension of the moment and they chuckled in relief.

"Let's settle down," Tim said. "We've been through enough excitement for today. The sun's setting and it's suppertime. We have lots of food in our backpacks, Tom, so no more fried monkey for you. After we eat, we'll act as if we've gone to sleep. If we keep quiet, it might help convince Narro that he succeeded in killing us."

The sun slipped slowly behind the green curtain of jungle and the village grew quiet. The inhabitants followed Miguel's instructions. They moved into their huts and stayed together. Miguel managed to plant a seed of doubt and suspicion about their medicine man in their minds.

Tim hoped it would serve him well.

During a nearly sleepless night, Narro heard nothing from the hut of the white devils and their brown friend. *"I hope my snake killed the new one. Regardless, tomorrow I'll deal with them all."*

Narro spent most of the night preparing himself and his potions while praying to his God to allow him to succeed against the white medicine man. After checking all his black magic pieces carefully, he gathered his bag of tricks together and eventually dropped off to a troubled slumber.

Tim awoke with a start from a short nap and was surprised to see Miguel and Tom asleep on the floor nearby. The sun was rising out of a steaming jungle. Dawn was greeted by a group of raucous monkeys swinging through the trees. A few white puffy clouds hung low on the horizon, but they appeared to contain no rain.

Tim shook Miguel's shoulder and smiled when the guide awoke startled. Tim said, "It looks like another beautiful day. I don't think we'll have any rain. We don't need anything to dampen our spirits or the fireworks tonight."

"The river won't be running as strong," Miguel said. "That will help Jose and Mister Frank when they get here tonight."

"We'll stay close to the hut today," Tim said. "Go ahead, Miguel – speak with the villagers and see how they made out last night. I hope they took your warnings to heart."

The three men took their morning meal outside, but Narro seemed content to remain inside his hut. There was no way Tim could judge Narro's reaction when he saw his supposed victims alive and well.

Miguel said, "Narro may be worried about his pet snake."

"Let him wonder," Tim said.

The noonday meal was a village-wide affair held in the large communal hut in the center of the clearing. With Miguel's help, Tim spoke again with the village chief.

After displaying the two pieces of the dead snake, which were now curled on a broad green leaf, Tim told the chief how he found the snake in his sleeping bag. He said, "The power of my God kept me safe."

Miguel whispered in Tim's ear, "The chief knows the snake belonged to the medicine man. From the looks from the other villagers, they know it too."

"Don't eat or drink anything they offer you," Tim warned. "We're not about to take any chances with Narro."

In the evening, the sun set slowly and darkness enveloped the village like a black blanket. As the natives prepared for the ceremony, the chief ordered a large fire lit in the center of the clearing.

Although Tim wasn't sure the walkie-talkie batteries were low, he changed them anyway. For tonight's work, he couldn't take any chances.

Miguel sorted through the remaining items in their backpacks. "There's not much we can take with us."

Tim passed out the remaining food and said, "Eat hearty, Tom, we have food left over. I checked the revolvers. They're ready if we need them."

Tom frowned and said, "Let's not talk about shooting anyone. Work your magic and get me out of here without hurting anybody else."

"I'll give it my best shot."

Tom shook his head, but smiled in spite of himself. "What a terrible pun."

Just before sunset, three miles upriver, Jose set the big bad bird down on the river. While powering the craft toward shore, he kept the blades moving until Frank could drop an anchor and pull them close to the riverbank.

Then Jose shut the engine down, waited until darkness overtook them and finally allowed the aircraft to slowly drift downstream.

Since they knew tonight all the natives would be in the village for the big ceremony, Jose and Frank didn't have any fear they would be observed; but they approached the village as quietly as possible. When Jose saw the light from the campfire, they poled the craft close to the bank and dropped the anchor once again.

After letting out line until the helo drifted close to the riverbank, Frank tied the anchor off and jumped onshore carrying a large backpack. An AR-15 was strapped over his shoulder, barrel down.

When Frank reached firm ground, he turned on a flashlight with a red filter to dim the light and pointed it into the jungle. He saw a small clearing thirty feet away and said, "This should do, Jose. Don't forget where I am."

For such a large man, Frank's voice sounded small against the strange noises emanating from the dense undergrowth.

Jose smiled wickedly. "You're a better man than I am, Gunga Din. Don't step on any crocs."

"You're not funny, Jose."

As Frank turned to make his way to the clearing, he didn't see Jose wave before allowing the aircraft to drift onward with the slow-moving current.

The sound of a drumbeat sounded as a signal to begin the ceremony. Wordlessly, the chief watched as the villagers gathered in a group near the campfire.

Since the natives couldn't understand him, Tim said, "Put some more logs on the fire, Miguel. I want Jose to be able to see the village."

Heat waves rose into the sky and seemed to make the surrounding shadows quiver, which only added to the eerie spectacle. Mist from the river drifted by as if ghosts were dancing to the beat of the drum. The sight made the scene even more surreal.

Tim stood to one side of the fire away from the riverbank and watched as Miguel kept feeding the fire.

Tim spoke quietly and reassuringly into the open mike of the radio beneath his shirt. "Two or three men have short spears in their hands, but most are unarmed."

Miguel added, "Two have machetes hooked to their belts."

Two clicks on Tim's radio told them their teammates heard and were aware.

Since he knew those in Obidos were listening, Tim said, "I doubt the villagers mean us any harm, Miguel. They're probably used to having the weapons with them at all times. Just play it cool and don't get excited."

Although Miguel's hands were shaking slightly, he said, "I'll do my best."

Two natives brought Tom from his hut and placed him on the side of the clearing near the riverbank. Tonight Tom chose to wear his Vestment with a white Alb and purple Chasuble. His reversed collar and purple stole with fringed ends added to his finery. Around his neck, Tom wore a gold cross on a thin chain.

Tim attempted to joke, but his eyes misted and his throat held a lump as big as one of Garfield's hairballs. "For a condemned man, Tom looks pretty elegant."

Miguel pointed to Tom's wrists and noted, "They tied his hands in front, but his legs are free."

Except for moonlight from the full moon above and the flickering fire, complete darkness surrounded the village.

When Tim's walkie-talkie clicked three times, he knew Frank was in place, ready with the fireworks, while Jose was poling the helo down the river.

Suddenly, with great flair, while swinging his machete in the air and screaming at the moon, Narro ran from his hut toward the fire.

Tim spoke into his mike for everyone's benefit, "Narro really outdid himself. His body is painted in different colors, so you won't be able to miss him, Jose. He has white circles around his eyes and a jagged yellow streak across his front, from his right shoulder down to his left hip."

The radio clicked twice, telling Tim that Jose heard his remarks and was ready.

Narro was dressed in his finest feathered cloak. It was hanging open around his painted torso and the feathers seemed to float around his body as he danced. Small gourds filled with tiny pebbles were tied to his hips and ankles. While his accouterments rattled merrily, he danced around the fire with another rattle gourd in one hand and a very large, highly-polished machete in the other.

Under his shirt, Tim tightened his grip on his revolver and thought, *"Make one move toward Tom and you're a dead man."*

When Narro stuck the long knife into the ground near the fire and continued to chant and sing as he danced, Tim's fears diminished.

Then Tim heard three clicks on his radio to signify Jose was in place and knew it was time to make his move. Above the noise of Narro's dance, he shouted, "Translate everything I say as quickly as you can, Miguel."

Miguel nodded. His hands were sweaty and he felt faint.

Tim clapped his hands together and heard the sound ring out across the clearing like a pistol shot. Then he threw his head back and shouted to the heavens, "Oh, God on high. I call upon you to display your great power. Send down the thunder from above."

Just as Miguel finished Tim's translation, the first bomb went off overhead.

CRACK--BABOOM!

A huge explosion echoed and reverberated through the jungle. Then a moment later, it was followed by another huge blast.

CRACK--BABOOM!

A few minutes ago, the jungle was alive with night calls of birds and the sounds of unseen animals. Now, except for the beating of hundreds of wings as frightened birds flew out into the darkness, it was deathly still.

Tim felt a slight concussion from the powerful explosions, and glanced down at Miguel. Although the guide knew of them in advance, Miguel appeared to be startled by the power of the bomb blasts.

Around the campfire, the natives were stunned. They dropped to their knees or fell to the ground, covered their heads and wailed. One old woman shook so badly Tim thought she might be having a heart attack. As they cried and screamed at the top of their voices, the children burrowed into their mother's dresses for protection.

Tim pointed at Narro, raised his hands high again and called out, "See and hear the power of my God, Narro. Do not tell me your medicine is more powerful than mine."

There was no answer from Tim's adversary, who stood quivering in his tracks. He was speechless and apparently paralyzed by the power of this white devil.

Tim stared into Narro's eyes and called out, "Now I will show you even more power. My God will turn night into day. Watch, Narro, while I call down fire from the sky."

Again, Miguel's translation was no sooner out of his mouth, before a huge star burst lit up the sky.

Above the village, a large circle of light suddenly glowed and expanded in the heavens. It was followed by a crack of a small explosion louder than any thunder the villagers may have heard in the past. By this time the natives were cowering on the ground, covering their eyes or staring in awe at the spectacle above.

The chief appeared to be in a trance. His arms were raised skyward as if in surrender to Tim's power. Although Narro initially recovered from his fear of the thunder from above, he was now completely overwhelmed by the fire from the sky.

Ten seconds later, another even more powerful star burst and explosion went off overhead. The natives continued to moan and cry out in fear. The old woman, who had been shaking so badly, finally fainted. Her eyes rolled back into her head and her body twitched spasmodically in time with her heartbeat.

Throughout the display, Tim waited to hear the sound of Jose's helicopter. Then he saw the dark shape flit through the flickering firelight and heard it hovering overhead.

In quick succession, two more bomb blasts went off.

Tim thought, *"Frank is putting them right on target."*

Overhead, Tim heard the rotor blades beating against the damp evening air. Suddenly, without warning, classical music filled the sky. He took his cue, pointed again to the sky and shouted, "Listen to my God's music. He is angry, for you have falsely accused one of my tribe of killing your people."

Miguel was having a hard time trying to keep up with Tim, but he thought, *"Although the fireworks did a number of their minds and they're petrified with fear, the chief and villagers will get the gist of what Tim is saying."*

Tim held his hand to his ear as if he was receiving a message. Then he pointed to Narro, who was still cowering near the fire. "My God tells me one of your own is guilty of the deaths of Santiago and the two children."

As Tim spoke, and Miguel translated, several villagers stared at Narro with hatred in their eyes.

Above the noise of the music, Tim shouted, "With His Holy beam of light, my God will point out the one who is responsible for these crimes."

After locating Narro from Tim's description, Jose engaged

the autopilot, pointed a small search light toward the head of the medicine man and hit the switch. "Gotcha, sucker."

Narro attempted to look up at the bright light, but he was blinded by the glare.

Tim watched as the painted devil shook his head to clear the cobwebs of fear. He could tell Narro was spooked.

By turning in a slow circle, the medicine man looked around the clearing at Tim, the villagers and his chief. Everyone was staring at him in hatred for the terrible consequences Narro had caused to their village with his dirty deeds.

Jose continued to hold Narro in the center of the light as if he was nailed to the ground.

Suddenly the father of one of the murdered boys ran toward Narro with a spear in his hand, screaming something Tim couldn't understand. Narro saw the man coming, so in an attempt to escape, he turned and ran toward the river.

His pursuer called out, urging other villagers to assist in his revenge. Several took up their weapons and joined in the chase.

As Narro reached the bank of the Amazon, the father hurled his spear. It stuck Narro squarely in the middle of his back, went completely through his body and emerged partway from his chest.

As if he was surprised, Narro stopped in mid-stride, wrapped his hands around the bloody shaft and attempted to pull the weapon from his chest. His eyes grew wider in fear. Then they rolled back in his head. He staggered slowly into the water, fell to his knees and slipped into the murky depths.

The current caught Narro's body and rolled it over until it was floating on its back. His dead face and blank eyes reflected the light from the helicopter. Then his body sank slowly underwater.

As if on cue, the light and music from above ceased. Tim heard Jose give the engine more power for a landing.

With respect in his eyes, the chief looked at Tim and gave the peace sign. Tim returned the greeting, smiled at their success, pulled his radio from under his shirt and said, "It's all over, Jose. Bring the helo down."

As the big black bird began to drop out of the dark sky in preparation of landing, trinkets by the hundreds rained down on the villagers.

When the wheels touched the ground, Tim shouted, "Get on board, Tom."

Tom didn't need a second invitation. He picked up the hem of his vestment and ran toward the aircraft. Jose held open the door to the rear compartment. Once Tom was aboard, he leaned out to pull Miguel into the helicopter.

Tim stopped long enough to salute the chief. Then he ran to the helo and quickly climbed into the front passenger seat.

Jose lifted off and turned toward the river where Frank was waiting. Above them, two more starbursts exploded and expanded.

Upriver from the village, Jose flared the helicopter into a hover over the water. The beam of a bright flashlight shone on the river, as Frank's worried voice came over the walkie-talkie, "Is everything okay? There's nothing in the water and plenty of space to land near the bank. You're a sight for sore eyes."

Slowly, Jose approached the riverbank and flicked on the powerful searchlight. Frank held his weapon at port arms and looked up. His eyes were as wide as if he had seen ghosts in the dark.

Calmly, Tim said, "We see you, Frank. Everything went better than planned. Put your rifle on safety so you don't accidentally shoot anyone. Then get your head down. Here we come."

Watching from the passenger's seat, Tim saw Frank click on the safety switch. Then he noticed some logs lying on the edge of the circle of light. He started to warn Jose, but when it didn't appear the logs would interfere with setting the helo down, Tim kept his silence.

Jose held the copter inches above the water with one float close to the riverbank until Frank handed Miguel his rifle and pack and quickly climbed aboard.

As Frank wiped perspiration from his eyes, he said, "Man, I'm glad to see you guys. I heard things in the brush. I think they were monkeys, but I'm not sure. The past hour was the worst I've spent in my life."

As if he had seen something funny, Jose shook his head and grinned as he lifted off the river and gained height prior to heading for Obidos.

Above the noise of the aircraft, Tom shouted, "My rescue is a real miracle. I thank God you were able to pull it off. I still can't believe the way things went. I feel sorry about the medicine man though."

From where he was sitting on the floor, Miguel stared up at Tom and said, "You're crazy to worry about Narro. He got what was coming to him, and his people got some well-deserved revenge."

Ever the pastor, Tom said, "You may be right, but I still regret the loss of any life."

Miguel was still pumped. "Did you see the reaction of the natives to the first two bombs? I think several of them thought they were about to die. They sure got a taste of your big medicine, Mister Tim."

Tim smiled at Miguel's comments and added, "I believe the next white man who sets foot in their village will be respected far more than he should be. I'm just happy no one else got hurt."

Jose's voice crackled on Tim's radio. "As I was listening to you on the walkie-talkie, I had the feeling the old chief knew all about his medicine man. I believe he wanted to get rid of Narro and you did him a big favor. When we left the village, I noticed the chief had a smile on his face."

"You may be right, Jose," Tim said. "Since we left our gear and the canoe, plus the trinkets you dumped on them, that will probably raise the chief's status in the eyes of the villagers."

Catherine's voice boomed out from Tim's walkie-talkie. "You guys sound like you're in a good mood."

Tom leaned over Tim's shoulder and spoke into the mike, "Tim told me about your help, Catherine. Thank you; you deserve a big kiss from us both."

"After you arrive, I'll take you up on the offer."

When they landed at Obidos, Catherine was waiting. Tim could tell she was as excited as they were. As they emerged from the helicopter, she ran up to them.

True to his promise, Tom hugged her and kissed the top of her head. Tim looked on in amazement and thought, *"Just the kind of a kiss a priest would give a beautiful woman."*

After Tom released her, he said, "Thanks, Catherine for all you did. Tim told me the original idea for this rescue plan was yours. You'll never know how glad I am to be back here in one piece."

"I didn't do much. I gave Tim an idea and he did the rest. You have a great brother, Tom."

"Yes, I know. I owe him a lot."

Then Catherine turned towards Tim. "I believe you said something about both brothers giving me a kiss."

She looked up at Tim and asked, "Well?"

Tim reached out slowly and pulled her to him. He kissed her warm mouth and felt his heart jump.

Catherine returned his kiss and for a moment she blushed. Then she took Tim's arm for the walk back to her house, as the others stood by watching. No one needed to be told something was going on between the two. They could see it in Catherine's eyes and the way Tim looked at her.

Miguel excused himself. "I'll meet you at your house, Catherine. Mister Tom will need some clothes. He's about my size."

After making their way down the potholed road to Catherine's house, the happy group discovered a big pot of coffee and a cooler of beer was waiting on the patio.

When Miguel arrived with a change of clothes, Tom excused

himself. Thirty minutes later, after taking a long, hot shower and having a shave, he looked and smelled much better. Miguel's shirt was a little short in the sleeves, but Tom rolled them up.

Tim handed his brother a cold one. "Have a beer, little brother."

"Thanks, it's been a while."

Tom downed half the brew in one long, satisfying gulp. Then he held the bottle high in the air as a salute. "I thank you all for rescuing me. It's a miracle I'm here, but I feel bad about the villagers we left behind.

"Because of my actions, and through no fault of theirs, four of them are dead. I'm ashamed of myself and will have to ask God for His forgiveness.

"I fooled myself by running around and looking for a solution to problems that I alone created. I plan to return to the U.S.A. to work with the youth of America. Maybe I can help change things for the better. One thing is sure; I'll be able to converse with the natives."

Tim slapped his twin on the back and said, "That was quite a speech, brother. To tell the truth, I'm tired of the jungle myself. Let's leave it to the locals."

Chapter 12

Austin, Texas

In her apartment on Bucknell Drive, Cheryl was sitting quietly on her sofa with a stiff drink in her hand while reflecting on her past life and the most recent developments.

"I wonder how I came to this end."

As always, most of the blame was placed on her ex-husband, Tim. Six months after she gave birth, Tim ran off to play war and left Cheryl alone and miserable.

Back then, all Cheryl wanted to do was party, so she left the kid with a babysitter and headed downtown. That's where she renewed her friendship with a man named Bob Stern. He was the guy Tim found her with when he came home from Viet Nam.

Once again, Cheryl had lost her latest job by being late too many mornings after drinking her blues away the night before. So she was easy prey for Bob, who first turned her on to marijuana and later cocaine.

Without realizing the consequences, Cheryl allowed Bob to move in with her. He had what she required – a steady supply of pot and coke.

As far as Bob was concerned, the arrangement was an even trade.

Cheryl possessed what he desired – her body.

Then Tim came home and wrecked it all, and Cheryl filed for divorce. Bob stayed in her bed for another six months until he grew tired of her. Then, like a pied piper, he moved on, leaving Cheryl alone once more. But now, instead of a desperate housewife, Cheryl was a craving druggie.

There came a time when Cheryl finally realized drugs were jeopardizing her life. She attempted to quit and actually did several times. Sooner or later though, she returned to her habit for the high.

While searching desperately for money to support her habit, Cheryl began to ask her male companions for cash or gifts. During the next ten years, she kept several men on a string. She would meet them for a quickie in a hotel or take short vacations with her latest conquest to various locations in Texas.

By the time Kate was fourteen, Cheryl had accumulated a wide selection of expensive jewels and a fair amount of cash from her men.

In a roundabout way, the jewelry gave Cheryl her big break.

One wild weekend while Kate was away with her grandparents, Cheryl made the mistake of inviting a new lover to her apartment. She seldom did that anymore, but the thought of George and Pearl discovering her secret made the liaison more dangerous, which only added to her pleasure.

The next morning Cheryl awoke to find her latest lover was missing, along with several pieces of her smaller trinkets. After she checked and found her stash of the more valuable items still secure in a stocking in her closet, she knew she had learned an expensive lesson.

To insure such an episode didn't happen again, Cheryl decided to take her remaining jewels to a bank and store them in a safe-deposit box. She drove to the nearest bank and made inquiries about renting a box. There, in the form of the bank manager, Wendell Grayson, fate walked into her life.

As she led Cheryl to his desk, the receptionist, Jane White, said,

"Mister Grayson handles new accounts."

Cheryl noted the man was fifty or a bit older and beginning to bald. On the plus side, his body was trim and he was handsome. A wooden plaque on his desk said his first name was Wendell.

Wendell asked, "How may I help you, Mrs. Fitch?"

"I want to rent a safe deposit box to store my valuables."

As they spoke, Cheryl caught Wendell's eyes straying from the paperwork to her breasts, and a plan began to take shape in her scheming mind. *"A bank manager must be wealthy. The suit he's wearing must have cost at least five hundred dollars."*

She leaned over the desk to read the contract and allowed Wendell a good view of the silky valley between her breasts. When he glanced up, Cheryl gave him her best smile.

After they completed the paperwork, Wendell said, "Please follow me."

He led Cheryl to a large vault at the rear of the bank, where he opened the gate to the inner portion. Then with a small bow and a wave of his left hand, he ushered her inside.

Cheryl watched as Wendell removed a key from his key ring and took another from a small envelope. Using both, he opened box number 716. Then he removed a long, slender container and repeated, "Please follow me."

She trailed along as he led her into a privacy room that resembled a small closet, where Wendell set the box down on a wooden shelf.

Cheryl moved closer and "accidentally" rubbed her breasts against his arm.

Wendell's face reddened and he said, "Pardon me, I'm very sorry."

"It's my fault," she replied. "In a small place such as this, accidents will happen."

Wendell removed a clean white handkerchief from his breast pocket and wiped his brow. "Please place your valuables inside the box. When you're finished, I'll show you how to lock it.

Then he asked, "Would you prefer privacy, or do you need

my assistance?"

Cheryl smiled again. "I would appreciate your help."

While they moved about in the small space, her breasts occasionally came into contact with Wendell's arms. From the look he gave her, Cheryl knew he was aware that this time it was no accident.

Although she felt Wendell was hooked, Cheryl wanted to be sure she could land him. She handed him her last item and said, "It's probably my bad luck that you're married and your wife wouldn't allow you to join me for a drink to reward your kindness."

Wendell smiled knowingly and winked. "My wife and I lead our own lives. After twenty-seven years together, that's the way it is with some couples. If a drink is really what you have in mind, or if it's something else, I'm free to join you."

"Wonderful, I know a quiet place – 'the Garden Room' at the Hyatt Regency. I'll be waiting at four-thirty this afternoon."

At four-twenty, Wendell walked into the bar and sat down in the booth next to Cheryl. They shared a drink. Then she moved closer and began to caress his leg. Wendell put his arm around her and pulled her close. When her warm hands roamed to his groin, she found he was very aroused.

By five forty-five, they were making love in the room she rented on arrival.

"*It was so easy,*" Cheryl thought and did her utmost to pretend Wendell was the best lover she had ever experienced. While Wendell struggled to reach his climax, she moaned, smothered him with kisses and stroked him everywhere.

After their first liaison, they met twice weekly at the same hotel. Although the desk clerk with a name tag identifying him only as Harry knew what was going on, as long as they were discreet, Harry didn't care. With a wink, he would say, "Good afternoon."

Cheryl always slipped him a twenty dollar bill and replied, "Hello again, Harry."

After making sure Wendell didn't suspect a thing, Cheryl bought a small video camera and hid it in a specially prepared purse. She sat the pocketbook on the dresser, where it would record the entire bed.

Just before Wendell arrived, she switched the camera on. While they made wild love, Cheryl arranged their position on the bed to insure Wendell's face and body were featured prominently in her first ever porno film.

When Wendell left, she rewound the tape, watched their performance and was very satisfied with the results. Then she took the camera home and made several copies. At the time, when she placed one in her safe deposit box, the move seemed ironic.

The next time Wendell arrived for his twice a week roll in the hay, Cheryl waited until they made love and he was dressed to leave. Then she said, "I have something to show you, Wendell."

She inserted the cassette into the VCR and let him view their production. A few moments later, thinking Cheryl was a blackmailer, Wendell said, "Okay, turn it off. You made your point, Cheryl. How much do you want?"

"I don't want money, Wendell. What I need is a job at your bank. I have previous experience as a secretary, so you'll get a fair return for a decent salary and we can continue our rendezvous. I like you, Wendell and enjoy making love with you. I'm only protecting myself in case you grow tired of me, as you seem to have grown weary of your wife."

While staring into Cheryl's eyes, Wendell took time to think things over. *"Well, she has me by the short hairs. I knew it was too good to be true, and just when I thought I had it made. Cheryl's a nice piece, but I hope she's not screwing around with me. Shirley hasn't wanted a thing to do with me for the past few years.*

"I'll give Cheryl the benefit of the doubt and see what happens. If all she wants is a job, that's easy to fix. And I keep getting into her pants? Now there's a real no-brainer."

"You didn't need the tape to find a job," Wendell said. "All you had to do was ask. You know I like you, Cheryl. I'm disappointed you felt you must do something so blatant."

Pointing toward the VCR, he asked, "How many copies did you make?"

"This is the only one," Cheryl lied. "I needed to know how you really felt. Here, take the tape and destroy it."

Just as she hoped, Wendell gave in. "I will. Okay, we understand each other. You come into the bank and apply for a job. I'll see you're hired."

Cheryl smiled and said, "Thank you. I apologize for my actions. How can I make it up to you?"

As he slowly unzipped his pants, Wendell smiled down at her and said, "There is one way."

Cheryl kept her end of the bargain, as did Wendell. After a year at her job with no mention of the tape by her lover, she removed the original from the safe deposit box and destroyed it along with the other copies.

Over the years, Cheryl's feelings toward her daughter slowly changed. At first, Kate was just another nuisance, something left over from her failed marriage. Finally Cheryl woke up and realized Kate needed a mother, one who really cared about her.

As she continued to be more communicative with her daughter, Cheryl thought Kate responded to her entreaties. At least they appeared to have a closer relationship.

Now several years later, Cheryl's memory drifted back to her main source of disappointment in her musings – her marriage to Tim.

"Maybe I'm wrong and Tim isn't the only one to blame. I did some stupid stuff myself and screwed up my life. Look at me now, sitting here and waiting to check out. I'm afraid of dying slowly and wasting away with

AIDS. If I wanted to kill anyone, I should have started with Bob."

Cheryl's mind drifted back in time again, to the day when Wendell reduced their liaisons to only once a week and she began searching for another sexual partner. She hadn't learned from her past mistakes, so Cheryl returned to her usual haunts, where she met an old friend, Freddie, who possessed a steady supply of drugs.

Freddie wasn't very cute, but she remembered he was good in bed. One thing led to another and Cheryl ended up getting stoned and staying overnight at his apartment.

Cheryl woke up the next day with her head in a fog of drug induced stupor. *"What did I do last night? I can't remember. Oh, God, I didn't use protection. What was I thinking?"*

Then she also recalled she used the same needle as Freddie to shoot up.

Her mind raced. *"What a stupid thing to do. Damn, I have a headache."*

A month later, after experiencing spells of dizziness and feeling very weak, Cheryl made an appointment with a doctor named Leslie. He took a blood sample and gave her pills to prevent the lightheadedness. The medicine didn't do much to relieve her illness.

When Doctor Leslie's nurse phoned and asked Cheryl to come to his office immediately, she knew it wasn't good news, but she went anyway.

"What's up, Doc?" she asked sarcastically.

Doctor Leslie didn't smile at Cheryl's flippant attempt at humor. His face was one of concern. "Come in and close the door. I'm sorry, but I have some bad news."

Still unrepentant, Cheryl said, "Go ahead, shoot."

"I'm afraid you contacted the HIV virus."

"You mean AIDS?"

"Yes."

She wasn't too shocked. "How much longer do I have?"

The doctor shook his head slightly. "I can't say for sure. Modern technology is constantly developing new drugs to combat this disease, so don't give up. With the medicine now available you may live a long time."

"Cutting through the crap, Doc; how much longer will I live?"

"Approximately two years, if you take your medicine, less if you don't."

Cheryl shook her head in disbelief. "Well, I asked, didn't I? Thanks, Doc. I appreciate your concern. What will happen first?"

"You'll begin to lose weight and may experience pain and fatigue."

"So it's a slow, one way ticket to hell."

Doctor Leslie didn't reply, but Cheryl knew.

After giving her more prescriptions, Doctor Leslie advised Cheryl to continue to take the medicine. The pills only seemed to make things worse.

Finally, Cheryl made up her mind she was not going to sit around and wait to die a slow, painful death.

She looked down at the list of names she had accumulated and said aloud, "To hell with reminiscing, there are people who need to pay. I have plans to make."

Chapter 13

Everyone who took part in the rescue attempt joined in the celebration, telling Tom how glad they were to have had a part in his release and safe return to civilization.

Catherine prepared a pile of sandwiches for the group and they drank a few more beers to wind down from the excitement of the day.

When Miguel was ready to leave, he said, "Come on, Frank. You can bunk at my house tonight."

"I'll sleep in my copter," Jose said. He waved goodnight and took along a can of beer to keep him company.

Catherine gave Tom some bedding and said, "Come with me, Tom. You can sleep in the schoolhouse. I hope a cot will be okay."

"After sleeping on the thin mats that covered the hard ground in my prison hut, this is heaven. Would you have a Bible I might borrow?"

"Sure, I have one in the schoolhouse."

When Tom was settled in, Catherine returned to the house to sit with Tim and share a glass of wine.

As she walked up to his chair, Tim asked, "Could I have another kiss? Our first one didn't last as long as I would have liked."

She bent down to kiss him and asked in return, "Why not?"

Mutually attracted to each other, they embraced for some time. When they finally pulled apart, both were out of breath.

"Wow," she said.

"Indeed," Tim said. "You're really something. I felt the kiss all the way down to my toes."

"You too? We may have started something. Do you mind?"

"Not me. The first time we met and I shook your hand, I felt a tingle in my body. I haven't experienced something like that for years."

Catherine moved back into his arms and murmured, "I think you need to kiss me again."

Tim did as she asked. Then he said, "We should finish our wine and get some sleep. I'm falling in love with you, Catherine and really want to take my time. Do I make sense?"

"Yes, Tim, you do. I feel the same way. I know how Cheryl hurt you, but I'm not her. I'm Catherine, someone who can love you like no one else. I'm willing to take as much time as we need to be sure."

"I knew you would understand," Tim said. "Give me one more kiss and then off to bed for us."

They both knew they had found someone special and didn't want to blow the chance, so their minds were filled with questions and neither got much sleep.

In the morning, Tim and Catherine were all smiles. When they kept looking at each other over breakfast, Tom noticed. "Am I seeing things, or are you two lovebirds hiding something?"

"You always were able to see through me, Tom. Yes, Catherine and I have a lot in common and want to see how things work out. We're not lovebirds in any sense of the word, but we're working on it. What do you think?"

"That's great. You've needed someone like Catherine, brother. You have for some time. I wish you both all the luck in the world."

"Luck and love is all we need, Tom," Catherine said. "Thank you for understanding."

In a few minutes, Jose arrived and ate breakfast with his three friends. Shortly after Catherine poured the last of the coffee, Miguel and Frank came in the door to join them.

"I'm ready to head back to Prainha," Frank said. "From there I'll catch a puddle jumper to Santare'm."

After writing a check for Frank's services, Tim said, "You really know your explosives. I don't know what we would have done without your well-placed ordinance."

"Thanks again, Frank," Tom said. "I owe you my life."

Then Frank made his own pun. "Except for the noises in the brush, I had a 'blast'. I'll remember last night for a long time. My hands were shaking so; I could hardly set off the fireworks."

As he interrupted their conversation, Jose wore a secret smile on his face. "If you want to get to Prainha before noon, Tim, it's time to load up and get a move on."

"Wind up the bird, Jose. I'll be there in a minute. I want to say goodbye to Catherine."

Tim held her in his arms and said, "I have to wind up my affairs and pay Jose for everything he bought, plus the cost of the hours we spent looking for Tom. As soon as I finish, I'll come back and get to know you better."

"I'll be here waiting," she promised and kissed him again.

As the others were loading the last of their gear, Tim arrived at the helicopter pad. He climbed aboard and said, "Let's head for Prainha."

When everyone else was loaded up and buckled in, Jose lifted the helo off smoothly and swung out over the river.

Miguel waved goodbye from the landing pad. *"With everyone gone, it's going to be awfully quiet around Obidos."*

The flight to Prainha, where they dropped Frank off was uneventful. In the terminal, Frank waved goodbye and said, "I'll have a great tale to tell my grandchildren."

Jose refueled the helicopter and they flew on to Belem.

After Tim booked Tom on a flight departing early the next morning to Bermuda; the twins stayed overnight in the Belem Airport Hotel.

Jose didn't seem to mind the delay. He had a list of items Juanita had given him that they either couldn't find in Prainha or could be purchased for less in Belem.

As the two brothers enjoyed a delicious steak dinner, Tim said, "When we were in the native hut, I promised you steak and potatoes, Tom. Doesn't that seem like a long time ago?"

While attacking his meat with gusto, Tom said, "I'm not complaining. This is great; no more fried monkey."

The next morning, Tim put his brother on board his flight. Then he decided to stay in Belem for another day.

When he asked Jose if it was all right with him, Jose said, "I'm only halfway through Juanita's list. If I don't return with everything, I'll be in the doghouse. Sure, it's okay if we stay over. I'll let Juanita know."

So Tim spent the day shopping. He bought several nice dresses and an engagement ring for Catherine. The next morning he and Jose flew back to Prainha where Tim stayed overnight in Miss Lela's hotel.

When Tim asked Jose for an invoice for his services, he was surprised at the total, but wrote a check gratefully. Jose was pleased with the bonus Tim threw in.

Tim hated to say goodbye to Miss Lela. She cried when he settled up his bill.

"I'll miss you, sweetheart," he said.

"Bring Catherine down for a visit," Lela said while wiping tears from her eyes. "I'll give you the honeymoon suite at a bargain price."

Jose was waiting at the helicopter pad. He looked very happy when he said, "Miguel told me you and Catherine have something going. You couldn't do better. She's one special lady."

"I agree, Jose. Are we going to stand around and talk all day, or do you plan to take me to Obidos anytime soon?"

"Get on board. You're like everybody else who thinks they're in love – always in a hurry."

"I don't think so, Jose, I know."

"Good for you, boss."

Although Tim had been away from Catherine for only a few days, he realized how much he missed her and was extremely nervous. While reliving the past few days in his mind, he was lost in thought. A few minutes later, Jose pointed ahead and said, "Catherine is waiting by the landing pad."

She wore a pair of shorts and a light blue blouse. As they got closer, she waved hello. When they landed, while Jose looked on and smiled, she ran to Tim. As Tim stepped down out of the helicopter, she threw her arms around him and kissed him hungrily.

When they both started to talk at once, Tim stopped what he was going to say to let her speak. "Did Tom get back to Bermuda okay?" she asked. "How was your flight? What did you bring me?"

"As far as I know, Tom is home with our parents. Although Jose thought I was nervous, the flight was fine. I don't know why. Maybe he thinks I'm in love."

"Go ahead," Jose said. "I'll bring the luggage and groceries to your house in about a half hour."

Tim and Catherine walked arm in arm down the muddy road toward her house. They spent the next half hour talking about everything in general and nothing in particular.

Although sharing a few sweet kisses, they didn't let their emotions get out of control. Jose would arrive shortly and they didn't want to embarrass him. Both knew what would happen when they were alone. They were willing to wait.

As Jose pulled his small wagon up to the door, he shouted, "Here are your groceries.

"Bring them in," Catherine said.

Jose knew he would be a third wheel on a bicycle, so he didn't stay to visit.

"Would you like some coffee," Catherine asked.

"No thanks, I have to get home. You two take care. When you want to be picked up, give me a call, Tim."

After Jose departed, Tim and Catherine were drawn to each

other. They kissed tenderly and passionately. Then Catherine reached down, took his hand and led him to her bedroom.

Then, while they made love for the first time, their movements were slow and tender. Tim knew this was love, not lust or just sex. Never before had he shared such a wonderful feeling.

Afterward, satiated and lying in each other's arms, they spoke of their future. Tim asked, "How long will you have to remain here?"

"I need to finish what I started, so I must complete this school year. I know I've made a difference in the lives of these children. I'll ask my supervisor to find a suitable replacement to begin in April. Okay?"

"Of course; anything you do is okay with me."

"How long can you stay?" she asked.

"I should have been in Fort Worth by now," he said. "Bill and Ken are probably snowed under. Seriously though, I need to phone to see for sure what shape the business is in. I usually do all the paperwork. After three weeks absence, they may be in over their heads."

Catherine tickled his chin and said, "You're Mister Important."

"Not really; when I'm not there the guys do well, but I need to catch up on everything. Then I'll turn the job over to a CPA firm and be free to return to you. If they can spare me for another week, I'm at your beck and call."

"Speaking of which, where were we?" she asked.

Slowly and carefully, they made love again. They both knew they had found something special and weren't about to let it go. Afterward, they fell asleep for a short time with their limbs entwined.

Later in the afternoon, Tim phoned and spoke with Ken and Bill on a very weak, static-plagued telephone line. "How are things going there?" he asked.

"Fair to middling," Ken said. "Did you find your brother?"

"Yeah, the big dummy got in trouble with a medicine man. "I'll tell you all about it when I get home. Seriously though, how are things?"

"They're not as bad as you may believe," Ken said. "Give us a little credit. Your secretary, Terri, did a great job of paying the bills and making sure the sheriff didn't evict us.

"You know how construction slows down in November. You have a few things to catch up on, but they can wait. When are you heading home?"

"I'd like to stay another week," Tim said. "The fact is I found a wonderful lady here and I plan to marry her."

"You work fast," Ken said. "Three weeks and you have a new gal? Congratulations; when do we meet her?"

"Not for a while; Catherine's a schoolteacher and wants to finish out the year."

"Now I know you're sorry you didn't listen to us last year when Ken and I told you to hire a CPA firm."

"I haven't proposed to her formally," Tim said.

"Take your time, but return next week," Bill said. "To save time when you do, I'll set up interviews with two or three CPAs. Give Catherine our love and don't lose her."

"Don't worry, I won't. Thanks for your understanding. I'll see you in a week."

As Tim hung up, Catherine returned from the schoolhouse where she went to check her schedule for the next day.

"What did your partners have to say?" she asked.

"Although they just found out about you, Bill and Ken send their love. I can stay for another week."

With her eyes aglow, Catherine said, "We'll have to find something to keep you busy, won't we? Do you have any ideas?"

"Only a few - what about you?"

"I want to know more about the man I plan to marry. Come out to the patio. I have a bottle of wine waiting."

After following Catherine outside, Tim watched as she poured two glasses of White Zinfandel. Then he touched his glass to hers in a silent toast, took a small sip and set his glass down.

He took her hand is his and said, "I never asked if you would marry me. I assumed you would, but now I'm asking officially. Will you be my bride, the new and last Mrs. Tim Fitch?"

As tears ran down her cheeks, Catherine kissed him and said, "Of course."

Tim reached into his pocket, removed a small blue box that held the engagement ring he bought in Belem and said, "I have something for you."

He took her left hand in his and gently placed the ring on her finger. It fit perfectly.

"Thank you, Darling," Catherine said.

Chapter 14

Twenty miles off the coast of South America

From the deck of their fifty-six foot yacht, "Miss Take", (which Jim named mostly in jest), Martha and Jim Ellis from Paris Island, North Carolina watched in awe as huge waves crashed over the bow. Now, Martha wondered if the name of the boat wasn't aptly applied; while Jim had his own doubts about such foolishness.

The storm that began as a tropical depression two days ago had quickly grown into a monster hurricane that now continued to rage around them. Their boat pitched up and down in huge waves that crested at more than twenty-five feet.

"I told you not to attempt to sail to Belem at this time of year," Martha said. "I doubt your boat will last very much longer."

"Have a little faith, Martha. This isn't too bad."

"No?" she asked. "Then I would hate to see what bad weather looks like. You should send out a Mayday message and ask the Coast Guard for help."

"I'm not sure of our location," Jim said. "The storm has blown us a long way off course."

"Great; what do we do now?" she asked.

"Pray, I guess."

Suddenly, above the sound of the roar of the wind and pounding rain, they heard a loud, ripping noise.

"There goes the mainsail," Jim said. "I'll cut it loose and let the canvas drift away."

"Give me a knife and I'll help," Martha said. "God help us, I don't believe we'll get out of this alive."

"*I named this boat appropriately,*" Jim thought. But he didn't say anything more to Martha. He didn't want her to know he was as frightened as she was – maybe more.

Sixty feet below the ship, in comparatively quiet comfort in contrast to the surface of the raging ocean above, the great white shark swam in slow circles. The huge beast was on its annual trek northward and its hunger increased with each passing hour. Then suddenly, it heard sounds of the yacht as it began to break up, so the beast paused on its long journey. It decided to wait and listen patiently to see what sweet treats might come its way.

Somewhere in the southern Atlantic, aboard the yacht, Miss Take, it had been a horrible night. Sometime around midnight, in waves of nearly fifty feet, the mast broke off. Water ran into cabins from splintered deck boards and there was no doubt the Miss Take was doomed.

Over the roar of the storm, Jim shouted, "Help me get the water and canned goods loaded aboard the dinghy, Martha. It won't be long and we'll have to abandon ship."

"Why don't we stay aboard?" she asked. "Even if the boat sinks, it won't go completely under, will it?"

"I'm not sure. Before we run out of time, let's put as many supplies in the small boat as we can. If the Miss Take breaks up, we won't have much to hang on to."

Suddenly the largest wave yet crashed noisily over the wreck and swept away nearly everything in its path. The dinghy was smashed against the rail at the rear of the ship. One side was crushed completely. Jim and Martha were saved from going overboard by their life lines.

"So much for the dinghy," Martha shouted. "Now what do we do?"

"We'll stay with her as long as she's afloat," Jim said. "The rest is up to God."

Fifty feet below the surface, the great white shark listened to the sounds above. Even with its small brain, the beast knew with luck, perhaps a meal or two might be forthcoming.

As it waited in patient anticipation, the great white continued to circle the area slowly.

The next morning, at 0617 hours, aboard the wreckage of the yacht, Miss Take, Martha clung to the side of the sunken vessel while she prayed to God to stop the storm.

The high winds, pouring rain and huge waves continued to pound the remains of a once-proud vessel. As water ran into the main cabin through broken and fractured boards, each hour the boat sank lower into the churning waves.

Finally, two hours ago, the Miss Take broke in two and both sections began to sink rapidly.

"It's the end of a great ship," Jim said. "I'm sorry I got you into this, Martha."

"I came along of my own free will," she said. "You can't be blamed for the weather. God, the water is cold."

"Let's move to the bow. It will probably stay afloat longer than the stern."

"How long can we hold out?" Martha asked.

"I got a Mayday out, but I doubt the Coast Guard will be able to find us in this weather. We'll have to pray for the storm to pass."

As a piece of the deck sailed by Jim's head, Martha screamed, "Look out, the ship is breaking apart."

"Tie yourself to the rail," Jim said. "Then hang on and pray."

While it had stayed with the wreckage of the boat throughout the last two days, the shark managed to gather a few small fish and one large tuna to appease its hunger.

As it continued to search for food in the maelstrom, the great white swam upward. On the surface, the waves were high, but beneath the water the current was nothing the predator couldn't handle.

Slowly, the beast approached the surface, where it encountered lines and shrouds of canvas from sails that hung in tatters and dragged along with the wreckage.

The shark listened for sounds of a struggle, felt the motion of feet as they splashed in the water and swam toward the noise.

Jim spotted the telltale fin of the great white as it cut through the water. He shouted, "Shark! It's a big one."

Martha attempted to climb higher on the bow, but the slope of the deck prevented her from pulling her legs completely out of the sea. She screamed, "Where's he at?"

"I don't know; he went under."

Suddenly Martha felt a tug on her leg. She looked down to see the shark's fin slide gently by. In panic, she kicked and scraped her shoes against the slick side of the boat while she attempted to gain a foothold.

Beneath her, the great white homed in on the noise, swam in a small circle and attacked. The beast grabbed Martha by her legs, yanked her from the wreck as if she was a rag doll, pulled her body underwater and silenced her screams.

Jim watched in horror and cried out, "Martha, oh, my God. No!"

After it cut Martha in half with one swift bite, the shark began to eat. As it pulled chunks of flesh from her body, the beast chewed for an instant; then swallowed and tasted the sweet nectar of human blood.

Jim forced his weary and heartbroken body to the top of the bow, where he clung precariously to a broken rail, as wave after wave beat at him. Tears flowed down his cheeks while between sobs of sorrow, he prayed for forgiveness.

After the great white finished its meal, once again the shark began to slowly circle the wreckage. It could see Jim where he clung to the bow and knew it was only a matter of time, so as it awaited dessert, the beast continued to swim in slow, small circles.

A day later, thirty-three nautical miles east/northeast of Belem, Brazil, aboard the Coast Guard Helicopter USCG 434, the pilot, Captain Harry Lightner asked, "What does it look like down there, Mike?"

The swimmer attached to Harry's helicopter, Mike Corman, said, "There's not much left of the Miss Take. I can't find any bodies or survivors."

"See if you can locate a written log in the cabin. The family will want to have some closure."

"I'll take a quick look, but I doubt if anything's left. It's lucky we found the stern. The wreckage is a long way off their original course."

"Let me know when you want hoisted out, Mike," Harry said. "We have thirty minutes of reserve fuel on board. Make your search thorough, but quick."

Three days later, after a passing tanker reported a near collision with a floating wreck, the Coast Guard dispatched a cutter to investigate the sighting.

They located the GPS beacon the tanker dropped and sent a diver aboard the bow of the Miss Take. He reported no survivors or victims were found.

Before they departed the area, crewmembers used their cannon to fire three shells into the wreckage. They blasted it apart, holed the main portion and allowed the remains of the Miss Take to sink into the depths.

Since he didn't have time to examine the forward portion of the bow closely, the diver failed to see the notation: "Shark", that Jim scratched into the blue paint shortly before he gave up trying to hold onto the wreckage and perished in the mouth of the great white.

Chapter 15

T he week Tim and Catherine spent together passed by too quickly. During the day, Catherine reopened the school and taught the little ones while Tim enjoyed watching the youngsters learn.

The children ranged in age from six to twelve and were mostly a mixture of Spanish heritage and other South American backgrounds. But they were well behaved and minded Catherine's instructions with no unruly behavior.

The little ones certainly weren't bashful. One six-year-old boy named Carlos seemed to adopt Tim. He preferred to sit on Tim's lap and listen while Catherine explained the lessons.

Proudly, Carlos proclaimed, "I know my alphabet and can count to one hundred."

While they filled their evenings with talk of their plans for the future and more intimate conversation, Tim and Catherine continued to learn more about each other.

When the week was over, Tim knew he must return to Fort Worth and the waiting paperwork, so with a heavy heart, he began to pack. Tearing himself away from Catherine was more difficult than he imagined. Reluctantly, he radioed Jose to pick him up the next morning.

As they spoke of their future together, Tim held Catherine in the crook of his arm. They talked until early in the morning and finally fell asleep in each other's arms.

When Tim awoke, he found his arm was asleep from Catherine lying on it. He removed his arm slowly, stood up and walked to the window to watch the sun rise over the river. A brisk, warm wind blew the mist around in circles.

Catherine stirred and awoke, saw him standing by the window and beckoned him to return to bed.

Tim was glad he packed the night before. When they heard Jose's helicopter overhead, they were still in bed.

"Oops" he said, "I better get up and get dressed. Jose will wonder why I'm not at the landing strip to meet him."

Catherine smiled and said, "Jose is a man. Believe me; he knows why you aren't there. I'll fix the coffee and we'll wait for him."

During the night, it rained and Tim knew the potholes would be overflowing again this morning. A few minutes later, Jose came to the door and scraped mud from his boots.

Catherine asked, "Do you have time for breakfast, Jose?"

"Sure, thank you. How have things been going with you two?"

"We're engaged," Tim announced. "Show him your ring, Honey."

Jose looked at the ring and said, "You're a fast worker, Tim. Congratulations to you both."

"Thank you, Jose," Catherine said. Then she asked, "How many tacos can you eat?

"Six will do."

Fifteen minutes later, Jose gave a small, polite burp behind his napkin and said, "I would like to sit here all day and watch you two lovebirds, but we should be going, Tim. Your flight leaves tomorrow at eight a.m. I know you don't want to miss it."

Tim shook his head. "I'd rather stay, but I know I'm needed at home."

Jose stood by politely and waited while Tim gave Catherine one more kiss and held her for a minute longer before they parted.

As they followed the river on the way to Prainha, Jose pointed downward. "There's a lot of debris on the river today. It must have rained upstream."

Tim watched a carcass of a dead cow float by. It reminded him of the white painted face of Narro as he slipped under the murky water.

When Tim reached Prainha and Miss Lela's hotel for the night, she met him at the door. "Welcome back, Tim. Headed home to the states, aren't you? How's Catherine?"

Tim hugged her and said, "When I said goodbye, she was fine. The good news is; we're engaged."

"Congratulations; but why didn't you bring her with you? Catherine and I could be putting her trousseau together."

"I'm sorry, Lela. Catherine didn't say anything about needing clothes or coming with me. She's busy with the children."

Lela asked, "When do you plan to be married?"

"We thought we would fly to Bermuda, where my parents live."

"I'll take care of her while you're gone," Lela said. "After I call to find a convenient time, Jose can fly Catherine down. At least you'll be out of our hair and we can accomplish something positive. That will be my wedding present to you."

Tim leaned over the counter, gave Lela another hug, kissed her on the forehead and said, "Thank you."

She gave him a kiss on the cheek and said, "Go to bed now. I'll wake you early enough to catch your flight."

At five a.m., Jose came by to drive Tim to the airport in Barreirinha. On the way, Jose shared a secret. "Remember when we picked up Frank from the riverbank and I switched on the search light? There were several crocodiles about one hundred feet from where he was setting off his fireworks. I never mentioned it to him. After Frank was alone on the riverbank for an hour in the darkness, he was freaked out."

Tim remembered how frightened Frank was and how he worried about the crocs. "I'm glad you didn't. In the back of my mind I saw them but I thought they were logs."

Jose smiled evilly. "Yeah, logs with very sharp teeth."

When Jose dropped Tim off at the airport and noticed he was carrying only one suitcase, Jose remarked, "You're traveling light."

Tim grinned and said, "Yeah, I left most of my warm weather clothes behind. Thanks for the lift, Jose. There's no reason for you to stick around."

"Okay, Tim; it's been great working with you. Thanks again for the bonus. Juanita already has it spent."

"When I plan to return, I'll phone, Jose. Thanks again for all your help."

The flight to Belem on the puddle jumper was becoming routine. On the way, Tim read a portion of his newspaper. When the plane landed, he was pleased to see the weather was clear.

After waiting for a short time at his new gate, when Tim's aircraft was announced, he climbed aboard and sat down.

A young stewardess asked, "Would you like a drink, sir?"

"Do you have a bloody Mary?"

"Sure – no problem," she replied.

Tim turned toward his newspaper as a young Brazilian took the seat next to him. The stranger said, "Good morning, I'm Fernando Lumas. Are you headed for Houston or beyond?"

Tim shook the offered hand and said, "I'm Tim Fitch. No, I'm going on to Fort Worth. What takes you to Houston, Fernando?"

"I'm attending a conference on oil exploration in Brazil."

Fernando carried a full briefcase of documents and he began to look through the papers, which ended their conversation rather abruptly.

Tim shrugged, picked up a copy of Newsweek and People magazine and thought, *I need to catch up on the news anyway.*

After Fernando finished looking through his important documents without making any further conversation, he apparently decided to sleep until they arrived in Houston. He covered his legs with a blanket and turned his upper body toward the window.

Tim continued to read until the aircraft entered the middle of the Gulf of Mexico, where it encountered turbulence. The rough ride woke Fernando, who now appeared more inclined to talk.

He covered a yawn with his hand and when he was finished, he said, "I'm a chemical engineer employed by the Brazilian National Oil Company. I plan to attend a conference in Houston with several representatives of an oil company that has expressed an interest in exploring for oil in Brazil."

"I don't know much about oil," Tim said.

In the next hour, Fernando told Tim more than he wanted to know, but he listened attentively. *"Dad always said if I took time to listen, I would learn something new every day."*

As Fernando rattled on, he casually mentioned his company had considered exploring an area near Barreirinha.

"I just came from there," Tim said. "If you ever need a good helicopter pilot, I know one."

Tim wrote Jose's telephone number on the back of his business card. Then he told Fernando a shorter version of his construction business, and they exchanged business cards.

With the aid of two more free drinks and a tender steak sandwich for lunch, Tim and Fernando soon became friends.

Another announcement informed the passengers the pilot was about to begin his descent into Houston. A few minutes later, the plane landed with a chirp of tires on concrete.

Tim took a look out his window and thought, *"It's good to be back in the U.S.A."*

He and his new friend shook hands, and Tim said, "Take care, Fernando."

"It's been a great pleasure meeting you, Tim. Have a safe flight to Fort Worth. I hope someday we'll meet again."

After a short wait, Tim caught his connecting flight to Fort Worth, where he met Bill, who was waiting in the baggage area. For once in his life, Tim's suitcase was among the first to slide down a chute onto the carousel. As it crawled by, Tim grabbed his bag and pointed toward the exit.

Bill asked, "You don't have any other luggage?"

Tim smiled and said, "I've learned to travel light."

As Bill drove out of the airport parking lot, Tim said, "Thanks for coming all the way out here, Bill. I wasn't looking forward to a cab ride to the office. How are things with you and Ken?"

"We're busy and everything is moving along well on all our projects. The Jenkins job is nearly completed. His wife drove us crazy with small changes, but we were finally able to make them happy."

"Wonderful," Tim said. "Are there any other problems I should be aware of before I get to the office?"

"There's nothing Ken and I can't bring you up-to-date on quickly. I set up three appointments next week for you to interview CPA firms. You'll be up to speed by then and ready to turn the paperwork over to whichever firm you choose."

When Bill paused, Tim said, "There's something I want to talk to you about, Bill. As soon as I get things straightened out, I plan to return to Brazil. Before I leave, I'll make sure you and Ken won't be snowed under.

"The Holiday season is coming up and you know the building industry usually slows from November until spring. You and Ken should be able to get by without me until then. I plan to be in Brazil until May, when Catherine's contract expires. She wants to finish this school year."

Bill shook his head in surprise. "Boy, you have it bad for her, don't you? Don't worry about us. We did okay without you so far, and we'll manage until you return for good. Will you be married here or in Bermuda?"

"Right now, we're both leaning toward Bermuda. Catherine has never been there. My parents will love to meet her and have the reception at their home."

Bill asked, "What's your fiancée like?"

"Catherine's from Des Moines, Iowa, of all places. After my first wife, I never thought I would find another woman to marry. Catherine is smart and good natured, but tough when she has to be. She loves children, is an excellent teacher and has her head screwed on straight."

"She sounds like my kind of woman," Bill said. "Why are you so lucky?

During the remainder of the drive, Tim continued to pump Bill about the business and what shape they were in financially.

"Invoices for our work are being paid on time and all our bills for material and other incidentals are up-to-date," Bill said. "You forget we have a very efficient secretary. Terri did a bang-up job of keeping the place running while you were staggering around in the jungle."

Fifty-year-old Terri Watson was the no-nonsense secretary to all three men. Everyone watched their step and mouths at the office.

Tim's thoughts turned to Miss Lela and how she and Terri would get along. While they drove, Tim told Bill of his adventures in Brazil. He gave most of the credit to Catherine and the others who assisted in the rescue.

"It's a fascinating tale," Bill said.

As they turned off the freeway, Tim said, "Drop me at the office, Bill. I'll catch a cab to the house."

"Okay, I need to get out to the new condominium job. Ken is there supervising two crews. Take care; I'll see you tomorrow at the office."

Terri greeted Tim with a hug and a kiss on the cheek. "Welcome home, boss."

After taking a quick look through the mass of paperwork on his desk, Tim soon found things weren't as bad as he thought they might be. He spent the remainder of the afternoon and worked into the early evening as he sorted things out.

At five p.m., when Terri left for home, she said, "Don't attempt to do everything in one day, Tim. Relax; your fiancée will wait for you. If I were she, I would."

At eight p.m., Tim's stomach growled to tell him it was time to quit and have something to eat. He glanced around his desk and realized he had done as much as possible today. *"As Scarlet O'Hara said, 'tomorrow is another day'. If I leave now, put some food in my stomach and get a good night's rest, I can easily complete the remaining tasks."*

Although the next few days were filled with work, Tim thought of Kate often and hoped somehow she would be able to attend his wedding. *"Maybe mom and dad can work a miracle and talk Cheryl into allowing Kate to attend."*

On the spur of the moment, Tim remembered Catherine's advice to call, so he phoned Cheryl's apartment. *"If Cheryl answers, I'll hang up."*

After the third ring, a younger voice answered, "Hello".

"Hello, Kate, this is your father. I hoped I would reach you. Do you have time to talk?"

At the news, Kate was flabbergasted. "I always wondered what your voice would sound like," she said. "Why haven't you called before?"

"I have, many times. Cheryl always told me you were busy or weren't there."

"I didn't know you called. Mom didn't say a word."

"Don't think ill of your mother, Kate. Years ago, she and I went through a rough period. Since our divorce, she's always been upset with me."

Kate sighed. "Yeah, I know. She told me things about you I find difficult to believe. I'm glad you called."

"Let me give you my cell phone number," Tim said. "During the day, you can reach me at Fitch Construction. Anytime you want to speak to me, I'll drop everything I'm doing."

After Kate wrote down the numbers and repeated them for verification, she said, "Thanks, Pops."

Tim thought, *"Kate's voice sounds a little more upbeat than when she first answered the phone and found her long-lost father on the other end."*

"I'll find a way to call," she said. "Soon, I promise."

"Call me anytime. I love you, Kate."

"I'm not sure how I feel about you, Pops. After all these years, this is a shock. You know I'm sixteen."

"Yes, I do. And I missed seeing you for nearly fifteen long years. The last time I saw and held you, you were eighteen months old. I've missed most of your life and I'm sorry. Take your time, think things through and then please, call me."

"I will, Pops."

After she hung up, Kate stood staring at the receiver. Her father's call came unexpectedly. She had dreamed about this moment for years. Now, before she knew it, the moment was over.

"Why did I hang up so suddenly? There were a thousand questions I wanted to ask, and when I finally got the chance, my mind went blank.

"I'm not surprised mom wouldn't let me talk to him before; but I wish she would have at least let me know he called. I wonder why she hates him so much. His voice was nice and he didn't say anything bad about mom.

"Every time I'm with Grandpa and Grandma Fitch, they always tell me how much my dad loves me. I wonder how many of mom's stories about him are true.

"I always wished mom and dad would get back together, but I guess by now that's a no-brainer. I wonder if he's seeing anybody. He didn't say, and I didn't ask. Man, was I stupid.

"I'm going to sit down and make out a list of questions to ask and then call dad on Saturday. Sally has a cell phone. I'll get her to go to the mall with me and I'll borrow it. What mom doesn't know won't hurt her.

"I didn't even let dad know I was going to Bermuda. I wonder what he's doing for Thanksgiving."

In his office, Tim felt as if he was walking on air. *"At last I heard Kate's voice."*

Terri noticed the difference in his attitude and said, "You're in an extra good mood today, Tim."

"After fifteen years, today, I spoke to Kate."

"Then you have a right to be happy."

"I gave her the number of the office. If Kate phones, find me no matter where I am. She and I have a lot to discuss."

Later in the evening, when Tim spoke to Catherine, he said, "I hoped Kate might call back, but she didn't."

Catherine said, "After all this time, she's probably getting over the shock of finally speaking with her father. For sixteen years, Cheryl has told her terrible things about you. No wonder Kate's confused. Give her time. I'll bet she's making a list of questions for you to answer. Be patient, Darling."

Tim decided to sleep in on Saturday morning. When his phone rang at ten, he was still in bed. After answering the call reluctantly, he was thrilled to hear Kate's voice.

"Surprise," she said. "I'm at the mall with friends and borrowed a cell phone. Mom gives me an allowance and I was saving for a new outfit. But, I figured talking with you is more important. I need to find out if you're as much an S.O.B. as mom says you are, or not."

Tim was taken aback by the reference, but took it in stride and answered honestly. "I like to believe I'm not what your mother calls me. I always wanted to be a father to you, but Cheryl wouldn't allow me to have any contact. She always hated me."

"Then why did you get married?" Kate asked.

"A very good question, Kate," Tim said. "For one thing, at the time, your mother was pregnant with you. I thought marrying her was the decent thing to do. We were young and believed we were in love."

"What happened to make you divorce?"

"Viet Nam for one thing," Tim said. "I was overseas and your mother was alone and had to raise you by herself, which was something she wasn't prepared for. I wish things had turned out better, but they didn't. What happened to us is strictly between Cheryl and me. We were both at fault and we both paid the price."

"At least you don't run mom down the way she does you," Kate said. "That's a point in your favor."

"I'm not attempting to make points, Kate. I'm sorry I didn't try harder to speak to you before now."

Although Tim couldn't see, there were tears in Kate's eyes as she said, "I'm glad you finally did."

"I'm very happy your mother allows you to have a relationship with your grandparents. They love you very much."

Kate smiled at the thought. "When I visit, I have a great time."

Tim thought, *"I don't want to be the one to tell Kate Cheryl was on drugs when we divorced."*

He changed the subject and asked, "How is your mother?

Kate surprised him. "She has a real problem. Mom's smoked pot for years and she may be into heavier stuff. She's been sick a lot lately. I don't do drugs and I'm worried about her."

"I didn't know," Tim lied. "I'm sorry you have to deal with drug abuse at your age. I'm also proud of you. It takes a strong person to say no to drugs."

At first, Kate didn't say anything in reply. Tim thought he heard her crying softly. Then she said, "I have to go now. Thanks for telling me the truth."

After Kate hung up, Tim sat staring at the receiver in his hand. *"I only hope Kate knows I was being honest with her."*

Over the weekend, as Tim struggled to pass the time, he phoned Catherine at Lela's hotel to say he heard from Kate.

"You were right about Kate wanting answers to questions. I tried to reply honestly. She sounds as if she has mixed feelings about me.

Cheryl's doing drugs, and I feel so helpless about what Kate has to go through every day. Damn Cheryl anyway. It must be hell to live with someone you love and watch her abuse her body."

"All you can do is support Kate when she asks you," Catherine said. "She sounds like a very smart and level-headed young girl."

Monday, Tim interviewed three potential CPAs. He decided to go with the second applicant, who maintained accounts similar to his. From their prospectus and a personal interview with the manager, Jerry Burns, Tim felt his business would be in good hands.

Tim phoned Mister Burns and said, "You won the contract."

"Thanks for your confidence in our firm. I'll have a contract prepared for your signature by day after tomorrow. When you feel the time is right, we're ready to supervise your account."

"If it's convenient, I'll see you Thursday morning at nine," Tim replied. "My partners agree your firm is the one to handle our business."

Tim thought, *"A few more days and I'll be on my way to Brazil, and Catherine."*

Terri broke into his thoughts as she asked, "What are your plans for Thanksgiving, Tim? The holiday is only a week from Thursday."

"I don't have any. I haven't spoken with my parents since I returned. They must think I'm an ungrateful son."

She suggested, "Why don't you go to Bermuda to celebrate Thanksgiving?"

"Thanks for watching out for me again, Terri. Yes, please, phone them. I'll have to tell Catherine I'll be delayed a few more days. When I finish speaking with mom and dad, try to reach her."

When George answered the phone and learned the caller was Tim, he said, "It's good to hear from you, Son. Your mother is at another of her bridge parties. She'll be sorry she missed you."

Then he got in a jibe at Tim's forgetfulness, when he added, "We thought we would have heard from you before this. What have you been up to? When did you return to Fort Worth?"

After telling his father about the development of hiring the CPA firm, Tim said, "I've stepped into a supervisory role again."

"I'm pleased to hear you finally came to your senses, Tim. You work too hard."

"I have a cashier's check for what's left after I rescued Tom, plus the receipts," Tim said. "How is he?"

"Tom's fine. Since he's not eating monkey anymore, he's gained a little weight. Tom told us how you took care of the crazy medicine man. I'm proud of you, Son."

Tim thought this was as good a time as any to break the news, so he said, "A lot of credit for the rescue plan goes to my fiancée, Catherine. She thought up the basic idea."

"Whoever is responsible did a great job," George said. "Wait a minute, did I hear you right? What fiancée? When did this happen?"

"Just before I left Brazil. You'll love her."

"Your mother will be thrilled with this news. I can't wait to surprise her."

"You do that, Dad."

Then George changed the subject and asked, "What are you doing for Thanksgiving?"

"That's why I called. Would it be all right if I come down for the holiday?"

"Your mother will be thrilled again. I am too. It's been a long time since we enjoyed a family reunion. Did you know Cheryl agreed to let Kate come here for Thanksgiving?"

"There's a shock," Tim thought. *"I wonder why Kate didn't say something. Maybe she didn't want me to know."*

"No, I didn't," he replied. "On the same subject, you won't believe it, but for the first time in fifteen years, I actually spoke to Kate."

George asked, "Why don't you surprise her when she arrives? We won't say anything about your visit. If Cheryl finds out, she may not allow Kate to visit. I guess you know I dislike your ex-wife immensely."

"I'm aware of your feelings, Dad."

As Tim thought about the situation for a minute, he was silent.

George grew impatient and asked, "Are you still there?"

"Yes, Dad; I was weighing my options. With no advance warning, I'm not sure Kate will be thrilled to see me. But I agree; I'll come. I haven't been allowed to see Kate for fifteen years, but if this causes problems between Cheryl and me, I don't care. I need to see Kate. When does she get in? I want to be there to meet her."

"Kate arrives on Wednesday, the day before Thanksgiving, George said. "Cheryl has actually allowed her to stay a week to see the islands."

Tim checked his calendar and said, "I'll ask Terri to make reservations for me to arrive on Monday. That way we'll have time to talk things over and get ready for Kate's arrival. What do you think, Dad; am I'm doing the right thing?"

"Yes, you are. You're overdue to spend some quality time with Kate. I should have put my foot down earlier and forced Cheryl to allow her to visit you."

"Kate told me Cheryl is on drugs," Tim said. "That worries me."

"I'm sorry to hear that," George said. "But it doesn't surprise me. Poor Kate; Cheryl is capable of anything."

"Kate's the one we need to think of now," Tim said. "I'll have Terri phone you with my flight info. I'll see you on Monday. Tell mom I'm sorry I missed her. Give Tom a hug for me."

After hanging up, Tim turned to Terri, who said, "I couldn't help but overhear, Tim. I'm glad you decided to go. It will make your parents happy. And Kate will be there too. That's a nice bonus."

"Yes, it is. Thanks again, Terri. I don't know what I would do without you. Would you see if you can reach Catherine?"

Much to Tim's surprise, Catherine was excited he was going home to see his parents for the holiday. She said, "They need to have their sons together. This Thanksgiving you all have a lot to be thankful for. I understand why you have to go, especially when Kate will be there. I hope you two hit it off. She has to love you. Be sure to take photographs. I want to see your entire family, especially Kate."

"Don't worry," Tim said, "I will. This is a big occasion for Kate and me. But I'm a little worried. I don't know if it's right to surprise her like this."

"Kate will realize you can't stay away for the rest of your life. You've missed too much as it is. Give her a hug for me."

"I haven't told Kate about you yet. I didn't want to throw her a curve by telling her over the phone I planned to marry again. I wanted to let her know in person. Do you understand?"

"Yes, I do," Catherine said. "I was a teenage girl and we're very impressionable at sixteen. When and if the time is right, tell Kate about me. I look forward to meeting her."

"I love you more than you'll ever know," Tim said. "Thank God Tom got lost in Brazil and I met you."

"We're both lucky. I love you too. Enjoy your holiday in Bermuda, but as soon as you've settled things, hurry home. I'll be waiting."

As promised, Tim signed the contract with Mister Burns on Thursday. Terri would remain as Tim's executive secretary, with a pay raise.

She chided him, "You're going to pay me more for doing less?"

"You earn every penny, Terri. You've put up with us three for several years now and you're still sane. Such an accomplishment is worthy of a raise."

After the turnover, Tim decided to spend the next three days shopping for Christmas presents for his parents, his brother and especially Kate.

Since Terri was the grandmother of a seventeen-year-old girl, she accompanied Tim to give him guidance. At the first stop, a toy store, Tim was prepared to buy Kate a stuffed bear the size of a small horse.

"Tim, your daughter is almost seventeen," Terri said. "Let's go to a TARGET store. They have good, fashionable clothes for a modern young girl. Those are what you should buy."

Following her advice, Tim bought a nice selection of skirts, blouses, jeans and T-shirts, plus a three-CD player/radio combination. A young man working behind the sight and sound counter picked out several CDs he thought a sixteen-year-old girl would like. "Believe me, sir; your daughter will enjoy the music."

While Tim's gifts were gift wrapped, he and Terri ate lunch in a nearby restaurant. Tim was amazed to find it was nearly two p.m.

After lunch, they strolled back to TARGET to find Tim's gifts wrapped in gaily colored paper with ribbons and bows. When the packages barely fit into the trunk of Tim's car, Terri laughed. "You'll need at least four extra suitcases. I hope you're prepared to pay for the overweight luggage."

Tim shook his head. "I don't care what it costs. This year, Kate will have the Thanksgiving of her life. I'll be in Obidos for Christmas, so Kate can open her presents a little early."

"That's a nice thought, Tim, but you can't buy your daughter's love. You have to earn it."

"You always have a way of chopping my ego down to size, Terri. Thanks again."

"The only advice I can give is to be you. Kate will see in you what we all do. You're a fine man, Tim."

Early Monday morning, Ken came by with his truck to drive Tim to the Dallas/Fort Worth airport. After helping load seven suitcases into the bed, Ken said, "I'm glad I brought my pickup. Are you sure you're taking enough? Don't they have washing machines in Bermuda?"

"Very funny, you clown. Most of these contain gifts. Haven't you ever heard of Christmas, or is your name Scrooge?"

Ken laughed and said, "There's such a thing as going overboard."

Tim grinned. "You may be right, but what's done is done."

When they arrived at the airport, Tim hired a porter to help with the bags. The redcap looked askance at all the suitcases and asked, "Is there another person in your party?"

Tim shook his head. "No, all the luggage is mine."

"With this many, you'll have to check in at the counter. On an overseas flight, the airlines allow only two bags per person. They charge extra for any overage."

Tim shrugged in resignation. "Let's go inside and I'll pay the freight."

Tim's flight route took him from DFW to Charleston, South Carolina, where he boarded another aircraft to Bermuda. The two-hour flight was smooth as silk. He enjoyed a pleasant conversation with his seat companion, Bryan Jessop, a young man of seventeen, who would graduate from a high school in Roanoke, Virginia, in May of next year. Tim discovered Bryan's parents were seated across the aisle.

After Bryan's father introduced himself and his wife as Bob and Marsha Jessop, Bob said, "If Bryan gets to be too much for you, let him know. Our son is excited about his first trip to Bermuda.

Then he added, "Nearly twenty years ago, Marsha and I went to Bermuda on our honeymoon. Now we're returning for a vacation and to inquire about purchasing a home. We always dreamed of owning a place in Bermuda. Since I'm ready to retire, perhaps our fantasy might come true."

When Bryan discovered Tim was raised in Bermuda, he asked a thousand questions. Tim didn't mind as it helped to pass the time away. He said, "You'll love the islands. There's a lot to do."

Bryan asked, "Is it true there are only twenty square miles of land?"

Quoting the Chamber of Commerce, Tim said, "Twenty-one."

He gave Bob his business card and added his parents' phone number. "If you don't find a home you like, phone me at this number. Dad knows everyone on the islands and will probably know of any bargains."

Tim informed Bob about the no-number addresses of homes in Bermuda and wrote instructions on the back of his card to give to the taxi driver. "I know it sounds strange, Bob, but that's the way things are done in Bermuda. Believe me; the taxi driver will know where to take you."

Bob looked at the instructions and laughed. "When in Rome... Thanks, Tim. I appreciate your offer. If we don't find what we're looking for, I'll phone."

Tim stepped off the plane into the wonderful sunshine and cool breezes of Bermuda in December to find George and Tom waiting on the tarmac.

Bryan seemed a little disappointed in the cool temperature.

"The weather doesn't look promising. I was looking forward to swimming a lot."

"It is wintertime," Tim said. Then he thought, *"There are other things to do in Bermuda than swim. Bryan's sure to find something to occupy his time. Maybe he'll meet a nice young girl to fall in love with. Stranger things have happened."*

As Tim walked to where George and Tom were waiting, he waved goodbye to Bryan and his parents.

Tom referred to the fact Pearl told the twins that Tim preceded Tom into the world by two minutes, when he asked, "How goes it, big brother?"

Tim shook Tom's hand and said, "Not bad, little brother."

Then he hugged Tom tight. "Since you stopped crawling around in jungles and eating fried monkey, you gained some weight."

Tom shook his head, frowned and said, "I wish I'd never told you or dad about that. You wouldn't believe the number of people who want to know how fried monkey tastes."

George allowed the boys to speak for a few moments; then he broke into their conversation with a hug of his own for Tim. Tears ran down George's cheeks as he said, "Welcome home, Son."

"I'm glad to be here, Dad. I'm sorry I spent so much of your money rescuing my brother. You can take the cost up with Tom."

"I already assured Tom that he doesn't owe me a thing," George said. "All I want is his promise to stay either in Bermuda or the United States to spread the word of God. There will be no more running around in the jungle. Tom gave me his word and I consider the matter closed."

Tim changed the subject and asked, "Where's Mom?"

"She remained at home so you would be more comfortable in the rear seat of the VW. With four people in my little car, I doubt we'd be able to go over twenty miles per hour."

Since Tim knew the speed limit throughout the Bermuda Islands was twenty miles per hour, he laughed at the joke. As a respected doctor, George knew he must maintain his genteel reputation, so he never exceeded the posted speed.

They walked to the luggage carousel, where they found Tim's seven suitcases slowly crawling around in a circle. When Tim began to take the bags from the carousel and stack them side-by-side, George and Tom watched in amazement. Then George asked, "How will the three of us fit in my car with all these bags? What's in them?"

Tim felt a little silly when he replied, "Presents mostly; I went shopping for the family and it appears I got carried away."

Tom laughed at Tim's discomfort. "Just a wee bit."

In resignation, George said, "I guess we'll have to hire a taxi to haul your bags separately. Find a porter to carry them outside, Tim."

When they arrived at "On a Hill", Pearl was waiting on the front porch for their return. She rushed out to greet them, caught Tim in a bear hug and gave him a kiss on the cheek. "Now we're all together again. Thank you, Tim, for what you did."

Tim laughed. "It was nothing. I've been getting this big dummy out of trouble all his life."

"You two," Pearl said. "It's good to have you both here for the holidays. How long can you stay, Tim?"

"I plan to leave a week from tomorrow and fly to Brazil to spend the next few months with Catherine. By the way, she sends her love."

"We're all anxious to meet her," Pearl said. "Your brother tells me you made quite a catch."

"Yes, Catherine is wonderful. I know you'll love her."

Pearl said, "I love her already for making your face shine as it does when you speak of her. I haven't seen you this happy in years."

"That's what love does to a man," Tom said. "Or so I've been told. Since he first laid eyes on Catherine, Tim has been starry-eyed."

George interrupted their merrymaking to ask, "Are we going to stand here all day while letting the meter run on your taxi, Tim? You better help the driver unload all those bags."

For the next three days, as he awaited Kate's arrival, Tim stayed on pins and needles. He spent some time giving his account of Tom's rescue. Pearl wanted to know all the details. She nodded knowingly and smiled in approval when Tim gave much of the credit for the plan to Catherine.

When Tim was done, Tom said, "I've applied through my bishop to work with troubled youth in New York City. Now, I'm waiting for his final approval. I hope he doesn't deny me this chance. It'll be a big challenge, but at least I'll be where I understand the customs."

"I don't know," Tim said. "Those kids in New York speak their own language."

Tom laughed. "While I'm there, I plan to take the advice of my superiors. Several young priests are already working there and have experience with the youth of New York. This time, I'll listen before I act."

"You better," Tim said. "The jungles of Brazil are nothing compared to the boroughs of New York. I'd hate to have to come to your rescue there."

Chapter 16

Austin International Airport

Whan her flight was announced, Kate hugged Cheryl close and said, "Thanks again, Mom for allowing me fly to Bermuda. I love you."

Since it would be the last time, Cheryl hugged Kate hard and said, "I love you too, Honey. Have a nice visit. I'll see you in a week."

Just then, Kate heard an announcement over the PA system.

"Miss Kate Fitch, please report to the counter."

Kate walked to the counter, identified herself and asked, "What's this about?"

The young male clerk said, "Your mother registered you as an unaccompanied minor." He handed Kate a small sign that was attached to a chained loop and intended to fit around her neck, and added, "You'll have to wear this."

Her face turned scarlet and Kate exclaimed, "Mom, you didn't. I'm sixteen; I can take care of myself."

Cheryl attempted to calm troubled waters. "I just wanted to make sure you get to the right gate in Charleston."

Kate continued to blush and said, "I've never been so embarrassed."

"Come with me, Miss Fitch," the clerk said. "I'll put you on board the plane."

"Goodbye, Honey," Cheryl said.

Kate didn't want other passengers to see her red face, so she kept her head down as she said, "Bye, Mom."

As soon as Kate and the clerk turned a corner in the gateway, where Cheryl could no longer see, he said, "Take the silly thing off, Miss Fitch. I'll tell the stewardess to make sure you get to the correct gate in Charleston. I know how you must feel."

Kate smiled in relief. "Sometimes mothers are too protective. Thank you."

Wednesday in Bermuda dawned clear and sunny, with an expected high forecast for the mid-seventies. As Tim walked out onto the patio with his breakfast coffee, small puffy clouds were drifting lazily across the sky. An aroma of saltwater hung in the air. Tim took a large sniff and smiled. *"Today Kate arrives, so it's a beautiful day in Bermuda. Last night I was so nervous I couldn't sleep."*

Pearl knew Tim was anxious to meet his daughter. She assured him Kate was a strong-willed girl. "Kate won't be swayed by what Cheryl says. She'll want to get to know you and form her own opinion. Be your normal self, Tim. Answer any questions Kate has, open and honestly."

Tim looked sheepish when he replied, "I received the same advice from two other women; my fiancée and secretary. Do all women think alike?"

"At one time or another we were young girls and know what they're like," Pearl said. "Over the years the events you experience as a youngster seldom change. Since you've heard the same thing from three of us, Tim, why don't you take our advice?"

Tim held his hands above his head in surrender. "I will. Thanks, Mom; I love you."

"I love you too, Son. Now relax until we leave for the airport. You're driving everyone crazy by walking back and forth through the house."

Time seemed to drag until Kate's plane was due at ten-thirty a.m.

Pearl took command of the situation. "You can drive us to the airport, George. When Kate arrives, we'll hire a taxi to carry her luggage. Then we'll determine who rides where by Kate's reaction to Tim's presence."

For the first time in Tim's life, he was upset with the speed limit in Bermuda. It seemed to take forever to arrive at the airport.

"Calm down, Tim," Pearl said again.

The long trip finally ended and they arrived thirty minutes prior to the arrival of Kate's plane. Tim was still pacing.

Finally Pearl gave up and let him work off his nervousness.

George said, "Tim's as anxious as an expectant father."

"If it had been fifteen years since you saw your daughter, you would be uneasy too," Pearl said sharply.

George saw "that" look in her eyes and apologized, "Sorry my love, I wasn't thinking."

With a smile, Pearl told George he was forgiven. "Over the years, I've often found men do that sort of thing."

A few minutes later, a large jet aircraft arrived, and Tim said, "I think that's Kate's plane."

Pearl said, "Your father and I will go out and meet Kate at the gate. You two boys stay here and wait until we come in."

As Tim started to protest, she raised her palm to stop his words. "I know it's difficult for you to wait, Tim. But it's best that I tell Kate you're here. That will give her a few minutes to compose herself."

"Okay, Mom; you know best. Just don't stay out on the tarmac too long."

Tom put his arm over Tim's shoulders. "Relax; you're worried about nothing. Kate will want to meet you as much as you want to meet her."

The twins watched the passengers disembark. Then Tim saw Kate. She looked beautiful in a two-piece, pale-blue suit with a white blouse. She had her hair pulled back into a ponytail that hung nearly to the middle of her back.

Tim thought, *"Mom must have told her I'm here. I saw Kate glance toward the terminal."*

After they spoke for a few moments, Kate and her grandparents finally turned to walk toward the terminal. Kate held her head high and she was smiling.

As she approached the twins, Kate said, "Grandma tells me my father is here, so one of you must be he."

Indicating Tom's reversed collar with a nod of her head, she said, "I don't remember a thing about my dad being a priest." Then she turned to face Tim. "So it must be you. Mom always said you were a handsome devil. I see what she meant."

When Tim didn't reply, Kate stuck out her hand and said, "Hello Pops."

Tim was so choked with emotion he could hardly speak. He clutched her hand in his and managed to squeak out, "Hello, Kate. Would it be okay if I gave you a hug?"

"Sure," she said. She moved forward and slipped her arms around Tim's waist.

After a moment, she broke their embrace and looked up at him. "I'm glad you're here. I've dreamed about hugging you for a long time. You are my father for better or worse. Now I can find out which."

While Tim wiped his eyes with a handkerchief Pearl supplied, he smiled and said, "I like your straightforwardness. I hope I live up to your expectations."

Kate seemed wiser than her years when she said, "We'll see. We have a week to get to know each other."

They collected Kate's bags, and Pearl decided she, Kate and Tim should ride in the taxi. George and Tom would drive the VW with the luggage to their home.

Tim leaned over to address the driver. "Take Middle Road so we can see the islands from one of the highest hills."

By the time they reached "On a Hill", Tim was relaxed. *"Kate has accepted the fact I'm here and she seems pleased to meet me after all these years. I know she's secretly studying me and comparing me to the tales Cheryl told. I only hope she'll see through those lies."*

As Tim knew she would, Kate fell in love with the elder Fitch's home. Pearl had prepared one of the bedrooms with "girl" stuff, as she called it. She led Kate to her room and helped her unpack so they could talk a while. The three men were left to fend for themselves.

"My father seems as nice as you said," Kate said. "I wish he would have contacted me sooner. While I was growing up, I missed not having him there. The only picture I have of him is one in uniform."

"Tim attempted to contact you for years," Pearl said. "I won't say a thing more except to tell you that he is not what your mother pictures him to be. He loves you very much and missed you as much, if not more than you missed him."

By this time, both women were crying again. Pearl hugged Kate to her breast and said, "Just give your father a chance to prove how much he loves you."

As Kate dried her eyes on a Kleenex, she smiled and replied, "Thanks, Grandma. I love you so much."

"We all love you, Honey. Enjoy your time here and have fun. Tomorrow, you can help me prepare the turkey dinner. This is a special Thanksgiving for us all. Did your father tell you how he rescued Tom from a crazy medicine man in Brazil last month?"

Kate was surprised. She said, "No, he didn't mention it. But the two times we spoke on the phone, I kept him busy with my questions. If I asked, do you think he would tell me the story?"

"Of course, he will. Tim will probably play down his role, but ask your Uncle Tom if Tim is telling the truth. That way you'll get the whole story."

Kate was intrigued by the thought her father was a hero and didn't tell her about it. She thought, *"His actions say a lot about who he is. Dad's not anything like mom told me or the picture I had in my mind. I have a lot of questions to be answered, but let's wait to see how things develop."*

When Kate and Pearl returned to the living room, George waved Kate into a seat between him and Tim. "Come in, Kate and make yourself at home. I won't allow Tim to steal all your time."

Kate leaned over and gave her grandfather a kiss on the cheek. "I forgot to tell you how pleased I am to be here. Bermuda is just as lovely as you said. I can't wait to explore the islands. Are there any shipwrecks here?"

"Any wrecks will have been pilfered long ago," Tom said. "Many years ago, your father and I dove on several old ships, but we didn't find any treasure. By now, I imagine time and storms have destroyed what few might have remained. Have you scuba dived, Kate?"

Kate nodded. "Only in fresh water, and I haven't been deeper than fifty feet. I understand with the currents and all, there's a big difference in ocean diving."

"Yes, there is," Tom said. "This is the wrong season to go out. In the fall, the waves and currents are too big and strong. If you return in the spring, I'll take you diving, and if they're still there, I'll show you some old wrecks."

"I'd love that," Kate said. Then she changed the subject. "How long have you been a priest, Uncle Tom?"

"Quite a few years – I just returned from Brazil, where I got in trouble and your father came to rescue me. I thought I was accomplishing something, but only made a fool of myself."

"You're being too hard on yourself, Tom," Tim said. "You couldn't help what happened. You just met the wrong people. At least you learned a lesson you'll remember for the rest of your life."

"Grandma told me you went down to Brazil and rescued Uncle Tom," Kate said. "Will you tell me about it? Grandma says it was exciting."

Attempting to downplay the story, Tim said, "I had a lot of help and good luck."

"Go ahead and tell Kate your tale, Tim," Tom said. "If you don't, I will, and my praise will probably make you blush."

So with the help of his brother and an occasional input from George, Tim told Kate a scaled down version of the rescue.

When he mentioned Sister Kate in passing, Tim noticed Kate didn't ask who she was. He thought he had got through Catherine's part of the story well and was about to finish his tale when Tom opened his big mouth. "Sister Kate isn't a nun. She and your dad really hit it off."

By the way Tim looked at him; Tom knew he had stuck his foot in his mouth.

"Thanks a lot," Tim thought. *"Now what?"*

"So you met a woman who has the same name I do," Kate said. "How well did you get along?"

Tim forged ahead with the news. "Well enough to ask her to marry me. I hope the news doesn't upset you."

Kate appeared to be deep in thought, but then she replied, "Not at all, Pops."

"I don't like being called Pops," Tim thought. *"I prefer Dad or Father. I'm not sure if Kate uses the term when she's upset with me or all the time. I can't read her very well yet."*

Then Kate asked, "I guess it means no reconciliation with mom, right?"

"No; to be brutally honest with you, Kate, there never was a chance. Your mother seems quite happy as a single parent. I thought you knew."

"I do, but it doesn't mean I couldn't dream when I was younger."

Tim said, "When I leave here, I'll return to Brazil. As I told you, Sister Kate is a school teacher. To avoid any confusion between you two, I call her by her given name; Catherine. Catherine plans to finish out this school year and then we'll be married here in Bermuda."

To Tim's surprise, Kate said, "I think it's great. Will I be a flower girl?"

"Why not?" Tim replied.

Chapter 17

"Pay as You Park" lot, Austin, Texas

In space thirteen, (an ironic parking spot as far as she was concerned), Cheryl sat in the rear seat of Wendell's car and watched the merry makers on Sixth street as they partied. She wished she could be happy on this night, Thanksgiving eve. But Cheryl was about to end her life, so tonight nothing seemed very cheerful.

She knew it would be difficult for Kate to understand her death. For a moment, she wondered what the future would bring for her daughter.

"Kate's young; but I know George and Pearl will take care of her."

Then her thoughts moved on to the past and her ex-husband, Tim.

"Kate will need him now. I have to admit; Tim made a success of his life. I should have been more patient. Who knows what might have happened?"

Over the past week, as she followed her evil plan to get even with many of the men who had used her throughout her life, Cheryl met and slept with everyone on her list except Tim.

"It'll take them a while to realize they have AIDS, but then they'll know how I feel."

When she met with her old nemesis, Bob; Cheryl traded her sex for five bags of good coke.

Earlier this evening, she met George at the hotel to hold her last session with him, just for old time's sake and also to even the score.

"I goofed and forgot the protection," she lied. "I need you Wendell. Can't we do without it tonight? I'm not going to get pregnant."

When Wendell sensed Cheryl's supposed passion burning, he gave in. "I guess one time won't hurt anything."

Cheryl made it a long and tiring session. When they were finished, Wendell fell asleep.

While pulling one of her best dresses over her scanty black bra and panties, she thought, *"When they find me, I want to be remembered as a woman of beauty."*

Cheryl left the hotel room with the keys to Wendell's car in her hand. She found his Cadillac and drove to a parking lot on Sixth Street.

"I want to see the nightlife of Austin one last time. I'm glad I could find Wendell's keys. I didn't want to screw up my car, and when they find me in his Cadillac, it'll create a scandal in the banking community. Wendell might claim his car was stolen, but how will he explain his keys in the ignition?"

But now, as far as she was concerned, Cheryl's life was over. Calmly, she cooked all five bags of coke in a dented lid from a small shoe polish can and waited until the drugs liquefied. Then slowly and professionally, she drew the fluid into a new syringe with a very sharp needle.

After allowing the deadly potion to cool for a few minutes, she found a firm vein, slipped the needle into her arm, and whispered, "Goodbye world."

Tears almost blinded her as Cheryl took a deep breath and pushed the plunger downward. Her arm burned momentarily and a pleasant warmness spread throughout her body. When the drugs reached her heart, her body convulsed, her heart stopped beating and her body slumped to the floor.

Early the next morning, after noticing there was still one unclaimed car in his lot, the parking attendant, Eddy Franklin found Cheryl's body.

Eddy called the police, who discovered Cheryl's driver's license in a pocket of her dress. When the investigating officer noticed Cheryl's purse was missing, he suspected Eddy had not been totally forthcoming.

Later in the day, while attempting to use Cheryl's credit card, Eddy was apprehended and arrested for theft. Inadvertently, Cheryl added one more victim to her list. At least, after Eddy was released from jail, Cheryl's last casualty would hopefully live a long life.

Chapter 18

After dinner, Tim asked, "Kate, would you like to walk down White Sands Road to see our private beach? It's a thrill to watch the winter waves break over the coral."

"Go ahead, you two" Pearl said. "Tom can help with the dishes. Besides, it's time for George to attack the crossword puzzle again."

As Tim and Kate stood watching large waves pound the coral, Kate asked, "Where's the white sand I've heard so much about?"

"The storms of winter take it back out to sea," Tim said. "With the gentle swells of springtime, the sands return."

Then he put his arm around her shoulders and said, "I'm glad we finally met."

She smiled up at him and asked, "Could I ask a favor of you?"

"Anything you want," Tim replied.

"I wish you would be 'brutally honest', as you call it, with me about you and mom. I've only heard mom's side of what happened between you two. You probably don't believe I would understand, but I will. I'm nearly seventeen now and close to being an adult. Why can't you?"

Tim answered as truthfully as he could. "For one thing, there might be things you wouldn't appreciate hearing about your mother. For another, I hate to reopen old wounds."

But Kate was persistent. "I really want to know. If you love me, you'll tell me the truth and let me decide. Don't you owe me that much?"

Apparently lost in thought, Tim nodded at her words. "I owe you more than I can ever repay, Kate. Let me think about your request. Today is Thanksgiving eve. Tomorrow should be a day of thanks for Tom being alive, and me too, after Narro's sneaky snake. Let's enjoy tomorrow. Then, if you still want to hear my side of things, we can go somewhere and talk quietly."

"Great, Pops. I can tell you now, I want to know everything."

Thanksgiving in Bermuda was wonderful. Everyone awoke at dawn, had breakfast and then walked several blocks down the road to a small chapel to celebrate Mass. As a visiting priest, Tom delivered a fine sermon about the first Thanksgiving.

Along with George and Pearl, Tim and Kate strolled back to his parents' home. Kate's grip was firm and her hand was warm. Tim felt like a king.

Pearl noticed Tim's satisfied look and was thrilled. *"I'm so happy for them both.*

With Kate's help, Pearl prepared a wonderful repast for the family. Of course, there was a large turkey stuffed with cornbread dressing and browned to perfection. It appeared the table was loaded with every vegetable known to man.

After Tom gave a short blessing, they sat down to eat.

George winked at Kate and commented dryly, "When it's time to eat, Tom never delivers a long prayer,"

Kate had never enjoyed a Thanksgiving more. When she was home, Cheryl didn't cook big meals. *"If it didn't come out of a box or can, ready to heat, mom didn't want anything to do with it."*

As he watched Kate stuff herself and then ask for seconds, Tim could tell she was enjoying her stay and the day. As a proud father, he couldn't keep his eyes off her. *"All this time wasted. I could kick myself for not standing up to Cheryl and demanding my visitation rights. What a fool I was."*

For dessert, Pearl served homemade pumpkin and apple pie with ice cream. She smiled when Kate finished her apple pie and asked for a piece of pumpkin. Then she asked, "Where do you put it all, child?"

"When it comes to your cooking, Grandma, I have the proverbial bottomless pit for a stomach. This is the best Thanksgiving ever."

While Kate and Pearl cleared the table and did the dishes, George and the twins went to the cellar to remove the Christmas decorations. As far back as Tim and Tom could remember; they ate Thanksgiving dinner and then decorated the house to use up the energy gained from the feast.

By the time they had moved all the decorations from the storage area to the front yard, the twins were worn. George let his sons do the heavy work – his forte was supervision.

With the dishes done, Kate and Pearl helped string lights, and hang wreaths and various other Christmas ornaments George strung or hung each year.

Kate laughed with the twins as they made good-natured fun of their father's obsession with Christmas. *"I've never had such fun."*

When the last string of lights was in place and every ornament met George's satisfaction, he threw a switch on a strip of electrical plug-ins. "Stand back and watch," he said proudly. The result was a blaze of lights."

"It was a lot of work," Kate said. "But the end result is spectacular.

While George wasn't listening, Pearl whispered in Kate's ear. "It's just a little gaudy, perhaps."

By the time everyone called it a night, Kate was worn out.

"I've never enjoyed an entire day so completely. My family is really something. I'm determined to discover more about mom and dad. But tonight, those things don't seem as important."

As Pearl and George got ready for bed, she said, "Things seem to have worked out well for Tim and Kate. I'm happy for them both.

Kate is a sweet girl. With a little luck, she'll realize it wasn't her father's fault that they never met before."

Just as in the United States, the day after Thanksgiving kicks off the traditional Christmas shopping craze in Bermuda.

Pearl woke Kate and said, "Come on, sleepy-head. It's time to hit the stores. The boys and George can sleep in, but we have work to do."

Shortly after Tom, Tim and George awoke and were eating breakfast, the telephone rang. Tim was closest to the phone, so he answered.

A somewhat familiar voice asked, "May I speak with Tim?"

"Speaking," Tim replied. He knew the caller's voice from somewhere recently.

"This is Bob Jessop. Several days ago, we met on the plane from South Carolina. My son, Bryan sat next to you."

Now, Tim remembered. "Good morning, Bob and a belated happy Thanksgiving. What can I do for you?"

"Marsha and I haven't found the type of home we had hoped to. I remembered your kind offer of assistance and wondered if we could get together tomorrow."

"Tomorrow will be fine," Tim said. "Why don't you come by for lunch at noon? My mother and father will want to meet you."

"If you're sure we won't interrupt any plans, we'll be there. I'll drag Bryan along, kicking and screaming because he can't go swimming. He's very disappointed by the lack of sand on the beaches."

"I knew he would be," Tim said. "Tell Bryan my sixteen-year-old daughter, Kate will be here. Perhaps that will make him more receptive to my invitation."

"A young girl, hmm, will he be interested?" Bob asked and then he laughed. "We'll see you tomorrow."

When Tim hung up, George asked. "Who was it? Someone we know?"

"No, Dad; I met Bob and Marsha Jessop and their teenage son, Bryan on the plane. They want to buy a home here. I told Bob you knew everyone in these islands and gave him my card. I told him to call if he experienced any trouble finding a place.

"Bob did, and he did. You'll like them. They'll be here for lunch."

"I'll let you explain to your mother why she has three guests coming to lunch tomorrow that she doesn't know."

"Mom won't mind. If I know Marsha, she's a shopper, so they'll get along well."

When Pearl and Kate returned in a taxi from shopping with their arms loaded down with purchases, Tim told his mother about the guests he had invited for lunch.

"Your friends are ours," Pearl said. Then she asked, "Does Marsha like to shop?"

"She's a woman, isn't she?" Tim asked in return. "Yes, Mom; I'm sure you and Marsha will get along splendidly."

"You say they have a son?" Pearl asked.

"Yes," Tim said. "Bryan is seventeen and a handsome young man."

While wondering how the news that a teenage boy was coming to visit would affect her, Tim glanced at Kate. She caught his eye over the edge of her glass and smiled.

"Bob and Marsha are looking for a home to buy," Tim added. "Bob is retiring soon. Since the day when they honeymooned here twenty years ago, they have wanted to return to Bermuda."

Pearl asked, "What should I prepare for lunch?"

"Anything you put on the table will be fine, Mom. I know your cooking, remember?"

"Speaking of food," Kate said, "We ate lunch at the Buckaroo Restaurant. It's really a neat place."

"Yeah," Tim said. "The Buckaroo has been here forever."

Tom patted his stomach and said, "We ate turkey sandwiches, so we're fine until dinner, Mom."

Then, Kate asked, "Dad, will you do me a favor?"

Attempting to make light of what he knew was coming, Tim said, "Anything for my daughter, who now calls me 'Dad' instead of 'Pops'."

"I want to talk to you alone about mom. Could we sit on the porch? I promise to have an open mind."

Tim could see no way to get around the subject, so he said, "Sure, everyone will excuse us."

As he followed Kate onto the porch, Tim wasn't sure where to begin. *"I told Kate about having to marry Cheryl. I guess I should begin there."*

"Shortly after you were born, I got drafted and sent to Viet Nam. Your mother was upset about the war and having to handle your birth all alone."

When he told the story of how he came home and found Cheryl and Bob together, Tim said, "One thing led to another and Cheryl filed for divorce.

"Your mother got a judge to sign a restraining order against me. As a result, I couldn't come within five hundred feet of your mother, Bob or you. She kept the order in effect for years."

Kate shook her head. "I knew mom hated you. But I didn't know about the restraining order. She never mentioned it. She let me think you left us all alone."

Tim reached out to pat Kate's hand. "That was a long time ago and Cheryl was under the influence of Bob and his drugs. But all that doesn't matter now. What really counts is the way you feel since you heard my side of the story."

Kate began to cry. "I feel as if I was cheated out of my father all these years. Mom shouldn't have made me suffer along with you. I don't know if I can forgive her."

Tim was upset with her reaction to his story. "If this is the way you're going to act, I'm sorry I told you the truth. No matter how much it hurts, you have to forgive and forget. Your mother isn't all bad. She raised you to be a wonderful person."

Kate dried her eyes and said, "I'm glad you told me your side of the story. Now that I know you didn't leave me on purpose, I feel better. The word, 'family' has begun to take on a new meaning for me."

"Good," Tim said. Then he put his arm around Kate's shoulders and led her back inside.

As they walked in the door Pearl asked, "Are you all right, Kate?"

"I'm fine, Grandma. I feel much better now."

Pearl echoed Tim's words. "Good. Take your time and think over what your father told you. Time heals all wounds."

Kate smiled and said, "I'm just glad I have my father with me again."

The next day, the Jessop family arrived precisely at noon.

Tim introduced everyone and made sure Bryan met Kate. "Kate; why don't you take Bryan out on the patio and show him the scenery?"

As Kate led her guest outside she said, "Come on, Bryan. The view is spectacular."

From the patio, she pointed to the beaches below. "There isn't much sand on the beaches at this time of the year."

Bryan nodded in agreement. "Yeah, I noticed. I was disappointed when I didn't see white sand beaches like the ones described in the travel brochures."

Kate laughed. "You'll have to come back to Bermuda in the spring. I plan to do some scuba diving then with my father and Uncle Tom."

Bryan looked amazed. "I didn't know priests scuba dived."

Kate laughed again. "They're human, just like you and me. Uncle Tom knows some shipwrecks we can visit. It sounds like fun."

"I graduate in June," Bryan said. "Maybe I can talk my folks into returning then. Then, again, if they do find a place to buy, they might be living here."

Kate asked, "If your parents move here, what will you do?"

"I have a scholarship to Virginia State University for the next four years and I plan to become a lawyer. Where I go afterward depends on who hires me."

"I'm a junior," Kate said. "But so far, I'm not sure what I want to do. I thought of becoming a nurse or teacher. I'm not sure which."

Bryan said, "Either one sounds like work." Then he asked, "How are your grades?"

"Not all As. I got two Bs last semester in Chemistry and Biology. I'm not very interested in those subjects. I hate to cut up grasshoppers and frogs."

"You and me both," Bryan said.

Kate shrugged and said, "We better go back inside with the old folks. After lunch we can take a walk on the beach to see what we can find."

When they rejoined the adults, Kate and Bryan found George and Bob were getting along fine. Pearl and Marsha were busy planning a late afternoon shopping trip. When they could get a word in edgewise, the twins joined the conversations.

George had discovered Bob was a stockbroker. After working for many years as a writer for a Virginia newspaper, Marsha retired recently and was now a homemaker.

When lunch was over, Pearl announced, "I'm afraid you and Tom will be stuck with the dishes, Tim. Marsha and I are going to town to shop. The stores will be closed tomorrow, so we must make do with the few hours we have remaining. I'll call a taxi, George. You can have the car to show Bob around the islands."

Kate begged off from the shopping trip. "I promised Bryan I'd show him your private beach."

"Well then, Marsha and I will leave now," Pearl said. "You two youngsters have fun on the beach, but watch out for the coral. It's very sharp. Don't climb on it."

George and Bob left a few minutes later in the Volkswagen. "I know several homes for sale," George said. "I hope one will be right for you and Marsha, Bob."

As they walked along the beach, Kate spotted something bright reflecting from the coral and asked, "What is that?"

"I don't know. Let me dig it out. Could it be gold?"

"I doubt it; I'm not that lucky."

"No," he said and laughed. "It's an English penny, worth about two and a half cents in American money."

Kate laughed with him. "Some treasure, but at least we found something. Since I discovered it, I'll give you the coin to remember your first visit to Bermuda."

As each group of people completed their trips, the day passed by quickly.

Windblown and exhausted, Kate and Bryan returned from the beach. Tim noticed they were holding hands.

Pearl and Marsha came home with yet another carload of packages.

George and Bob also returned, weary, but in good spirits. "We looked at four homes," Bob said. "You'll like at least two, Marsha."

"Would you allow us to take everyone out to dinner?" Bob asked. "It's the least I can do to repay your hospitality."

"We accept," Pearl said. "After shopping all afternoon, I'm not about to cook, and I'm tired of leftover turkey. Let's go to the Castle Harbor Country Club."

"I'll call a cab for you girls," George said. "We men will ride in the VW."

At the club, after displaying his "treasure", Bryan got a laugh from everyone.

"We may have to buy more suitcases to hold all the things I bought," Marsha said.

"Tim could loan you some," George said dryly.

His statement resulted in yet another report of Tim's woes by bringing seven suitcases to Bermuda.

The day ended as the Jessops departed for their hotel by cab. Everyone in the Fitch household crammed into George's small car for the ride home.

"Bryan was fun to be with," Kate said. "It's too bad he lives so far away from Austin. But maybe we'll both return to Bermuda again soon. Who knows?"

Sunday, everyone relaxed after the busy Thanksgiving week-end.

Monday dawned bright and breezy and promised to be a very nice day. It would also be a day everyone would remember for a long time to come.

When the phone rang, the family was almost finished with their noon meal. Pearl answered the call and then motioned for Tim to take the phone.

"Tim, this is Terri. Is Kate with you?"

"Yes, what's up?"

"Is there some way you can get to another phone and call me? I don't want Kate to hear what I have to say or see your reaction to the news."

Tim wondered what could possibly be wrong, but he said, "Yes, of course. I'll get the information and call you back in five minutes."

"I'll be here in the office. It's very important."

"Okay," Tim said.

As he hung up, Tim thought, *"From the tone of Terri's voice, the news is not good."*

Turning to the others, he said, "Terri needs some information on one of our new developments. I'll call her from my room. Go on with your meal. I won't be long."

Terri answered on the first ring and Tim asked, "What's going on?"

Terri's voice shook when she replied, "Cheryl is dead. Apparently she overdosed on drugs. A detective named Samuel Wise called and said he was attempting to locate you and Kate. After the police found Cheryl's body, they broke into her apartment to search for information on her family. They found your number in her address book and the neighbors told them about Kate. This is terrible for poor Kate."

Terri's news hit Tim hard. *"Not now, not after the wonderful time Kate spent here. How do I tell her about her mother?"*

Terri was shaken at Tim's lack of a response. She asked, "Tim, are you still there?"

Tim realized that since he heard Terri's first words, he had been staring into space. "Yes, I'm here, Terri. I'm sorry; your news hit me hard. I don't know how to tell Kate. You say Cheryl overdosed? Where can I get more information?"

"Detective Wise left his number. He's waiting for your call at 210-555-2222, extension 17."

Tim copied down the number and said, "I'll call immediately."

"Oh, Tim, I'm so sorry to be the bearer of bad news. I feel so bad for Kate. Cheryl's death will be difficult for her to understand."

"Thanks again, Terri. I'll be in touch. We'll have to make arrangements for Cheryl's funeral. I don't believe she has any living relatives. I'll talk to Detective Wise and get back to you."

When Detective Wise came on the line, Tim said, "This is Tim Fitch. My secretary says you've been attempting to locate my daughter, Kate and me."

The detective seemed to be relieved. "Yes I have. Is Kate with you?"

"Yes, I'm calling from Bermuda. My parents live here and Kate is visiting them for Thanksgiving."

"Thank goodness," Samuel said. "We've been looking for her. Is she an only child?"

"Yes, she is. I'll inform her of her mother's death, but first, I'd like to know what happened."

"Your ex-wife's body was found in the backseat of a car that was parked in a lot on Sixth Street. When the officers arrived, Mrs. Fitch was deceased. She was alone in the vehicle with a needle still stuck in her arm. We believe it's a simple case of an overdose, but we're checking further. The car wasn't hers. We're tracing the owner as we speak."

"Are you sure it's Cheryl?"

"Yeah," Samuel said, "we're positive. She didn't have her purse, but she was smart enough to carry her driver's license in a dress pocket. We're sure her death wasn't foul play. She just took one too many hits of cocaine."

Tim sighed and said, "A few days ago I found out she was experimenting with drugs. I'm sorry Cheryl had to die this way."

"Yeah, but we all have to go sometime, don't we? It's not that I'm callous, Mister Fitch, but I'm tired of finding people who are dead from drugs."

"I understand. When will you release Cheryl's body for burial?"

"Unless something unusual comes up during the investigation, and I doubt it will; her body will be released within two days. If you come to Austin to settle her estate, you can check with me."

"I don't believe Cheryl has any family in Austin," Tim said. "Thanks for your help. I'll be in touch. If you need to speak to me before I arrive in Austin, you can reach me here in Bermuda." Tim gave the detective his number and then hung up.

While sitting alone for a few minutes, Tim thought things through. Then he stood up, opened the door and called, "Tom, could you come here for a minute?"

When Tom entered the bedroom, Tim told his brother about Cheryl and asked his advice.

Tom said, "We have to tell Kate. It's going to shake her up. She may feel it's her fault."

"Why should she?" Tim asked. Then he paused to think clearly and knew the reason. "She'll believe by being there she could have prevented Cheryl's death, won't she?"

"Possibly," Tom said. "I believe I should be the one to tell her. After your talk with her about Cheryl, and although Kate now knows more than she did about your ex-wife, she may not appreciate hearing of her mother's death from you. It will be difficult enough as is. Do you agree?"

"Yeah, I do; thank you, Tom. Break it to her as gently as possible. God, I hate this. Why now? Kate was having such a good time and we were just getting to know each other."

Tom attempted to console his brother. "God works in mysterious ways. We can't question His motives. The living must go on. I'll take Kate to the den to tell her the news. You can tell mom and dad what happened."

They returned to the dining room, where Tom asked, "Kate, could I talk to you in the den for a minute?"

"Sure, Uncle Tom," she said and followed Tom toward the den. He closed the door quietly behind them.

Pearl asked, "Oh, Tim, what happened? You look as pale as a ghost."

Tim sat down at the table and said, "You know Terri called. She said the police in Austin found Cheryl's body. She's dead from an apparent drug overdose."

Pearl clutched her arms to her chest and sobbed, "Oh no, poor Kate. Is Tom telling her about this now? I should go to her."

"Please wait until Tom calls you, Mom. In the next few days, Kate will need all the love we can give her."

"Good Lord," George said. "I can't believe it. I didn't care for Cheryl, but I would never have wished a death like this on anyone."

"No one would," Tim said. "I'll have to change our plane tickets. Kate and I will fly to Austin to complete the details of Cheryl's burial."

When Pearl heard her only grandchild crying in the den, she could contain her grandmotherly instincts no longer. She ran to the door, opened it, entered and then closed the door softly behind her.

George said, "Your mother knows best, Tim. She'll be able to help Kate now more than any of us. She'll call you when she thinks you should come in. Sit down and I'll fix you a drink. You look like you could use one."

"Thanks, Dad; yes, I'll have a small one. This hit me hard."

Regardless of what Tim asked for, George prepared a strong drink, handed it to his son and asked, "What about notifying your fiancée?"

Tim took a small sip of his drink and thought for a few seconds. Then he said, "Catherine expects me to return to Brazil next week. I'll have to phone and cancel those plans until we get through with Cheryl's service."

"Wait until your mother calls you to speak with Kate," George said. "Your daughter will need you now more than ever. This will have a lasting effect on you both. What you do in the next few hours will make a big difference in your daughter's welfare. Slow down and think."

Tim set the unused portion of his drink down on a table and said, "That's good advice, Dad. I don't need this anymore. Thank you."

In the den, when Kate was seated, Tom said, "Kate, I have some bad news."

From the way Uncle Tom and her father acted, Kate knew something was wrong. "Is this about my mother?"

"Yes, I'm sorry to say, it is. Your father just found out your mother passed away yesterday morning. He wanted to tell you, but I thought it would be best if I did. I'm very sorry, Kate."

Through tears that coursed down her cheeks, Kate sobbed, "What happened to her?"

"I'm not sure. All I know is Cheryl is gone. Your father may know more. He's very worried about you."

Kate continued to sob. "Why now? Maybe if I hadn't come here, I could have prevented her death from happening."

"I doubt it, Kate. You can't blame yourself for a thing. God calls us when our time is up. You need to be strong for your father. He's all you have left now. God must have been the force behind your mother suddenly allowing you to visit us. This way, when you heard about her, you weren't alone."

Suddenly, Pearl entered the room and cried out, "My dear child; I'm so sorry about your mother. Go ahead and cry; it will make you feel better. I know you loved your mother."

Pearl took Kate's hand in hers, sat on the edge of the chair and held Kate to her breast.

Eventually Kate calmed down, stopped crying and asked, "How is my father taking the news?"

"Not well," Pearl said. "He will need you as much as you need him, Kate. Let him know you love him. He's been longing for your love for a long, long time."

"I know. Would you tell dad its okay for him to come in?"

Tom moved to the door and called Tim into the room.

When Tim entered, he walked to Kate and knelt down beside her, took her other hand in his and whispered softly, "I'm so sorry Cheryl's gone. I know her death is a shock. Are you okay?"

Through fresh tears, Kate replied, "I'm fine, Dad. I feel so terrible for mom being all alone when she died. What happened?"

Tim didn't want to let Kate know how Cheryl died, so he lied. "I don't know all the details. I spoke to a detective in Austin. All he knew is that Cheryl was found in a car. She may have suffered a heart attack. Detective Wise said all the information wasn't in yet."

Kate dabbed at her eyes with a tissue and asked, "What happens now?"

"You and I will leave for Austin as soon as possible. We need to plan a memorial service and burial for your mother. Are you up to the trip?"

As she shook her head, Kate said, "Not really. I don't know what needs to be done. Do you?"

Tim had never dealt with the death of anyone, but he didn't want Kate to know. "I'm sure when we contact a funeral director he'll tell us what we need to do. I'll call my secretary and have her change our tickets. Do you know where yours are?"

"They're in my purse," Kate said. "I'll get them."

"Stay where you are, child," Pearl said. "I'll get your purse and bring it to you."

Tim asked, "Are you feeling better, Kate?"

"A little bit. The news is finally sinking in – mom isn't here anymore. What's going to happen to me? Where will I live?"

Fresh tears welled up in Kate's eyes and she attempted to blot them out with her balled fists.

Tim handed Kate his handkerchief, gently rubbed her back and said, "You can live with me or you can stay here with your grandparents. I know they'd love to have you."

Kate's tears continued to flow as she sobbed, "What hurts most is that we were having such a wonderful time. I couldn't wait to get back home to tell mom about it. Now I'll never have the chance. Why did this have to happen now?"

"There's no easy answer," Tom said. "We have to accept things as they happen and move on. Your mother loved you and wouldn't want you to grieve."

Pearl returned with Kate's purse and handed it to her. Kate found her airline ticket, gave it to Tim and asked, "When can we leave?"

"I'll know as soon as I speak to Terri. I know you want to get home to Austin as soon as possible. I hope we can leave tomorrow or the next day."

"You take care of the tickets, Tim," Pearl said. "I'll look after Kate." She took Kate's hand in hers and said, "Come with me, Darling. You should lie down and rest for a while."

Terri was still in the office and answered on the second ring.

"Terri," Tim said, "Kate and I will need our tickets changed. I'd like to get out on the first available aircraft."

"The airlines have bereavement fares," Terri said. "But I know you'll want to fly first class, right?"

"Right now, Terri, I don't care if we fly coach. Just do your usual best. Can you do another favor and call Detective Wise? Ask him to arrange for a reputable funeral home to pick up Cheryl's body and prepare her for viewing. I don't want Kate to know how Cheryl died. Tell him to ask the mortician to do a special job."

"Let me get busy," Terri said. She hung up without saying goodbye.

Tim knew he was in good hands.

It took some time for Tim to reach Catherine. The connection was so bad the operator was forced to repeat most of his message.

"Do what you must," Catherine said. "Stay with Kate until you're sure she's okay. Don't worry about me, I'll be fine. I'll miss you every night, but I understand what you and your family are going through. What a horrible thing to happen just after Thanksgiving."

They spoke a while longer, but the connection didn't improve. Hearing an operator relay Catherine's "I love you", wasn't the same as hearing the words from her. Finally Tim gave up, told the operator to tell Catherine he loved her and hung up.

As Tim replaced the phone in the cradle, it immediately rang again. This time the caller was Bryan, who asked for Kate.

"I'm sorry, Bryan," Tim said. "Kate just received the news that her mother passed away. She and I will leave for Austin very soon."

Bryan was shocked, but he recovered and said, "I'm sorry. Is there anything I can do?"

"It's very nice of you to ask, Bryan. But I can't think of anything right now. Kate is resting and I'll tell her you called. Give me your number and she can phone you later."

Thirty minutes later, Terri phoned. "I got both tickets changed. You leave the day after tomorrow, at six-thirty a.m. and arrive in Austin at four-thirty p.m. Your tickets will be waiting at the Eastern Airlines counter at Kindley airport."

Then Terri changed the subject and asked, "How is Kate? How did she take the news?"

"Better than I thought she would," Tim said. "She's worried about what will happen to her now."

"Take good care of her," Terri said.

"I will. Thanks again for a superb job. I assume you told Ken and Bill."

Terri said, "Yes, and they said to take as much time as you need. They understand. Have you told Catherine?"

"We changed our plans for now. I'll go to Brazil after I find out what Kate wants to do. Good job on the tickets, Terri. Now you know why I gave you a raise."

"Thank you," she said and hung up.

As Tim walked back into the living room, he asked Pearl, "How's Kate?"

"She's sleeping like a baby. I just checked on her. She's been through quite a bit. It's amazing how resilient young people are."

Tim gave his mother a kiss on the cheek. "Thanks for taking care of her."

"That's what grandmas are for."

An hour later, when Kate heard a murmur of voices from the living room, she awakened. She still wasn't over her mother's death, so she didn't feel up to talking to anyone just now. After all the new information her father had given her in the last few days, plus the news of her mother's death, the pain was almost too much to bear. *"I know now mom must have hated dad. Either that or the drugs she took affected her mind. I feel sad about mom, but I don't know if I feel bad for her, or because of her."*

While she was still attempting to make sense of everything, Kate fell to sleep again.

When Kate awakened the next morning, Pearl was sitting in a chair by her bed and drinking coffee from a pretty Christmas cup.

Pearl smiled when she saw Kate was awake and asked, "Feeling better?

"Much," Kate said and stretched full length. "I mean it. I feel better today. It's nice to have my grandma nearby."

She took Pearl's hands in hers and said, "Thank you, Grandma, for everything. I love you."

Fighting back tears, Pearl replied, "I love you too. You're quite a young lady for your sixteen years."

"Sixteen and a half," Kate said proudly.

"Oh, yes," Pearl said knowingly. "That's important at your age. Oh, by the way, your young friend, Bryan phoned last night. He said he's sorry about your mother. He seems like a nice young man."

"He is. Did Bryan leave a number where I can call him?"

"Yes; Tim left the number by the phone. Why don't you get dressed and phone Bryan? It will do you good to get out in the fresh air. It's a beautiful day for a drive. Does Bryan have his license yet? If he does, he can drive in Bermuda."

In response to Pearl's question, Kate shook her head. "I don't know. Even if he does, I doubt Bryan has had any experience driving on the wrong side of the road, the way you Bermudians do."

Pearl said, "Well, there's no time like the present to learn. I'll leave you to your bath and go fix a big breakfast. Take your time, Bryan will wait."

After taking a shower and washing her hair, Kate examined her eyes in a mirror. *"Bummer, my eyes are swollen from crying last night. I hope Bryan won't notice. It will be nice to spend some time with him. It might take my mind off mom."*

Pearl insisted Kate should have breakfast before she phoned Bryan. "Your young man will probably be waiting by the phone for your call. You need some food in your stomach. Sit down and eat."

When Kate began to eat, she realized she was starved. She finished three eggs plus several pieces of bacon.

Pearl buttered a piece of toast, gave it to Kate, smiled at the sight of Kate's empty plate and said, "There, you see, grandmas always know best. Now you can phone your young man. I'll bet he answers on the first ring."

Pearl was wrong; Bryan picked up after the second ring.

"Hello," Kate said. "What were you doing, hatching the phone?"

"No," Bryan said and laughed. But then his voice turned somber. "I'm sorry to hear about your mother. If you don't feel up to going out, I understand. I was sitting here, reading a travel brochure on Bermuda. Have you heard of Devil's Hole? It sounds interesting. Would you like to go exploring?

"Why, Bryan Jessop. Are you asking me for a date?"

"I suppose I am."

Kate smiled at his response. "Grandma says it's time you learned how to drive on the 'right' side of the road, which in Bermuda is the left. She wants to know if you have a driver's license."

"Yes; but is my license good in Bermuda?"

"Grandma says it is," Kate said. "Hold on."

"Grandma, will grandpa let us borrow his car? Bryan wants to see Devil's Hole."

"If George wants to eat any more of my cooking, he will," Pearl said. "Tell Bryan to take a taxi here. Devil's Hole isn't far."

"Bryan, did you hear grandma?"

"Yes; it shouldn't be too difficult to drive on the wrong side of the road at twenty miles per hour. If your grandfather will trust me with his car, I'll take good care of it. I'll be right there."

"Wonderful," Kate said and hung up. Then she jumped up from her chair and ran around the table to give Pearl a big hug and a kiss on the cheek. "You're fantastic, Grandma. Do I look like I've been crying? Are my eyes still swollen?"

"Sweetheart, Bryan won't look at your eyes. He'll stare into them, but won't see beyond them. Don't worry. Let's go tell your grandfather he's volunteered his car. I can't wait to hear his reaction."

All George said as he handed Kate the keys to his prized VW was; "I hope your young man can adapt to driving on the correct side of the road."

As Tim and Tom entered the room, Kate announced, "Bryan is coming by and we're going for a drive. Isn't it wonderful?"

Tim gave Kate a hug. "You're in good spirits this morning. I'm glad you feel better. Did grandma mention we have reservations for Austin and depart at six-thirty tomorrow morning?"

Suddenly Kate looked dejected. "No, she didn't. That means I have only today to see Bryan. The Jessops leave at the end of the week."

"I'm sorry, Kate, but we have to take care of things in Austin."

"I know; I'm being a pain. Ignore me. I'll be ready in the morning. Oh look, there's Bryan now."

Kate ran to the door and waved at Bryan, who was paying the cab driver. Bryan waved back and smiled.

George greeted Bryan with a warning. "Watch out for pedestrians and especially tourists. They don't pay any attention to cars and always look the wrong way. Take your time and remember, left is right."

As Tim laughed at his father's attempt to fluster Bryan, he said, "You'll do fine. If you make a mistake, remember what you did wrong. That way you'll learn quickly. Have fun."

"Here's a map of the islands," Pearl said. "I marked the way to Devil's Hole. Have a good time."

"Buckle your seat belts," George ordered.

After Bryan pulled away from the curb, he started down the road in the right lane.

"He's on the wrong side of the road," George shouted.

Either Bryan heard George or suddenly realized his mistake. He quickly moved the VW to the left-hand side of the road.

George watched as Bryan continued on slowly to the intersection of South Shore Road. There he turned safely and correctly into the left lane of traffic.

"They'll be fine, Dad," Tim said.

"It is strange to drive on the left," Bryan said.

"Count it as another adventure," Kate replied.

They found Devil's Hole; which is a beautiful grotto built into the side of one of the hills bordering the coral shoreline.

"When we're done here, let's go to the Buckaroo for lunch," Kate suggested.

Bryan was pleased to see the death of Kate's mother wasn't affecting her happy mood. There were several sad moments, when Kate mentioned her mother's name in connection with an old memory. Other than those, Bryan knew she was enjoying their day together.

While they were eating a hamburger and fries, Kate said, "It's too bad our time together can't last."

Bryan was surprised. "What do you mean?"

"Tomorrow morning I have to leave for Austin. My father and I have to take care of my mother's affairs."

Bryan reached out to hold her hand. "I'm sorry; I've enjoyed your company. If it wasn't for you, this trip would have been a bummer."

She squeezed his hand and said, "Thank you, kind sir."

After lunch, they drove around the islands in an attempt to see all the sights mentioned in Bryan's travel brochure.

Out of the blue, Kate asked, "Do you enjoy living in Virginia? I've never been there, but I hear it's a pretty state."

"Yes, it is. I love to drive through the countryside. Everything is so green. Virginians keep the state very clean."

"Did your family originally come from Virginia?"

Bryan smiled and then chuckled. "Our family goes way back in history. Dad likes to tell everyone our ancestors came over on the 'Wallflower' – the second ship after the 'Mayflower'. He gets a laugh from their reaction."

All too soon, their day together was over. As the sun was setting, Bryan turned the car toward home. Kate laid her head back on her seat and let her hair fly in the wind as warm air blew in the side window.

Bryan broke into her reverie by shouting, "Look out!"

Kate sat up in time to see a moped rider headed toward them in their lane. Bryan stomped on the brakes and the car slid to a stop.

Unabated, the moped driver continued on as if he hadn't seen them and ran into the front of their car.

On impact, the driver flew over the handlebars and ended up spread-eagled on the hood. After recoiling from the force of impact and landing on its side, the small motorcycle slid to the side of the road. The back tire continued to make a humming noise as it spun around for a few seconds. Then the engine stalled and it was deathly still.

Bryan quickly shut off the motor, unbuckled his seat belt and climbed out. He moved to the side of the moped rider and asked, "Are you all right?"

The stranger looked up at Bryan with bloodshot eyes. His breath smelled of alcohol and he slurred his words with a European accent. "I'm as well as can be expected after I've been run over by someone driving on the wrong side of the road."

Bryan could hardly understand the stranger. As Bryan helped him to his feet, the man didn't appear to be seriously injured. Except for a few small scratches on his hands and face, there was no other blood. He was barely able to stand erect and continued to sway back and forth.

Kate looked closely at the stranger, frowned and said, "He's drunk as a skunk."

Still slurring his words, the stranger said, "Not quite, my lovely; but I'm getting there."

A police van with a flashing blue light appeared around a bend in the road, slowed and then came to a stop fifteen feet from the front of George's car.

A policeman stepped from the van, adjusted a tan pith helmet on his head and walked to where the trio stood. He took one look at the drunk driver and asked, "You again, Jock?"

Kate asked, "Do you know this man?"

"Jock's what you might call our town drunk," the policeman replied. "For five years, he has claimed to be drinking himself to death, but he hasn't managed it yet. I will say he keeps trying.

"Another motorist phoned to report a moped rider on the wrong side of the road. We were attempting to stop him before he hit someone. I see we weren't so lucky."

From out of the darkness another man's voice asked, "Is anyone in your vehicle injured?"

The stranger belonging to the voice was dressed in a dark suit, white shirt and pale blue tie. He approached them so quietly neither Kate nor Bryan heard him. Kate was startled by his sudden question.

"No," she and Bryan said almost simultaneously.

Then the stranger asked. "Is there any damage to your car?"

After examining the front of George's VW closely, the policeman said, "There's only a dent in the bumper where the moped struck and some scratches on the bonnet where old Jock landed."

The stranger took the time to inspect their vehicle closely. Then he asked, "Isn't this Doctor Fitch's car?"

"Yes, it is," Bryan said and pointed to Kate. "This is his granddaughter, Kate. Doctor Fitch gave us permission to use his car for sightseeing. We're both here on vacation."

"Check it out, will you, Bill?" the stranger asked. "Call in and see if headquarters can contact Doctor Fitch to verify this young man's statement. What did you say your names were?"

As he produced his Virginia driver's license for verification, Bryan said, "My name is Bryan Jessop. This is Miss Kate Fitch. As I said, she's the doctor's granddaughter."

The mysterious man asked, "Do you have any identification, young lady?"

"Yes, I do," Kate replied. She rummaged through her purse, found her student ID and handed it to the stranger. "I don't have a driver's license yet. I'm only sixteen."

After studying their identifications for a minute, the man returned the documents and said, "I must apologize; I haven't introduced myself. I'm Inspector David Smythe. I know your grandfather quite well, Miss Fitch. George and I play an occasional round of golf."

Bill returned from the police van to report, "It checks out, Inspector. Headquarters contacted Doctor Fitch, and he hopes they won't be detained. Doc Fitch understands about Jock. He's treated him off and on for years."

"I'm dreadfully sorry you met up with Jock," David said. "You're free to go. We'll let Jock sleep it off in a cell again tonight. We should reserve one for him permanently. It would save a lot of our time and energy."

"Thank you for your courtesy, Inspector," Bryan said.

"And thank you for yours, young man," David said. "In our profession, we don't meet many well-mannered gentlemen. I hope you'll enjoy your stay in our islands."

David turned and walked back to the police van, while Bill attempted to help Jock roll his damaged moped to the van to load. The front wheel was bent and scraped noisily against the fender.

Bryan saw Kate was shaken by the close call. He said, "If Jock hadn't been so drunk; he might have been seriously injured,"

While taking Bryan's head in her hands, Kate looked into his eyes, smiled and said, "It wasn't your fault and everyone knows it, including my grandfather. You're a good driver. Being able to stop before Jock hit us proves it. I'm glad you weren't hurt."

"When he sees the bent bumper and scratches on his hood, I won't earn any awards from your grandfather."

"Well, here's one from me," Kate said and kissed him tenderly on the lips.

"Pardon me, young lady," Bill said. "You need to move your car, young man. In the dark, this is a bad curve."

"We were just leaving," Kate said. "Before we did, I wanted to reward Bryan for his good driving."

Bill laughed, waved them on and said, "Lucky Bryan."

After starting the motor and pulling back on the road, Bryan blushed, but managed to say, "Thank you for the reward."

"You're welcome. I wish you weren't leaving in the morning."

There was a moment of silence. Then Bryan said, "I never asked what you're going to do, now that your mother is gone. Where will you live?"

"My father says I can live with him. There's only one problem; he's getting married again to a woman he met in Brazil. I can't see them on their honeymoon with me along to tie them down."

"What about your grandparents," Bryan asked. "Can't you stay with them?"

"That's probably what I'll do. I'll have to change schools in the middle of the year. It's a bummer, leaving old friends behind and having to make new ones. But what other choice to I have?"

"I don't know," Bryan said. "I hope my parents find a house here. If they do, and you come here to live, we could see each other often. I have to attend college in the fall, but I could spend my school vacations here. What do you think?"

"I'm leaning more and more toward staying with my grandparents," Kate said. "Would that make you happy?"

"Very much so; maybe I would do something to earn more of your rewards."

Kate smiled and said, "You never know."

When they arrived at the Fitch residence, George was waiting alongside the road. Bryan was afraid to drive the final few feet to where Doctor Fitch stood glaring at the damage to his prized VW.

Kate got out first, met her grandfather's stare and defended her beau to the death. "Bryan's not to blame for any damage to your car. Inspector Smythe was there and can tell you who was at fault."

"I'm not upset with Bryan," George said. "A few minutes ago, I spoke with Inspector Smythe. David is my friend and a good judge of character. He has nothing but praise for young Bryan. David said if Bryan hadn't stopped in time, I might be down at the hospital now, patching up Jock again. I have better ways to spend my evenings."

When Bryan heard George's words, he finally climbed from behind the wheel, handed George the keys and said, "I'm sorry, sir."

George reached up, patted Bryan on his back and said, "I know you are, Bryan. Don't worry about it. Jock is a friend of mine, but I wish he would quit drinking. One of these days, his luck is going to run out. I'm glad it wasn't tonight."

The twins and Pearl were waiting inside. Pearl rushed up to Bryan and put her arms around his shoulders. "Thank you for bringing our granddaughter back in one piece. I'm sorry you met Jock the way you did. When he's off the sauce, he's a nice man."

Tim interrupted with his own observation. "The only trouble is; Jock is always into the booze. It's his middle name."

"Doctor Fitch is taking this quietly," Bryan said. "I thought he would want my skin for damaging his car."

"George is upset," Pearl said. "But he won't use profanity around young people or in mixed company. Under his breath, he's probably saying some nasty things about Jock. Don't worry; George doesn't blame anyone but Jock."

"Kate and I had quite a day," Bryan said. "I hate to see it end, but I should get back to the hotel. My parents will be wondering what's become of me."

"Don't worry, Bryan," Pearl said. "I phoned your mother and told her what you two were up to. She's surprised you wanted to drive on the 'wrong' side of the road; you Americans."

"Thanks, Mrs. Fitch. I'll phone for a taxi to take me to the hotel."

Pearl held up her hand and said, "I'll do it for you."

After dialing the number from memory and listening to the cab company's response, Pearl said, "Your taxi will be here within fifteen minutes, which gives you two young people time to say goodbye. Did Kate inform you that she's leaving in the morning, Bryan?"

"Yes, Ma'am; I hope she decides to stay with you after she returns from Austin. If my parents find a house here, I'll be able to visit her often."

"Got it all planned out, don't you?" Tim asked. "I'm glad you two hit it off. I like your style, Bryan. Anyone who manages to damage my father's car and gets away alive has to stand tall in my eyes."

"Oh, Tim, leave them be," Pearl said. "Can't you see they want to say goodbye without us around? Don't you remember when you were sixteen? I do. Remind me to tell you about it sometime, Kate."

Without waiting for a reply, Pearl reached out, grabbed her oldest son by the top of his right ear and held on firmly as she led Tim into the kitchen. Tim yelped all the way.

"I like your father," Bryan said. "He's quality people."

"Would you believe I met him for only the second time in my life a few days ago? Remind me to tell you the story another time. Right now, I'd like to know if I earned any rewards today for my companionship."

"Only a couple," he said and reached out to take her in his arms.

They shared exactly two kisses before a horn blew outside.

Bryan said, "Just my luck. Leave it to my taxi driver to be early. Thanks for a wonderful day and some great rewards. I'll treasure them for a long time."

"So will I," Kate said. "Take care and please write. Send your letters to my grandparents' address. I've made up my mind. I'm coming here when we're finished in Austin."

The horn blew again.

"I have to go. I'll see you soon."

When George saw Bryan run to the taxi and jump in, he waved, but Bryan didn't notice. His eyes were glued to Kate where she was standing on the front porch. *"I'm in love."*

Tim watched Kate stroll slowly to the front door. She seemed to be walking on air and lost in thought.

She was.

Tim thought, *"I'm glad I met Bryan and his parents on the plane. He's taken Kate's mind off her troubles."*

As Kate walked in humming an old song, Tim broke into her

happy mood. "You still have to pack for tomorrow's trip. We'll leave at four thirty a.m., which means we have to get up very early."

Kate nodded and said, "I'll leave most of my clothes here. I brought mostly light-weight clothes for the warm weather and won't need them in Austin. I have plenty of warm clothes at home."

"So, you plan to return," Pearl said. "I'm glad. You're always welcome here. I'd love to have another woman to talk to."

"Yes, Grandma, if it's okay with you, I want to come here to finish my junior year in high school. Dad can see about my transfer from Reagan high in Austin."

"Of course it's all right, Dear. You'll be happy here. You make friends so easily. As pretty as you are, the boys will be phoning all hours of the day. It'll be fun, you'll see."

Tim said, "If that's what you decided, Kate, it's fine with me. Let's make it through the next few days, one at a time. When we have your mother's affairs settled, I'll put you on a plane to Bermuda."

"Super, Pops," Kate said and smiled brightly. "As you say, I need to pack. See you in the morning."

There were a wide variety of dreams that evening.

Kate dreamed of Bryan.

Tim dreamed of Catherine.

Tom dreamed of his new assignment in New York City.

Grandma Pearl dreamed of things to do when Kate returned.

George experienced a nightmare about the scratches on his car. Then he dreamed of somehow getting even with Jock.

Across town, as all boys do who believe they are in love, Bryan dreamed of Kate and their future together.

Marsha dreamed of their new house in Bermuda and how to furnish it.

Bob dreamed of the mortgage payments and had an upset stomach all night.

Chapter 19

When they arrived in Houston to make connections, Tim and Kate found that although the weather was chilly, there were no delays. Their flight arrived in Austin on time, and to their surprise, Terri was there to meet them.

"I thought you might need some clerical help," Terri said as she gave Tim a kiss on the cheek. "Introduce me to your lovely daughter, Tim. Don't stand there with your mouth open."

"Of course; Terri, this is my daughter, Kate.

"Kate, this is Terri, my very dependable secretary."

"It's nice to meet you, Terri."

After Terri hugged Kate, she kissed Kate's cheek and said, "I was so sorry to hear about your mother."

"That's very kind of you."

"I made potential reservations for you at the Hilton," Terri said. "I didn't know if you wanted to stay there or at your apartment, Kate. I'm rooming with a friend on Ben White Boulevard, which isn't far away from either location."

Tim asked, "What do you want to do, Kate?"

"I'll save you some money and we'll go home. You can sleep in mom's room. We have to go there anyway to get my clothes, so why not stay?"

"Okay," Tim said. "Can you cancel our hotel reservations, Terri?"

"Sure, and I have the phone number of your apartment, Kate."

Terri handed Tim a slip of paper. "Here's the number and address of the mortuary where they've taken Cheryl. The funeral director says he'll be available to speak to you about the service any time today. There's no rush. Whenever you say, he'll set up a private viewing for the family. The second phone number is where I'm staying."

When Terri saw tears in Kate's eyes, she put her arms around Kate and said, "Honey, I'm very sorry about your mother. You're a brave girl. She'd be proud of you."

"Thanks for your help, Terri," Tim said.

As they rode in a taxi toward her apartment, Kate said, "Mom's apartment is off Cameron Road, in the University Hills area of northeast Austin. We have a two bedroom, two bath unit with a parking garage located under the building. It's the one thing mom always insisted on. She wouldn't let her car be parked outside."

The taxi dropped them in front of the building, where Kate led the way to an elevator and the third floor apartment.

After she unlocked the door, Kate held it open so Tim could enter first with their bags. Although not big by Texas standards, the apartment was very nice. Tim found he was standing in a large living room with a well-appointed kitchen to his left and a hallway to the right that led off to the bedrooms and baths.

As Tim remembered, Cheryl was never a serious homemaker. Books and magazines were strewn here and there around the living room, but it was fairly clean and orderly. *"I can see Kate's work here."*

Kate took her bag into her room and then returned to the living room. She clutched her arms across her body and surveyed the apartment. "It's not much, but its home. Mom's room is down the hall from mine, and you'll have your own bath. Would you mind waiting while I clean her room?"

"Not at all; take all the time you need."

Tim sat down on the couch, picked up an old copy of People magazine and absentmindedly thumbed through it.

When Kate returned again, she said, "I cleaned out two drawers in the dresser for you. Mom's closet is full of clothes, so there isn't much space to hang anything."

"That will be fine. I can live out of my suitcase. After the services, we'll worry about Cheryl's clothes. Right now, we should concentrate on the funeral."

Tears formed in Kate's eyes as she asked, "Can you call the funeral home and ask when we can see mom?"

Tim handed Kate his handkerchief. "Sure, Honey, I'll phone right now."

"You can view Mrs. Fitch's remains after eight p.m. tonight," Mister Worley said.

"Fine," Tim said. "We'll see you at eight."

As Tim relayed the news to Kate, he suddenly realized they hadn't eaten since breakfast. "Are you hungry, Kate? I'm starved."

"Yes, I am. Can I change clothes first?"

"Sure," Tim said. "I'll change too."

When they met at the door, Kate looked like a model from Teen magazine. Her long blonde hair was tied into a ponytail, and she wore Levi jeans and a bright printed shirt. A small scarf was tied around her throat to accent her natural beauty. She appeared much older than her sixteen years.

Tim asked, "Ready to go?"

"Sure, Dad - you look like a dude in your western outfit."

Kate walked to his side, kissed his cheek and said, "Thanks for being here for me. Where do you want to eat?"

"Is the Service Station still in business?"

"I believe so."

Tim started to call a taxi, but Kate stopped him. "Here's the key to mom's car. It's a mint condition Mustang you might remember. Mom said you bought it for her."

"And she kept it all this time?" Tim asked incredulously. "I can't believe it."

"She loved the car. Let's put the top down. When mom was feeling blue or was in a good mood, we'd ride around with the top down, and we both would fly our hair in the wind. We'd drive out Route 290 and take Highway 71 through the beautiful hill country."

They walked downstairs to the garage, where Kate pointed to a car covered with a thin blue cover. When Tim pulled the tarp off, he was surprised. The car was in mint condition, as if it just came off the show room floor. He remembered how happy Cheryl was when he bought it for her.

Tim climbed in and fired up the engine. The motor purred and the exhaust rumbled satisfactorily. He drove out of the garage and pulled to the curb to put the top down. Kate helped him button a cover over the folded canvas.

Tim slowed for the exit from I-35 to Barton Creek Road and turned right. Since he attended school here, Barton Creek Road had been expanded from a two-lane road to a very nice, wide, four-lane highway. It snakes along the left bank of the Colorado River in downtown Austin.

They enjoyed the ride and looks they received from other motorists and pedestrians. Kate let her ponytail fly in the wind and laughed when someone gave her a "wolf-whistle".

"No matter how old you are, you still love an old Mustang, Tim said. "This is a fine car."

At the Service Station restaurant, Tim found a parking spot where he hoped no one would ding the doors of Cheryl's car.

Then he asked, "Do you know the history of the Service Station, Kate?"

"Not really."

As they walked through the door, Tim said, "It's actually an old service station. Look at the Model T Ford setting on top of a grease rack in the middle of the dining room."

Kate pointed to two antique gas pumps. "Do they really serve beer from those?"

"Yes, they do, but check out our table. It has a steering wheel and hood ornament from a Chrysler imbedded in plastic."

"Neat."

Tim added, "They serve the best Nachos in Texas – especially if you order a bowl of Texas chili and dump it on top. Man, the thought makes my mouth water."

"Then that's what we'll order," Kate said.

Once Kate tasted the finished product, she declared her father a genius.

"Speaking of cars," Tim said, "I'll see about having the Mustang transferred to your name. We should keep it in the family. I can drive it to Fort Worth and store it in my garage until you decide what you want to do."

"I don't even have a driver's license yet. I love the Mustang too. It reminds me of mom and the fun we shared. I definitely want to keep it."

"Okay, it's a done deal."

After supper, they drove to the mortuary. Kate was quiet and seemed composed. But when they approached Cheryl's coffin, she became apprehensive. "I've never seen a dead person before."

They spent several moments by Cheryl's side, and Tim thought, *"The mortician did a great job. She looks as lovely as I remember."*

Cheryl's hair was brushed back and lying on both sides of her head. Tim was pleased to see the mortician dressed her in a long sleeved dress, which hid any needle marks on her arms. Kate didn't seem to notice. She placed her hand on her mother's and stood there, trembling and crying.

Finally between sobs, Kate managed to say, "She looks very nice. Oh, Mom, I miss you so much."

Cheryl's service, which was held two days later, was a simple but dignified affair. There weren't many mourners. Terri was there, and a few of Cheryl's fellow workers from the bank arrived to pay their last respects. Several neighbors that Tim didn't know also attended.

Tim made the arrangements and together they picked a wooden casket for Cheryl. Pearl, George, and Tom sent a large floral arrangement, which was placed at the head of Cheryl's casket. Tim and Kate picked out a floral blanket for the coffin made of Cheryl's favorites, red roses. Father Flannigan, a wiry, old and wise Irishman delivered a fine eulogy.

There were no graveside services. Only Father Flannigan, Terri, Tim and Kate followed the hearse to the graveyard for a private interment. Although Kate cried during much of the main service in the church, she was strangely composed at the gravesite.

Kate was pleased with the service and appeared to have made peace with herself. She didn't ask Tim any more questions about the way her mother died.

The next morning, they saw Terri off at the airport. She was returning to Fort Worth and the business. She hugged Tim, kissed Kate and wished them well.

Tim and Kate spent a few days picking out items Kate wanted to keep. She said, "I'd like to donate Mom's clothes to the Goodwill store."

While they were looking through Cheryl's belongings, Tim discovered a key to a safe deposit box at nearby First National Bank. He phoned the bank and discovered the box was still active, with Kate as a co-signee.

After Tim explained Cheryl's death to an assistant manager of the bank, Mister Baxter, Tim was informed when he and Kate opened the box they would need a lawyer present.

Mister Baxter said, "The lawyer will inventory the contents of the box for any valuables which might be a part of Cheryl's estate."

Tim contacted a local lawyer named Larry Rhodes, who agreed to meet them the next morning at the bank at ten a.m. and do the inventory.

"All we need is a copy of your ex-wife's death certificate," Larry said.

"I have one," Tim said. "We'll see you tomorrow at ten."

As they returned to the task of packing, the telephone rang. Kate answered and then handed the phone to Tim.

An unknown man asked, "Mister Fitch?"

Tim replied, "Speaking."

"This is Wendell Grayson, Manager of the First National Bank. If it can be arranged, I need to speak to you in private about a delicate matter."

"Does this have anything to do with my ex-wife's death?"

"In a round-about way, yes, but I can't speak of my problem over the telephone. Can we meet today to discuss the matter?"

Tim wondered where this conversation was headed. "Your request is very unusual. Can you give me any particulars?"

Mister Grayson said, "My concern is something Cheryl may have put in her safe deposit box. The item could be embarrassing for us both. That's all I can tell you. Please, I implore you; give me a chance to explain in person."

Tim decided to find out what this was all about. "When and where would be convenient to meet?"

"Would the Embassy Room at the Hyatt Regency Hotel at two p.m. today be agreeable?"

"I'll be there," Tim said. "How will I recognize you?"

"I'll be seated at the bar and wearing a dark blue suit. Thank you for agreeing to my request. I'll explain everything to you then."

Wendell hung up before Tim could reply.

Kate asked, "Who was it?"

"Someone from the bank," Tim said. "You don't need to come along. It shouldn't take long."

At one forty-five, Tim drove to the Hyatt Regency Hotel and found the Embassy Room. Wendell was the only person seated at the bar in the middle of the day.

Tim walked up to him and asked, "Mister Grayson?"

As he shook Tim's hand, Wendell said, "Thank you for meeting me. Let's sit at a table in the corner, where we can't be overheard."

"Your secrecy has me puzzled," Tim said. "What's this all about?"

Wendell sat down and waited until Tim was seated. Then he said, "I'm attempting to avoid an embarrassing situation. You see, for the past two years I was involved in an affair with Cheryl."

Tim shrugged and asked, "Why is that any of my business? Cheryl and I have been divorced for fourteen years,"

Wendell leaned forward and said, "The outcome might embarrass your daughter. Your wife was a very conniving woman. Without my knowledge, while we made love, she made a video tape and used it as blackmail to secure a job at my bank."

Although it did, Tim said, "It doesn't surprise me."

"In her attempt to get ahead, I wouldn't put anything past Cheryl."

"Let me continue," Wendell said. "Cheryl assured me there was only one copy of the tape, which she gave to me after we made a deal. I destroyed it so my wife would never know. Now I'm not sure Cheryl didn't make extra copies. That's what concerns me and where you come in."

Tim said, "I still don't understand,"

"Cheryl's body was found in my car," Wendell said. "She and I met every week at this hotel. The night she died, I fell asleep. She took my keys and drove downtown.

"What happened there, I don't know. I reported my vehicle as stolen, but the police want me to explain how Cheryl had my keys. I'm afraid she may have hidden a copy of the videotape in her safe deposit box. Now do you understand?"

Tim nodded and said, "Yes, now I do. You want to be there when we open the box to see if any tapes are present."

"Yes, please. If there are, I ask you to give them to me. You wouldn't want your daughter to see them."

"Do I have your word you had nothing to do with Cheryl's death?"

"Yes, I swear. I'm attempting to prevent embarrassment for all concerned. If you wish, you may view the tapes before you turn them over. You won't like what you see, but it has nothing to do with Cheryl's death."

"We meet with the lawyer tomorrow, at ten a.m.," Tim said. "Be there, and we'll see what's in the box."

Wendell's hands almost shook in relief as he said, "Thank you. I only hope I can save my marriage. I was an idiot to become involved with Cheryl."

"Cheryl made fools of us both," Tim said.

The next morning, after Tim and Kate met Larry Rhodes in the lobby, they gained entry to Cheryl's safe deposit box. Wendell met them at the entrance to the vault and introduced himself as if they had never met.

As Wendell escorted them into the vault, he asked for, and Tim gave him, Cheryl's safe deposit box key. Wendell unlocked the locks and carried the long metal box to a waiting table. Tim noticed perspiration was dotted on Wendell's brow.

"Let's see what we have," Larry said and opened the box slowly.

There wasn't much inside, but there were no tapes. Tim heard Wendell give a sigh of relief.

Larry said, "We have an insurance policy, a registration and title for a Ford Mustang, plus several pieces of fine jewelry." Then he asked, "What's this?"

A manila envelope that contained a large amount of one-hundred-dollars bills was lying at one side of the box. After Larry finished counting, he said, "The money totals seven thousand, seven hundred dollars."

He laid the envelope aside and reviewed the insurance policy.

Then he said, "The insurance policy in the sum of thirty-five thousand dollars names you, Kate as the sole beneficiary. I'll make a list of the jewelry and give you a copy, Mister Fitch.

"I can release the documents that pertain to the vehicle so you can transfer ownership to Kate's name. In order to have the vehicle registered, you'll need the death certificate, the documents I'll give you and a copy of Mrs. Fitch's will to take to the state comptroller's office.

"The comptroller has the necessary forms to complete the transfer from your mother's name to yours, Kate. Since you're underage, your father can sign for you.

"You may give your father verbal permission to drive the vehicle, but before you take any trips, I would contact the insurance company to change the information on the automobile policy immediately.

"The insurance company will also need to see the life insurance policy. You can take it with you when you leave the bank.

"I'll have to keep the cash and the jewelry until we have it appraised. As soon as possible, I'll file the will for probate and you'll receive the items when that is complete. You're fortunate your mother maintained a will."

After Larry wrote a receipt for the money, he said, "Unless you can find proof that your mother already paid it, you may have to pay income tax on the cash. It's usually difficult to establish such validation. If you are notified to pay the taxes, I suggest you do so. It's much easier and less time consuming."

Tim gave Larry the information he needed and said, "I'm going to Brazil for a few months. Kate will stay with her grandparents in Bermuda. I hope this doesn't pose a problem. I'll give you my address at my construction company and you can send your bill there."

"We shouldn't have any trouble," Larry said. "If I need to speak with of either of you, I have your numbers. I'll be in touch."

Before he departed, Larry turned to Kate and said, "I'm sorry for your loss."

"Thank you," Kate said and watched Larry walk away. "He didn't even know mom. That was nice of him."

As they left, Wendell gave Tim a nod of thanks.

"Consider yourself lucky, Mister Banker," Tim thought. *"Not many of Cheryl's victims got off so easily. I hope this is the last of your troubles. Cheryl had a way of reaching out to disturb people's lives, even from beyond the grave."*

After he paid for Cheryl's funeral and the services performed by the mortuary, Tim and Kate contacted the insurance company and filed the proper papers for Kate to receive thirty-five thousand dollars from Cheryl's policy. Kate thought the amount was a fortune.

Tim said, "In today's market, it's not much. But it was nice that Cheryl thought enough to leave you a nest egg. If you invest the money wisely, it'll grow and by the time you graduate from college, you'll be able to buy a nice home."

The next morning, after he rented a small U-haul trailer, Tim unhooked it in the basement parking garage. They spent the remainder of the day hauling boxes and small pieces of furniture Kate decided to keep to the parking garage and packing the items inside the trailer.

When everything on Tim's list was done, they reattached the U-haul to the Mustang. Tim hated to install even a temporary hitch to the rear of Kate's prized vehicle. *"I hope the damned thing doesn't mess up the paint job."*

Then, after they bid Austin farewell, Kate and her father headed for Fort Worth to begin a new life together.

They arrived at Tim's house a little after three p.m., where he backed the U-haul onto the grass at the side of his driveway and unhooked it.

Tim said, "Come in, Kate, and I'll give you a tour of the house. Make yourself at home. I'll be out in the garage putting the boxes away. If you want, you can help."

"Sure, Dad; let me put my bags in my room first."

As a team, they made short work of the project. Then Tim pointed to the trailer. "Let's get rid of this thing. On the way home, we'll stop for groceries and I'll grill steaks for supper."

"Super, Pops. Your home is very nice."

When they returned, Tim carried in the groceries and Kate began to prepare a large salad. After he put the steaks on the grill over low heat, Tim called Terri to let her know they were in town.

"How are things going?" he asked.

Terri brought him up to date on the status of all ongoing projects that were being handled by the construction firm.

Then she asked, "When do you plan to leave for Brazil? And when is Kate returning to Bermuda? I need a day or two to get your tickets. With it the middle of the holiday season, tickets may be hard to schedule on such short notice."

Tim shook his head and said, "I haven't forgotten Christmas, but we've been so busy I haven't paid attention to the date."

"Today is the eleventh of December," Terri said. "There are only two more weeks until Santa slides down your chimney. Have you talked to Catherine lately?"

Tim was amazed. "It's so late in the month? Yes, I called Catherine twice from Austin. I'll phone tonight to tell her we arrived here safely."

"If you and Kate are ready to travel, I'll call the airlines and see what I can do about tickets. Would day after tomorrow be too soon?"

"That will be fine," Tim said.

Terri said, "Let me get busy. I'll get back to you."

Kate overheard the conversation and asked, "When can we leave?"

"Terri will schedule our tickets for day after tomorrow. It gives us time to do some Christmas shopping."

As Tim happened to glance out the window, he saw smoke pouring from the grill. He shook his head, took off at a run and shouted over his shoulder, "I forgot about the steaks."

He ran outside, lifted the lid and found one steak ablaze and the other well done. Kate arrived at his side, and with a wry smile, Tim said, "Let's salvage what we can. I'll eat the charred one."

During the night, Tim was awakened by thunder. When he awoke the next morning, it was still raining. Water poured down in buckets and the gutters overflowed. Dark clouds filled the sky and it looked like a long dreary day ahead.

At eight-fifteen, the phone rang. When Tim answered, Terri said, "I have your tickets reserved for the thirteenth of December. Kate leaves first, at eight-thirty a.m., first class to Charleston and then on to Bermuda.

"You leave at eleven-ten the same morning to Houston with a two hour layover before your plane departs for Belem.

"Kate arrives at a halfway decent hour; five p.m. local time, so your parents can meet her. I'll notify them of her arrival time.

"You arrive late in the evening, Tim. Your plane lands at eleven-seventeen, Brazilian time. I reserved a room for you at the Western Inn so you can get some sleep and make arrangements to fly to Obidos the next day.

"I attempted to notify Jose, but he didn't answer. Do you want me to keep trying, or do you want to contact him when you arrive in Belem?"

"I'll call Jose. You did great, Terri. Thanks for your help."

"Pick up your tickets at the counter. Have a nice flight and enjoy the holidays. Give Kate a kiss for me."

In the evening, Tim phoned Catherine and for once, the connection was clear. After he gave her his flight info, Tim said, "I get in very late, so I'll stay overnight in Belem. The next day, Jose can fly me to Obidos."

Catherine said, "Jose has been flying some oil company official around lately. He said you gave this guy his name. I hope Jose's not too busy to bring you home. I've been waiting too long."

"If Jose isn't available, I'll get someone else. I don't remember giving Jose's name to anyone. Don't fret your pretty head; I'll get home somehow."

The next day, in a jewelry shop in Highland Mall, Tim saw a diamond bracelet he thought Catherine would like.

He asked, "What do you think, Kate? Would Catherine like this?"

"I'm sure she will. It's lovely."

Although Kate knew she probably wouldn't see him until next year, still, she bought Bryan a Christmas present – a very nice Texas Longhorn sweatshirt and cap combination. "Bryan may be from Virginia, but if he wants to date me, he'll have to support the Longhorns."

Tim asked, "What happens when Texas plays Virginia?"

"We'll both root for our own teams, but Texas will win. Then I can console Bryan in his grief."

My little girl is growing up fast. Bryan better watch out. It appears Kate has set her sights on him."

Their last evening in Fort Worth, Kate and Tim spent an hour rearranging boxes and furniture in the garage so Tim could park the Mustang inside, out of the Texas weather. To insure the vehicles would start when he returned, Tim disconnected the battery on the Mustang and his Ford pick-up.

"We'll decide what to do with the things you brought from Austin later," he said. "I made arrangements for a taxi at five-thirty, tomorrow morning."

Tim waited with Kate until she boarded the plane and watched as she waved a small goodbye before she disappeared down an enclosed ramp. He stayed at her gate until her plane moved away and then found his departure gate, bought a newspaper at a nearby store and sat down to wait for his boarding call.

Two hours later, he boarded his aircraft and found his seat in first class.

"No one has the seat next to you," a stewardess named Sue said. "You can stretch out and relax."

"Thanks," Tim said and was suddenly very tired. *"The last few days must be catching up with me. I'm beat."*

"Could I have a bloody Mary, Sue."

"Sure, Mister Fitch."

While he waited for the remainder of the passengers to board the aircraft, Tim enjoyed two drinks and hoped the liquor would dull his senses enough so he could sleep on the plane.

When they were airborne, Tim pushed his seat back, closed his eyes and drifted off to sleep, with Catherine at the center of his dreams.

Chapter 20

Aboard Flight 764
to Charleston, South Carolina

Kate was wide awake and enjoying the company of a young woman named Judy Boyer, who was seated next to her in first class. Judy was from Fort Worth and on her way to Charleston to visit her son, Andrew and his bride, Mary. Judy's daughter-in-law just gave birth to her first grandchild, a boy they named Thomas.

Since the air conditioning on the plane must have been set at sixty-five, Judy adjusted a blanket around her legs and said, "You know, it seems the women of our family are giving birth earlier each generation. My mother was nineteen when I was born. When we graduated from high school, John and I married and I gave birth to Andrew when I was eighteen. Now Mary had Thomas at the ripe old age of seventeen. I'm only thirty-six and I'm already a grandmother."

Judy's mood turned somber and Kate saw tears form in the corner of her eyes. As she watched Judy dab at her cheeks with a Kleenex, Kate knew something was bothering her.

Judy sighed and said, "I'm sorry. I was thinking of my husband, John and how nice it would have been if he could have seen our first-born grandchild. John was killed last year in a hit and run accident. I miss him so."

As fresh tears ran down her cheeks, Judy sobbed, "I'm sorry. Please forgive me."

"There's nothing to forgive," Kate said. "Did they catch the driver of the other car?"

"Oh, I'm sorry again, John wasn't driving. He was walking from his law firm office. There was only one driver involved, a punk rock star named "Hambone" of all things. Have you heard of him?"

Kate shook her head, "No, I haven't. What happened to the driver of the car?"

Judy's voice turned harsh. "The fool was driving under the influence of drugs or alcohol and speeding. I doubt he even saw John, who was killed instantly. The driver didn't stop, but there were a number of witnesses who wrote down his license number. He was caught a few blocks from the scene.

"There was no doubt of his guilt. He was tried, convicted of vehicular homicide and is currently serving a five year sentence. But I don't believe five years is long enough. That doesn't bring John back. With good behavior, in two years this guy will be out of jail and able to make more money. It makes me sick."

Kate asked, "I don't mean to pry, but did John have insurance? How are you getting by?"

Judy indicated she was well off financially when she said, "I work as an accountant for another attorney. Both my husband's firm and mine are suing Hambone for fifty million dollars. The lawyers tell me the case is nearly over and we'll win.

"The punk has millions in record sales, so he can afford to settle out of court. The money won't bring John back, but it will allow me to help other women who have suffered this type of trauma in their lives.

"If I receive a large settlement, I plan to set up a charitable foundation in my husband's name to assist other widows and their children."

"You have great plans," Kate said. "I'm sorry about your husband."

"Thank you, Kate. I apologize for burdening you with my personal troubles. Every time I think of what John is missing, I want to scream. It's so unfair."

"I know how you feel," Kate said. "I recently lost my mother to drugs."

"Oh, my dear," Judy said. "And here I am, bothering you with my problems. You have enough of your own to deal with. I'm sorry to hear of your mother's passing."

Kate decided to change the subject. "Have you been to Bermuda before?"

"No, I haven't. Since I was about your age, I've always dreamed about going there. I couldn't afford it then, but I can now. Perhaps someday we'll meet again in the islands."

"That would be nice," Kate said.

Although Judy was older than Kate, they seemed to hit it off. Before she and Judy parted company in the Charleston airport, they exchanged addresses.

"If I do come to Bermuda, I'll call," Judy said.

Kate's connecting flight was packed with vacationers. There were a number of young students aboard who were flying to Bermuda for the Christmas holiday break. Kate hoped she might see Bryan among them, so she scanned their faces as they passed by.

"I haven't heard from Bryan since we parted. I still remember those two sweet kisses we shared before the taxi's horn interrupted us."

As they came on board, several young men smiled at Kate. She was a very pretty girl and they were impressed with her looks. All of the lookers would have mistaken her for eighteen or nineteen years of age.

Then, a pretty blonde woman said, "Excuse me, my seat is next to the window."

After she was seated, the stranger held out her hand and said, "My name is Lorna Hayden. I'm from Peoria, Illinois."

Lorna appeared to be in her late twenties, with long blonde hair, blue eyes and a ready smile. She also drew longing glances from the young men and some older gentlemen.

There was a twinkle in Lorna's eye and she displayed a mischievous smile.

Kate gave Lorna her hand and said, "I'm Kate Fitch; originally from Austin, Texas, but I'm on my way to live with my grandparents in Bermuda."

As they shook hands, Lorna said, "It must be nice to have grandparents who reside in such a beautiful place. I envy you."

Kate asked, "Have you been to Bermuda before?"

"No, Honey, I haven't. From everything I've read, the islands must be beautiful. It's a great place to meet rich men. At least I hope so."

"I don't know," Kate said. "It's also where young people go. Look how many are on board."

"True," Lorna said. Then she glanced around the first class cabin, noted several mature men were also headed to Bermuda and added, "Still, there are some older men in first class. You never know."

A stewardess stopped by and asked, "Would you care for something to drink?"

Lorna nodded and said, "I'll have a martini."

"A diet coke, please," Kate added.

Lorna surprised Kate when she said, "I'm going to Bermuda to find a rich husband. I know my dream is probably a fairy tale that won't come true, but I'm going to give it my best shot."

Kate asked, "What do you do in Peoria? Have you lived there long?"

"I'm a nurse and I've lived in Peoria for so long I can't remember anyplace else. I have two weeks to find my man, but if I don't, I'm still going to have fun. I saved for this trip for years."

"You have the right attitude," Kate said and laughed. "You do know there won't be much white sand on the beaches, don't you? The winter storms take the sand out to sea."

Lorma joined in the laughter and said, "Shucks Honey, I plan on lying around the heated indoor pool of my hotel and look for Mister Right. I won't need any sandy beaches."

Kate continued to laugh at Lorna's straightforwardness and determination to find a rich husband. "I wish you luck."

The remainder of the flight went by quickly while they gossiped about many things and men in general.

When they came down the stairs to the tarmac, Kate and Lorna parted company. Pearl and George were waiting and gathered Kate into their arms. She didn't have time to introduce Lorna. Kate's new friend disappeared in the crowd of passengers who were entering the terminal.

While she and Pearl spoke quietly outside, George went inside and waited at the carousel for Kate's bags.

Pearl asked, "How was your mother's service?"

"It was nice. There weren't many people, but the ones who came were friendly to dad and me. We picked out the stuff I wanted and took it to Fort Worth. I guess Austin is a thing of the past. I'll miss my friends."

Pearl rubbed Kate's back and said, "I know, but you'll make new ones here."

George and a porter appeared with Kate's two bags, and Kate handed the redcap her carryon. "I brought most of my clothes," she said. "I'll probably have to buy some new things for school. Can you help me shop, Grandma?"

"There's a silly question if I ever heard one," George said.

Pearl ignored her husband's comment and asked, "What are your plans?"

"I told dad I would stay with you for the rest of this year. I have to enroll in school as soon as possible. I have my records from Austin."

"Of course you can stay here with us," Pearl said.

"For as long as you like," George added. "You'll love Bermuda as much as we do. The schools are wonderful."

"I plan to finish high school here. That means you'll have to put up with me for two years."

Pearl said, "Honey, you're no bother. It will be wonderful to have a young woman around. I'll teach you all the ins and outs of shopping."

As Kate climbed into George's VW, she noticed the vehicle sported a new bumper and the scratches on the hood had been repaired. She winked at Pearl and said, "Your car looks like new, Grandpa."

George replied, "Never better; all traces of Jock have been removed. One of these days he'll finally drink himself to death and we can all rest a little easier."

"You don't mean that, George, and you know it," Pearl said. "Jock's one of your favorite patients."

At first, George shook his head as if the mention of Jock and his drinking problem had upset him, but then he smiled and said, "He's also my most recurring. I lost count of how many times I've patched him up. Jock still owes me for the last two visits. I would file a claim against him for the damages to my car, but it wouldn't do any good. Jock drinks up every penny his parents send."

"Enough about Jock," Pearl said. "Remember your high blood pressure, George. Kate doesn't need to hear this nonsense."

The drive home was filled with fond memories for Kate. *"I remember Bryan taking me on a tour of the islands in grandpa's car."*

She asked, "Have you heard from the Jessops?"

Pearl asked in return, "Are you talking about any particular Jessop or all of them? Bryan is back in Virginia, as are Bob and Marsha. They've closed up their Virginia home for the winter. Bob and Marsha bought a very nice house on Blue Waters Drive and will close on it after Christmas. I don't know the exact date they plan to return to Bermuda."

"Will Bryan be with them?" Kate asked. "He has to finish his senior year in Roanoke High School."

Pearl smiled and said, "You'll soon discover for yourself. There are a half dozen letters from Bryan waiting for you."

With a sparkle in her eyes, Kate said, "Grandma, how mean!" Then she asked George, "How long will it be until we get home?"

"Patience, girl," George said. "Those letters have been lying in a basket by the front door for days. They won't fly away before we get there. I won't speed for anything, not even your boyfriend's letters."

When they arrived at "On a Hill", Kate flew out of the vehicle and ran to the front door, only to have to wait until George unlocked it. She rushed inside, picked up the letters, checked the postmarks and arranged them by postage date marks.

Then she asked, "Will you excuse me?"

Without waiting for a reply, Kate ran to the back door, unlocked it and walked out onto the porch, where she sat quietly in a chaise lounge to read Bryan's letters.

George watched helplessly from the curb. Then he shrugged and began to carry in the luggage, while under his breath he mumbled something about not having any help.

With a wave of her hand, Pearl shushed him. "Be quiet, George. Go grumble somewhere else. It won't hurt you to carry those bags. Leave Kate alone. Can't you see she wants to read her letters? Honestly, sometimes I get so mad at men. You don't understand women."

Aboard Flight 23 to Belem, Brazil

When the stewardess named Sue gently shook Tim's shoulder, he awoke with a start. "I'm sorry to disturb you, Mister Fitch, but it's time to serve our in-flight meal. Would you prefer a baked chicken breast with dressing and mashed potatoes or a small steak with broccoli and rice?"

"I'll take the steak, please. Thank you."

Tim stretched his sore back, stood up and walked to the lavatory. He glanced at his watch and saw he had slept for two hours.

When he returned to his seat, he found his dinner waiting. The food was tasty and the steak tender.

Sue handed Tim a cup of coffee and said, "You had a nice nap. We're still several hours from arrival. If you want to sleep a while longer, after everyone finishes their meal, I'll turn the lights down"

"Thanks, but I think I'll read instead."

Sue smiled again. Then she turned and walked down the aisle and into the small serving area, which gave Tim a nice view of her shapely legs.

Those thoughts brought Catherine to mind. Tim pictured her in the kitchen of her home. She was wearing a pair of dainty panties and his shirt, the same as she did the morning after their first lovemaking. With only one button hooked near the bottom, Tim was afforded an exquisite view of her lovely breasts.

In an effort to take his mind off Catherine, he removed a magazine from a bracket on the wall. The periodical contained an article describing a search for new oil reserves in Brazil. Tim was surprised to see the town of Barreirinha listed.

The remainder of the flight was smooth as silk. As they approached Belem, Tim's heart beat faster. *"Why couldn't I get in earlier? Here I am, with my thoughts on Catherine and I have to spend my first night alone in a hotel."*

After making his way through customs and immigrations, Tim managed to be fourth in line for a taxi. The night was sweltering, and while waiting in line, Tim's suit jacket made him perspire. Of course, his taxi didn't have air conditioning.

By the time Tim reached his hotel, he had removed his jacket and loosened his tie. His pants were mussed and wrinkled. With a wry smile, he thought, *"Looking the way I do, no one's going to recognize me as a successful building contractor. Man, let me find my room and get some sleep."*

The young lady behind the counter with a name tag reading: "Maria" greeted Tim with a smile. For some reason, when she saw the name on his passport, her smile grew larger. "Oh, yes, Mister Fitch; we've been expecting you. I hope you enjoy your stay."

Maria reached behind her, found Tim's room key and handed it to him along with a small white envelope. She said, "You have a message from a friend."

Tim opened the envelope and removed a folded paper. The letter was from Jose:

"Welcome Back, Tim. Thanks for giving Mister Lumas my name. He chartered my copter for the next two months. I appreciate your help. As a way to say 'thank you', I asked room service to put something special in your suite.

"When you're ready to fly to Obidos, give me a call, and we'll have lunch. I'm staying with my sister. Her number is enclosed. Thanks again, Jose."

As Tim thought, *"I wonder who Mister Lumas is,"* he thanked Maria, who continued to beam like a cat waiting for hot milk.

At this late hour, there was no bellboy on duty, so Tim had to carry his own bags to the elevator. Glancing down at his key number, he was surprised to see he had been given a room on the top floor. After dragging his bags into the empty car, he punched a button for the fourteenth floor.

As the elevator doors closed, Tim suddenly remembered who Mister Lumas was. *"It's Fernando, from the plane ride home – my drinking buddy, the chemical engineer. So Jose is flying Fernando around. I wonder why?"*

The bell rang to signal the arrival at his floor. Tim hefted his two suitcases and walked down the hall until he found his room, where he set the bags down and attempted to open the door with a plastic keycard. It took three attempts before he was successful.

As he moved his luggage into the hallway, the door swung shut and a suitcase banged into his knee. "Damn it," he said aloud.

Then Tim heard a noise behind him and turned to see what it was. To his surprise, he found he was in the hallway of a large suite. *"This is either the penthouse or a honeymoon suite. How do I rate these accommodations?"*

There was a large living room to his left. To Tim's right was a small nook where a desk set with a lamp aglow.

Tim heard the noise again. It seemed to come from the bedroom, so he walked to the door. Sitting up in bed and wearing only a smile and a gown of flimsy, white material was Catherine.

In her right hand, she held a tall glass of red wine. In her left was a long stemmed red rose she had been using to stroke the satin sheets.

When Tim looked closely at the top of Catherine's gown, he noticed she wore a nametag. In large block letters, it read: ROOM SERVICE.

Tim was so startled he couldn't speak.

Catherine continued to smile at him. "Here I am, waiting for your first words, and they're 'Damn it'? I'll remember them the rest of my life."

At last, Tim found his voice. "I'm sorry, I didn't expect you."

He let his bags drop to the floor and moved to her side.

Catherine set the wineglass on the bedside table and spilled a few drops on the white sheets in the process. She dropped the rose to the floor and reached for his hand.

As she stared up at him with stars in her eyes, Tim cupped his left hand under her chin.

"God, you're beautiful," he said. Then he bent his head and kissed her lips tenderly. Her tongue searched hungrily for his.

When they finally broke their embrace, Tim said, "What a surprise. When I read the note from Jose, I was looking forward to a nice bottle of wine. I never suspected a thing."

Recollection dawned and Tim said, "Now I know why the young girl at the desk smiled so much. You two were in on this, weren't you?

"Yes, Darling; Maria is a dear. She's Jose's cousin and she arranged for this honeymoon suite at a reduced rate. I'll always remember you standing there, holding a suitcase in each hand and staring at me. You should have seen your face."

Tim sat down on the edge of the bed and held her hand. "Remind me to give Maria a large tip. How in the world did you get here from Obidos so quickly? I spoke to you last night and you didn't say a word."

She shook her head. "I had no idea I would be here. An hour after you phoned, Jose landed and came to see me. Mister Lumas accompanied him and says he knows you. Do you remember him?"

"Yeah, Fernando and I shared a drink or two on the plane to Houston. What's he doing with Jose?"

"He hired Jose to fly him over this area. His company believes there's oil in the jungle. That's why Jose stopped by. When Jose heard you would arrive tonight, he told me he and Mister Lumas were flying here for a meeting and invited me to come along if I wanted to surprise you. So here I am."

"Remind me to also give Jose a huge tip," Tim said. "His note set me up. I'm so glad to see you. On the plane, I thought how much I hated to spend my first night alone. I was worn out when I walked in. Now I'm wide awake."

"Good, we have a large amount of lost loving to make up for. By the time I get through with you, you'll know what tired really is."

As he took her in his arms again, Tim asked, "And, where should we begin?"

"Enough talk," Catherine murmured.

The next morning, a few minutes before ten a.m., the phone rang. Tim reached across Catherine's warm body and grabbed the receiver.

With his Spanish accent, Jose said, "Howdy, Tim. Did I wake you? How did you like our little surprise?"

Tim chuckled. "I owe you, Jose. You put one over on me last night."

At the sound of Tim's voice, Catherine stirred, reached out and tickled him on his stomach.

"I thought you would be up by now," Jose said. "Aren't you hungry? I'm starving. It's been three hours since I ate. Let's have breakfast. Bring along the wicked woman you found in your bed last night."

Tim smiled at Jose's enthusiasm. "Where do you want to eat?"

"The hotel has a great restaurant," Jose said. "I'm downstairs waiting."

"Give us thirty minutes."

"I can wait," Jose said. "Don't rush on my account."

After Tim hung up, Catherine tickled him a little lower on his anatomy. Then she said, "You only gave me fifteen minutes to dress. What were you thinking?"

As he responded to her urging, Tim said, "I should have said forty-five minutes. Come here."

Forty minutes later, the two lovebirds arrived at Jose's table just as the waitress removed an empty plate with only a large puddle of syrup remaining.

At the sight, Catherine shook her head and said, "I guess Jose couldn't wait."

Jose smiled at his two friends. "Since you two were late, I ate a small appetizer. There's coffee in the carafe."

As the men shook hands, Catherine poured two cups of coffee and handed Tim his. "After you phoned, something came up," she said innocently.

Jose roared with laughter, which caused several customers to glance their way. "Sometimes the same thing happens to Juanita and me."

Tim attempted to change the subject. "Catherine tells me you have a big charter with Fernando. What's going on?"

Jose shook Tim's hand again and said, "Thank you for your reference. The Brazilian National Oil Company seems to think there may be oil in our neck of the woods. I've flown Fernando here and there to check out different areas. So far, he hasn't found anything yet, but he is optimistic."

Jose paused to look around the room. Then he continued in a low tone. "I have a secret to tell you and Catherine. But this isn't the place for idle talk."

As he wondered what Jose was so excited about, Tim said, "Then let's order; didn't you say you were hungry?"

"Yes, I did," Jose said. He reached for the menu.

When their orders arrived, Jose said, "You two aren't eating much. After last night, I thought you would devour half the menu."

Tim blushed again, but Catherine wasn't fazed.

Jose ate three plates of eggs, ham, sausage and grits, plus a multitude of assorted breakfast meats and fruit, while he consumed half a loaf of bread and drank several cups of coffee.

When the waitress presented the check, he said, "I'll get the tab. You two are my guests."

As they left the hotel, Jose led the way and walked across the street into a park. He took a seat in one of several chairs at a round table that set on a patch of concrete surrounded by small flowerbeds. Then he waved them into two others.

Jose glanced around his surroundings once more and said, "I want to tell you my secret." He acted as if spies were hiding in the flowers and listening for his words. "You're my friends and I know you'll keep my secret."

"Go ahead, Jose," Tim said.

Jose leaned closer and said, "It involves the possibility of oil in Barreirinha. So far, I've led Fernando on a wild goose chase. I could tell him where there might be oil, but I waited until I could speak to you, Tim."

Tim was puzzled by Jose's words. He said, "Thanks Jose, but I don't know a thing about oil. How can I help you?"

"You already have. Let me to tell you my story. Then you'll understand."

"Okay, Jose," Tim said. "Fire away."

"It all began shortly after you left for the states, Tim. I was flying groceries to a town north of Prainha and ran low on gas. To save fuel, I decided to fly cross-country instead of following the river. You know how I hate to fly over the jungle.

"Anyway, a big storm brewed up right in front of me. With it filling the whole sky, I knew I was in trouble. I also knew I had to find a spot to set the bird down.

"There wasn't anything below me but jungle. Then I saw what I thought was a small lake. It was black like the river. Right then, it looked like heaven to me, so I flew over and set the bird down.

"The storm hit and rain poured down in sheets. When the big drops hit the copter it sounded like hail. Then I noticed something strange about the lake.

"The drops of rain hit the water and instead of just splashing a little, they made big dents on the surface, just as if the surface was thicker than grease. Whatever made the water black slopped up and adhered to the glass at the front of my helo. As I sat there and watched my windscreen turn black, it was eerie.

"The storm lasted an hour and then fizzled out. Afterward, my helo looked like a creature from the tar pits. I thought for sure the engine wouldn't start. When the rain finally quit, I climbed out of my cockpit and almost fell into the lake. The floats were slippery with a tarry goop.

"The engine was okay. The black stuff didn't splash up that high. To get the windscreen clean, I had to loosen a fuel hose and drain a few drops of valuable gas onto an old rag.

"My clothes were covered with the sticky black junk. When I finally got home with a nearly empty gas tank, the bird was a mess. I tried everything I knew to clean the crap from the helo.

"Finally I rented a steam cleaner. The steam blew the tarry stuff off the aircraft, but it stuck together and formed clots at the side of the landing pad. It took two days of hard work to finally get my helo back to looking like the Big Bad Bird of old.

"Then out of the blue, here comes Mister Lumas to charter my helicopter. Thanks again, Tim."

"You're welcome, Jose. But what's your point?"

Jose smiled and said, "The point is; the goop is oil."

Now it was Tim's turn to be surprised. "Oil - how do you know?"

"When Fernando saw the residue from my little excursion over the jungle, he got excited. He told me the tar was what came out of the ground when there's a heavy oil deposit located nearby.

"Fernando wanted to know where I picked up the goop, but I told him I had no idea. I don't think he believes me. Now you know why I wanted to speak to you."

"I'm still in the dark, Jose. I told you, I don't know a thing about oil. What do you need me to do? I'll help any way I can."

Catherine said, "Let him finish, Honey."

Tim smiled at her and said, "Okay, go ahead, Jose."

Jose pointed to a far-off tangle of trees and vines composing part of the jungle. "Our government has a program whereby you can purchase jungle land. Each acre costs five hundred dollars. I checked and if we're partners, we can buy as much land as we can afford. Now do you see where you come in?"

Finally, Tim understood Jose's remarks. "Yeah, I do, but as a U.S. citizen, how can I file on the land? I would think it would be restricted to local people."

Jose nodded and a smile spread across his face. "It is, but if you're my partner, we can buy as much land as we have money. The government doesn't care. They think of the jungle as wasteland. If they can make anything from it, they will."

Tim asked, "Won't someone get suspicious about the sudden interest in jungle property?"

Jose shook his head. "No, I don't think so. There are many other people buying up the jungle to burn it off for farm land."

"How many acres do you want to purchase?" Tim asked. He was becoming interested in Jose's plans.

"I have the thousand dollar bonus you gave me and Juanita says I can have four thousand dollars of our savings to invest."

"So you want Tim to put up an equal amount?" Catherine asked. "If my math is correct, ten thousand dollars would buy you two partners a total of twenty acres. Is that enough?"

"Yeah," Jose said. "If there's oil where I found the lake, it should be within the twenty acres surrounding the area. I also believe it's worth taking a chance on the land. If we strike oil, we'll both be rich."

Tim smiled and said, "Well, maybe not that rich. After the oil company subtracts their share to drill the well, lay the pipes to take the oil to a holding tank etcetera, we'll be lucky to receive fifteen to twenty percent of the net profits."

"That's still not a bad return for the amount of money Jose is asking for," Catherine said. "Can we afford it?"

Tim laughed. "Yes, <u>we</u> can. I have quite a bit of money saved from when I was a struggling, bachelor doctor. Do you believe this is a gamble worth taking?"

"Only if Jose is sure," she said.

"You seem to be positive this is oil, Jose," Tim said. "What if you're wrong?"

Jose shrugged as if it didn't matter. "Then we'll just lose five thousand dollars apiece. I'm willing to take the gamble, but I want you as my partner, Tim. So, what do you say?"

Tim stuck out his hand and said, "You have a deal, Jose."

Jose took Tim's hand and pumped it vigorously. "Thank you, my friend."

"You and Jose should contact a lawyer to establish a partnership," Catherine said. "Have him check into this government land offer to make sure you aren't doing anything illegal. I would hate to visit you in jail for my conjugal rights."

Jose roared with laughter again. Then he said, "Fernando will be stuck at his conference for several days. I'll call a lawyer I know and we'll have time to finish our business before I pick Fernando up. Then I'll fly you to Obidos."

"Great, Jose," Tim said.

As they parted, Tim's new partner beamed with pleasure. "I'm headed home to give Juanita the good news."

During the night, Tim dreamed of oil wells dotting the skyline of Prainha, while he, Catherine, Jose and Juanita celebrated a new well's 'coming in' with a bottle of imported champagne.

Catherine dreamed of making babies with Tim and how she would raise the children in Fort Worth. She had never been there and was looking forward to becoming a real Texan.

Chapter 21

The next day, Jose again phoned bright and early, and asked sarcastically, "Don't you two ever get out of bed? It's nearly eight a.m. I've been up for hours and I'm starving."

"We'll meet you in the restaurant in a half-hour," Tim said. When Jose disconnected without another word, Tim turned to Catherine and said, "Get up, you wanton woman. Jose is waiting. We can't delay the oil baron this morning. Besides, he's starving."

Catherine stretched, yawned and asked, "So, what's new with Jose?"

The day was bright and the sky cloudless. Tim looked out onto the square below and the small park across the street where he and Jose sealed their new partnership with a simple handshake.

A flock of pigeons was eating popcorn someone threw on the sidewalk. Their strutting reminded Tim of German soldiers on parade. As the birds swallowed the snow white kernels, their necks stretched up and down and bobbed like a bobble-head doll of a San Francisco Giant baseball player might in a category five earthquake.

When they arrived at the restaurant, to Tim's surprise, Jose wore an off-white suit, a freshly pressed and starched white shirt and a paisley tie, but he hadn't ordered yet. His rotund stomach protruded over the vast expanse of his belt, and the buttons of his shirt strained against his bulk.

In spite of his size, this morning Jose looked very respectable. *"Almost like a true oil baron, albeit a very fat one,"* Tim thought and then said, "You look like a real businessman, Jose. I like your suit."

"And your tie," Catherine added.

While he poured them each a cup of coffee, Jose said, "You two are in good spirits this morning. We should drink some wine to celebrate our venture."

"Let's have a toast with this mud they call coffee," Tim said. "It's thick as oil. Maybe it will bring us good luck."

"To our venture," Jose said and "clinked" his cup first with Tim and then Catherine. "We have an appointment with our lawyer, Mister Lopez at nine-thirty. We should order breakfast or we'll be late."

Tim was surprised again when Jose ordered only two scrambled eggs with a side order of toast. Tim and Catherine split a large Spanish omelet with an extra order of wheat toast. When Jose's meal arrived, for a change he ate slowly, almost delicately.

At nine-thirty, the trio walked into the office of Mister Hector Lopez. Hector's secretary, Gloria announced their arrival and then led them into his well-appointed office. Their new lawyer was a thin, mustachioed man at least fifty years old, who was dressed in a black suit, white shirt and grey tie. His shoeshine would have earned points from any drill sergeant.

After they shook hands, Hector motioned the trio into soft, comfortable leather chairs next to a large mahogany desk. He sat down in a wooden rolling chair and offered the men cigars, which Tim declined. Jose accepted his with a polite nod.

"From Mister Hernandez' initial inquiry, I understand that you would like to establish a limited partnership for the purpose of purchasing several acres of forest land for possible development," Hector said.

He rolled the big words out of his mouth with the ease of a practiced lawyer. Then he asked, "Am I correct?"

"Yes, sir," Tim said.

Jose was busy lighting his cigar and didn't appear to have anything to add.

"Yes, sir," Tim repeated. "Mister Hernandez and I want to purchase twenty acres of government land. Can we can do so legally?"

"As an American citizen, you could not obtain any land in Brazil. On the other hand, if you are partners with a citizen of Brazil, you can purchase all the land you desire."

Jose took the cigar from his mouth, smiled and said, "See, I told you so."

While Tim and Hector were speaking, Jose lit his cigar and puffed merrily away. As a cloud of grey smoke gathered in a ring around his head like a musty halo, he wore a satisfied smile.

Hector coughed lightly and said, "I can provide you the documents you need, plus those which the government of Brazil will require. All I need are your names, addresses and a birth certificate from Mister Hernandez.

"Mister Fitch will furnish a copy of his driver's license, together with the number from his passport, and you'll be in business."

Then Hector turned to Catherine and asked, "Will you be joining in the partnership?"

"No, sir," she replied politely. "I'm Mister Fitch's fiancée. He brought me along to explain how business is transacted. I'm just a spectator to these proceedings. Is that okay?"

"Certainly, Miss Thomas," Hector replied. "When you and Mister Fitch marry, have your name added to the ownership documents. Either that, or Mister Fitch should make provisions for you to take over his portion of the partnership in the event of his death."

Catherine smiled and said, "Thank you, sir. After we're married, we'll make sure those things are done. You're a very thorough man."

"I try to be, Miss Thomas." He turned back to Tim and Jose. "Now gentlemen, please give the information to my secretary, Gloria, and I'll begin work on the documents. They should be completed and ready for your signatures in two to three days. Leave a telephone number with Gloria and I'll be in touch. Is there any other way I may assist you?"

"No, thank you," Tim said. "This is all we require."

"So far, during the entire proceedings, Jose muttered, 'I told you so' and smoked half his cigar. Other than managing to pollute Mister Lopez' office for some time to come, he didn't say another word.

"I'm beginning to understand why Jose wanted me as his partner. He's a novice when it comes to dealing with lawyers and needed my assistance and money. But I'm being cynical. Jose is a good friend. It was nice of him to include Catherine and me in this oil discovery."

As smoke curled around their heads, and with the cigar stuck in one side of his mouth, Jose shook hands with Hector. After Jose walked out the door, Tim heard Hector cough lightly.

Tim and Catherine shook Hector's hand and thanked him for his courtesy, while Tim thought, *"I'm beginning to feel better about this idea."*

They supplied Gloria with the information the lawyer requested, and the trio walked back to the hotel.

Then Jose asked, "What about a drink to celebrate?"

"It's only ten-thirty," Tim said. "But okay."

Of course, the drink made Jose hungry, so he told a waiter, "I'll have a small steak sandwich and an order of fries."

After covering the potatoes with ketchup, Jose waded into them. When some red sauce dripped onto the front of Jose's shirt, Tim realized why Jose hadn't eaten a big breakfast. *"He was afraid he would soil his suit and look like a peasant to Mister Lopez."*

When they finished their drinks, and Jose's stomach was once more satisfied for the next few hours, Jose said, "I'll meet you outside at one p.m. to take you to the airport."

Tim and Catherine packed their suitcases. In Catherine's case, it didn't take long. Her sexy gown didn't take up much space.

As planned, Jose met them and loaded their suitcases aboard his truck. He said, "It's hot, but thank God we have a cool wind blowing out of the north."

Jose had changed from his suit into his usual flying outfit – shorts and another ungodly, ugly shirt. Instead of following the river to Catherine's hometown, Jose flew over the jungle.

Tim wondered where they were going, and suddenly he knew. *"Jose is taking us to his lake of oil. This should be interesting."*

He leaned over to Catherine and said, "I believe Jose is taking us to see his lake."

Catherine sat staring at the forbidding jungle below, while she said nothing in return and looked anxious.

Jose continued to fly for ten minutes above the treetops. It appeared he was searching for a landmark. When he pointed at a large, dead tree to the left, Tim knew Jose had found what he was looking for.

Then Jose lifted the aircraft to a higher altitude and scanned the surrounding jungle. Tim followed Jose's eye movements and saw a dark lake in the middle of all the green.

As Tim watched, Jose lowered the copter slowly until it was approximately twenty feet above the lake. Tim noticed the downdraft of the rotors didn't make ripples on the water. Instead, the surface sort of "quivered". The black mass below appeared to be thicker than chocolate mousse.

When Jose didn't attempt a landing, Tim knew why. *"He doesn't want any telltale splotches of black tar on his aircraft. Not with Fernando riding with him day after tomorrow."*

Jose pointed with his finger at the lake. "See, I told you so."

Tim nodded. "I see what you mean. It's amazing you could get the copter out of there after you found the place."

Jose responded by raising the helo slightly and heading toward the river. For the remainder of the way to Obidos, he didn't say a word.

When Jose set the aircraft down gently, there was a big smile on his face. Tim knew Jose was happy he had shared his discovery with his friends.

The blades of the helicopter slowed and then stopped spinning completely. A buzzard flew over and landed next to it. The bird looked like it had found a long lost cousin.

Tim unplugged his headset and hung it on a hook. Since they were once again on dry land, Catherine also wore a big smile.

As Tim helped her climb down from the cabin, he said, "It's good to be home again."

Not accidentally, her breast pressed against his arm, and Tim could feel the heat of her body. When she looked into his eyes, Tim could almost read her thoughts. "Welcome home, Darling," she said. Then she kissed him chastely on the lips and smiled again.

"You two go on ahead," Jose said. "I have to deliver the groceries before they spoil. I'll be by your place with your luggage and food in less than an hour."

"Here are your perishables," he said and handed Tim a large cooler. It was heavy, but Catherine came to Tim's aid. They strolled down Main Street swinging the container back and forth.

Suddenly Tim noticed where they were walking. "What the devil? When did they do this?"

The potholes were filled with heavy gravel and the road was graded flat.

"Isn't it wonderful?" Catherine asked. "I saved this as a surprise."

"If I hadn't seen it, I wouldn't believe it. When did all this happen?"

"Just last week - one day, a big barge arrived with two backhoes, a diesel bulldozer and road grader. The remainder of the barge was loaded with gravel and sand. The government finally realized there are taxpayers out in the jungle. It's amazing, isn't it?"

"I hope it survives the next heavy rain," Tim said.

When they arrived at Catherine's house, she stopped and motioned for them to set the cooler on the ground.

Then she looked up at Tim and said, "I always wanted to be carried over the threshold of my home by my husband. Since we're not going to be married here, that won't happen. But right now, if I'm carried through the doorway by my fiancée, it would be just as nice."

Tim used his best impression of Cary Grant and said, "At your service, my dear."

He bent down, scooped her off her feet and into his arms. Catherine kissed him and held it as he pushed the door open with one foot and carried her into the interior.

She whispered in his ear, "It's too bad Jose is coming by, or I'd have you carry me into the bedroom and do wicked things to my body." Then she bit him gently on the earlobe.

Tim continued with his impersonation. "Judy, Judy, Judy, what a wicked woman I chose to marry. If only I had known before we met."

"And what would you have done?" she asked as he sat her down again.

"Why, Judy, Judy, Judy, I would have met you sooner," he said, laughed and kissed her.

They broke their embrace reluctantly, and Catherine said, "Hurry up, Jose."

Behind them, Jose said, "No sooner said than done Miss Queen of the Amazon. Your wish is my command."

Although Jose's comments startled her, Catherine recovered nicely and said, "You and Tim can bring in the cooler and I'll put the perishables away. Leave the groceries in the box and I'll take care of them later. The suitcases can go in the bedroom. Thank you, Jose."

Tim asked, "What about a cold beer, Jose?"

"No thanks, I don't drink and fly. I'm glad you're back, Tim. As soon as Fernando calls me, I'll be in touch."

Tim motioned toward Catherine's desk. "Before you go, I'll give you a check. Go ahead and buy the acreage. There's no way to tell how long you can steer Fernando in the wrong direction. He impressed me as a smart guy. Watch your step."

Jose took the check and said, "Thank you, Tim. And thanks for your trust in my judgment – you and Catherine won't be sorry."

Tim shook Jose's hand and said, "After I saw the lake of black sludge, there has to be oil somewhere in the vicinity. Have a safe trip home."

"Goodbye, Catherine," Jose called. "See you soon."

When Jose had departed, Catherine cast Tim a knowing look. "I thought you two were going to talk all night long. Can you find your way to the bedroom without my help? The rest of these groceries can wait until tomorrow."

"Judy, Judy, Judy, what will the neighbors say?

She attempted to sound like Clark Gable when she replied, "Frankly, my dear, I don't give a damn!"

It was late the next morning before Tim and Catherine finished putting the groceries away. The ice in the cooler had melted, so after Tim carried it outside, he poured the water over some flowering plants.

In the distance, he heard two or three church bells peal together in unison, but not in harmony. He knew he missed services again and wondered, *"What would Tom think?"*

He shrugged helplessly and returned to the chore at hand. "I'm glad Jose stayed long enough for you to store the perishables. What's on the agenda for today?"

Catherine looked up from where she was storing canned goods in the cabinet and said, "The children will know I'm here, so tomorrow it's school for me. They expect me to be there and I can't let them down. They've made so much progress in the past year. I know I'll miss them."

Tim asked, "What about teaching our own? We should have enough for a baseball team."

"You have great plans," she said and grinned. "I'm thirty-three, which leaves me with only seven years of possible child production. We'll need to have several sets of twins."

"They run in my family," Tim said.

"Two at a time - can we handle it?"

Tim matched her grin. "I hope so. My parents are anxious to have more grandchildren."

Catherine had a few questions. "From what you've told me, I know I'll get along well with your father. What about your mother? What's she like?"

"Mom's great and you'll love her. She's retired from doctoring now and lets dad work in the emergency room. He's actually semi-retired too, but likes to 'keep his hand in tune'."

"Let's take a walk before lunch," Catherine suggested. "If we see some of my children, I'll tell them to come to school tomorrow and they'll spread the word to the remainder of the class. I need to get back to work."

As they walked through the village, Tim and Catherine were soon aware everyone knew the schoolteacher and her beau were back in town. The children were excited to see them again, especially Carlos. He grabbed onto Tim's pants leg and held on for dear life.

The next day, while Tim sat on the veranda and read a book of short stories, his eyes grew weary. He realized he wasn't getting much sleep at night. He laid down on the chaise lounge intending to take a short nap. He was surprised when Catherine shook his shoulder and awakened him much later in the evening.

Tim glanced down at his watch to see it was nearly six O'clock. School had been out for two hours and Catherine let him sleep.

She laughed. "I guess I wore you out. When I came in, you were sawing logs. I hope I won't get any complaints tonight."

Tim reached up for her and said, "I'll never object to you being in my bed."

She came into his arms and seemed to meld into his body. Tim had never known a woman as warm and wonderful as his new love.

Tim often thought about his unique situation and thanked his lucky stars he came to Brazil and found Catherine.

Not realizing he was speaking aloud, Tim said, "Tom always said God moves in mysterious ways."

When Catherine looked at him, Tim knew she had heard his remarks, so he continued. "It's true. Every day, I thank God for you. Catherine. Just think of the story we can tell our grandchildren of how we met – a lost priest. Who would have guessed?"

Book II

"The Lost Spirit"

Chapter 1

Hamilton, Bermuda

On a bright, sunshiny day, Lorna Hayden thought she was a fool for coming to Bermuda to find a husband. This was the third day of her visit to the islands, and still, she hadn't met a rich man she might marry.

Small wispy clouds were scattered across the far horizon, but the azure sky and deeper turquoise color of the water in Hamilton Bay only matched Lorna's blue feeling. After spending a bundle on this trip, she was disappointed with the prospects.

Although Lorna looked a few years younger, she turned twenty-nine two months earlier and worked diligently to stay in shape. As an operating room nurse at the Methodist Hospital in Peoria, Illinois, she had seen what an unhealthy lifestyle could do to a person.

Until now, Lorna stayed busy with her career, but lately she realized the years were passing her by.

Lorna liked men and dated occasionally, but her career always came first. Cute in a sensuous way, after her long, luxurious blonde hair and dark blue eyes, her greatest attributes were her ample breasts and shapely body.

Today, Lorna was once again experiencing second thoughts. So far, back home in Peoria, "Mister Right" had not made his presence known. Lorna knew she wasn't getting any younger. She wanted to get married and have babies, so she was placing a lot of faith in this trip. If she didn't strike pay dirt here, Lorna didn't know what she would do.

"A life as an old maid spinster might be in the cards after all."

Her first full day in Bermuda, Lorna walked around the town of Hamilton viewing the various sights and visiting many unique shops. There were a large number of tourists in town from a ship named "The Royal Princess", which was docked alongside the quay.

The gangplank was busy with passengers flowing from the ship to enjoy the day. They were mostly young pairs or older, very married couples.

In the afternoon, Lorna wore her new bikini and positioned herself on a lounge chair alongside an indoor, heated swimming pool at her hotel. Although it was sunny outside, the temperature was only in the high sixties and not conducive to lying outdoors on a beach in a skimpy swimming suit.

As Lorna glanced around the pool, she found she was surrounded by mostly teenyboppers and young mothers with small children. There was an occasional husband, (who wasn't out playing golf on one of the many courses dotting the landscape), who was swimming and splashing in the pool with his children. The pickings looked very slim.

An older man sat down in a chair nearby and bought Lorna a glass of iced tea. Deeply tanned, with snow-white hair that added to his distinguished appearance, he introduced himself as Sidney Graham, a lawyer from New York City.

Instead of going in the water immediately, Sidney remained

seated with his eyes focused on the swell of Lorna's breasts. If he was unattached, (which Lorna doubted since he wore a gold wedding band), Sidney would be quite a catch for someone.

They were conversing quietly when Mrs. Graham arrived on the scene. Her wrists and fingers were covered with jewelry. Lorna noticed Sidney's wife's presence when the sun's rays reflected from the many diamonds adorning her hands and arms.

Lorna thought, *"From the number of diamonds she's wearing, Mrs. Graham must support at least one South African diamond mine and all its workers."*

She would have known the woman was from New York without another clue, when Mrs. Graham said in a deep nasal inflection, "Oh, there you are, Sidney. Who is your young friend?"

Sidney introduced Lorna to his wife, who shook hands with a limp grip and said, "Just call me Dolly."

Dolly's arrival was a sign for Sidney to become active and less attentive of Lorna. As Dolly stared darts at him, Sidney got up from his chair, dove into the pool and began swimming laps.

While watching her husband's antics, Dolly sighed. The reflections from Dolly's rings sparkled as bright spots on nearby umbrellas as she remarked, "Sidney has this thing of meeting younger women. I hope he didn't disturb you. He can be an old fool at times."

Lorna counted four diamond bracelets on one of Dolly's wrists and three on the other, and thought, *"Perhaps, but he takes good care of you."* Then she smiled to relieve Dolly's fears and said, "He was a real gentleman."

Dolly continued to follow her husband's movements in the pool and nodded absentmindedly. "I can count on Sidney to pick the youngest woman with the largest breasts every time. I hope you know he doesn't mean any harm. You're a lovely young woman."

The women continued to gossip until Sidney completed his laps. Then they watched as he dried his hair and body with a large, fluffy towel provided by a pool boy.

Dolly stood up and put her arm possessively through his. "We should return to our room, Dear. You know the doctor told you not to be in the sun too long."

As the couple moved away, over her shoulder Dolly said, "It was nice to have met you, Lorna." She didn't wait to hear Lorna's reply.

After a night of fitful sleep, the next morning, Lorna decided to try tennis. In Peoria, she took lessons from a professional at the tennis courts in Bradley Park. This meant she had to get out of a warm bed early on her two off-duty days and travel halfway across town from her small apartment on Garfield Avenue.

Then she endured another two hours of instruction and practice, plus the long drive home. Lorna hoped her dedication was worth the price. Her instructor said she was progressing nicely.

Vindictively, Lorna thought, *"Whatever that means!"*

Although the courts were packed with players, Lorna managed to join a trio of two men and one woman for a doubles game; but soon discovered she was overmatched. Her new friends were approximately twenty years old and in better shape than she. When Lorna and her partner were beaten soundly, she knew most missed points were her fault.

In the afternoon she rented a moped and went touring. Of course, since she was unaccustomed to driving on the wrong side of the road, at first Lorna experienced trouble remembering to stay to the left. Finally she got the hang of it and managed quite well for the remainder of the day. Lorna enjoyed the drive, but still fate didn't allow her to meet any new men. *"I'm frustrated. Here it is, my third day in Bermuda with no prospects."*

Today, Lorna decided to spend the day visiting the small boutiques along Main Street, where she hoped she might strike up a conversation with a male customer. *"Who knows what could happen? It's worth a try. So far, my other plans have failed miserably.*

She spent the day talking with several shop owners and other female customers. Except for several young servicemen from a nearby Air Force base, who were trolling the streets for a companion, there were no unattached, available men.

Late in the evening, when Lorna returned to her hotel, she was feeling dejected, so she decided to stop for a drink at bar in her hotel named "The Fox and Hounds".

At this late hour, the small pub was nearly empty. Two couples were seated in separate booths against the wall. They appeared to be lost in each other's eyes.

Lorna thought, *"They look like newlyweds. I should be so lucky."*

The only other persons in the bar were the bartender, Jesus, and a man sitting on a stool at the far end of the bar. Jesus hurried to take Lorna's order, and she opted for a Mai Tai. As Jesus filled her order, Lorna sat and studied the male customer.

The tall, blond-haired stranger appeared lost in thought. He had placed his stool at a ridiculous distance from the bar, until he was practically lying down from his hips to shoulders.

While resting his chin on a folded left arm, his eyes were nearly level with the top of the bar. He appeared to be staring into the mirror at his reflection, but seeing nothing.

Near his right hand was a tall tumbler filled with a dark substance Lorna knew was whiskey. Several other glasses were stacked on the bar to form a crystal pyramid.

Lorna wondered, *"Did he empty all those tonight?"*

One look at his sunken and bloodshot eyes in the mirror told Lorna he did. *"If it's true, he can't be feeling any pain."*

Jesus returned with her drink, placed it on a napkin in front of Lorna and asked, "Would you like to run a tab?"

As Lorna slid a ten dollar bill across the bar, she replied, "No, thank you. I just stopped in for one drink. It's been a long day and I needed something to cheer me up."

After ringing up her drink, Jesus returned with a five dollar bill and some loose change.

Lorna nodded toward the two couples. "There's not much business tonight."

Jesus agreed. "No, there isn't. If it weren't for my buddy, Jock at the end of the bar, this place wouldn't pay my wages."

"I noticed him when I came in. What's his story? Did he empty all those glasses piled on the bar?"

Jesus shook his head at the sight, but then nodded a reply.

"Yes, I'm sorry to say he did. Jock comes in almost every night. He claims he's drinking himself to death. If he keeps on his quest, one of these days he may succeed."

Almost as an afterthought, Jesus added, "His wife was killed while they were on their honeymoon, here in Bermuda. He blames himself and can't let go of her memory."

Lorna took a closer look at the man called Jock. *"How sad he appears. He once was very handsome and still is, in a battle-scarred way. I wonder what happened to his wife."*

Down the bar, Jock was lost in thought and tortured by the same ghost that haunted him nightly. As he attempted to erase the memories of the death of his wife, Lorelei, tonight he was drinking steadily again.

He remembered vividly the day they decided to go scuba diving to explore an old wreck off the coast of Bermuda. *"That's when it happened. While we were having fun and exploring, we stumbled upon several gold bars in the hold of a wreck."*

As Jock's thoughts continued, he silently cursed himself for his greed. *"Instead of being content with one bar, I returned to the wreck for a second. I didn't know a great white shark was nearby, so I sent Lori up the anchor rope to the boat.*

"When I got to the surface, Lori wasn't there. After seeing her carried off by the shark, Leroy, the captain of the boat was in shock. When Leroy told me what happened, I knew it was my fault. God I miss her. It's been five years last spring since Lori was taken. I hope I'll join her soon. Life without her is lousy._

"I know I'm being stupid by drinking so much, but I want to die. I've been in several accidents; any one of which could have killed me. Just a few days ago, I ran into a Volkswagen carrying two youngsters.

"I know it frightened them. Then I found out the girl is the granddaughter of George Fitch, my doctor buddy who always seems to patch me up. He keeps after me to get off the booze."

Jock's mind returned to the present. Down the bar he heard a woman laugh. Through the fog of a whiskey-dulled mind, Jock saw a lovely vision of a tall, longhaired blonde woman with deep blue eyes. In his drunken state he made a fateful decision. *"It's Lori; she's come back to me."*

He called out, "Lori, my love," turned toward the vision of loveliness and attempted to raise himself from the bar. But his hand slipped and he tumbled from the stool. As Jock fell, his right hand flailed out and smashed into the pile of glasses.

Pieces of flying glass gashed Jock's hand in two places, and blood spurted from the wounds. He continued on his downward spiral, hit his head on the brass rail at the bottom of the bar and blackness overcame him.

At his outburst, Lorna's and Jesus' attention was drawn to Jock. They watched in amazement as he appeared to rise up from his stool and then fall forward. The pile of glasses shattered into millions of pieces, and Jock's head made an ugly sound as it struck the brass rail.

Instinctively, Lorna's nursing skills took over. She hopped down from her barstool and hurried to Jock's side. Jesus followed and watched as Lorna felt under Jock's head to see if there was a wound.

When her hand came away with no trace of blood, Lorna thought, *"He knocked himself unconscious, but there's nothing I can do about that. The cuts on his hand are another matter that require immediate attention."*

She looked up at Jesus and asked, "Can you find a towel, Jesus? I need to stop the bleeding."

"Sure," he said. He ran behind the bar, grabbed a large towel, leaned over and handed it Lorna. "Here, I'll phone for an ambulance. He shouldn't be moved until we know how seriously he's been injured."

After Lorna wrapped the towel around Jock's hand, she applied pressure to the point under his arm where a main artery is located and watched the flow of blood slow to a trickle.

A male voice at her side asked, "Can we help?"

Lorna glanced up and saw a young men and his female companion looking down at her. "Yes, thank you. Could you wait outside for the ambulance and direct them to where we are?"

"Of course," the young man said. He grabbed the hand of his young wife and hurried out the door. "Come on, Ann."

From behind the bar Jesus handed Lorna a wet towel. As she carefully washed Jock's face and brow, Lorna saw his eyes blink open.

He stared up at Lorna, reached to take her hand and sobbed, "My Lori, come back from the dead. After all this time, I can't believe it."

Lorna didn't know what to say. Jock held her hand so firmly she was afraid her circulation might be restricted. Softly she said, "My name is Lorna, not Lori."

When Jock continued to look deeply into her eyes and didn't respond, Lorna knew he didn't hear her words.

"Don't leave me again," he said.

His eyes were so sad, Lorna felt like crying. *"Lori must be his lost wife."*

Now, this close to the stranger, Lorna could tell Jock was about her age, but the booze had aged him and made him appear older. *"It's terrible for such a young man to drink the way he does."*

In the distance, Lorna heard the wail of a siren and knew help was on the way. A few minutes later, two tall attendants ran into the room. Each carried a large black leather bag full of emergency gear.

Close behind, a smaller man dressed in a dark suit, crisp white shirt and black tie walked into the bar. The stranger took one look at Lorna's patient, shook his head and said, "So it's you again, Jock. When will you ever learn?"

An EMS technician took over for Lorna, but Jock wouldn't release her hand. She moved to one side, looked up at the stranger in the dark suit and asked, "Do you know this man?"

"Yes, I'm afraid I do." He held out his hand and said, "I'm Inspector David Smythe. We've dealt with old Jock many times in the past. May I ask your name?"

With her free hand, Lorna reached up, took his and said, "I'm Lorna Hayden, a nurse from Illinois. I saw Jock fall and cut his hand. Now I'm afraid he has me confused with his wife and won't let go."

Inspector Smythe studied Lorna's face for a moment. Then he nodded and said, "Yes, I've seen a photograph of Jock's wife, Lori, who was lost at sea. You do bear a striking resemblance to her. I can see why Jock could be confused."

The technician stood up and said, "I patched up his hand temporarily, but he'll require one or two stitches there. He needs to have a doctor examine the bump on his head to be sure he didn't suffer a concussion. I'll bring in a gurney and we'll transport him to the hospital."

"Very well," David said.

Lorna continued to kneel at Jock's side. He didn't say anything else, but held her hand as if his life depended on it.

"I don't know what to do," she thought.

With a wry smile, and an unintended pun, David came to her aid. "It appears your patient has formed a solid bond with you. Would you mind accompanying him in the ambulance? I believe I would have to break his hand to free yours, which would only create more work for the doctor."

"I don't mind; I'll be happy to help."

"That's kind of you, Miss Hayden. Jock could use a true friend of the female persuasion. Since his wife went missing so long ago, he's been a wreck. Perhaps you can help Jock climb out of the bottle and back on his feet."

Lorna smiled at the inspector, but shook her head. "I don't know how. I'll be here for only eleven more days, and it appears it will take much longer than that to dry him out. Jock's been drinking too long. I can tell by looking at his eyes."

The two EMS technicians arrived with a gurney and busied themselves with loading Jock onto the wheeled apparatus. After they lifted him aboard and strapped Jock down, as he was wheeled from the bar, Lorna walked alongside. She noticed Jock's eyes were wet with tears and she could feel his body shake through his hand.

In the ambulance on the way to the hospital, Lorna sat on a cushioned seat. Several times during the short drive, she heard Jock mumble, "Lori, Lori."

"He's hurting, not only from his injuries at the bar, but deep down in his soul. I hope somehow I can help. It's just my luck – I come to Bermuda to find a rich man to marry and end up with the town drunk holding my hand. Spinsterhood, here I come."

When the ambulance pulled up to a hospital emergency entrance, an elderly, distinguished gentleman stood waiting on the sidewalk. He was dressed in a white doctor's smock with a nametag attached that read "Doctor Fitch".

After the rear doors of the ambulance were opened, Doctor Fitch climbed inside to check his new patient. When he noted Jock's tight grip on her hand, he looked inquisitively at Lorna.

"I'm Doctor George Fitch. Old Jock is a recurring patient of mine. They always call me when he's involved in an accident. He seems to be very attached to you."

Lorna smiled at the pun and extended her free hand to the doctor. "You might say so. I'm Lorna Hayden, a nurse from Peoria, and I attempted to assist him. Now he has me confused with his wife and won't let go of my hand."

George said, "Yes, you are similar to Lori. Jock has shown me her picture several times. It was a tragedy when she was attacked by a great white shark. Jock still blames himself for her demise, when there really wasn't a thing he could have done. Now you know why he's in such bad shape."

As Jock returned to his senses, he looked up at George and smiled crookedly. "Doc Fitch, you old bugger. Look who has come back to me, my Lori." He pointed his damaged hand toward Lorna. "It's a miracle."

"The real marvel will be getting you off the sauce," George said. "You've frightened this young lady, Jock. She isn't your Lori and you know it. Lori's gone and you have to accept the fact."

"I'm not Lori," Lorna added. "My name is Lorna. I'm from Peoria, Illinois – a nurse who tried to help you."

Tears ran down Jock's face and he appeared to be lost with nothing to live for. His brain kept trying to tell him Lori was there, but she wasn't. The lovely apparition by his side was only someone who resembled his lost love. But Jock couldn't take his eyes from her face.

George reached over and took hold of Jock's hand. "Please let go of Lorna's hand. You're frightening her."

Slowly and reluctantly, Jock released his grip.

Lorna smiled down at him and said. "Don't worry; I'll stay for a while."

The doctor signaled to the EMS technicians and then watched as they pulled the gurney from the ambulance and wheeled Jock into the hospital.

Turning to Lorna, he said, "Thank you for looking after him, Miss Lorna. But you don't have to stay. Jock will understand."

"I told him I would be here when you finish and I'll keep my promise. Jock looks like he's been hurt too many times in the past. Perhaps I can help."

"You're a good woman," George said. "If you feel up to it, you may come in and watch me work."

Lorna grinned and asked, "So you're about to put me to the test, are you Doctor? As the head nurse and a good anesthesiologist in the OR of the Methodist hospital in Peoria, I've passed gas with the best of them."

Although George had heard the old joke many times before in his life, he laughed appreciatively. "Then let's go in, patch up Jock and get him back on his feet."

Lorna followed George down the hall to the emergency clinic where Jock was lying on a steel table that was covered with a white sheet. The smell of alcohol and disinfectant told Lorna she was back in her environment.

First George cleaned the wounds with antiseptic. Then he sewed the worst wound with three stitches as Lorna covered the smaller cuts with gauze and tape.

As she was bandaging Jock's hand, his eyes followed Lorna's every movement and she saw him staring down her blouse. She glanced sideways, saw a smile on his face and felt her own grow hot. *"What's with you, girl? Don't tell me you've fallen for the town drunk?"*

"It appears you cheated death again, Jock," George said. "If you keep trying, someday he'll win."

Jock looked ashamed and said, "I know."

George's face grew stern and his voice was harsh. "You need to face up to the fact Lori is gone. This young lady would make a fine replacement, but I doubt she'll be attracted to you if you continue to drink the way you have in the past."

George glanced at Lorna and noticed the color in her cheeks. "I'm sorry, my dear, but I'm only telling the truth. Jock needs someone like you to chase away the ghosts of his past."

Lorna didn't know what to say. She was surprised at the course of events that allowed Jock to enter into her life. Suddenly, the name Fitch struck her. *"It's the name of the young woman on the plane to Bermuda, Kate Fitch."*

She asked, "Are you related to Kate Fitch?"

"Why, yes, I am. Kate's my granddaughter. How do you know her?"

"Three days ago I met her on a plane to Bermuda. Kate's a sweet girl and I remembered her last name was the same as yours."

George nodded and said, "That's the great thing about Bermuda. The islands are so small you get to know everyone. Kate didn't mention you, Lorna, but she's been busy with thoughts of her new boyfriend."

Jock asked, "Am I free to go, Doc?"

"Yes, Jock, you are. I'll give you extra gauze and tape. Knowing you, you'll need them. Be sure to wash the wounds well each day and put on new bandages. If I never see you in the emergency room again, it'll make me happy."

Jock's voice sounded apologetic when he said, "I'll try."

George thought, *The way he's been looking at Lorna, perhaps Jock actually means it this time. I hope so. He's a good man. I don't want to have to pronounce him dead some night.*

When Lorna looked for her handbag, she suddenly discovered it wasn't with her. *"In all the excitement, I forgot and left it on the bar. What will I do now?"*

"I'm missing my purse," she said. "I left it on the bar at the hotel. All my traveler's checks, money and credit cards are inside."

"That's a shame," George said. "But don't fret; the people of Bermuda are very honest. Perhaps the bartender retrieved it. I can phone and check."

"Would you, please?"

As George picked up the telephone, the door opened and Inspector Smythe walked in. Dangling from his shoulder was Lorna's handbag.

"There you are," he said. "With your purse slung from my shoulder, I've received obvious stares from the hospital staff. By this time tomorrow, rumors will be circulating about me being gay."

"Thank you, Inspector. I just missed it. You're a life saver."

"No thanks are necessary, my dear," David said. "You've worked wonders on our young friend, Jock. He actually looks halfway sober."

Then he looked down at her companion and asked, "How are you, Jock?"

"I'm fine, David. Have you met Lori's look-alike?"

David shook Jock's un-bandaged hand and replied, "Yes, I have." Then he turned to Doctor Fitch and asked, "How are you tonight, George? I see you were called in to work on our mutual friend again."

"I'm fine, thank you, David. But I'm tired of patching up Jock. Before you walked in, I was giving him 'what for'. Jock claims he will attempt to stop drinking."

David asked, "How many times have we heard that old, sweet song from you, Jock?"

"Too many, I know, but Doc believes Miss Lorna may be the solution to my drinking problems. It appears she adopted me."

Lorna blushed again and was surprised how easily Jock flustered her.

David noticed the color in Lorna's cheeks and smiled.

"She is lovely, Jock. Thank your lucky stars Lorna was in the bar tonight. Before anyone else came to your rescue, you might have bled to death. She seems to be heaven sent."

"Gentlemen," Lorna said. "It isn't nice to talk about a person in the third party when she's standing here able to defend herself."

David apologized. "You're right, my dear. And, I'm sorry. We're not accustomed to Jock being so docile after one of his accidents. You have had a wonderful effect on him. We're grateful."

Jock said, "David and George, you're embarrassing Lorna." Then he climbed down from the table and turned to Lorna. "George says I am free to go. Will you assist me in leaving this place of mercy and returning to my home?"

Lorna nodded her head in surrender. "To quote an old English saying; I'm 'in for a penny, in for a pound'." She walked to Jock's side and helped him climb down from the table. He was a little wobbly on his feet, but with him leaning on her shoulder, they made their way toward the hospital exit.

George and David watched as Jock and Lorna departed, and George said a little prayer things would work out between them. *"I must remember to tell Kate I met her friend, Lorna."*

When they reached the street, Lorna didn't know where they were headed. After all the excitement, she was tired. *"It's been a long day. I just want to take this man home, wherever that is, and return to my nice, warm bed in the hotel."*

She asked, "Which way?"

"We need transportation," Jock said.

From behind them, David said, "I can provide it."

Although Lorna recognized his voice, David had approached so silently, for a moment she was startled.

"Inspector Smythe to the rescue," Jock said. "Thank you, David. You do remember the way?"

"Of course; how could I forget?" In way of explanation, David smiled at Lorna and said, "At least once a week, I usually provide Jock with a ride home. If I didn't, I would only have to answer another accident call. Sometimes an ounce of prevention is truly worth a pound of cure."

Lorna smiled at David and said, "It must be nice to have friends like you and Doctor Fitch."

David returned her smile and said, "In Bermuda, everyone looks out for their fellow men and women. We have a high regard for what's right or wrong. If you stay here long enough, you'll discover the fact."

They walked to David's small, black automobile, where Lorna and Jock climbed into the back seat as Lorna thought, *"I still have no idea where we're going."*_

David drove slowly and carefully over hills and around sharp curves. In a few minutes they arrived at a cottage located on North Shore Road, where David said, "Jock lives near the highest point on the island. His home is one hundred and sixty feet above sea level and provides a fantastic view of the surrounding ocean and beaches."

"You sound like an announcer for the travel channel," Lorna said.

"Here you are, home safe and sound," David said. Then he added, "Well, in your case, Jock, perhaps not so sound, but safe. Do you want me to wait for you, Miss Hayden?"

She asked, "Can I get a taxi at this time of night?"

"Call 555-2323 and they'll be here in a matter of minutes. You plan to stay with Jock then?"

"In case he needs anything, I'll stay a while. I really don't know why, but I feel obligated to see this adventure through."

David leaned out his window and said, "See Jock, I told you this woman would be good for you."

Lorna frowned and said, "There you go again, talking about me in the third party."

"Off with you then, David or we'll wake the neighbors," Jock said. "You wouldn't have them believing I was drunk again."

David chuckled. "Heaven forbid. Behave yourself and treat Lorna like a lady or you'll answer to me."

"Don't worry; I will. Goodnight and thank you, David."

With a wave of his hand, David departed. He left Jock and Lorna standing at the bottom of a short driveway leading to the cottage. As he waved his hand in the general direction of his home, Jock said, "Follow me, and I'll give you the cook's tour of my mansion."

He led Lorna up a short staircase to the porch. On his second attempt Jock managed to unlock the door.

Lorna thought, *"Jock seems happier than before. Perhaps my presence has helped. I'm glad I decided to stay."*

With a wave of his hand to complete the gesture, Jock bowed

Lorna through the door. Then he lost his balance, hit the doorknob with his injured hand and yelped in pain as fresh blood seeped through the bandage.

"You're an accident looking for a place to happen," Lorna said. "Sit down and I'll check your hand."

She removed the bandage and inspected the sutures. "The wound has reopened, but there's no new damage done."

Lorna used a clean bandage to apply pressure until the bleeding stopped. Then, as she applied a new bandage, she said, "There; from now on, will you please watch what you're doing?"

With a half-smile Jock said, "Yes, Ma'am. I'm beginning to sober up, and I apologize for the trouble I put you through. I know you aren't Lori. It was the alcohol and my thoughts of her that caused my muddle-brained confusion. Thank you for your aid and assistance. If you wish, I'll call a taxi now."

"I would like a drink of something cold. I'm suddenly thirsty."

With a crooked grin, Jock said, "You ask a drunkard if he has anything to drink. Surely, you jest."

His reply exasperated Lorna, so she remarked rather unkindly, "You must stop feeling sorry for what life has given you and not call yourself a drunk. It makes you look like a fool."

Jock was taken aback by her comments. "For a nurse, you don't have very good bed-side manners."

Frustrated, Lorna cried out, "Is everything a joke to you? You don't know how lucky you are to have good friends watching out for your interests."

At Lorna's outburst, Jock realized how sincere she was. Suddenly he did feel like a fool for his actions. "I apologize again. I know I must appear foolish to you, but you don't know my story."

Lorna wasn't done. "I heard a portion and I'm sorry for your loss. But your wife wouldn't want you to carry on the way you do. You don't do her memory any favors by drinking so much. If the shark got you instead, do you actually think Lori would do the same thing?"

For a moment, Jock was struck dumb by Lorna's frankness. *"She's right. Lori wouldn't want me to grieve so long, or become a drunkard to prove how much I miss her. No, Lori wouldn't have done the same. She would have gone on with her life, always remembering me, but not wallowing in self-pity."*_

Lorna was surprised when Jock didn't make some smart remark. He appeared to be thinking about her comments. She waited for him to speak.

It took several long minutes before Jock finally said, "You're right. I believe this knock on the head, combined with your sharp criticism has made me see the light. On three separate occasions my father sent one of his minions here to ask me to return to Germany and go to work in the family business.

"I told them all the same thing; I wanted to stay here and die. Now I see how pitiful I've appeared over the past five years. You've opened my eyes, Lorna. I thank you more than you can know."

Lorna's smile returned. "If I've helped you, then this night hasn't been in vain."

Jock nodded his agreement and then remembered her previous request. "But you asked for something cool and wet. I'll be right back."

He walked into the small kitchen at the rear of the cottage and returned in a few minutes with two glasses. He handed one to Lorna and said, "A nice glass of ice water. Just what the doctor would have ordered. Will you join me in a toast to a new beginning?"

While they raised their glasses high in unison and stared at each other over the rims of their individual glass, Lorna thought, *"I wonder what he's thinking."*

As if he could read her mind, Jock said, "I would like to know you better, Lorna. To repay your kindness tonight, would you permit me the honor of having lunch with you tomorrow at noon?"

"Yes, I will. But now, I need to call a taxi and return to my hotel. It's nearly two a.m. and I'm very tired. Will you be all right?"

Jock raised his hand as if he was about to take an oath. "I assure you tonight only clear, cold water shall pass through my lips. The next few days will be rough, as I attempt to quit after drinking myself silly for so many years. Can I count on you to help?"

"Let's wait and see. I have only ten more days until my vacation is over. I'll meet you in my hotel dining room at noon and we'll talk."

Jock nodded his acceptance of Lorna's terms, picked up the telephone, asked for a taxi, listened for the response and then he said, "The cab will be here within ten minutes."

They stood silently for a few moments, each wrapped in their individual thoughts. Then Jock said, "Let me walk you to the road. The driveway is steep."

"Are you sure you're okay? I can make it by myself."

"Never," he said. "From now on, I'm a gentleman. I'll be fine."

As they walked together down the steps from the porch and the driveway to North Shore Road, a crescent moon was shining on the water below and a cool wind blew softly out of the north.

As it slipped behind a light layer of clouds, Lorna gazed at the moon and its reflection on the ocean. *"If this were any other night, I would call it romantic."*

A pair of headlights appeared around the nearest bend and a taxi pulled to the curb. Jock held the door for Lorna, watched as she climbed in; then bent and kissed her hand in the European manner. With a smile, he said, "Goodnight, my guardian angel."

Lost in thought, Lorna didn't reply.

Jock leaned in the open window across from the driver, handed him a twenty pound note and said, "Take this young lady to the Palms Hotel. Keep any change for your trouble."

With a small roar from its muffler, the taxi pulled away. Jock stood watching until the vehicle disappeared around a bend; then he shook his head slightly at his good luck tonight.

Across town, George returned weary and tired to his home on White Sands Road. As usual, Pearl was waiting up. When he walked in the door, she handed him a bottle of his favorite beer.

George thanked her with a small hug, kissed her cheek and said, "You're a mind reader. Since I left the hospital, I've been dreaming of a cold bottle of beer."

She asked, "Was it bad?"

"Not as bad as it could have been. By a turn of fate, a nurse was on hand. She acted correctly and probably saved Jock the cost of a transfusion. Her name is Lorna Hayden. It appears she and Kate are friends. They met on a plane to Bermuda."

Pearl shook her head in resignation. "That man, Jock. One of these days, there won't be an angel of mercy handy to protect him. When will he ever learn?"

George said, "I asked him the same thing. Strange, but I believe perhaps Lorna may be the one to change Jock's life back to normal. Although bearing a striking resemblance to Lori, she didn't put up with any of Jock's nonsense."

"Good for her," Pearl said. "Someone needs to knock some sense into Jock's head before he kills himself. If he dies in one of his accidents, such as the one with Kate and Bryan, some poor soul will have Jock's death on his conscience. I wonder if he ever thinks of the possibility."

George shook his head and said, "Probably not. I left him in Lorna's capable hands. She told me she was, 'in for a penny, in for a pound'. I haven't heard that old saying in many a year. I believe she means it. Although they just met tonight, Lorna took Jock home to look after him."

"I hope Jock keeps his hands to himself," Pearl said.

With a laugh, George said, "Oh, I doubt you have to worry about a thing. I'm impressed with Lorna, both as a lady and a nurse. She knows her way around an emergency room. She says she's the Chief of OR, somewhere in Illinois."

A thought occurred to Pearl. "I wish you would speak to her about remaining here to work. Mary Taylor, the head nurse will leave soon. Two years ago, she married a young naval flyer. Now she's six months pregnant and they'll soon be transferred to a base in the United States."

"I didn't get Lorna's number, but she's staying at the Royal Palms hotel," George said. "That's where the call for the ambulance originated. Remind me tomorrow, and I'll tell Kate about Lorna. Between the three of us, perhaps we can talk her into accepting the position. Operating room nurses are hard to come by. We'll be lucky to find a suitable replacement for Mary."

"Maybe fate is working for more than Jock," Pearl said.

"As Tom would say, 'God works in mysterious ways, his wonders to perform'."

George smiled at the old cliché. "True; but do you have another bottle of beer on ice? One more should put me right to sleep. Strange, but I feel very good about what happened tonight."

Chapter 2

The next morning Kate was up early. Yesterday in school, she received a heavy load of homework. For three hours after she came home, she did her assignments. When she completed the difficult job, she was extremely tired, so she went to bed early.

Late last night, the ringing of the phone awoke her. It was a periodic occurrence in a physician's home, so Kate snuggled deeper under the bedcovers and soon drifted off to sleep again. She didn't hear George leave or return.

Knowing there was time for a cup of hot chocolate before her school bus arrived; Kate put a kettle of water on the stove to heat. A few seconds before the pot would whistle, she lifted it from the burner.

After duping a pack and a half of instant chocolate mix into a large mug and pouring in the hot water, Kate stirred the mixture until it reached the rich, dark consistency she loved. Then she added a spoonful of sugar, took a sip, insured it was exactly the way she wanted and walked out onto the back porch with the mug in her hand.

The morning was cool, but a clear sky filled with sunshine promised warmer temperatures for later in the day. Kate sat down on a chaise lounge and warmed her hands over the hot chocolate. As it cooled, she sipped the tasty mixture.

"So much happened in the last few weeks, I'm amazed and a little frightened. I wonder what the future will bring." Kate reached into her notebook and withdrew Bryan's latest letter. *"He writes nice letters and doesn't go in for mushy, romantic stuff. Bryan says he likes me, but didn't mention the magic four-letter word, love. We're a little too young for that yet, but who knows, perhaps with a little more time..."*

She wrote once in reply, a letter of several pages to tell Bryan all the things that happened on her trip to Texas.

The day after Kate returned to Bermuda, Pearl accompanied her to Washington high school in Hamilton to register for classes and buy her books. The school buildings were old, but well maintained.

"I'm surprised how far behind I am. Even though it's only been three days, I know it will be difficult to keep up with the other students. Everyone seems so bright. The kids I met so far are friendly and have welcomed me. Plus, I made several new acquaintances. Things are looking up."

Although Kate had maintained nearly a straight A grade point at Reagan High School, she knew she was still behind the average student here. It was an eye opener. *"No wonder dad and Uncle Tom earned scholarships to Texas colleges."*

Glancing up from her cocoa, she saw Tom come through the door. It appeared the cool temperature didn't faze him. He was wearing shorts and a t-shirt.

"I can understand. Compared to sleet, snow, blizzards and sub-zero weather in much of the United States during the winter, a temperature of sixty degrees in Bermuda is wonderful.

"Most of my schoolmates wear shorts. When I become accustomed to the weather, I'll do the same. Right now, it's jeans and a long-sleeved blouse for me."

"Good morning, Kate," Tom said. "You're up early. Isn't this a beautiful day?"

"Yes, it is," she said. Then she set her empty cup on a table, stretched her arms over her head and added, "It's a great day to be alive."

Tom nodded in agreement. "Those are my sentiments exactly. Every morning when I see the sun come up, I say a prayer of thanksgiving. If it weren't for your father and his friends, my shrunken head might be hanging around some native's neck."

Kate grimaced and said, "Ugh – what a thought to begin the day."

"Yes, but the truth is the truth."

Changing the subject, she said, "I should get my books for school. Grandpa tells me if I pass the driver's exam and receive my license, he'll buy me a motor scooter."

"Dad has a thing against riding buses. When we were your age, he bought us motor scooters. They're fun to ride. From the first day, you'll learn to drive on the wrong side of the road, so it'll be easy."

Kate said, "I look forward to that, but I have to run." Then she stood up, gave Tom a kiss on the cheek and added, "Thanks for saying such nice things about my father."

Tom reached out to rub Kate's back. "They're all true. Have a nice day in school. Tomorrow begins a new weekend. It's not long until Christmas."

Kate walked inside to her room to gather her books and purse. When she turned down the hall, she met her grandmother, who asked, "Is one cup of hot chocolate all you're going to have for breakfast? How will you survive until lunch? Do you have money?"

"I'll be fine, Grandma. I have money to buy something to eat. If I get hungry, they have machines at school."

George came into the room and overheard their conversation.

"Those snacks in packages will kill you, Kate. You should eat a good breakfast every day."

"Beginning tomorrow, I will. I promise. I really have to run or I'll miss my bus."

George said, "If you'd prefer, I can drive you to school."

Kate shook here head. "No, thank you. I'm meeting my girlfriends at the bus stop. I have to go."

Before her grandparents could protest further, Kate kissed them both on the cheek, slipped out the door and walked briskly down the winding, blacktopped road.

"Kate appears to be adjusting nicely," George said. "Girlfriends already; next the boys will come to call."

Pearl shook her head in resignation and said, "I still wish she would have eaten a better breakfast,"

The morning after his evening with Jock and Lorna, when David arrived at the police headquarters, he remembered his supervisor; Jim Marshall expected a report on their mutual problem. The thing was; David couldn't speak of the mystery to his friends or colleagues. Jim told David to keep his review low-key and private.

Since they were considering the disappearance of several missing people, David said aloud, "Well, they weren't all still missing."

The victims had been gone for such a long time, there was no doubt they were now dead. The Coast Guard and other searchers found a few pieces of wreckage; but these and other strange clues provided nothing to solve the problem. This only added more mystery to each individual case and the combination of them all.

Each case was separate from the others and there was no clear-cut evidence leading to a final resolution. Six years ago, first there was a missing fisherman.

After the authorities found his boat, or to be more accurate, part of the vessel, it appeared someone or something tore the craft apart. Doctor Lyon, a marine biologist who assisted in the investigation believed he discovered teeth marks of a shark on one broken board.

His findings weren't much to go on and there was no way to confirm the good doctor's suspicions. In the end, the disappearance was written off as another mysterious occurrence that happens periodically in the Bermuda Triangle.

Then the next spring, Lori, the wife of David's friend, Jock, was killed by a great white shark. There was a witness to this occurrence. At an inquest, Leroy Jones, the owner and pilot of a boat named "Tern" swore to the fact under oath.

The government of Bermuda, especially those connected to the tourist trade did their best to downplay the incident. They claimed the shark attack was a one-in-a-million occurrence and nothing to be excited about.

The Governor said, "There have been no other shark attacks, so why alarm the tourists? Surely this one was a fluke."

With the exception of David, Jock and a few of the victims' friends, the attack was soon forgotten. But over the next four years others went missing. Most Bermudians were not aware of the fact; the main reason was the lack of evidence.

So far, David was investigating six cases that continued to haunt him. Three of the missing person reports concerned scuba divers. The others were individual cases where a single boater or a lone fisherman foolishly went out alone on the ocean blue and were never heard from again.

Only one case pertained to a multiple disappearance and it was also the only one bearing a distant resemblance to another mystery. The incident occurred two years after Jock's wife; Lorelei was killed while they were scuba diving.

The strangest thing about this last incident was that it involved the same boat owner who witnessed Lori's attack, Leroy Jones. From what David could determine; Leroy and his live-in girlfriend, Sherry Lee were attempting to dive over the same wreck.

"Coincidence is the most logical explanation, but the disappearance of the two lovers continues to puzzle me."

In reality, no one reported Leroy and Sherry as missing. They were private people who seldom associated with their neighbors. During the subsequent investigation, drug paraphernalia was found in their small apartment, which might have provided the reason for Leroy and Sherry's wish to remain anonymous.

Since the cases spanned a period of seven years, no one connected the mysterious disappearances.

"Perhaps there isn't anything," David surmised aloud. But then he thought, *"The only consistent factor linking the cases is the time of year. All the disappearances occurred in the springtime, from April through late June."*

David sighed again and said aloud, "It's a puzzle. My worst fear is that a great white shark has been prowling these waters every spring. If so; it could ruin the tourist trade."

Jim Marshall was well aware of the cases David was reviewing. Both men were concerned and neither wanted the media to stumble upon the open cases. As David closed another folder, he thought, *"I'm surprised a bright young reporter from the local newspaper hasn't already discovered the similarities."*

Since it was December, spring seemed a long time away. From past experiences, David knew the most difficult part of police work was the waiting game.

One last time, although he knew there weren't any to be found, David thumbed through each case file searching for an unseen clue. Then he gave a sigh of discontent, leaned back in his chair and lit his pipe. While praying silently that his supervisor would be satisfied, David carefully stacked the reports back into his bottom drawer, closed it and wrote a short report to Jim stating there were no new leads.

Chapter 3

When Tim arose early from the bed he shared with Catherine, he did so quietly to avoid waking her. Today he was going fishing with his friend, Miguel. After spending some time in a canoe on the Amazon with Miguel during Tom's rescue, Tim swore he would never ride in a boat again. Patient and persistent, Miguel kept after him until Tim finally agreed to go fishing this morning. *"I hope we don't catch any Piranha. I hate those evil-looking creatures."*

During the night, Catherine had kicked off the sheet, so now Tim was afforded an erotic view of her nude body. He gathered the wrinkled sheet and while running his fingers along the flank of her hip, he replaced the sheet tenderly.

She murmured softly, "That feels wonderful."

Playfully, Tim patted her bottom. "Miguel will be here shortly. It was either cover you or have the entire village hear about our sex life."

Catherine yawned and said, "They probably know already, but I don't care."

Tim bent down and whispered in her ear. "I may be forced to make you an honest woman soon or the tribal elders will shoot me. Do you want coffee?"

"Yes, please; thank you."

Catherine stretched, the sheet slid off again and she smiled up at him. "Care to have a little fun, G.I.?"

Tim chuckled and covered her again. "You know I would. But as I said, Miguel will be here in a minute or two. We're going fishing, remember?"

Catherine yawned again and said, "I'm hungry for fish." Catch me a nice trout for supper."

In a poor imitation of the jungle king, Tim beat his chest with his fists. "Tarzan of the jungle will do his best for Jane. I would give my jungle yell, but it might frighten the children."

She shook her head but smiled at the same time. "Spare me and bring my coffee, please. Then go meet Miguel outside so I can take my shower."

"Your wish is my command, my love," Tim said and walked into the kitchen.

After pouring a cup of coffee and carrying it into the bedroom, Tim placed it alongside the sink in the bathroom. Before he left, he gave Catherine a deep kiss and a sharp slap on the bare derriere.

As he quickly ducked out the door, Catherine yelped and threw her shoe at him.

From the patio, Tim checked the outside thermometer to find it was another warm morning. It was nearly eighty degrees already and the sun was shining brightly. Rain hadn't fallen in or near Obidos last night, so the current on the Amazon shouldn't be very strong today.

The swirling wind blew up a small dust devil which quickly died from lack of support. It reminded Tim of his days spent driving through the cotton rich region of Plainview in west Texas.

Miguel arrived a few minutes later and said, "We'll fish the back water ponds today. The current will be less there."

Before Tim could reply, they heard the roar of a helicopter passing over the house. They both looked up and spotted Jose's helicopter at a hover one hundred feet above. Jose was alone. He waved his microphone back and forth to tell Tim he wanted to speak to him on Catherine's radio.

Tim thought, *"He's either excited or agitated."*

As Tim ran into the house, Catherine was emerging from her shower wrapped in a large towel. He knew she hadn't heard the copter over the noise of the water, so he pointed upward. "I need to use the radio. Jose's up above signaling me."

Clutching her towel tightly around her body, Catherine ran to her radio and flicked some switches. Several dials glowed green as she tuned to the same frequency Jose used in his helicopter, and said, "Go ahead, Jose."

"I need to speak to Tim. Tell him to meet me at the landing strip and be prepared to fly to Belem. Over and out."

As Jose's copter flew off toward the edge of town, Catherine shrugged and hung up the microphone. "Jose didn't give you much choice, did he? Take Miguel with you, Tim. If you have to leave, he can come back and tell me why."

Tim motioned for Miguel to accompany him and led the way down the newly repaired road at a fast trot.

Miguel said, "Jose was in a hurry today. I wonder what he wants."

"It's hard to tell. He just said come meet him."

As they approached the helicopter, the long blades were still spinning slowly. Jose waved them over to the side of the helo.

Tim ducked unnecessarily under the blades, walked up next to Jose and asked, "What's up?"

Jose leaned out of his seat and said, "I need you to fly to Belem with me and sign some papers."

"I thought the deal on the land was still a few days off. Why the rush?"

"Fernando has become suspicious. I left him about thirty miles upriver. I'm on my way to Belem to pick up some equipment. Mister Lopez says the final paperwork is ready for our signatures."

"So Fernando is on to you," Tim said. "I doubted you could stall him much longer. Okay, I'll fly down and sign the papers. What about the survey? Has it been completed?"

"Yes – we'll get a copy when we sign the papers. That's another reason I want you there. When it comes to reading technical reports, you're better than I am. You can look things over before we sign. Then we'll be sure we have the right property."

Tim nodded and chuckled. "Yeah, I'd hate to wind up owning the wrong twenty acres of jungle land. How accurate are they in laying out jungle property?"

Miguel broke in to add his two cents worth, "Believe it or not, the surveyors are fairly accurate."

Tim asked, "How do you know, Miguel?"

"The government keeps tight control of the land in Brazil. They want to get every cent they can. Believe me, the officials don't want anyone complaining and causing others to have doubts. The Amazon has been mapped very thoroughly. Every curve and bend is recorded."

"I'll take your word for it, Miguel, but just the same, when we arrive at the lawyer's office, I'll look over the plats. I'm sure he can assist us."

Then Tim turned to Jose and said, "Wind the bird up, Jose and let's go. I want to get back as soon as possible."

As he climbed into the opposite seat, Tim turned to Miguel and shrugged in helplessness. "I'm sorry about the fishing trip, Miguel. We'll go another day. Will you let Catherine know what's going on? Tell her we'll be back shortly. When I return, I'll explain all of this."

Miguel nodded and said, "You better hope she didn't want you to pick up something in Belem."

"It's too late now. She should have let me know earlier."

The flight to Belem was quick and quiet. Jose didn't have much to say. Tim knew he didn't need to strain his eyes anymore, so he sat and relaxed and enjoyed the trip. *"It seems like years ago."*

Sunlight glistened off the wide green leaves and threw out bright rays that cut through the darkness of Tim's sunglasses and almost blinded him. Heat waves bounced off the river to make wavy mirage lines along the bank.

At Belem, Jose landed at the airfield and they caught a taxi to their lawyer's office. Gloria seemed to expect them. She quickly ushered the pair into Hector's inter sanctum.

Hector greeted them both with a firm handshake. "I see Jose found you, Mister Fitch. Welcome back to Belem. I believe you'll find the papers for your joint purchase are in order, but we'll go over each document carefully. I want you to understand what's involved in your venture."

Tim smiled and said, "Thank you, I appreciate your thoroughness."

As Hector led them carefully through the entire transaction, he held up two documents. "This is a copy of the plat for the twenty acres and the property deed that is made out in the name of the J & T Construction Company. Your land borders on a curve of the Amazon, with a five hundred foot frontage on the river. The remainder stretches out on each side and resembles a slice of pie.

"The top of the plat depicts a rounded portion, which makes the pie shape comparison even more accurate. You now own nineteen point four-three-five acres of jungle, including the mineral rights."

After comparing the plat with a map of the Amazon provided by Hector, Tim found the figures and location matched perfectly and said, "I'm satisfied."

When the documents were signed, Jose wrote a ten thousand dollar check, plus another for five hundred dollars for Hector's services, and the meeting adjourned.

As they were leaving the office, Hector offered Jose another Cuban cigar.

Tim smiled inwardly and thought, *"Now you're being smart, Hector. The last time you gave Jose a cigar; he lit up and polluted your entire office. Besides being thorough, you have a good memory."*

The equipment Fernando required was ready, so Tim helped Jose load the boxes into the baggage compartment. Then Jose refueled for the trip to Obidos and to continue upriver to where Fernando was waiting.

On the way to Obidos, Jose was very chipper. For most of the trip, he kept the unlit cigar clamped in his teeth and hummed a country western tune.

Then he removed the stogie and placed it in his pocket. Over the intercom he said, "That went well, Tim. We are now landowners in Brazil. How does it strike you?"

"I'll be happy if your prediction about the oil comes true."

In Tim's mind, he was considering his new position in life as a land owner. *"I know Jose is excited. I am too. This could turn out to be something big. That would be nice, especially for Jose."*

Tim spoke into his mike and asked, "If we strike it rich, Jose, what will you do with your millions of dollars?"

It appeared Jose had been thinking things through in advance. "I'll buy Juanita a very nice home and me a new truck, plus a newer and more sophisticated helicopter. Then I'll spend a large portion of my money to help friends who aren't so fortunate."

"Good selection," Tim said. "I think I'll attempt to help the orphans here. Poor little Carlos is such a nice kid. His aunt and uncle have had a rough time, but they took him in anyway. That shows character. How difficult would it be for someone to adopt an orphan from Brazil?"

Jose shook his head to indicate he didn't know. Then he said, "I'll bet with a nice cash donation, more orphans could be adopted. Your plans are also nice."

"When are you going to explain to Fernando that we just 'happen' to own property that 'appears' to show signs of oil, Jose? I doubt that he'll be amused."

Jose smiled and said, "I'll let him know soon."

Tim said, "I owe you two hundred and fifty dollars for my part of the lawyer's fee. The next time I see you, I'll write you a check."

As always, Jose set the bird down gently. Tim climbed out and ducked under the blades as Jose kept them spinning. Then he waved as Jose lifted off for upriver. *"I hope Jose can handle Fernando. We'll have to wait and see. To quote a few old worn out clichés: 'the fat is in the fire', and 'we're in the ball game'."*

Jose's feeling of well-being was contagious. On the way to Catherine's home, Tim whistled a happy tune.

Chapter 4

It was Saturday in Bermuda and the beginning of a new weekend. In the Fitch household this fine sunny morning, everyone was sleeping late – everyone that is except Pearl.

When she heard the pieces of her lighthouse wind chime spank together, Pearl knew the day would be windy with a slight threat of rain. *"Our water tanks are low. Although it means a wet day, I hope we receive a good, soaking rain."*

Pearl was not happy when her granddaughter skipped meals, so in case Kate asked for a decent breakfast, she got up early. *"I know it's important to girls her age to remain slim, but there's such a thing as going too far."*

She prepared a batch of pancake batter and had a bowl of eggs waiting when sleepyhead Kate finally arrived in the kitchen.

Pearl was drinking her second cup of coffee. She said, "Sit down and read the newspaper, Kate, while I make you a healthy breakfast."

When Kate ate three pancakes with two eggs and washed her meal down with a cup of hot chocolate followed by a glass of milk, Pearl said, "There, you see, that didn't hurt a bit."

Kate was finishing her last bite, when Tom and George arrived in the kitchen. They saw the pancake batter and asked Pearl for three pancakes and three eggs apiece.

When he looked for and didn't find what he wanted, George complained, "There's no butter,"

"Sometimes we have to suffer," Pearl replied sagely.

George shrugged at the fickle finger of fate, changed the subject and said, "Kate, I met a friend of yours. She said to tell you hello."

"Who was it, Grandpa?"

"Lorna Hayden, your companion on the flight from South Carolina."

Kate's eyes told George that she knew Lorna. "I remember her. She was outspoken, very pretty and is searching for a rich husband in Bermuda. I hope she had some luck."

George said, "She met a man."

"Good for her. Do you know him?"

With a sly grin, George said, "Yes, and you do too."

Puzzled by his remark, Kate asked, "I do? Who is it?"

"Does the name Jock ring a bell?"

Kate was amazed. "You don't mean the town drunk? How did Lorna meet him?"

"Another accident, I'm afraid," George said. "Jock fell off a bar stool and cut his hand. When Lorna came to his rescue, in his drunken state, Jock confused her with his wife, Lori, who was eaten by a great white shark."

Kate was surprised at her grandfather's remark. "She was what? Eaten by a shark? When did it happen?"

George replied, "Over five years ago. Lori's the reason for Jock's drinking. Jock blames himself for her death, when there was absolutely nothing he could have done to prevent the attack. It was extremely lucky the shark didn't kill them both."

Kate said, "That sounds so tragic."

Tom nodded knowingly. "The tragedy is, while he has mourned his wife for so long, Jock continued to drink like a fish. Dad attempts to make him stop, but Jock won't listen."

George grinned and said, "That situation may change."

As George told them the story of Lorna and Jock, his grin became a smile.

Kate sat with her mouth wide open. She was hardly able to believe what her grandfather said. She thought, *"Poor Lorna."*

George ended his tale. "David claims when he left them, Lorna and Jock were getting along fabulously. He also says Jock has sworn off booze. I hope David's right. But it appears I strayed from the reason for informing you of Lorna, Kate. I need your help."

She asked, "In what way?"

"Lorna is a registered nurse. In fact, she's the chief of the operating room where she's currently employed, somewhere in Illinois."

Kate remembered and provided, "Peoria."

"Very good," George said. "To get to the point, our head OR nurse here will soon depart for the states. I would appreciate your assistance to convince Lorna to stay here and take over the position. I discussed my suggestion with the hospital administration and they're prepared to offer her a very nice salary. Do you believe Lorna would approve of my plan?"

Kate shook her head. "I have no way to know, Grandpa. I do know Lorna said she isn't very happy in Peoria. It seems there aren't many eligible men there. I gather she's ready to get married, settle down and have children."

She paused for a moment and then added, "If she does find the right man in Bermuda, it might upset your plans. Of course, if she was employed here, she would have more time to find a rich husband."

George asked, "Then you'll aid and abet my scheme?"

"Of course Grandpa; what do we have to lose? The least she can say is 'No.'"

"Good," Pearl said. "I'll phone Lorna and ask her to join us at lunch."

The day before, precisely at noon, Jock arrived at the Palms Hotel at the wheel of an Austin Healey automobile, (a small, two-seated convertible), with the top down. The day was sunny and the temperature hovered between seventy-two and seventy-five degrees, so it was ragtop time.

Jock loved his little roadster, but seldom drove the vehicle. When he was drinking in excess, he was smart enough to realize he was a menace to others on the road.

Killing yourself was one thing. In his eyes, taking some innocent person with you was murder. So his pride and joy remained in the garage. In his sober moments, Jock remembered to keep the vehicle repaired and periodically recharge the battery.

On the way to the hotel entrance, Jock paused for a moment to watch two frisky squirrels chirp in anger as they chased each other across a closely clipped lawn and up a huge Banyan tree.

When Jock entered the dining room, he saw Lorna already seated and waiting for him with a glass of white wine in her hand. *"I wonder if it's for courage. I could use a stiff drink myself, but I've sworn off alcohol."*

The previous evening, after Lorna departed for her hotel, Jock held a long talk between himself and the ghost of Lori. *"I know I've been stupid for some time with my continual drinking. Now, by the grace of God and help from the beautiful woman seated at this table, I've seen the light."*

As he approached the table, Jock held his right arm behind his back. In his right hand was a single, long-stemmed, pale yellow rose from his garden. After placing the flower on the table, Jock said, "Beauty for the fair maiden from the tamed beast. Good afternoon, Lorna. You look lovely."

"Thank you, Jock. By the way, is Jock your given name? Or is it a nickname?"

"Actually, my name is Jocquin. It's an old German name. When they see my name written, no one can pronounce it properly, so over the years it has been shortened to Jock. At first, it fit my life style. Now, I don't mind. I love sports, although I haven't been active for a while."

He smiled and Lorna caught his meaning. *"At least Jock hasn't called himself a drunk today. I'm pleased."*

Lorna looked deep into his eyes and found they were still bloodshot. It would take some time for the whites to recover.

"Jock's feeling the effects of withdrawal, but he does look nice."

"You look rather well yourself," she said. "I like the shorts and sports jacket approach. I've seen many gentlemen wearing knee socks in Bermuda. Is it an English tradition?"

"I believe it is," Jock said. "I just follow suit. You know, when in Rome..."

She asked, "How do you really feel?"

"I'll admit I'm dying for a drink, but I will stick to water."

To demonstrate his resolve, Jock held his glass aloft and took a deep drink. His hand shook slightly and perspiration formed on his brow.

"Let's order," Lorna said. "Perhaps a nice lunch will help settle your stomach."

Jock glanced at the menu, but then he put it aside. "I don't feel like eating, but I'll try. Maybe something light like a salad."

Lorna said, "While I waited, I checked the menu. I must admit I arrived a half hour early. I didn't want to miss you. Do I seem forward?"

"Not at all," he replied. "What would you recommend?"

"I'll have a small shrimp salad and a bowl of clam chowder."

Jock agreed. "I'll have the same." He signaled to a waiter who was hovering nearby, gave him their order and added, "I'll have a glass of iced tea to drink. Would you like more wine, Lorna or would you prefer iced tea?"

"I'll have tea please. Thank you."

While they waited for their drinks to arrive, Lorna said, "I got here early and ordered a glass of wine for courage. I don't usually drink with my lunch."

Jock asked, "Are you pleased to see I'm sober?"

"Yes, Jock, you seem to be an entirely new man today. I hope I had something to do with your transformation. I especially hope you'll continue on the straight and narrow path. It would mean the world to me."

He took her hand in his. "Lori and I had a long talk last night. We both agree I've been a fool and wasted five years of my life. Instead of drinking myself silly, I should have done something positive in her memory. I promise her and you; I'm finished with alcohol."

He paused to wipe perspiration away with his napkin. "I know it will be difficult, but I would appreciate your assistance. Although you only plan to be here a few more days, it would please me immensely if you were by my side to keep me on the straight and narrow. I admire the chewing out you gave me last night. You don't pull any punches, do you?"

Lorna continued to hold his hand and said, "No, I don't. I came here to search for a rich husband, but so far my plan hasn't borne fruit. So, I might as well enjoy the remainder of my vacation and do something besides look for a man. If you need my assistance, perhaps we can help each other."

She paused to tap a map of Bermuda that was lying near her right hand. "Since you've lived here for years, you should know several places I haven't seen. Let's explore the islands together and see what happens. It takes a strong-willed person to make the decision you have. For the next ten days, I'll support you in any way I can."

"Wonderful," Jock said.

They spent the remainder of the meal planning several day trips around various parts of the islands and decided to begin their exploration this afternoon.

Jock glanced at his companion with new interest in his eyes. *"So far, everything has gone exceedingly well. In the days ahead, there may be rocky roads, but now, Lorna and I are a team with a definite purpose in mind."*

Chapter 5

E arly Sunday morning, Pearl phoned Lorna at her hotel. Yesterday, when she attempted to reach her, no one answered.

Kate said, "More than likely, she's exploring Bermuda. Call her again tomorrow morning."

On the third ring, Lorna answered with a sleepy voice, "Hello."

"Oh, my Dear," Pearl said. "I'm sorry if I woke you. This is Pearl Fitch, the wife of Doctor Fitch."

Lorna said, "No, it's all right. I should have been up by now. What can I do for you?"

"If you're not busy later today, Kate and I want to treat you to lunch. My husband informed us he met you at the hospital. Kate would like to see you again."

"Mister Becker and I have a date this morning," Lorna said. "He's taking me for a drive around the islands. Can we arrange to meet you somewhere? I'm sure Jock will know the place you choose."

Pearl chuckled. "That's the first time I heard Jock called Mister Becker in years. Would the clubhouse at the Castle Harbor Golf Course be satisfactory? They serve a very nice brunch."

Lorna replied, "We'll meet you there at twelve-thirty. Thank you for the invitation. I'm anxious to meet you and speak to Kate again. She spoke very highly of her grandparents."

After she hung up and glanced at the clock, Lorna realized it was nearly eight a.m. She was due to meet Jock at nine. *"I'll have to rush. It'll be nice to see Kate again. I wonder what she'll think of Jock."*

Jock arrived promptly at nine. He carried another rose, a red one this time. He kissed Lorna's hand again and she blushed. *"What is it about this guy?"*

When he was informed of Pearl's call, Jock gladly accepted the invitation. "I admire Pearl. She's another no nonsense lady. I'll be pleased to see Kate again. I wonder if she'll remember me."

They spent an enjoyable morning at Saint George's Golf Course in Saint George's Parish, a difficult, nine-hole layout, which is mostly uphill and downhill. Lorna laughed when Jock's tee shot on number two rolled across the green, up an embankment and plunged into the sea.

Mutually agreed, they didn't keep score as they played their shots and enjoyed the walk in bright sunshine. It was a delightful but warm day, with the temperature well over seventy-five degrees. They were happy to approach the final hole.

At the small snack shop, Jock bought them ice cold sodas and remarked, "I believe we completed our round in sufficient time for a leisurely drive to Castle Harbor."

Although they arrived before their hostesses, they discovered the head waiter had a table waiting. First he pulled out a chair for Lorna and then did the same for Jock. Another waiter took their folded napkins from the table and spread them on their laps.

Jock could tell Lorna enjoyed the individual attention. He glanced around and saw several men seated at other tables in the club take notice of her natural beauty. She was especially pretty today, in a white skirt and pink blouse.

The waiter was pouring their water when Pearl and Kate arrived. Jock stood to greet them. When they were seated and everyone was introduced, Lorna said, "I believe you've met Jock before, Kate."

Jock smiled at Kate and asked, "Haven't I run into you somewhere?"

Kate laughed at his pun. "Yes, you could say so. I'll never forget the first time I saw you. You were spread-eagled on the hood of my grandfather's car."

At the memory of that night, Jock shook his head. "That was a night to forget. Since that day, I've wanted to apologize to you in person. I do so now. Please accept my humble apology."

"Thank you," Kate said. Then she turned to Lorna. "You look lovely today, Lorna. I'm pleased we could have lunch with you. Thanks for accepting grandma's request."

"I wanted to meet you again, Kate. How have you found the schools in Bermuda? I knew you were worried how well they compared with Austin."

"They're much better. I have to work my fingers to the bone to keep up."

Pearl broke in and changed the subject. "George informs me that you're a nurse, Lorna. How well do you like the hospital where you're employed?"

With a wry smile, Lorna replied, "As far as hospitals go, it's all right. They do have all the latest gadgets for the doctors and nurses. Overall, the staff is easy to work for and with. I can't complain. Why do you ask?"

"Kate and I have an ulterior motive for asking you to lunch. My husband wants me to see if you would consider joining the staff at Hamilton Hospital as head nurse of the OR."

Jock knew Lorna was surprised by the offer, so he said; "Now there's a shock."

Lorna regained her composure and said, "I agree with Jock, it is a surprise. Why me? And, if I was interested, how can you be sure the hospital would hire me?"

"Our head nurse will leave soon," Pearl replied. "The position will be open with no other qualified nurse available. As to why the hospital would hire you, George will have a definite say. As a member of the board of directors, his recommendation carries a significant amount of weight. If he wants you, you're a shoo-in. The salary is also very nice."

Lorna said, "Based on the short time we spent together, I'm flattered at your husband's faith in me. I'm also overwhelmed and don't know what to say. May I think about your proposition and give you my answer in a few days? I need time to think things through."

"Of course," Pearl said. "You don't have to decide this minute. Take as long as you need. When it's convenient for you, George will provide a tour of the hospital. He's justifiably proud of 'his' hospital and takes great pains to find the best employees."

Lorna nodded and said, "Jock and I have plans for the next two days. Afterward, I'll be pleased to visit. Thank you for the opportunity."

"Now may we order?" Jock asked. "I'm starving."

"Please excuse my companion," Lorna said. "After he's been on a liquid diet for so long, Jock's just now re-discovering how good food can taste."

While they ate, Kate stole a look at Lorna's face and noticed how her friend kept her eyes on Jock. *"I'm surprised at the bond she's apparently formed with Jock. She doesn't seem to mind the way things are. In fact, Lorna looks very happy."*

As she and Jock made their way upward through the interior of Gibb's Hill lighthouse, which is situated on a high bluff, Lorna said, "This is frightening."

The stairways, one up and one down on opposite sides of the lighthouse are steep and the steps are narrow.

Sagely, Jock said, "Don't look down on the way up and don't look up on the way down."

Then he laughed as Lorna paused, glanced back, frowned momentarily and said, "You're not helping, Jock."

Today, their third day together, Jock intended to show Lorna the southern part of the Bermuda Isles. Yesterday, they spent the day climbing over many of the exposed coral formations along North Shore Road and watching large black fish play in the turquoise water.

It was another lovely day, with the sun shining brightly overhead. A few puffy clouds provided shade periodically, but they were small, so the relief was short lived.

A flight of six sea gulls were gliding on an updraft with their wings spread wide to provide more lift. Their shrill cries could be heard above the sound of waves as they broke on the coral below.

After they reached the top of the stairway, Jock and Lorna exited through a very small door and had to duck their heads to avoid hitting a metal door frame. They found themselves on a narrow circular walkway at the top of the tower, where a thin, fragile-looking railing approximately three feet high is installed around the exterior of the walkway.

"Should they trip and fall, I doubt such a flimsy rail would prevent anyone from tumbling off the tower," Lorna thought. *"The way up was frightening, but the view is worth the effort."*

She pointed and said, "Look at the colors of the houses. They look like paint on an artist's palette."

They took a few minutes to admire the view. Then they descended the equally steep and narrow stairway on the opposite side of the lighthouse and emerged at the bottom into bright sunshine.

As they stood side-by-side and admired the wonders of nature, Jock asked, "Would you mind if I kiss you?"

Lorna thought, *"I've wondered when you'd ask. After three days together I'm surprised you haven't discovered that I'm in love with you."*

In response to his question, Lorna placed her hand on his cheek and kissed him tenderly. Their lips parted and she asked, "Does that answer your question?"

"Most certainly and thank you. Since I met you, I feel alive again."

"I'm pleased, Jock."

He smiled, chuckled softly and said, "I know I'm far from your expectations, but it appears you're stuck with me. I hope you don't mind. I've enjoyed our time together."

Lorna said, "I intend to keep my promise. If you feel up to it, you may kiss me again."

He did, and he did. When they finally broke apart, they smiled at each other and knew nothing more needed to be said. They joined hands and walked to Jock's automobile.

After Jock opened the door and helped her into the vehicle, Lorna said, "I must contact Doctor Fitch today to set up an appointment to speak with the hospital staff and tour the facilities. I hate to interfere with our fun, but I'm seriously considering his offer."

Jock smiled and said, "I'm pleased. I don't want you to leave. There is much more of the islands to show you."

She asked, "Is that the only reason?"

He shook his head and continued to smile. "I want to know you better. You took me from the town drunk to a man of responsibility again. I can't thank you enough. But to be truthful, I believe I've fallen in love with you."

Lorna blushed, but at the same time she smiled and said, "I believe the feeling is mutual."

Then she felt the heat in her cheeks and asked, "Why is it I blush so much around you? You do have a strange affect on me."

Jock shrugged. "I don't know, but, getting back to George, if we must interrupt our day, we will."

When they arrived at "On a Hill", they found George and Pearl at home.

"Come in," Pearl said. "We were just talking about you."

Lorna said, "I hope it was all good."

"It was," George said and chuckled. "What brings you our way?"

After shaking George's hand, Jock said, "We came by to see if you were available for a tour of your hospital, George. Lorna would like to meet the staff and check out your facilities."

George looked earnestly at Lorna. "I sincerely hope you'll consider our offer, Lorna. I know you'll enjoy the work here. We aren't as big as the hospital where you're currently employed; however, we do have all the bells and whistles of a modern medical facility.

"The staff is handpicked, with only the best qualified personnel in their particular specialties. But I tend to brag. When you meet them, you'll discover I'm telling the truth. I'm available anytime you are."

"Would tomorrow at ten a.m. be convenient?" Lorna asked. "I want you to know I'm seriously considering joining your staff. If things are as you say, I see no reason why I shouldn't."

"Wonderful," Pearl exclaimed.

Then George asked, "Jock wouldn't be another mitigating factor, would he? You have the blush of spring in your cheeks, my dear. You can't fool an old country doctor."

"Yes, you might say my companion has been a slight influence in my plans."

Jock asked, "Only a slight one?"

"Well, perhaps a little bit more," Lorna said and laughed.

"Give George his rightful due," Pearl said. "He can spot a pair of lovebirds a mile away. You'll stay for lunch, won't you? I know George wants to extol the virtues of Lorna remaining in Bermuda."

"I didn't think to ask about the cost of living here," Lorna said. "From what I hear, it's not cheap."

"Purchasing a home is expensive," Pearl replied. "However, there are other ways to survive. A number of houses and apartments are available for rent at a reasonable price. And, there's always the possibility you could stay with friends until you have your feet on the ground.

"We have four bedrooms and only three are being used. Tom is awaiting a calling of employment in New York City. When word comes, he'll be leaving. So you see; we have ample space available.

"George and I discussed this the other day and we both agree, as does Kate. It would be wonderful to have another woman in the house."

"Thank you, Pearl," Lorna said. "Your kindness never seems to cease. If things work out tomorrow and I decide to remain, I'll consider your offer for a roof over my head. I admit it would be to my advantage to live with someone who knows the islands and people so well."

"Until tomorrow then," George said. "Let's drink a toast to a successful tour and pray you'll join us."

"Make mine iced tea, please," Jock said.

In the evening, after an afternoon of exploring, Jock and Lorna ate a tasty meal of broiled flounder at a small restaurant on the edge of Hamilton bay.

As the waiter lit a candle on their table, they stared into each others eyes, held hands and spoke of their days together and the ones to come. A cool night wind brought the aroma of salt water to their nostrils, while small dew drops dripped from the roof and splattered quietly onto bricks below.

Overhead, a half moon slid behind a dark cloud to hide and watch the two lovers.

Afterward, Jock drove Lorna to her hotel and walked her to her room, where she unlocked and opened the door. Then she turned to meet Jock's embrace and he kissed her.

Lorna reached behind her, pulled Jock into the room and closed the door. Without another word spoken, she took Jock's hand and led him to her bed. After they made love passionately, they fell asleep in each others arms.

At three a.m., Jock departed for home to allow Lorna to dream of things to come. She awakened refreshed and smiled at her memories of the night before.

She ate breakfast and then walked to the hospital grounds, where she met George near the entrance. He was speaking with another doctor. As Lorna approached, George introduced her. "Lorna, meet Doctor De Wayne Peters. Pete is our resident surgeon."

Tall; six feet, three inches, with a shock of white hair cut in a flat top style, Pete wore small glasses perched on the end of his nose.

Pete stared at Lorna over the top of the rims, shook her hand and said, "I'm pleased to meet you Nurse Hayden. George has been singing your praises. Welcome to Hamilton Hospital. We're small, but we provide every service a larger facility would. We're very proud of our reputation. I hope you'll like what you see."

"I'm sure I will."

Lorna spent the morning on a tour of the facilities. She was impressed with the staff and the equipment. Doctor Peters was right; the hospital possessed all the latest technology. The operating rooms were spotless, well-lit and modern.

She admired what she saw, and at the end of the day, she reached a decision. "If you'll have me, I would love to join your staff."

"Congratulations," George said.

They spent the next hour discussing salary and nursing shift schedules. Lorna met the three nurses on duty and was assured she would like the six others who were currently off-duty.

"I must return to Peoria and inform my supervisor of my decision," she said. "I'm not sure if they'll require me to stay on until a suitable replacement is found, or if they'll agree to an immediate release. How soon do you want me to report?"

"We thought your current employer might require you to remain a week or two," George said. "Whenever you're free to begin, the position is yours. Take what time you need and keep us informed." Then he said, "I'll drive you to your hotel."

They reached the hotel shortly after five p.m. and parked near the pub, where George asked, "What about a drink to celebrate?"

Lorna replied, "Why not?"

When they walked into the Fox and Hounds, Lorna realized it was the first time she had set foot in the bar since the night she met Jock. It brought back memories.

Jesus was behind the bar polishing glasses. He waved a greeting to her.

George said, "It appears you're well known here. Hello, Jesus."

"Good afternoon, Doctor Fitch and Miss Lorna. It's a little early in the afternoon for a drink. What's the special occasion?"

George was beaming. "I just hired Lorna as our new head nurse."

Jesus reached out to shake George's hand. Then he turned to Lorna and said, "Congratulations, Lorna; the drinks are on me. After the way you took care of Jock the other night, I owe you one. How is he, by the way? I haven't seen him since; which in itself is a small miracle. I hope he didn't take his business elsewhere. If so, I might be searching for a new job. Jock practically kept this bar afloat."

"You'll be pleased to know Jock has given up the sauce," George said. "I know it's difficult to believe, but you can also thank Lorna for that miracle. She's had quite an affect on our friend."

"Great," Jesus said. "I'm happy for Jock, but sad to see my profits go down the drain."

After a glass of white wine, George headed for home, while Lorna retired to her hotel room to think things through. *"There are still several days remaining before my vacation is over. Should I stay for the full two weeks, or return early and tell the hospital in Peoria of my decision to leave?"*

With thoughts of her future employment interrupted by remembrances of Jock and the previous evening, Lorna easily reached a decision. *"I'll stay until my vacation is over. Jock and I have a lot to discuss and discover about each other. As far as I know, my lover isn't rich, but I can't believe my luck in finding him. Wealthy or not, my dreams have come true. I found my future husband in Bermuda. What more could I ask for?"*

Chapter 6

As Kate left Washington high school behind for the last time until after the Christmas and New Year's vacation, she shouted, "Free at last. Hallelujah!"

Someone on the bus tore his corrected homework into small pieces and threw them into the air, where they drifted down around the other students like confetti.

The bus driver, Clarence Clowers knew before he could turn his bus in, he must clean up the mess, so he frowned.

"Cheer up Mister Clowers," Janice Simpson said. "Just think; you don't have to contend with us for another two weeks."

Clarence smiled and thought, *"Suddenly, I feel like I could throw some confetti myself."*

Although Kate had only attended school here for a week, it seemed like much longer. She waved goodbye to her new friends and got off the bus. *"It will be wonderful to have a few days to relax."*

As Kate approached the house at the top of the hill, Pearl was watching out the window.

Every time Kate saw the sign in the front yard, she smiled. "On A Hill" was certainly aptly named. The view of the beaches and homes below was lovely. As each day passed, Kate grew to love Bermuda more. She was content for the first time in her young life.

For the time being, there appeared to be no more turmoil ahead. She thought, *"I love my new family."*

Although she still missed her mother, the memories of Cheryl grew dimmer with time. Kate wished her father would hurry back to Bermuda with his fiancée. *"I'm dying to meet my new step-mother."*

Before Kate could reach for the doorknob, Pearl opened the door. She wore a pretty apron with a sprinkling of flour adorning the front. Pearl enveloped Kate in her daily hug and kissed her on the cheek. "Good afternoon, sweetheart. You look relieved at the thought of no school for the next two weeks."

Kate laid her books down on a bookcase and said, "I am. I never thought school could be so difficult. I'm slowly adjusting to the way they do things here, but it's a far cry from my old school in Austin. I'll need the next few days to relax and gather myself for the months ahead."

"Don't worry, Honey," Pearl said. "You'll do fine and make the honor roll next semester."

Kate said, "I hope so." Then she sniffed the delicious aroma coming from the kitchen and asked, "What are you baking?"

"Christmas cookies and banana bread," Pearl answered. "Here, tie this apron on. You can help me cut out cookies and decorate after we bake."

This was something new for Kate. *"Mom and I never baked anything. I don't think she knew how."*

While she cut dough and added decorations to the finished product, Kate wondered if Bryan and his family would spend the Christmas holidays in Bermuda. *"In his last letter, Bryan said his parents were shuttering their home in Virginia and would come to Bermuda soon to close on their new home on Blue Waters Drive. I don't know what 'soon' meant. Is it tomorrow or next month?"*

Almost as if she could read Kate's mind, Pearl asked, "Did Bryan tell you his parents are coming here to close on their new home?"

"Yes, but I don't know when they'll arrive or if Bryan will be with them. In his last letter he wasn't very clear concerning the date."

Pearl asked, "Would you rather wait for him to clarify the issue or should I tell you?"

Kate hugged Pearl and in the process got flour all over the back of Pearl's dress. She grinned and said, "Grandma, you can be so mean at times."

"I declare, child, when it comes to Bryan, you have a one-track mind. I shouldn't spoil the surprise, but I never could keep a secret. The Jessops will arrive on the twenty-third of December."

Instead of acting like a sixteen-year-old young lady, Kate skipped around the room like a six-year-old child. She wore a smile a mile wide and exclaimed, "Thank you for not being able to keep a secret."

At dinner, Tom and George noticed Kate's gay mood. Tim asked, "Why are you so happy tonight, Kate?"

Pearl answered for her. "Kate's boyfriend and his parents will arrive in a few days."

"Now I understand," Tom said. Then he asked, "Was there anything in the mail for me, Mother?"

Pearl knew Tom was still concerned about the lack of a reply to his application, but she said, "No, Tom; I'm sorry. Perhaps we'll hear something tomorrow." Then she thought, "*I wish he'd hear something.*"

She decided to change the subject. "I told Marsha there was no reason to spend money for a hotel and then have to rent a car or pay taxi fare back and forth between their place and ours. She finally saw the wisdom in my words, so we'll entertain the Jessops for a few days until they close on the house. Marsha says their furniture is already on the way by ship."

"It'll be nice to see them again," Kate said.

Pearl asked, "All the Jessops, or just one in particular?"

"Grandma, you know I like them all."

"I know, Honey. I enjoy teasing you, just as your grandfather does. It will be nice, and I know they'll be happy living here. Bermuda is such a lovely place."

Kate wrapped her arms around Pearl's waist and gave her a big hug. "I love my new family and I'm learning to like the islands more and more each day."

"We love you too, Honey; we always have. It's so good to have you here. Let's stop chattering and get things done, or the Jessops will be here before we're ready."

The next two days flew by, as the women planned the meals and shopped for a Christmas goose, which was a tradition in George's family for generations.

"I've never tasted goose before," Kate thought.

Then before Kate was ready, the twenty-third of December dawned bright and cool. The Jessops' flight was due at ten-thirty a.m. The entire Fitch family was on hand to meet them at the airport.

Bryan was the first person to deplane. As he searched through the crowd of people who were waiting for friends and loved ones on the tarmac, he spotted Kate and waved.

Kate returned his greeting while she jumped up and down in excitement. *"I know grandma thinks I act like a child around Bryan, but I don't care. It's going to be wonderful to spend time with him again."*

After making his way through the crowd, Bryan approached Kate with a smile on his face. She was prepared for anything, but he only hugged her. Still, it took her breath away.

Close behind were Bob and Marsha, who smiled as they approached the Fitch family. Marsha said, "It's wonderful to see you all again."

Bob echoed her sentiments. "Kate, you look lovely. Bermuda has put the blush of spring into your cheeks, or is it the fact that Bryan has returned?"

Kate put her arm through Bryan's and smiled in reply. "Oh, Mister Jessop, you love to tease me just as grandma does."

Bryan and Kate held hands all the way home and didn't care who noticed.

Chapter 7

Since Tim returned from the states, he kept busy helping Catherine. In the evenings they took long walks through the village. Tim discovered the local people were preparing for Christmas, just as they did everywhere.

"It's the same here as in Bermuda," he said. "While they decorate their homes, each resident attempts to outdo the others"

Strings of colored lights were strung throughout the village. Children made chains from colored construction paper rings, exactly the way Tim did when he was small in Bermuda.

Catherine said, "No matter where you are in the world, when it comes to Christmas, nothing much changes."

While she examined the many boxes under a small fir tree in the living room, Catherine thought, *"I wonder what Tim bought me."* Her curiosity was getting the better of her.

When Tim caught her shaking a package, he said, "If you continue to rattle presents, you're liable to break something."

Coyly, she asked, "Why can't I open just one?"

Tim shook his head. "One would lead to two; two to three etcetera. I'm not asking about my presents, am I? Be a good girl and wait."

As Catherine slunk around the room seductively, she asked, "Can't I persuade you somehow?"

Tim remained adamant. "I'm above bribing."

She came into his arms, kissed him fiercely and smiled coyly as she asked, "Are you sure?"

"Your wiles will work on me for anything but Christmas presents. But if you're looking for a good time, lead on."

Catherine needed no more persuasion. She forgot about the packages and led Tim to the bedroom.

On Christmas Eve, Tim and Catherine placed a phone call to Tim's family. For a change, the line was clear as a bell. Tim thought, *"Perhaps Tom's Boss is watching over us tonight."*

Catherine enjoyed every minute she spent speaking with everyone, especially Kate. After she hung up, Catherine asked, "Do we still have to wait until Christmas morning to open our presents? In my family, we opened them after church on Christmas Eve. While we were gone, Santa always arrived. I never did figure out how my parents arranged that."

With her fingers crossed, she asked, "What does your family do?"

"We open our presents the morning after Santa arrives," Tim said. "It is always late in the evening before he gets to Bermuda."

She asked, "Whose family tradition will we follow?"

Tim knew this was time to surrender. "We'll do it your way."

"Wonderful," Catherine cried. She threw her arms around his neck and kissed him. "Which may I open first?"

He handed her a small box that contained the diamond bracelet, and said, "Kate would like you to open the one she picked out."

Excitedly, Catherine tore the wrappings from the box like a small child opening her first gift on her initial Christmas Eve. She opened the box, saw the diamonds sparkle as they reflected lights from the tree, and Tim heard her intake of breath. "Oh, Darling, this is beautiful."

On Christmas day, the children of the village serenaded their teacher with holiday carols. Catherine gave them candy canes and small packages of school supplies as gifts.

As she prepared their Christmas feast with the traditional turkey dinner and all the vegetable dishes associated with Christmas, she said, "Now you will see my wifely attributes."

Tim cast his gaze over her body, smiled and said, "You have many good attributes."

Miguel, his wife, Pauline and their two children, Julia and Jonathan joined them for dinner. They listened to Christmas Carols on the radio until late in the evening.

The lights from a small Christmas tree spread a glow through the living room.

In Bermuda on Christmas Eve, there were still three days remaining of Lorna's vacation. She and Jock spent the last several days getting to know each other and expanding their love. Although they made love occasionally, Jock didn't rush her into bed every time he felt like it. Usually, it was the other way around. Lorna made her desires known and he cooperated.

"Even though Jock says he's not comparing me to Lori, I know, he must be. There's no way to avoid it. I only hope his appraisal is positive. I know I'm in love with him, but I'm not entirely sure of his feelings."

During the week that followed Lorna's decision to stay in Bermuda and enjoy her vacation with her new love, she and Jock met twice with Pearl and George for lunch.

"What do you have planned for Christmas?" Pearl asked. "If you're free, we'd love to have you for dinner."

"We accept," Jock said.

Christmas day dawned bright and sunny, with a slight breeze from the north, but the weather did nothing to chill the spirit of the day.

Lorna and Jock joined the Fitch family and their guests, the Jessops for worship at a small church nearby. Afterward, Jock drove to "On a Hill" while their hosts and the Jessops walked the few blocks.

When they arrived, Lorna and Jock stood outside his small roadster for a while and watched a flock of sea birds fly high above and circle on the wind's currents.

Then, Jock reached into a pocket of his suit jacket and retrieved a small, blue box. While he looked deep into Lorna's eyes, he opened it slowly and said, "I've searched for a nice place to give this to you. Lorna Hayden, will you do me the honor of becoming my wife?"

Between sobs of joy, as she stared at the ring in surprise, Lorna said, "Yes, of course."

Jock placed the ring on her left hand and smiled at her answer. As Lorna threw her arms around Jock's neck and kissed him, the Fitch family and their other dinner guests walked up the driveway.

Pearl stared in admiration and surprise at the gleaming ring on Lorna's finger and asked, "Do my eyes deceive me, or are congratulations in order? What a lovely Christmas present."

"Look, we're engaged," Lorna cried. "Isn't it wonderful?"

Since they didn't open gifts before they went to church, Kate was anxious for the activities to begin. A huge pile of presents was under the tree. Forewarned of the gift giving, Lorna and Jock supplied several boxes of their own. Likewise, the Jessops brought their Christmas gifts to each other and their hosts.

Pearl said, "Why don't you play Santa, George?"

"Find one of mine first," Tom said.

They took turns and unwrapped one gift at a time. An hour passed before they had opened every present and acknowledged the giver. Then Pearl said, "It's time for dinner. Gather round the table and Tom will say a blessing."

"A very short one," Tom said, and everyone laughed.

Jock glanced at the abundance on the table. "You outdid yourself again, Pearl."

In addition to a huge roast goose, the feast featured baked ham, walnut dressing, gravy, mashed and sweet potatoes, slaw, green bean casserole and rolls. After dinner, Bryan said, "I'm stuffed."

"Tom and George will do the dishes," Pearl said. "Then we'll play a game of scrabble or cards."

Kate excused herself and her beau. "Bryan and I are headed for the beach. We want to give and receive our personal gifts in private."

The teenagers stopped near the spot where they found the penny and Kate handed Bryan his gift. Bryan took the wristwatch she gave him from the box and said, "Thanks, I'll think of you all the time."

"Bad pun, but cute," Kate said. "Let me open mine."

Inside a heart shaped locket, Kate found Bryan's and her photos. She thanked him with a tender kiss and Bryan returned the favor. As they smiled and savored the moment, they continued their stroll along the beach.

Kate thought, *"This is the best Christmas of my life."*

Bryan was sure he was in love.

Chapter 8

With the dawn of a bright and cheerful day, Pearl knew the good weather was also a welcome sign for the second day of a new year.

"Soon, Tom will travel to New York City and return to work. He's so relieved to be able to serve the Lord again."

Pearl's New Year's Eve party was a magnificent success. Everyone who was anyone attended.

On the twenty-seventh of December, Bob and Marsha closed on their new home. Now they were busy moving their furniture into the house. But they took time to assist Pearl and George as they hosted their annual party. Pearl introduced the Virginia pair to all the right people on the islands.

George commented, "Pearl and Marsha are kindred spirits – they both love to shop. Or is it they live to shop? I swear it's the latter."

Pearl's mind continued to wander. *"Bryan leaves for Virginia today. I know Kate hates to see him go. She enjoyed the time they spent together for the past two weeks. It seems they're inseparable; however, I hope they don't become too serious. After all, Kate is only sixteen, (well, make it sixteen and a half, to hear her tell it), and Bryan is eighteen. They're far too young to be serious about each other.*

"Tim and Catherine phoned on Christmas Eve and spoke with everyone."

"I'll be so happy when they arrive from Brazil," Pearl said aloud. "I'm already making plans for their wedding. It will be an affair to remember."

Then she thought again, *"Sometimes I wish Tom hadn't made the choice he did. It reduced George's and my chances of having grandbabies by fifty percent.*

"Such is life. If we could choose our children's careers, there would only be doctors and lawyers on this planet. The doctors would treat the lawyers for depression and the lawyers would sue the doctors for malpractice. What kind of a world would that be? Tom made his choice, so we'll have to live with it.

"A New Year is beginning. I only hope it will bring peace and joy to everyone I know. There's enough heartache in the world."

Pearl shut down her thoughts for the morning and moved on to the chore of making breakfast for two grown men and one young lady. Then she glanced out the window and noted once again what a lovely morning it was, and had one last thought, *"With the new year beginning like this, how could it not be a wonderful one for everyone in my family?"*

Three days into the New Year George checked the mail and said, "You have a letter, Tom."

As Tom read the letter and looked at the enclosures, George stood by quietly and waited for a response. Then Tom said, "I've been assigned to a small mission in New York City. They sent an open-ended, one-way ticket. All I have to do is contact the airline and inform them when I want to leave."

George asked, "When will that be?"

"As soon as possible – I've been inactive too long."

Tom phoned the airline's service counter at Kindley Airfield and arranged a flight for the seventh of January.

When Tom arrived safely in New York City, he drifted along in the sea of humanity that daily clogs the arteries of the city. Amid the mass of human beings, he realized just how insignificant he was in the scheme of things. He used a map provided by his mentor and took a subway to Harlem.

Through a combination of luck and help from several passing pedestrians, Tom found the mission, which was located in an old, abandoned warehouse district.

The complex consisted of an administrative office and classroom area housed in a small, rundown building. There was also a fairly large gymnasium/recreational building, with the mandatory basketball hoop at one end and a broken and splintered black pole at the other.

To one side of this structure was a huge parking lot/playground area that was paved with a fairly thick coat of recycled tar, pea gravel and asphalt. Bricks and concrete peeked through the crumbling paving and made it look like a patchwork quilt done in black and white.

In an attempt to beautify the place, it appeared someone began to paint the side of one building. But whoever it was must have grown weary or been interrupted. The once bright green paint, now faded and stained, was rolled in uneven layers to a height of five feet and it stopped two yards short of the corner.

Tom thought, *"It looks like the Marlboro man was mugged for his cigarettes while he attempted to put up an advertisement."*

The entire area was decrepit, but after his long vacation, it looked like a small piece of heaven to Tom. He carried his luggage inside the administration building and met the other priest assigned there.

Guy Mendez was a short, thin Hispanic man of forty years who was given to speaking in short sentences in a combination of Spanish and English. His hair was long and black and he needed a trim. Except for a thin moustache, his face was clean shaven.

Guy shook Tim's hand to welcome him and said, "Here, let me lock your bags in a wall locker. I'd hate to see them to come up missing."

Then Guy walked his new assistant around the complex, while he explained Tom's duties. "The main purpose of the mission is to serve the community by keeping youngsters away from the unsavory influence of many street gangs. It's a job that requires tact and self-discipline. Combating gangs is a never-ending job.

"What we do here is give the children a place to come to instead leaving them to roam the streets and get into 'who knows what' kind of trouble. When the weather cooperates, we allow the kids to play basketball in the gym or baseball in the parking lot."

A wide variety of scuffed, worn tables and chairs were in the classroom portion of the building. Along the walls, mismatched shelves housed a collection of games and puzzles – some were complete while others were ragged from use or abuse and/or missing pieces.

A group of teenagers and younger boys and girls from a wide variety of ethnic backgrounds were playing games and speaking in loud, accented voices.

Tom said, "I'm amazed at the number of children who are present."

In response, Guy asked, "It appears we're the babysitters for the entire neighborhood, doesn't it?"

Tom laughed and asked his own question. "Yes, is it always this busy?"

"This is a light day. Wait until the week-end when things get hectic. We have to be on our toes to prevent fights. Sometimes rival gang members attempt to gain entrance to recruit our young people. You'll need to learn who they are and deal with them in a forcible manner. It is a challenge."

"After a month of lying around, I'm ready," Tom said. "I often wondered if I would ever get another chance."

Guy changed the subject and asked. "Where do you plan to live?"

Tom was surprised at Guy's question. "I don't know. I assumed the Church would have a place for me. Was I wrong?"

"Yes, you were. We receive a housing allowance each month,

and maybe I can help. If you don't mind sharing a bathroom, I have a spare bedroom in my apartment. You'll also have to share the rent. If you're agreeable, we can also split the expenses of our food."

"Thanks," Tom said, "I accept."

"Don't thank me until you've seen the place," Guy said. "The apartment's not much, but it's clean. After my shift is over, I'll show you your new home."

For the remainder of the afternoon, Tom watched Father Guy interact with the children. He was a friend to everyone he spoke to. The children laughed at his antics and the street language Guy used to communicate.

Although Tom assisted where he could, he felt like an outsider. *"I see the children watching my every move. I hope I can achieve an easy rapport with them, the way Father Guy has."*

Time passed quickly and the day ended at seven p.m. After he closed and locked the facility doors, Guy carried one of Tom's suitcases while he led the way to his apartment through streets littered with rubbish.

Tom's new home was on the second floor of a multi-leveled apartment building with two apartments on each landing. A stairway crisscrossed back and forth across the front of the building. At each level, residents could exit onto a balcony that provided a small, shared patio for relaxing.

"We have a large, living room/dining room combination," Guy said. Then he pointed to a small kitchen to the right and added, "I don't cook much, but everything in there works."

A long hallway led from the living room to two bedrooms and a large bathroom in the rear. "I've used the second bedroom as a storage area," Guy said. "There's a single bed, a four-drawer dresser and chest of drawers. None match, but they're functional."

"The room is fine," Tom said.

Guy said, "The rent is five hundred dollars per month. I have prayed for someone to help with the payments. The Lord truly works in mysterious ways."

"I can afford it," Tom said. "Thanks again."

Guy smiled and said, "I'll haul my junk out and you can move in."

After the switch was completed, Tom's stomach rumbled and he asked, "Where do we eat?"

"My treat," Guy said. "There's a great little bistro down the street."

As Guy and Tom walked into the restaurant, where most customers were black or Hispanic, a few heads turned. As he ignored the stares, Tom thought, *"I'll have to get used to being the only white man around. Come hell or high water, I'm here for the duration."*

The first night, the constant wailing of emergency vehicles, combined with loud noises from the surrounding ocean of humanity, resounded, echoed and reverberated off the walls of the concrete and steel canyons of the city.

The next morning Guy asked, "How did you sleep?"

Tom looked worn. He yawned and said, "I didn't."

Guy asked, "Have you ever tried ear plugs?"

During the next few weeks, Tom met most of the other tenants in his building. He enjoyed his talks with the neighbors next door, Irene and Paul Snyder. Paul was a laid back kind of guy who worked as a mechanic in a garage across town, while Irene was a clerk in a hardware store.

One night, Tom asked, "Have you noticed an aroma of liquor on Irene's breath?"

Guy replied, "Yeah, but it's none of our business."

Late another night, Tom said, "I heard Paul and Irene arguing last night."

"Get used to it," Guy replied. "Don't attempt to save everyone, Tom. Take them one at a time."

Tom especially enjoyed his work with the children of Harlem, who gradually grew accustomed to his ways and accepted Tom for what he was – a servant of God. Although he didn't have the same rapport with them as Guy, Tom attained an easy truce.

He soon fell into the mission's routine. They opened the center early in the morning and ended the day late in the evening. The days passed by quickly. In mutual arrangement, Tom and Guy grabbed meals when and where they could. They usually ate most evening meals in the bistro down the block.

One evening in March, following a long day's work, Tom retired early. Just after he reached the point of slumber, he was awakened when he heard glass break outside his window. *"What's going on?"* he wondered.

Tom arose and looked out the front window to see Irene in a drunken state on the street below. She staggered about while she frowned at a broken bottle of liquor she apparently dropped on the pavement. He heard her growl like a cat that spilled its milk, "Damn it!"

As Irene stumbled up the stairway, across the porch and into her apartment, Tom felt the pain of a headache from the stress at the mission. He walked into the kitchen and reached into the cabinet above the sink for an aspirin bottle.

Suddenly he heard a loud pop. At the same time, something struck Tom's arm and chest with such force he was thrown violently against the wall that led into the living room. In an instant, the small room was filled with a white powder that caused him temporarily blindness.

With the breath knocked from his lungs, Tom stumbled into the room and sat down on the couch. After he wiped the grit from his eyes, Tom glanced down at his body to find his hair; t-shirt, right arm and the upper portion of his body were covered with a thin film of a mixture of plaster and sugar.

"Where did it come from?"

White powdery dust hung heavily in the air of the kitchen area/ dining area and the living room. A thin layer of the same material covered almost all the furniture. Finally, when Tom began to breathe normally again, he checked his arm and body for damage. Near his elbow, blood slowly flowed from several small puncture wounds that resembled tiny volcanoes, and there was pain from his chest.

He removed his T-shirt and found several more similar wounds on his chest. *"What the Devil caused these?"*

Suddenly, the front door burst open. Tom glanced up to see Paul in the doorway. He looked frightened and said, "My God, Tom, I'm sorry - my gun went off accidentally. How bad are you injured?"

Guy, who had been asleep in his bedroom, ran into the room, stared at the white dust floating in the air and asked, "What happened?" Then he saw the blood on Tom's arm and remarked, "Tom, you're bleeding."

Tom glanced into the kitchen to see the dust had begun to dissipate. In the wall over the stove, there was a large hole approximately four inches across. A light from Paul's apartment was shining through. Then the answer struck him. *"I've been shot."*

Paul continued to explain the circumstances of the accident, but Tom couldn't focus on his words. He realized he might be going into shock, so he attempted to relax and get his heart rate back to normal.

Guy went into the bathroom, returned with a wet towel and used it to mop Tom's brow. Then he attempted to remove some of the mixture of sugar and plaster. Finally, after not making much headway, he said, "We should get you to a hospital, Tom."

Guy nodded to Paul, who rushed to the phone and dialed 9-1-1.

Several minutes later, they heard the wail of an ambulance. But with the constant sound of emergency vehicles in this area, they couldn't be sure this one was for Tom. While they waited, Guy asked, "Why were you working on a gun at this time of night, Paul? How could you not know the weapon was loaded?"

Paul offered two or three explanations, but none of them were convincing. Tom thought, *"I believe Paul's lying."* At the same time he wondered, *"How bad am I injured?"*

With a screech of brakes and the slowly decreasing wail of a siren, an ambulance pulled up outside the building. Two EMS attendants rushed up the stairway and into the apartment.

One young black man wrapped a blood pressure cuff around Tom's arm, while the other began to clean Tom's wounds with a swab.

As the EMS attendants worked, Tom counted the holes in his arm and chest. There were six in his arm. They included a very painful one located near his elbow. His chest was riddled with eight additional small holes. *"My extended arm must have kept me from being struck in the face by pellets. That may have saved my sight."*

Slowly, Tom looked around the apartment and the mess created by the shotgun blast. He noticed a plastic sugar canister lying near the far wall of the living room. It was torn and shattered. A small trace of sugar remained in the bottom. The force of the shotgun blast had thrown it thirty feet. *"That's where the majority of the shotgun pellets hit. Thank God I refilled the container this morning."*

Tom returned his attention to the attendant who had taken his blood pressure and pulse. The young man said, "It doesn't appear anything vital was damaged, but we'll transport you to the nearest hospital for an examination. There'll be a charge for the ambulance. Are you agreeable?"

Guy broke into their conversation and said, "Yes, of course. We have insurance. I'm sure if they don't pay, Paul will."

Guy stared at Paul and waited until Paul nodded and said, "Of course; it was my fault."

Although Tom assured the attendants that he could walk to the ambulance, as a precaution, they loaded him onto a gurney and carried him down the stairs.

At the hospital, Tom was rushed into the emergency room, where his wounds were cleaned and painted with an orange substance that stung like the dickens. A young black doctor examined him and ordered X-rays of Tom's arm and chest.

With a worried expression on his face, Tom asked. "Will you cut the pellets out?"

The doctor chuckled. "No, they only do that in the movies. In time, the pellets will calcify and you'll never know they're there."

After the X-rays were taken, the doctor read them and said, "You're in good health, but we'll keep you overnight for observation."

The next morning, when Tom was released, he called Guy, who came as quickly as possible with a clean change of clothes.

The arrived at their apartment to find Paul had stuffed a pink towel into the hole in the wall between their two residences. Guy had cleaned up the mess, and aside from the damaged sugar container that set on the countertop as a reminder of a close call, there was no evidence of the accident.

Tom didn't realize how much the near miss on his life had affected him. He attempted to continue functioning at the mission, but any loud noise made him nervous.

At the apartment, every time he had to go into the kitchen, he experienced anxiety. After completing whatever task took him there, Tom almost ran from the room. Guy noted Tom's nervousness and said. "You're certainly jumpy anymore."

Tom attempted to grin, but a frown flickered at the edge of his lips. "I realize now how lucky I was. I wonder if the landlord will ever repair the hole."

Guy frowned and said, "Probably when pigs learn to fly."

As the days passed, Tom thought he would get better, but it didn't happen. Instead, he became moody and more depressed. Guy noticed the changes in Tom's demeanor and asked, "Is there anything I can do?"

"Thanks Guy, but I have to work this out myself."

For the next two weeks, Tom's attitude didn't change. If anything, his feelings of despair grew worse. Finally, Guy spoke to their bishop, who advised Tom to take two weeks vacation with his parents in Bermuda.

Lately, while thinking back on his life as a priest, Tom was becoming disillusioned.

"I don't feel I've accomplished the goals I set when I first decided to become a man of the cloth. Perhaps the priesthood isn't my calling after all. I'm having doubts again, and they're serious. Perhaps two weeks with mom and dad will help. It couldn't hurt, could it?"

Chapter 9

Belem, Brazil

Today was a lovely day for an explosion.

Frank Moses, a partner in the demolition company tasked with this job looked across the room at the co-owner, Harold "Red" James, and said, "Do one more security check, Red. Then we'll blow this puppy."

Red replied, "Roger, Boss." Then he picked up his radio and spoke into the microphone, "All stations check in."

They both listened carefully as eight guards and spotters made their reports. Red and Frank were pleased to hear there were no intruders or protestors inside the buildings they were about to implode.

Rumors had circulated that the Green Peace organization and/or other protest groups might attempt to occupy the buildings to prevent their destruction.

An undercover informer told them, "They're concerned about the amount of pollution associated with the imploding of such a large complex."

"We don't need any delays," Red said. "The spring rains will begin soon."

Frank nodded in agreement. "That's all we need – mud after two months of work."

The job entailed imploding a complex of six buildings that formerly housed a hospital. The tallest building stood seven stories tall. All others were at least three stories high.

"It's one of the most complicated shots I ever attempted," Frank added. "Let's get on with it. Raise the flag, Red."

Frank watched as Red quickly lowered a white flag, unhooked it, put a bright red flag in its place and raised the signal to the top of the pole.

Behind them, Frank heard a murmur of expectancy and excitement run through a crowd of people that was gathered to observe the forthcoming explosions.

Red shook his head slightly and said, "Man, the cops have their hands full attempting to control all the people who want to see the shot."

"They've done a fantastic job of keeping them away from any falling debris," Frank added. Then he asked, "Are you ready buddy?"

After he gave Frank the thumbs up sign, Red crossed himself and silently asked for a blessing of safety and success.

Over a loud speaker, Frank bellowed, "Fire in the hole!" Then he flipped a protective cover back from his master firing switch and pushed down on a red button with his right thumb.

At the bottom of the buildings, a series of small explosions appeared and then continued to move almost as if in slow motion throughout the complex. Each one appeared to grow in power. Then, even louder blasts reverberated throughout the area.

At first, nothing happened. The buildings shuddered in protest and everyone could see small white clouds of smoke where explosions had taken place.

Then slowly, but inevitably, the buildings collapsed toward the middle, floor by floor, while the walls fell inward and slipped toward the center. As they disintegrated, huge columns of dust rose over the entire complex.

Red grinned in appreciation and said. "For the small amount of explosives we used, it's a massive display of power,"

"Yeah," Frank agreed. "I never get tired of seeing the results."

In the sudden silence that followed, they heard shouts and the applause of pleased spectators. Several onlookers broke through the police barricades to collect small pieces of the buildings' remains as souvenirs.

Red walked over to Frank, shook his hand and said, "It was another great job, partner." Then, while shaking his head in disbelief that things had gone so well, Red added, "I'm happy to see this job done. I thought for sure the protestors would screw things up at the last minute."

"If there was anyone inside, they're flatter than a pancake now," Frank replied.

Red asked, "What's next on our agenda?"

"I'm about to take a well-deserved break as I head up the Amazon to visit friends and fish," Frank said. "I'll be back in two weeks and we'll see then what else we can find to blow up or down."

Red yawned loudly and said, "I'm going to bed and sleep for two weeks. I've worried about this shot so long I haven't slept in a month."

Frank grinned and replied, "Then we'll both have much-needed rests. I'll check in when I return."

Before the dust was completely settled, Frank noted the cleanup crews had begun to move their equipment into place. He thought, *"The developer of the condominiums to be built on this property isn't wasting any time. With the money from this project, Red and I could retire. Sometimes I feel like I should hang it up, but the thrill of watching another building go down is too much to resist."*

While he walked to his vehicle, Frank thoughts were centered on the past and how he came to be in Brazil and using the name of Frank Moses.

His real name was Ben Hillman. Born in Spokane, Washington fifty-seven years ago, Ben cut his teeth on dynamite. His father, Frank was a "powder monkey" who drilled holes in a rock quarry, loaded them with dynamite and then proceeded to blow the place up, (in a controlled fashion).

By the time Ben was a teenager, he had graduated from dynamite to nitroglycerin. His father taught him everything there was to know about powder and liquid explosives.

During his off duty moments, Ben's uncle, Fred, a reformed robber who specialized in safes, also taught Ben everything there was to know about safe cracking.

After Fred was apprehended and served five years in prison, he turned his illegal knowledge into legal profit when he was hired as a consultant to a safe company to help them build stronger, more burglarproof safes. (Of course, as a hobby and behind their backs, Fred devised his own clever ways to defeat his inventions.)

Naturally, he passed these techniques on to his favorite nephew. Fred and Ben spent many a happy hour as they blew apart safes in a field behind Fred's farmhouse on the edge of town. Everyone knew Fred worked with explosives, so there were no questions asked of the periodic detonations that took place on his property.

Shortly after he graduated from high school, Ben decided not to pursue a college education. Instead, he worked for a short time with his father. In his spare time he kept up with his uncle's latest inventions.

Then Korea came along.

Drafted and sent overseas in 1952, Ben served as a rifleman until his expertise in explosives was discovered. During the advance in the other direction, (commonly known as a retreat elsewhere), Ben was called upon to destroy U.S. equipment to prevent it from falling into the enemy's hands.

As a result of Ben's performance of these duties, he was transferred to his company's explosives and demolition team, where he was assigned to mine and destroy roads and bridges, often under enemy fire. He performed these missions bravely, and for a short time Ben actually found war to be fun.

Then the conflict wasn't amusing anymore. One of Ban's team members didn't check his work properly and the explosives detonated prematurely. The idiot's action resulted in injury to six team members and death to three others. Ben was one of the injured; his left leg was broken in two places. The fool at fault was one of those killed.

The broken limb took Ben out of action and he was transferred to Japan for medical treatment. By the time he recovered, the conflict was over.

When Ben returned home, he found his father had retired from the quarry, and his uncle was once more residing behind bars. It appeared a large payroll at a nearby factory was too much for Fred to resist. The unique techniques used to blow the safe led the cops to Fred's door.

With the massive unemployment due to the sudden influx of veterans as they returned from Korea, jobs were few and far between.

Ben thought, *"What is a young man supposed to do?"*

Naturally, he turned to robbing safes, but not the large type his uncle favored. Instead, he specialized in smaller wall units full of money and jewels, and found his niche in life by robbing the stars of Hollywood.

In 1954, Ben moved to Los Angeles and became lost in the multitude of people there. He rented a rundown apartment, spent what money he owned on tools of his trade and soon became an expert lock-picker. Before long, Ben found he could bypass or defeat completely any security system in the world.

To his amazement, Ben found most rich people in town didn't have security systems. Instead, they depended on hidden safes to keep their valuables secure.

Ben read the local gossip columns to discover which movie star was where. If they were out of town, he would strike. With each robbery, his expertise grew. Ben soon discovered every place where a safe could be hidden.

To become invisible at night, Ben wore a dark black turtle neck shirt and mask with large eye holes. To prevent leaving any fingerprints behind, he wore skin-tight, latex gloves.

First, he would drill small holes in the safes and then used the latest in plastic explosives to surgically remove each door with a minimum amount of noise. Quickly, Ben became a master of his trade.

He found a fence for the jewelry, but kept the cash he stole and the money he received from the jewels in several safe deposit boxes throughout the city.

Soon, due to his elusiveness, the police and press dubbed Ben "the Artful Dodger".

Then one night fate stepped in.

A well known movie star, Daniel Steel was rumored to be headed for Paris on the Concord. Since Ben knew where Daniel resided, he planned his robbery for the day the star was due to depart for France.

After breaking into the house with ease, Ben found a safe hidden behind a large painting in the living room. Everything appeared to be normal, so he drilled four small holes in the face and was packing them with plastic explosives when the overhead lights came on. Before Ben could duck behind the furniture, a young man and woman walked into the living room and saw him.

"What are you doing here?" the man asked.

Although Ben instantly recognized Daniel Steel from his films, he didn't know who the young woman was.

With murderous intent written in his eyes, Daniel advanced toward Ben. Ben imagined Daniel must be living out one of his scripts. He outweighed the actor by thirty pounds and doubted Daniel really knew how to fight the way Ben was taught in the Army.

Daniel threw a punch, which Ben easily blocked. Then he feinted with his left hand, drove his right hand into his opponent's chest, and the actor dropped like a stone.

The woman screamed and attempted to run, but her high heels did her in. In her fright, one caught in a rug and she fell to her knees.

Ben caught her easily, forced her to the ground, coveredeHH her mouth with his hand and used a small arm cover from a chair to stuff into her mouth. She stared in disbelief and fear while she watched him tear a strip of cloth from her blouse to tie the gag in place.

Then Ben snatched a cord from a telephone extension, ripped it from the wall and wrapped her arms and legs tightly.

Once she was secured, Ben turned his attention to the unconscious movie star.But Daniel wasn't unconscious; he was dead!

At the autopsy, it would later be discovered that Daniel suffered from a heart condition. Ben's blow stopped his heart and killed him.

Ben was horrified. At first he didn't know what to do. But then, he knew there wasn't another viable choice, so he decided to flee. *"The woman won't be able to identify me, but it's no longer a game. I've outsmarted myself this time."*

Quickly, Ben gathered all his equipment and left the house. There was no way the police could find him, but he knew the pressure would be increased. From a minor irritant of a cat burglar, the authorities were now faced with a murderer.

The next day the newspaper headlines blared, "Playboy Movie Star Murdered in Home".

After the plane developed problems, the Concord flight was cancelled, which prompted Daniel's return to his mansion.

Over the next few days, Ben removed the money from his safe deposit boxes and converted it into cashier's checks. He knew a man who specialized in phony passports and other identification, so for ten thousand dollars, Ben purchased a complete new identity package. He chose the name of Frank Moses from the combined first names of his father and grandfather.

As soon as Ben received his new identification, he bought a one way ticket to Brazil.

"I'm leaving town," Ben told his landlord and gave him a phony forwarding address. He used a phony name and disposed of his burglar tools and other equipment through pawn shops. As much as he hated to part with his Cadillac, Ben placed an ad in the local newspaper asking a ridiculously low price. He sold the vehicle the next day.

Pressure was building on the police to solve the murder of Daniel Steel. The public was outraged, (or so the newspapers in LA said). Ben believed it was probably the movie studio's PR department making waves.

The next day, he departed, headed for Belem, Brazil, a city he picked from a map. The large town was on the coast, which provided easy access to the Amazon River or other parts of the country. *"If I don't find work there, I'll search elsewhere."*

Ben secreted his cashier's checks in various places in his luggage and hoped they would pass through customs as just another piece of paper. *"It's far better then attempting to take cash into the country."*

So here Ben was, in Brazil for the duration.

Upon his arrival in Brazil, Frank Moses was hired as a construction worker, a job that paid a fair wage, but it was nothing compared to the money he made from robbery. But, that was not an option here. Over the next few months he deposited his cashier's checks one at a time in different bank accounts. No one ever questioned where his money came from.

While working his way upward in the construction firm, Frank made contacts with other workers. That was how he met Red.

In idle talk, Frank told Red of his explosive background and knowledge of the field. Red was currently involved in a project requiring a demolitions expert, so he took a chance and decided to test Frank's ability.

When Frank proved he knew his business, Red hired him permanently. Soon they became partners and opened their own demolition business. Fate smiled on them and they both had become wealthy. With Frank's ill-gotten gains in the bank and his new riches, there was no reason for him to consider a renewed life of crime.

To Frank's relief, the robbery and murder of Daniel Steel slowly faded into obscurity.

Now Frank was on his way upriver to see his friends, Miguel and Tim. He had enjoyed the small adventure his friend, Jose involved him in a few weeks ago.

"Saving the priest's life should make up in some small way for taking the life of a movie star. Perhaps the good Lord will place a plus mark in my ledger to balance the minus one from Mister Steel. I hope so."

Chapter 10

In late March, Tim asked Catherine, "Guess who's coming to dinner?"

Catherine didn't have a clue, so she answered with her own question, "Martha Stewart?"

Tim laughed. "No, silly – it's Frank Moses, our buddy who is frightened of crocodiles. He's coming to fish with Miguel and me. Me, reluctantly, I might add."

She asked, "Are you still afraid of those little Piranhas? What happened to my big, bad medicine man?"

"You're in fine form this morning," Tim said. "Anyway, Frank will arrive tomorrow. Jose will fly him here from Belem. It seems Frank blew up a big hospital complex there yesterday and needs to get away to relax."

Catherine grinned. "That's our Frank; he's always blowing something up or down. He's had a lot of work lately. No wonder he's tired. I hope you and Miguel don't wear him out fishing."

"There's no chance," Tim said. "I'm going along as Frank's friend. Jose saved me the last time. Maybe he'll need me to go see our lawyer again and I can skip out of this fishing trip too."

"You better behave and go along with the boys," Catherine said. "Miguel will think you're attempting to avoid him. He loves to fish. Don't be a spoilsport. He won't let the Piranha eat you."

The next day Frank and Jose arrived in his two man helicopter.

Tim watched them land and thought, *"I wonder how Jose wrangled a free day from his new charter boss, Fernando. As far as I know, Jose still hasn't said anything to him about our property."*

After they walked to the landing pad at the edge of town, Catherine and Tim waited to greet their guests. Tim knew Jose preferred to sleep in his copter, while Frank would stay with Miguel and his family.

Catherine greeted Frank as a long lost brother. She gave him a hug and a kiss on the cheek. "It's nice to see you again, Frank. Tim tells me you've been blowing up things again."

"Yeah, I have and I'm tired. Sometimes I wonder if I'm in the right career field. Then I remember the fun I had shooting off fireworks for your friend and mine. I wouldn't have missed that for the world."

Jose smiled and asked, "Should I tell him, Tim, or would you rather?"

"You go ahead, Jose," Tim said. "You got such a kick out of it when you told me. I know Frank will enjoy your story."

"What story?" Frank asked.

"The tale of logs that shared the riverbank while you shot off those fireworks," Jose said. "We saw them in the light. They weren't logs, my frightened friend. Those were crocs."

Frank's mouth dropped open. "Crocs, – and you didn't say anything? Thanks a lot buddy. I knew I heard noises in the brush. You'll never get me on another of your adventures again. I don't want to be eaten by any animal."

Catherine asked, "How long can you stay, Jose?"

"Just this afternoon - Fernando has me on a short leash."

Frank was exuberant about the project he and Red just completed. "We dropped the sucker just as I told them we would."

"You always do good work, Frank," Tim said.

Jose was also full of news. "I told Fernando about our lake. He wasn't too surprised about the possibility that he might find oil there. I believe he was aware I knew where the oil-bearing mud on my landing pad came from.

"Fernando also wasn't too happy at being kept in the dark, but he understood the need for secrecy. I took him for a ride over the lake and Fernando was very excited at the sight.

"I hovered over the goop while Fernando lowered some vials on a long pole to get samples. Two days ago, he sent them to his company by express mail.

"Fernando says he should have a report within two weeks. The only way to know for sure is to sink a well and see what comes up the pipe."

"What did he say about the cost of drilling the well?" Tim asked. "Is his company interested in making an offer for the land, or will they want us to drill our own?"

"We didn't discuss it," Jose said. "Fernando says to wait until the report comes back. Then he'll meet with his boss and let us know."

Tim said, "I'm glad he wasn't upset. I suppose he's pleased to find oil. It has to be a thrill for a chemical engineer. And if an oil well comes in, that may earn him a promotion."

Frank broke in and asked, "So, when do we go fishing?" He thought, *"I'm tired of hearing about oil and talking business. I'm here to relax. Nothing is going to stand in my way of a good time for the next two weeks."*

"We go out early tomorrow morning," Miguel said. "At last, I'll get Tim in my boat. You interrupted our last fishing trip, Jose. Don't do it again. Business can wait until the next two weeks are over."

"I second that notion," Frank said. "But on another subject, where can a guy get a cold beer around here? It was a long, hot flight. For the price he charges, you'd think a good charter pilot would have cold beer or two on board."

Jose grinned at Frank's comments and said. "I don't drink and fly."

"One cold brew coming up," Tim said. "Follow me to Catherine's house. He thought, *"Even if it means I'm going out on the Amazon in another canoe, it's good to have friends together again."*

Hamilton, Bermuda

The annual April showers arrived right on schedule. But George hoped the rain would dissipate by the time of the annual Floral Parade.

Various organizations always sponsored floats for the parade. One was the Odd Fellows' Club, of which George was a member in good standing. Every year, they produced and entered a silly, satirical float. This year the men would don women's garb, put on an abundance of exaggerated makeup and dance to rock music.

"It'll be hilarious," George said.

Since Pearl knew of George's earlier experiences, she said, "I see no reason to doubt your statement. I've seen your past presentations. Your members are really odd."

So far, the events of the New Year were fairly eventful. Tom wrote to say he was extremely busy with the youth of his district.

Pearl thought, *"I'm so happy Tom's letters are so upbeat,"*

When Tim phoned, Pearl reported, "Kate's progressing nicely in school. She maintained at least a B average the first semester and has improved her grades this past six weeks. She seems to have adjusted to her new environment. You should see the house on weekends, Tim. It's always crowded with her friends."

"The government found a replacement teacher," Tim said. "She'll report at the end of April. Catherine hopes to sell her house to the new teacher. Then she'll spend a week introducing whoever shows up to the students and assisting with the transition. We plan to leave Brazil in late May."

Pearl continued her thoughts. *"I hope I can talk Tim and Catherine into waiting until June to be married."*

"Lorna and Jock are planning a June wedding," Pearl told Tim. "After Lorna returned to Peoria late last year, she secured her release. The hospital was not pleased with her decision to resign and move to Bermuda, so as a concession, she agreed to stay on for two weeks until a replacement could be found."

"I'm happy for them," Tim said.

When Lorna returned, she confided to Pearl that she didn't have any heirlooms of any kind, family or otherwise. She only shipped a few boxes of clothes and personal items she felt she couldn't part with. The remainder was sold at a garage sale or donated to the Salvation Army.

For two months, Lorna lived with the Fitchs. One third of the nights she spent at Jock's home, where they made love and loved each other. After a while, Lorna finally faced up to the fact that people knew she and Jock were co-habitating.

After she explained her reasoning and thanked the Fitchs for their kindness and generosity, at the end of March, Lorna moved into her lover's home permanently.

Since Lorna's departure, Pearl missed her, but understood her feelings. *"Love knows no boundaries."*

Now busily employed at Hamilton hospital, Lorna was the supervisor of the nursing staff and served as head nurse in the OR.

"She and I performed several operations together," George said. "I'm impressed with her skills."

The Jessops had moved into their new home, were very happy in Bermuda and now were considered a part of the Islands' upper society. Marsha joined Pearl's bridge club and they enjoyed weekly luncheons with other women of the community.

Since Bob retired, he found his golf game had steadily improved. Within three months of being able to play three to four times a week, he consistently shot in the middle eighties.

Due to, (or perhaps in spite of), George's instructions, Bob once shot a seventy-nine. It was cause for yet another celebration and party at the Jessops' home.

Pearl's thoughts and plans were interrupted by the ringing of the phone. To her surprise, she found herself speaking with Tom.

She asked, "How are you, dear?"

"I'm not doing too well, mother. I had a small accident three weeks ago and it's bothered me since. When I see you, I'll explain. The bishop believes I should take two weeks vacation, so I'll arrive in Bermuda on the tenth of April at ten-thirty a.m."

"You sound melancholy," Pearl said. "Are you sure you're all right?"

"I'm basically fine, mother. I just need time away from my duties here. I'll enjoy your home cooking."

She asked, "Is there anything special you'd like me to prepare for dinner the day you arrive?"

"No, I can't think of anything. Whatever you fix will be fine. I'm tired of eating out all the time. Tell dad I said hello. I love you and will see you on the tenth."

After he hung up, Pearl sat and stared at the phone. *"It isn't like Tom to be so short with me. There must be something that's bothering him deeply to put him in such a foul mood. I'm pleased he's on his way home – I've missed him."*

As George came into the kitchen, he asked, "Who was on the phone?"

"Tom; he'll be coming home for two weeks. He didn't sound well. Something is bothering him. He said he had a small accident."

George looked concerned and asked. "What kind?"

"Tom didn't say, but he did say he would tell us about his problem when he arrives. I hope it wasn't anything serious. He was doing so well in his new work. All Tom needs is one more disappointment and I swear; he'll resign the priesthood."

"You're jumping to conclusions without knowing the facts," George said. "Wait till Tom arrives and tells us his story."

Chapter 11

L orna didn't believe she was being nosy. It was "that time of the month" and this morning she experienced a bad case of cramps, so she called in sick and remained in bed until Jock departed for his weekly round of golf with David and George. Since he expected to return home with several more English pounds in his pocket than when he departed, Jock was in a good mood.

David and George were easy prey for a man who played golf almost every other day. The trio played for a pound for winning each hole; two pounds for a birdie; five pounds for the best score after nine holes and ten pounds for the best score after they completed the round.

Jock grinned and said. "When it comes to earning money by playing golf, I love suckers."

Lorna lay in bed and wondered what she would do when her cramps eased, while she also thought about her lover. It was then she realized, for all the time they spent together, she didn't know what Jock did for a living. *"It never occurred to me to ask."*

In a passing conversation, George mentioned something regarding the fact that Jock received monthly checks from his parents in Germany. But until now, George's comments hadn't registered.

"Where does Jock get the money to live so high on the hog? Five days a week, I go to work and leave him either in bed or seated at the table and drinking his coffee. I'm shocked I haven't questioned his ability to take life easy every day."

Lorna's thoughts led her to Jock's desk in the den. Again, she didn't believe she was being nosy. She was just "curious".

"There is a difference," she thought.

After she opened the first drawer, she peered inside. But before she attempted to move any documents within, Lorna took note of their position. *"I don't want Jock to know I was curious."*

The first few documents were letters in German. Since she didn't understand the language, Lorna laid them aside and continued her curious search. A few minutes later, she struck pay dirt. *"Jock has a file of deposit slips from a local bank. Each is for the same amount – two thousand pounds."*

Lorna turned the slips over and discovered they each reflected the same item, one check per month drawn on the Becker Hotel chain with headquarters in Dusseldorf, Germany. *"I've never heard of the firm, but the name is the same as Jock's last name. What's his connection to this hotel chain? He never mentioned it."*

Carefully, Lorna replaced the documents and attempted to insure they appeared to be in the same order that she found them when she began her curious search.

"Now I know more than I did, but still, it's a puzzle. Should I ask Jock about the Becker Hotel chain or should I keep my mouth shut until he's ready to tell me?

"If I ask, he'll know I've been prying into his personal affairs. That may be all right after we're married, but I doubt he would appreciate my curiosity. He might think I was being nosy."

She decided to wait. *"Where and how Jock makes his money is his business. In a few weeks it will also be mine. Perhaps that's best."*

Before Lorna finished her curious search of the desk, she opened the middle drawer and found Jock's personal check book inside.

Astonished, Lorna read the balance contained on the last page. *"It's over twenty-five thousand pounds!"*

Now she was furious with herself. *"My nosiness, (Yes, that's what it was, clear and simple), has caused more questions than it provided answers."*

Lorna's mind raced a mile a minute. *"I wonder if Jock's involved in something illegal. I pray not. If there's one thing I know, he's honest."*

Her second thought was almost impossible to believe. *"Is Jock actually rich? How could he be and not say anything? If he is, how will it affect our future together? Why would he withhold such information?*

"Does he think I'm a gold digger? Jock knows I came to Bermuda to search for a wealthy husband. Am I a fool to believe in him?"

With so many questions on her mind, and no answers in sight, Lorna's head pounded until it ached. As her stomach cramped again, she threw herself down on the bed, wept into her pillow and cried aloud, "Good Lord, why was I so nosy?"

Chapter 12

Becker's Conglomerate, Dusseldorf, Germany

When Dieter Becker's executive secretary, Emily informed him there was a long distance phone call from Bermuda on line three, Dieter experienced a feeling of dread. He was positive the phone call would be from some governmental official in Bermuda, who was calling to inform him of his only son's death.

Dieter glanced out the window and remembered it was the middle of April. Weeks ago the last snow storm of the past winter came and was now melted. Outside in several flower boxes, the blossoms of spring had begun to push their way through the earth.

"Who wants to prepare for the funeral of a son in the springtime?"

For five years, Dieter had tolerated Jocquin's strange and defiant behavior. Three different times, he dispatched his associates to Bermuda to seek out his son and attempt to sway him from drinking himself to death. Since the demise of his wife, Jocquin was dispirited and remorseful. He rejected all their pleas.

Jock, as he preferred to be addressed, continued to wallow in self-pity until he lost his common sense.

When Emily saw Dieter's despondent face, she smiled and said, "It's your son, Jocquin."

Dieter was astonished. "And he's phoning me? I can't believe my ears."

In his haste, Dieter pushed the wrong telephone button twice.

"Line three," Emily said.

Finally he hit the correct button and asked, "Jocquin?"

"Good afternoon, Father. Surprise; it's your long lost, stupid boy, sober and well. Can you believe it?"

His stunned father asked again, "Jocquin? How are you son?"

"Sober and well," Jock repeated.

Dieter thought, *"Is it possible after all this time? If his statement is true, that's a miracle."*

"Wonderful," he said. "That's great news."

"Thank you, Father. And, there is more good news. To your great surprise and mine, I'm sober and intend to remain that way."

"Thank God. That is wonderful news, my boy. What brought you to your senses?"

"Her name is Lorna and I know you'll love her. To add to your surprise, I'm engaged to be married again."

Now Dieter's emotions were completely overwhelmed by Jock's latest statement. He asked, "Engaged? When did this happen? Who is Lorna?"

In a few short minutes, Dieter went from being afraid to answer the phone, to feeling flabbergasted by his son's announcements. The news was almost more than his heart could take. For a few seconds Dieter felt faint and couldn't speak.

An anxious Jock asked, "Are you still there Father?"

Dieter took a few deep breaths and soon regained his composure. Then he replied, "Yes, Son, I am. Your news startled me and took my breath away. What are your plans for the immediate future?"

There was still concern in Jock's voice when he said, "Since she wishes to be a June bride, Lorna and I are to be married here in Bermuda. It's an old American custom. Lorna is from the state of Illinois and a nurse at the hospital in Hamilton where we met. It's a long story, which I'll be happy to relate to you and mother when we return to Germany."

"You plan to return home?" Dieter asked. "I am amazed. Your Lorna must have had quite an affect on you. Your mother and I will welcome her with open arms. How soon will you return?"

Jock said, "I haven't told Lorna of my position, vis-à-vis the business. I assume I'm still the heir apparent to your throne?"

Although Jock couldn't see, Dieter nodded his head. "Yes, you are and happily so. Your mother and I nearly gave up hope of your returning to Germany and the business. You don't know how happy your news will make her."

"Give mother my love and apologies for my being such a wayward son. I owe you both much more than I can say for still believing in me after my stupidity of the past five years.

Then Jock paused to take a breath. "But back to Lorna – I haven't told her I may some day soon be a millionaire. I didn't want to shock her. She has no idea of our company or the family fortune. She made me see I was wasting my life and Lori wouldn't want me to be a drunk in her memory. My fiancée is one special lady."

"If Lorna brought you back to your senses, we owe her a great deal of gratitude," Dieter said. "Bring her home to meet your mother as soon as possible."

Then a stroke of genius came to Dieter's mind. "Better yet, we'll fly to Bermuda for the wedding. I know when your mother hears the news; I won't be able to stop her."

Jock was all smiles. "That would be wonderful, Father."

Dieter also continued to smile. "Phone us when you have the details of your marriage confirmed. We'll make arrangements to arrive a week in advance and stay a few days afterward to see the islands."

"I will, Father. Thank you for your understanding over the past five years. I love you and will phone again soon. Goodbye."

In the doorway, Emily was also crying softly. She had remained nearby to hear the latest news from Bermuda and was relieved to hear the details of the conversation. She walked to Dieter's desk and handed her boss and good friend a small package of Kleenex.

Dieter looked up and said, "Thank you, Emily. What a wonderful day this is."

Chapter 13

On the advice of his bishop, Tom returned to Bermuda in the early part of April for a sabbatical.

As Tom came down the stairway from his plane and they could see him well, Pearl whispered to George, "Look at his eyes - they're bloodshot."

George noticed Tom's hands and said quietly, "His fingernails are bitten to the quick."

When they arrived home, Tom told them of his experiences in New York City; especially the shotgun blast late at night.With a small laugh, he said, "Now I don't expect to hear any more snide remarks about the amount of sugar I put in my tea."

It was the first time his parents had seen a smile on Tom's face since his arrival.

"You've heard the last of them," George said. "I'm glad you can joke about the matter."

As a mother concerned about her son, Pearl asked, "After your long plane ride, why don't you take a nice walk on the beach to relax and clear your mind?"

Tom nodded absentmindedly and replied, "At least the sand is returning to the beaches. That's a good sign."

Pearl patted Tom's back and said, "Take your time and enjoy the day."

George spoke up and said, "If you don't mind, Tom, I'd like to accompany you."

As they walked down the path to the beach, Tom put his arm around his father's shoulders and said, "This is like old times."

The sun reflected off small waves as they rubbed gently against the sandy beach below, while Tom thought of his life in Bermuda. He recalled his younger days and the richness of his life then. *"I'm still the same. Nothing has changed."*

When Tom and George returned from their walk, they found Kate was waiting. With a small cry, she ran up to Tom, threw her arms around his neck, kissed his cheek and hugged him tight for a few moments."It's so good to see you again, Uncle Tom. You've lost weight again. Grandma will have to work her magic to put the pounds back on your body and a smile on your face."

Tom stood back to admire Kate. *"Tim is a fortunate man to have such a wonderful daughter. The young man who claims Kate's heart will be a very lucky person."*

Then without waiting for his answer, Kate changed the subject. "Bryan is coming to visit for the spring break. Isn't that wonderful? Will you take us scuba diving, Uncle Tom?"

Tom shook his head slightly. "I don't know if I'm up to it, Kate. When does your young man arrive?"

"Four days from tomorrow. If you rest up and get your strength back, you'll be in great shape to show us some shipwrecks. Remember, you promised me."

Kate's joy and youth were contagious. In spite of feeling fatigued, Tom laughed. "All right, I'll do my best. You have a way of infecting people with your happiness, Kate. It's a joy to be near you. Bryan is a lucky guy."

"Wonderful, thank you," Kate cried.

Tom's thoughts were elsewhere. *"Perhaps the bishop knew what was good for me after all. Coming home was a wonderful idea. I feel better already and there are still thirteen days of my vacation remaining. What can go wrong?*

Ten nautical miles offshore, northeast of Belem, Brazil

The waters around Brazil were growing colder. It was time for the great white shark to move on.

Since the day it met and ate Marsha and Jim, the man killer had been denied the taste of human flesh. The ocean here was filled with an abundance of small fish and mammals that it easily caught and devoured, but the sweet taste of humans was ingrained in its small mind.

North was Bermuda and the hunting ground off the United States. It was a long trip, but during its winter vacation the shark had put on weight. By the time it reached the familiar killing fields off Bermuda, the beast would be sleek, and very hungry.

Chapter 14

Ten days into Frank's vacation, just as the fish had begun to bite for the day; Jose arrived overhead in his helicopter. The noise and downwash from the blades stirred up the water and scared away the fish.

Three tall white Egrets that had been standing on one leg each and waiting patiently for a bait fish to swim by were disturbed by the noise. Hurriedly, they spread their wings and lifted off into the sky.

As Jose smiled down at them from his lofty perch, Tim could tell Frank was ticked off. Tim took one look at the set of Frank's jaw, laughed and said, "You look like you could skin Jose alive, Frank. You'll have to get used to his arrival at always the wrong time. Jose didn't mean to disturb our fishing. It appears he doesn't know how to use a telephone."

First Frank shook his fist at Jose. Then he gave Jose the number one sign, but with the wrong finger.

Jose continued to smile down as if nothing was wrong. Finally he got the message and flew off toward the landing pad. The three fishermen watched as the copter disappeared behind some tall trees.

"I wonder what Jose wants this time," Miguel said. "If I didn't know better, Tim, I'd think you sent for him to get out of fishing again."

Tim shook his head. "No, I didn't. I've actually enjoyed the last few days. I wasn't aware there was such a wide variety of fish available in the Amazon. I don't want anything to stop us."

Frank still looked irritated when he said, "Well, the day is shot now. I suppose we should go find out what the big fat bird man wants. He really ticks me off."

"I had no idea," Tim said. "Especially after you told Jose he was number one in your book. You're a hard man to read, Frank. You hide your feelings well."

"Go ahead and laugh, but I'll figure out a way to get even with the fat man. Maybe I'll plant a grenade under his butt and blow off some blubber."

Tim continued to laugh. "My, Frank, your anger knows no bounds, does it?"

As they paddled across the small overflow pond where they were so rudely interrupted, Frank stewed in his own juices. When they entered the main channel of the Amazon, they found the current was moving along rapidly.

"It must have rained upstream," Miguel said. "Pull like the devil."

Their arms soon grew tired from the unusual exertion and they were glad to see the far riverbank approach. Miguel pulled the canoe close to shore and held it there while they rested from their labors.

When Frank and Tim regained their strength, Miguel led them as they paddled downriver to the landing strip area. Jose was seated on the dock, swinging his legs over the water and smoking a thin black cigar.

He waved casually to the three men and asked innocently, "How's the fishing? Catch any big ones?"

Frank displayed his middle finger again, and Jose roared with laughter.

By the time they tied up the canoe and gathered their rods and fishing gear, Frank had calmed down. Then Jose reached down to help them from the canoe. As he gave Frank a hand, Jose pretended to accidentally drop him into the water, but stopped short at the last moment.

"Not funny, Jose," Frank said, but he kept his temper.

Tim wanted to separate the two as soon as possible, so he asked, "What's up, Jose?"

Jose jerked his head toward town and Tim's place. His face looked sad when he said, "We need to talk. It's about our property."

"You're among friends, Jose. Tell me what your problem is."

With a half smile, Jose relented and said, "Fernando got the report and it indicates a strong possibility of oil on our land."

Tim said, "That sounds like good news. Why the long face?"

Jose continued to look downtrodden. "His company wants us to drill for oil before they'll come in as our partners. It's either that or they'll purchase our property outright. If we sell, we only retain ten percent of the mineral rights. I don't know what you want to do."

Tim shook his head. "It appears they might have us over a barrel, Jose. We don't have money to pay for drilling a well, and they know it. What kind of a purchase price did they offer?"

They were all surprised when a large smile spread across Jose's face and he replied, "Fernando says he can probably get the company to pay a half million for the property. I didn't know if that was a fair price or not. All I knew was it was a large return on our initial investment."

Tim nodded in agreement. "If there's oil there, it could be worth many millions of dollars. Everything depends on how big the field is. It could just be a small pool or a monster. Those are the chances you take when you wildcat an oil field."

Frank interrupted their conversation and said, "It sounds like you've done well already. It's none of my business, but I think you should take the money and run. That's a fantastic return on your investment without your having to do any work."

"I vote the same as Frank." Miguel said. "Cash in hand is worth more than a pool of oil in the jungle."

As Tim studied his friends and partner, he knew their advice was the correct road to take. What Fernando offered wasn't the millions he and Jose envisioned when they first agreed to this venture. However, it was a windfall of major proportions as far as Jose was concerned.

Tim's thoughts centered on Jose and his share of the fortune. *"Jose could live very well for the rest of his life on this amount of money.*

"But who am I kidding? Half of five hundred thousand is two hundred and fifty thousand. That's not chump change for a five thousand dollar investment on my part. What the devil, all I did was lend Jose a few dollars and play a role when we spoke to the lawyer. No, this isn't small potatoes at all."

Finally Tim made up his mind. "I tell you what, Jose. If our buddy Fernando 'believes' he can get them to pay a half a million, it means we can bargain with them for a little more.

"What do you say we go for seven hundred and fifty thousand and see what happens? What can they do; say 'No'? I'll bet some other oil company will meet our price."

Jose's eyes lit up. "Now you know why I asked you to be my partner," he said. "I like the way you think."

Tim asked, "When must we tell Fernando of our decision?"

Jose shrugged in reply. "He didn't set a date. Fernando said he wanted to speak to us both whenever we could find the time."

"Where is he? Can we reach him by radio? If so, let's call and set up an appointment. I'm free to fly anywhere to settle this matter."

"Fernando is at his company's office in Belem," Jose said. "If we radio or telephone, I know they can get in touch with him. Let's go to your place and see."

Tim agreed and the foursome left the riverbank, headed for Catherine's home. Tim's mind naturally switched to his lover.

"I liked Jose's reference to 'your place'. I think of Catherine's home as mine. Just a few more weeks and we'll make my home hers and our dreams will come true."

Catherine was conducting classes, so her home was vacant for their use. Jose contacted Fernando's company headquarters and left a message for Fernando to radio them in Obidos.

Now all they could do was await his call.

Miguel busied himself by cleaning the fish they caught before Jose interrupted their pleasure. He preferred to work alone. Miguel was a master at cleaning fish and owned what Tim believed were the sharpest knives in the world.

Catherine returned from school shortly and greeted them all with hugs and a peck on the cheek – even Tim. "You smell like fish. If you want a real kiss, go take a shower and change your clothes."

Frank heard her comments and made tracks for the bathroom.

After he filleted the fish, Miguel gave half the finished product to Tim for supper. "What you don't use, Catherine can freeze for later. I'm headed home. I'll see you tomorrow morning."

Tim let Frank shower first and when he finished, Tim quickly did the same. When both men reappeared in the living room, they smelled and looked much better.

They were kicking back with a cold beer when the radio crackled and Fernando's voice echoed, "Calling Jose."

Jose answered and between them, they worked out an arrangement to meet in Prainha at noon the next day.

Then Jose used the radio to call Father Mendez in Prainha. He asked the priest to tell his family he would remain in Obidos overnight. "Juanita expected me to stay. But I like to keep her assured of my safety. Thank you, Father."

Jose thought, *"When Juanita learns of the amount of money we may receive, she'll appreciate my efforts."*

Catherine said. "I have an extra cot in the schoolhouse, Jose."

Jose thanked her with a smile but then shook his head. "Thanks, but I prefer to sleep in my helo. It fits me well."

The next morning, in case something came up that might cause a delay; Tim packed an overnight bag with a change of clothes and toilet articles.

Catherine accompanied them to the landing strip, where she kissed Tim goodbye. Last night, after Jose departed, the two lovers talked over Fernando's proposition.

"I agree with your plan of action," she said. "You know the oil company will attempt to purchase your land for as little as possible. Where oil is concerned, their first offer is usually not the last. Stick with your original plan and be firm. I believe they'll meet your figure. I could be greedy and tell you to ask for a cool one million dollars, but why? Your percentage of profit is already phenomenal."

As they approached the landing strip, Jose pointed to his shack/office. "It appears Fernando is already here."

"It's a good sign he's early and waiting for us," Tim said. "He has to know there's oil on our property. Fernando may have told you he only believes it, but he has the report and will attempt to make the best deal he can. Play it cool and let me do the talking."

Tim and Jose walked from the helicopter to the office, while in a nearby group of trees, a gathering of raucous monkeys that were upset at being disturbed, chattered and screamed loudly at the intruders.

Jose laughed at their antics and said, "They sound ticked off."

Tim grinned and replied, "They're probably saying, 'there goes the neighborhood'."

Fernando greeted Tim as if he was a long lost cousin. He shook Tim's hand and patted him on the back. "It's good to see you again, Tim."

"It's a pleasure to meet you again, Fernando."

"Thank you, my friend. Should we get down to business? Tim asked, "Can we use your office, Jose?"

"Sure," Jose replied.

Tim glanced sideways at a subdued Jose. *"Once again, it appears Jose will be a man of very few words. Oh well, this is why he brought me in on this deal. I suppose I should earn my money."*

"Lead on," Tim said and bowed Fernando through the door ahead of him. Jose followed quietly behind. They pulled chairs away from the desk and sat down in a small circle in the middle of the room. Then Fernando asked, "Did Jose inform you of my company's proposition, Tim?"

Tim folded his arms across his chest and replied, "Yes, but your initial offer appears a little low. I'm sure you realize there may be a large amount of oil on our property. You also know we don't have the funds to allow us to drill our own well. Still, your company should be able to pay a bit more than five hundred thousand for our land."

Fernando smiled shyly and asked, "And how much more is a 'bit more'?"

"I believe eight hundred thousand would be a fair offer," Tim said.

When Tim glanced at Jose out of the corner of his eye, he saw Jose appeared to be concentrating on lighting another huge cigar, but his hand shook slightly.

"I didn't tell Jose I planned to start a little higher and bargain down to our original seven hundred and fifty thousand. I hope my offer didn't upset him."

Fernando acted as if he was surprised and asked, "Eight hundred thousand? I'm not sure my company would authorize me to agree to such an amount. As my first offer to you appeared a bit low, your offer seems a little high."

Tim chuckled loudly. "And how high is a 'little high'?"

Fernando grinned and asked in return, "How would the sum of seven hundred thousand appeal to you?"

Tim came back with another suggestion. "What if we split the difference and agree on seven hundred and fifty thousand?"

"You drive a hard bargain," Fernando said. "But enough, I agree."

"And ten percent of the mineral rights when the oil well comes in?"

"I have already agreed to that figure with your partner, Tim. A bargain is a bargain."

Tim chuckled again and said, "I still believe you and your company have made a better deal than Jose and I. This find should earn you a promotion, my friend."

"Perhaps it will," Fernando said. "It certainly can't hurt my chances. I'll have the transfer of ownership papers drawn up by our office within a week. Is that satisfactory?"

In response, Tim stuck out his hand to shake. "Sure; tell Jose when you want us there. He'll fly to Obidos and bring me to your office to sign the paperwork. It's been a great pleasure doing business with you. May we buy you dinner?"

Fernando nodded and said, "I'll be pleased to dine with you, but only if first you'll join me at the bar for a celebratory drink."

That evening, they enjoyed a wonderful dinner at Miss Lela's restaurant. She was pleased to see Tim again, as well as Jose. Tim had just introduced Fernando when a sudden storm interrupted their conversation. Rain pelted the tin roof overhead. It sounded like Rosie the riveter was hard at work.

Lela raised her voice to be heard over the din. "It looks like you'll be staying over. I'll have the padre radio Catherine to let her know you were detained."

"It appears my return flight will also be cancelled," Fernando said. "Do you have a room available, Miss Lela?"

"Of course," she said. "You'll have your old one tonight, Tim. I only have two other guests. Enjoy the rest of your meal. I'll see if it's raining into the kitchen."

At midnight Jose said, "I have to get home. I know Juanita will be upset with me because I stayed so late, but when she learns of the deal we made, she'll forgive me."

Early the next morning, Tim and Fernando parted company. Fernando's pilot radioed in to say he would arrive at eight thirty a.m., so there was barely time to enjoy a cup of coffee and toast before he departed.

On the way to Obidos, Jose radioed Catherine. She was waiting at the landing pad to greet them.

"You should have seen Tim," Jose said. "I almost swallowed my cigar when he raised the ante. We sold the land for just what you said, Catherine."

"You hid your surprise well," Tim said.

Catherine smiled at them both and said. "I'll give you a special kiss as your reward, Tim,"

Tim smiled knowingly and thought, *"I wonder what other gift she might have in mind."*

As Jose prepared to depart, he said, "Thank you, my friends. I could never have done this on my own."

Tim shook Jose's hand and said, "Thank you, Jose, for including us. We both earned our money last night. I'll see you when Fernando calls. Let's get our checks as soon as possible and celebrate then. Have a safe return flight."

Catherine and Tim waved and watched as Jose lifted off and turned the copter downriver toward Prainha.

As they walked toward their home, Catherine whispered in Tim's ear to tell him of the reward she had planned.

Tim thought, *"She can read my mind."*

Chapter 15

As she pointed toward the steps leading down from the plane, Kate said. "Look, there's Bryan. He's coming down the stairs." She jumped into the air, waved and called, "Bryan, over here."

The plane from South Carolina was packed with young students on spring break. On the flight, Bryan overheard several conversations revolving around swimming, snorkeling and scuba diving. It appeared Bermuda was the "in" place to be this year.

In a way, Bryan was sorry. With his new hometown so popular with the younger set, he and Kate would experience long lines at restaurants and other venues. But the tourists' money, helped keep Bermuda green. *"In return for their dollars, I'll never be the one to deny the students their fun."*

Bryan was anxious to see Kate again. It had been a long four months since they held hands and kissed. She had become very important to him. He hoped she felt the same. In Kate's letters, she said she missed his company and looked forward to being with him again.

After Bryan passed through the crowded gateway to the tarmac, he found Kate and Pearl waiting, but there was no sign of his mother or father. He wondered if there was some problem.

Pearl calmed his fears when she said "Bryan, your parents are waiting for you at home. Since Kate and I planned to meet you, they thought they would wait to greet you there. With this crowd, I can see they were smart to stay away. How are you, dear?"

"I'm fine," Bryan said and smiled down at Kate, who was now firmly attached to his arm.

Kate reached up, kissed him lightly and said, "Welcome back, big guy."

"Hi yourself; you're very pretty this morning."

"Thank you," she said and continued to smile at him with a secret twinkle in her eyes. "I have a surprise for you."

Bryan asked, "What is it?"

"Uncle Tom is home on a sabbatical and promised to take us scuba diving. Isn't it wonderful?"

"Great," Bryan said.

Kate replied, "I can't wait."

Pearl stood by silently and let the youngsters talk while her mind drifted back to her teenage years. *"I remember how puppy love affects young men and women. Bryan is a handsome boy and polite too. I'm pleased with Kate's choice for a boyfriend."*

Then she asked, "Are you ready to leave?"

"I'll get my luggage and we'll be ready to go, Mrs. Fitch."

"I'll wait outside," Pearl said. "These crowds are too much for me."

Kate took Bryan's hand and they made their way to the baggage area. "We'll be right out, Grandma."

As Pearl watched, she noticed they were holding hands. *"They do make a nice-looking couple."*

On the trip to Bryan's parents' home, Pearl concentrated on her driving. From the back seat the air was filled with laughter. Bryan and Kate sat, talked and caught up on each other's news of the past four months.

When they arrived, Bob and Marsha were waiting on the front porch.

"Welcome home, Bryan," Bob said. "I know you're glad to see Kate again. Good morning, Kate."

"I'm looking forward to my vacation," Bryan said. "Kate's uncle is taking us diving."

After Marsha hugged and kissed Bryan, she said, "Wait until you see how I've furnished our new home."

The ladies gossiped and made polite conversation while Bob and Bryan carried his luggage into the house.

As Kate and Pearl left for home, Bryan said, "I'll borrow dad's new car and drive over later, Kate. What about a movie in town?"

She smiled and said, "Anything you choose will be great."

The fourth day of Bryan's vacation, he and Kate asked Tom about the scuba diving expedition.

"So you're ready to dive," Tom said. "I feel better and I'm also ready for some action. Dad gave me name of a man who owns a boat – Samuel Scoggins. Sam's willing to take us out to pay off his son's doctor bill. We can rent our gear in town and enroll in an eight-hour diver training course."

Bryan asked, "How long before we can actually dive?"

"The training takes three days and we can dive the next," Tom said.

"Wonderful," Kate said. "Let's begin."

The day before the dive, in the form of Lorna and Jock, fate stepped quietly into their lives. Jock approached Tom and said, "We heard you were going diving tomorrow. Lorna wants to come along. Sam says he knows a spot where you can dive and we can collect sea shells."

"You're welcome to come with us," Tom said. "The more, the merrier."

Jock looked pale as he said, "When I remember what happened to Lori I'm still a little apprehensive. But Lorna says the trip will be good therapy. I hope so, but I doubt I'll ever lose my fear of sharks."

The next day dawned bright and sunny with a blue sky overhead. As the sun rose behind a far-off cloud bank, it turned the grey mist into red, orange and pink tones.

Lorna said, "Look at the sunrise."

While Tom helped carry the diving equipment and other gear aboard Sam's boat, he heard her remark and said, "Red sky in the morning; sailor take warning."

Lorna brought along a large basket of sandwiches, chips, drinks and some fresh fruit. When Sam saw bananas, he was upset. "It's bad luck to have them on a boat."

Lorna couldn't believe Sam was serious. "How could bananas cause problems, Sam?"

He shook his head and said, "I don't know why, but every time someone brings bananas on board, either we don't catch fish or someone is injured. I know its superstition, but I've seen it work."

Tom took the bananas, stored them in Jock's car, walked back aboard and asked, "There now, Sam; isn't that better? We don't need bad luck to accompany us."

Suddenly, Jock felt an overpowering urge to stay behind. *"I don't care to hear anything about bad luck. I'm not too happy with this trip as is."*

Lorna saw Jock's ashen face, smiled at him and said, "Thank you for coming with me." She reached up and kissed Jock's lips. "I hope this adventure will help you."

In his heart, Jock knew his fear of the past was unreasonable, so he fought off his fright and remained aboard.

As the boat pulled slowly away from the dock, Sam noted the seas were calm and the wind light from the southeast. He and Tom had discussed the trip in advance.

"I believe we should dive on a wreck situated in fairly shallow water," Tom said. "My niece has never been deeper than fifty feet underwater. Her boyfriend is making his first dive."

Sam nodded knowingly and said, "I know of an old tug boat that ran aground on a reef not far from the south end of the islands. It'll be easy to dive on. At the same time, I can pull into shallow water to allow Miss Hayden and Jock to beach comb. You and the other divers can easily swim from the beach to the wreck."

Lorna pointed out the lighthouse standing tall on a bluff. "You can see a long ways from up there."

"We haven't been to the lighthouse yet," Kate said.

"You'll enjoy the view," Lorna replied.

Sam kept the boat on slow speed, which allowed his passengers to fully appreciate the beauty of Bermuda's beaches and coral outcroppings. The wreck he was searching for was only a short distance from the last small island that is considered a part of the Bermudian chain.

Near that point, a sharp outcrop of coral lurks a few feet beneath the surface. A small island behind the reef, but not connected to the mainland, gives boaters a false sense of security.

Unwary boat captains could easily pilot their vessels to destruction on this reef, and in the past, several had. The pilot of the tugboat they planned to dive on was one of the unlucky ones. Now he couldn't find an owner who would trust him with their boat.

After Sam slowed his trawler to a crawl, he located the hidden reef, stayed well to the seaward side and piloted his craft safely around the dangerous crags. Once clear, he pulled the boat slowly toward shore until he felt the bottom scrape on the smooth sandy beach. Then Sam dropped anchor and announced, "Here we are. Beachcombers head to the right; divers move to the left."

Kate and Bryan applauded.

Sam knew they were anxious to get on with the dive.

Jock and Lorna helped the three divers into their diving vests and lifted individual air tanks onto their backs. As they struggled to tighten straps around their waists and chests, Kate and Bryan discovered their weight belts made it difficult to walk naturally.

Tom paused for a moment and then took the time to strap a long-bladed knife in a leather scabbard to the side of his right hip. He handed a similar device to Bryan and said, "Strap this on your leg, Bryan. If you or Kate gets caught in ropes or rigging, you can cut your way out. It's better to be safe than sorry."

Lorna and Jock watched the three adventurers climb down a ladder into the clear blue light surf. The water was only knee deep at the bow, so after removing their footwear, Jock and Lorna waded to the beach. They turned to watch the divers move into deeper water. Then the trio swam toward a coral outcrop where the half-submerged tugboat was bobbing gently on small waves.

Lorna thought, *"I envy Kate and Bryan for their young spirit of adventure. I'm afraid to attempt to dive. The thought of being at the mercy of water is too much for me."*

She turned her attention to Jock, took his hand in hers and they strolled slowly down the beach.

Tom, Kate and Bryan had progressed well. As they slowly became accustomed to the weight of the air tanks, they remembered how their instructor told them the tanks would appear lighter as they descended into the deep.

The wreck was more than sixty feet long and mostly submerged. Approximately six feet of the bow stood upright, with the stern completely underwater. Air trapped within kept the boat afloat in place, and it bobbed slowly up and down.

Before Tom signaled his two companions to begin their dive, he stared into their eyes to make sure they were listening. Then he said, "We will stay down no longer than forty-five minutes, which gives us fifteen minutes of reserve air. I'll make sure we head up in time. Watch for my signals."

Then as they began their initial dive, he watched carefully to insure Kate and Bryan didn't become frightened by the sea life around them. The water was clear and they could see for a long distance.

As they submerged and began to breathe oxygen, Tom started his diving watch. *"It's time for Kate and her boyfriend to enjoy the day. I kept my promise. There's nothing to interfere with the young couple as they enjoy their first dive together, is there?"*

Chapter 16

Five nautical miles south of the Bermuda Isles

Once more, the great white shark was in familiar waters. The warmth in the current of the Gulf of Mexico felt wonderful on its skin. The water temperature was much better than the cool waters off the Brazilian coastline. A month ago, the killer departed that far shore and slowly made its way north, always moving and constantly searching for food.

The waters that surround Bermuda are alive with schools of fish and other sea creatures. Just minutes before, the shark attacked a pod of unwary porpoises 'and was successful in killing two. The others fled into shallow water, where they escaped the shark's killing field.

As it cruised at a depth of fifty feet, the shark suddenly sensed movement above. It felt the vibrations as if they had occurred within a few feet. A shark's senses are that acute. The sound was one the predator knew well - small boat propellers.

Over the years, the great white shark identified this sound with a food source. The stealthy hunter turned to follow the noises. It remained submerged forty feet below the surface and continued to trail the boat at a safe distance.

In the past, the shark's small brain registered the sound as divers fell or jumped from a boat into the water. On those occasions, it followed the sounds of their breathing apparatus to find food waiting in the form of one or more tasty humans.

A creature of habit, the shark followed age-old instincts that told it there might be a source of food at the end of its quest.

Abruptly, the sound of propellers ceased. For a minute or two, the great white was confused. While the beast attempted to retrieve the source again, it swam in circles. After a few anxious moments, it was about to give up and search elsewhere, when the monster heard the familiar sound of swimmers splashing in the water.

A large reef came into view. Instinctively the shark knew its body was too large to rise above the sharp coral formation, so the killer detoured around the reef. The change in direction caused a momentary loss of the signal.

At the end of the reef, the great white turned slowly in a circle until it reacquired the vibrations from its prey. Although its stomach was half-full from the porpoises, its voracious appetite drove it onward.

As Tom emerged from the shadow of the shipwreck into the sunshine once more, he checked his watch and discovered they had spent the last thirty minutes swimming around the wreck and examining it closely. He thought, *"It's time to return to the boat."*

He swam over to where Kate and Bryan were looking at the damage to the underside of the tugboat, and motioned for them to follow him upward. They nodded and the trio slowly ascended to the surface.

When they were able to breathe fresh air again, Kate removed her mask and said, "Wow; that was fun, Uncle Tom. Thanks."

Tom was unhappy with the way his oxygen tank was riding on his back. He said, "My air tank is giving me problems."

Bryan asked, "Can I help?"

Tom shook his head in frustration. "I'll take it off and float back to the boat atop it. Thanks anyway, Bryan."

As he bobbed along in the water between the wreck and Sam's boat, Tom reached up and hit the "quick disconnect" button. The straps came lose and Tom began to move the tank beneath his stomach to use as a flotation device.

Without his air tank, Tom's weight belt caused him to sink underwater. He came up sputtering. Quickly, he removed the belt and secured it around the top of his air tank. Then he straddled the cylinder like a bucking bronco and paddled after the two teenagers.

No one had an inkling of the danger that was approaching from seaward, so Kate and Bryan swam ahead toward the boat.

As he propelled his metal transportation forward, Tom relaxed and enjoyed the day while he thought, *"I'm glad Kate talked me into this trip."*

He watched Bryan and Kate swam in tandem. As they raced each other the short distance to the boat, they easily outdistanced Tom.

The shark paused for a moment. It sensed his prey was far above him on the surface. The predator preferred to attack unseen at a deeper depth. All sharks know instinctively the inborn danger of exposing themselves when their dorsal fin emerges from the water. As a result, great whites seldom attack on the surface.

Hunger drove the shark onward, so it ignored the danger, turned in a half circle and swam a short distance out to sea. Then it rose to the surface and began its attack on the nearest creature – Tom.

After completing their search of the small island, Lorna and Jock were returning to the boat with a collection of shells and rocks in a bag Sam furnished for their souvenirs.

While he was assisting Lorna aboard the boat, Jock watched the three divers returning to the craft. He noticed Tom was lagging several yards behind the others. Suddenly, approximately two hundred yards behind Tom, a huge dorsal fin appeared in the water. *"It's a shark and it's headed for Tom."*

Jock pointed behind the swimmers and shouted, "Shark"!

As they neared the boat, Bryan and Kate heard Jock's call and looked back at Tom. Tom also heard Jock's warning. He turned to see the approaching dorsal fin and thought, *"There's no way I can reach the boat before it overtakes me. I've only got one chance."_*

He turned to face his attacker and allowed the air tank to rise to the surface between him and the shark. His mind raced. *"If I can deflect its initial attack, maybe I can reach shallow water and the boat. I doubt the shark will follow me. At least I hope not."*

Bryan and Kate swam like never before to reach the safety of shallow water. After Bryan felt his feet on the sandy bottom, he hit his quick release button. As quickly as possible, he dropped his air tank and weight belt into the water. Then he turned to Kate and did the same to her equipment. Now unencumbered, they ran to the side of the boat.

As soon as Jock shouted a warning, he ran to the stern, where he and Lorna helped Kate and Bryan scramble aboard. Then they all turned seaward again in time to see the shark attack Tom.

The shark wasn't fooled by Tom's ploy, but still the air tank deflected its attack slightly. Tom's left arm, halfway between his elbow and shoulder was caught in the beast's mouth. Tom screamed in terror and pain.

With the speed of its attack, combined with Tom's actions to repel it, the shark miscalculated the water's depth. Its own momentum carried the beast and Tom into shallow water. Momentarily beached, the great white was shocked into near paralysis.

Throughout the attack, Tom remained conscious. Now he found he was staring eyeball to eyeball with the beast. Blood flowed from Tom's torn left arm and he saw splintered white bones had pierced the skin. The pain was terrific. Tom knew he was in serious trouble.

When the shark momentarily ceased its movements, Tom reached down with his right hand and removed his knife from the scabbard. He struggled painfully to his knees alongside the monster, and with all his remaining strength, drove his knife downward into the eye of his attacker.

Pain shot through the shark's body. As it recoiled from the attack, its mouth flew open and the beast released Tom's arm.

Tom fell backward and watched in awe as the great white thrashed in agony while it attempted to rid itself of the object that was causing so much pain.

With his one good arm and both feet, Tim pushed and crawled away from the beast. Blood drained from Tom's wound and stained the water red. Tom knew he would soon go into shock and if he wanted to live, he had to reach the boat.

Suddenly, Tom felt an arm encircle his waist and drag him to safety.

Jock stood in fear, nearly paralyzed by the attack on his friend. Although he hadn't witnessed Lori's attack, Jock knew what happened to her. Now he was reliving the scene as if in slow motion. He watched helplessly as the shark brushed aside Tom's air tank. Then Jock saw Tom's arm disappear into the mouth of the awesome beast.

Lorna and Kate screamed in tandem. Their terrified cries brought Jock out of his trance and shocked him into action.

He swallowed and thought, *"I have to help Tom somehow."*

When the shark beached itself in the shallow water, Jock watched in amazement and admiration as Tom stabbed the monster in the eye. Then to everyone's amazement, the shark released Tom's arm. Without a thought for his own safety, Jock jumped into the water, splashed through the shallows that separated them and grabbed Tom around the waist. *"God, Tom's arm is almost torn from his body."*

The shark continued to thrash about, and Jock kept a wary eye over his shoulder. As he struggled with his burden toward the boat, Jock's mind raced. *"I doubt the shark can attack from where it's at, but I damn sure don't want to find out. Move, feet!"*

Sam and Bryan reached down, grabbed Tom as carefully as possible and dragged him onto the deck. Then they hurriedly pulled Jock from the bloody water.

As he watched the shark finally attain enough buoyancy to swim away from the beach, Jock gave a sigh of relief. It seemed as if the beast shook its head in apparent anger at the escape of its prey. In reality, the great white was attempting to rid itself of Tom's knife.

Lorna sprung into action. She ripped a length of cloth from her dress, placed it around Tom's arm near his armpit and clinched the cloth as tightly as possible. Then she turned to Sam and asked, "Do you have a screwdriver or some other straight piece of metal, Sam? I need to tighten this tourniquet to stop the bleeding."

Sam ran to a tool box and returned with two long-handled screwdrivers.

Quickly, Lorna slipped one through the tourniquet, turned the tool clockwise and watched the flow of blood diminish.

With an ashen face, Sam stood transfixed with the other screwdriver clutched in his hand, and stared at Tom's arm. Then he turned and vomited his breakfast over the railing.

Tom was in agony, but Lorna knew there was nothing available for his pain. She laid his head on her lap and rubbed her hand across his brow. Tom's teeth were clenched tight against the pain.

After he regained his composure and wiped vomit from his chin, Sam started the engine while Jock and Bryan pulled in the anchor. The boat roared backward from the beach. Then Sam turned the wheel and threw the throttle all the way forward. They seemed to fly out of the small bay. The keel barely cleared the coral outcrop by inches. Everyone aboard heard and felt the powerful engine respond as the large craft sped across the water.

Tom's left arm lay useless at his side. Lorna could tell the bone was broken in at least three places. Huge teeth marks pocked his skin. Tendons and sinew were visible along with torn and frayed muscles. She knew, *"The pain must be unbearable."*

Apprehensively, Kate approached with a bottle of water and held the flask to Tom's mouth while he drank deeply. She poured some of the cool liquid onto a clean rag and handed it to Lorna, who wiped Tom's brow and face.

"I feel so helpless," Kate thought.

Sam used his CB radio to notify the authorities in Hamilton harbor of the shark attack. He reported he was bringing in a victim of the attack who would require immediate medical treatment.

A voice boomed out of the speaker overhead. "We'll have an ambulance and EMS technicians standing by."

Lorna called out, "Tell them Tom needs an immediate operation or he'll lose his arm."

After Sam relayed the information to the authorities, the port authorities asked the name of the victim.

"It's Tom Fitch," Sam said.

"Oh my," Lorna thought. *"I can imagine George being called in to the emergency room only to find his son is the victim."*

Kate continued to sit by Lorna's side and sob uncontrollably. She cried out, "Why did I have to beg Tom to take us diving? It's all my fault."

Lorna thought, *"I can only take care of one patient at a time."* She called to Jock and nodded in Kate's direction. When Jock saw Lorna's predicament, he went to her aid and took Kate aside. He held her close and said, "Don't blame yourself, Kate. The shark could have attacked anyone. It was just your bad luck and Tom's that you were the ones it chose. Tom doesn't blame you."

Through his pain, Tom heard Jock's words and reached out his good hand toward Kate. She grabbed his with hers and said, "I'm so sorry, Uncle Tom. Please forgive me."

Tom fought off the pain and whispered, "It's not your fault, Kate. It was an act of God. I don't blame you."

Sam completely ignored the "No Wake" signs in the harbor, and powered his large craft as fast as it would go across the bay and into the docking area.

As he sped past million dollar yachts and sailboats bobbing at anchor in the bay, Sam thought, *"To hell with them and their fat cat owners who do nothing all day except sit around in their glass mansions atop the hills that surround the bay. If they raise hell, I'll tell them to sue me."*

Sam didn't care. The young man who was lying on the deck with his arm mangled was the son of a man he respected. Tom wasn't the son of some fat cat who might be smoking a Cuban cigar on his yacht. This was the time for action, not niceties.

As Sam approached the dock, under his breath, he said "Screw 'em."

With ease of past experience, approximately seventy feet from the dock, Sam threw the engines into reverse. The boat slowed enough to turn broadside to the dock and collide softly with several recycled rubber tires that acted as bumpers.

An ambulance was parked at the edge of the dock. Two EMS technicians and a small crowd of onlookers watched as they docked. Jock and Bryan tossed ropes to two willing men, who quickly tied off the boat and held it tightly alongside the dock.

Then the medics jumped over the rail and ran to Tom's side. Lorna let go of Tom's hand and got to her feet. When the medics recognized Lorna as a nurse from the hospital, they awaited her orders.

She pointed to Tom and said, "Twenty minutes ago, I placed a tourniquet on his arm. It should be released shortly to prevent further damage. His arm is broken in at least three places and he has severe muscle damage. Tom needs an immediate emergency operation. Try to be as gentle as possible, but get him on a gurney and to the hospital quickly."

In unison, both medics replied, "Yes, Ma'am." Then they vaulted over the rail again, ran to the ambulance and returned momentarily with a folded gurney. With the assistance of Jock and Bryan, the stretcher was manhandled over the rail and onto the deck.

Quickly, but professionally the medics moved Tom onto the gurney. As they secured his injured arm, Tom screamed in agony.

Cold shudders ran up and down Kate's back. She continued to sit on the damp deck and cry.

The medics strapped Tom down tightly and raised the gurney above the rail and onto the dock. Then they lowered the wheels and rushed Tom to the ambulance. Within minutes, with its siren wailing, the ambulance sped from the area toward the hospital.

Inspector David Smythe was among the authorities who came aboard to question the witnesses. With his permission, Lorna excused herself and Jock. *"The others can tell the story. I have to go to the hospital and assist whoever will operate on Tom. I hope another doctor besides George is on call, but I doubt it. George likes to handle emergency calls. It's his forte."*

On the short drive to the hospital, Jock broke every Bermudian speed law. He left a trail of smoke from his spinning wheels behind on the dock and never slowed until they approached the emergency entrance. *"If a policeman arrests me afterward, so be it. Lorna wants to be at Tom's side, so to hell with the speed limit."*

The vehicle screeched to a halt, and Jock shut down the engine. Lorna opened the door and ran from the car. Jock left the vehicle where it was. If it needed to be moved, the keys were in the ignition. *"I doubt anyone will bother me about where I parked, but if they do; then to hell with them too."*

He raced down the hallway after Lorna.

Chapter 17

O nce again, George was attempting to complete at least one crossword puzzle from the stack by his chair. The pile seemed to grow daily. *"I wonder if they're mating and reproducing faster than I can solve them. Although it's against the laws of nature, I wouldn't put it past them."*

The phone rang to interrupt his efforts. *"Not again. Just when I settle down to enjoy life, some fool does something to injure himself and the phone inevitably rings. It must never be my day to relax."*

A woman's voice asked, "Doctor Fitch?"

George replied, "Speaking." *"It's one of the nurses in the Emergency Room, but I can't put a name to her voice."*

"This is Nurse Jennings, Doctor. There's been a shark attack and you're needed in the OR."

"I'll be right there," George said. *"She appears nervous. I wonder why."*

As he started to hang up, Nurse Jennings said, "I called in Doctor Peters to assist you."

George thought, *"I wonder what that's all about."*

Other than multiple injuries, such as a serious automobile accident, it was strange for Doctor Peters to be called in for any emergency.

"Very well," he said, hung up and made his way to his bedroom, where he changed from his lounging clothes into a respectable shirt and dark pants.

He was aware his son, granddaughter and Bryan were on the water, (or, to be more correct, in the water). He also assumed the shark attack happened on one of the beaches that surround the islands, so he didn't connect the phone call with Tom in any way.

He whistled a chorus of "Hi Ho, Hi Ho; it's Off to Work I Go", while he walked to his VW in a happy mood.

Nurse Harriette Jennings was aware of the name of the shark attack victim. Harriette's standing orders were to phone Doctor Fitch for any emergency, but this one was a bit unusual. Therefore, she called Doctor Peters first.

When Pete heard the news of Tom Fitch's injuries, he said, "Phone Doctor Fitch as instructed, but inform him I will assist. If Doctor Fitch asks, don't tell him who the victim is. I'll let him know when he arrives. If George knew ahead of time, he might have an accident on the way to the hospital. Then we would have two victims on our hands."

Nurse Jennings said, "Thank you Doctor. This is terrible news for Doctor Fitch. Will he be up to operating on his son? The medics say Tom's injuries are terrible."

"Doctor Fitch is a professional," Pete said. "I'll watch carefully for any undue stress. When will Tom arrive?"

"I'm monitoring the radio and the medics are leaving the dock now. They should be here momentarily."

"I'm on my way and should arrive in five minutes. Wait a few minutes before you phone Doctor Fitch. I want to be there when he arrives."

Harriette heard the wail of a siren as it approached the hospital, so she hung up and hurried to help the medics wheel Tom into the Emergency Care Unit. Five minutes later, she phoned Doctor Fitch.

When George arrived at the hospital, he was surprised to see Doctor Peters waiting inside the door. He asked, "How are you, Pete?"

"I'm fine, George. But we need to talk about your new patient. Please come into the lounge."

George looked inquisitively at his colleague. But when Pete offered nothing more, George shrugged and followed him into the lounge.

Pete said, "There's no easy way to tell you this, George, so be prepared."

George saw Pete's face was grim; so he knew bad news was on the way. He still didn't connect the patient with a member of his family. He asked, "What's the problem with the shark attack victim, Pete?"

Pete watched George carefully for his reaction as he made the statement, "It's your son, Tom,"

George's hands shook as he reached for his spectacles. "Why didn't the nurse inform me?"

"She kept it secret at my request. I couldn't afford to have you involved in an accident on the way here. I know how you love your sons."

Tears started to form in George's eyes as he said, "Yes, I do. How bad is Tom?"

"The injuries are to his left arm. I'm sorry to say the damage is severe. I doubt we can save his arm, but I'm willing to try. I examined Tom's wounds carefully and feel the muscle and tendon damage is irreparable.

"The staff is prepping him now. Are you up to examining Tom and confirming my diagnosis, or would you prefer I call in another doctor?"

"Take me to my son," George said.

Small tears continued to flow from George's eyes, but his face was set in determination. Pete knew in this case George was a physician first, a father second.

They walked through the double doors of the ECU, where they found three nurses and several orderlies scurrying about, while they set up trays of instruments and prepped Tom for the operation.

A bottle of whole blood hung upside down from a steel support, and from it, a thin plastic tube led to Tom's right arm. It appeared he was already under the effects of anesthesia.

As if he could read George's mind, Pete said, "I gave Tom a general anesthesia to put him under and ordered an I.V. drip. He lost quite a bit of blood, so I ordered one pint to stabilize his condition. If Tom needs more, we have it. He's lucky he's O Positive. We have six pints on hand. The pain must be horrible, but he didn't say a word. Tom knows he's seriously injured."

"I wish I could speak with him, but thank you for your kindness," George said. "I don't want him to suffer. Let's scrub and examine his wounds."

After they walked through a door to a scrub room, both doctors washed their hands thoroughly. A nurse stood by to assist them into rubber gloves.

When George's hands were cleaned to his satisfaction, he accepted the nurse's help to don the gloves. Then he followed her into the ECU. Inside, another nurse waited with sterile gowns, caps and masks. Both helped George tie the straps behind his neck and back.

Pete completed the same routine and joined George at Tom's side, where the injured limb was covered with a sterile cloth. George raised the cloth, removed the cover and was shocked by the devastation to his son's arm. He noted three different breaks with pieces of bone protruding through the skin. He knew Pete's diagnosis was correct.

The damage was severe. The muscles in Tom's lower arm were ripped and torn. Teeth marks were deep and wide.

George wondered, *"How did Tom escape from the jaws of death with such damage? No, there's no way to save his arm here. If we were in some big hospital, say Bethesda in Maryland, and had the greatest team of surgeons in the world, there might be a very slim chance. However, we aren't and we can't. I must face reality. If we are to save Tom's life, he'll have to lose a portion of his arm."*

George turned to his fellow physician. "I concur with your diagnosis, Pete. I hoped we might be able to save the entire limb, but I see the damage is too severe."

Tears blinded George's eyes for a moment, but at his signal a nurse rushed to his side and wiped his eyes. "I'm sorry," George said. "That won't happen again. I would appreciate it if you would take Tom's arm, Pete. I'm not in the best frame of mind to operate. I'll assist in any way I can."

Pete reached out to touch George's arm and said, "As you wish. I'll save as much as possible. I believe from the elbow down will need to be removed."

Then Pete turned to the head nurse. "Nurse, are we ready to proceed?"

"Yes, Doctor," she replied.

When George glanced down to see who was serving as anesthesiologist, he was amazed to see Lorna Hayden seated at the head of the table and monitoring Tom's respiration. The last time George heard, Lorna was on the boat with Tom.

George acknowledged her presence with a slight nod, and Lorna managed a weak smile.

Aboard the boat, Kate finally stopped sobbing. "Are we free to go, Inspector? Has anyone told my grandma about Uncle Tom? She needs to know."

"How stupid of me," David said. "In the excitement, I completely forgot to notify Pearl. I'll drive you and Bryan home, Kate and tell your grandmother of Tom's misfortune."

David assisted Kate and Bryan into his small car and then waved to a policeman, who guided them through the crowd and away from the dock.

In the rear seat on the short trip to the Fitch residence, Bryan held Kate in his arms. As David pulled into the driveway, they saw Pearl in the back yard hanging clothes on a line to dry. From her actions, David knew Pearl was unaware of her son's troubles.

He knew the chore ahead would be difficult, so David said, "Please stay in the car until I speak with Pearl. It would alarm her to see you crying, Kate."

Without another word, David walked to where Pearl stood looking at them with a curious expression. When Kate and Bryan didn't join David, Pearl suspected something was amiss.

She said, "You look nervous, David. Is something wrong?"

"Yes, Pearl, I'm afraid there is. Earlier today, Tom was a victim of a shark attack."

Pearl's hands flew to her mouth and tears welled up in her eyes as she cried out, "Oh my God! Is he alive?"

"Yes, but his left arm was severely injured. When Tom managed to escape from the beast, Jock jumped into the water and pulled him to safety."

Pearl voice quaked as she asked, "Where is Tom?"

"He's in the emergency room at Hamilton hospital. Doctor Peters and George are there. I'm sure they'll perform the operation together."

Pearl glanced apprehensively toward David's car. "Are Kate and Bryan okay?"

"They're fine, but I asked them to wait until I told you of Tom's accident. Kate's very disturbed about the attack, as is Bryan. He seems to be taking it better. Kate believes she's to blame for asking her uncle to take her diving."

"Poor Kate," Pearl said. "Tell them to come into the house. I'll speak with them and then I must go to the hospital. George will need me by his side, as will Tom."

Four hours later, after Pete was able to save Tom's arm from the shoulder down to within two inches of his elbow, George thought, *"Pete did a hell of a job. I'll say a small prayer for the good doctor being available. I don't know if I could have made it through the operation on my own."*

During the procedure, when George felt Pearl's presence in the operating room, he realized someone notified her of Tom's accident.

He glanced over his shoulder to see Pearl was masked, gowned and gloved, and ready to assist, but she never said a word.

As the nurses wheeled Tom into the Intensive Care Unit, the three doctors removed their masks and gloves. George said, "Thanks Pete," and shook his hand.

Then he took his wife into his arms and rocked back and forth with her as Pearl sobbed. George was amazed at Pearl's ability to withhold her sorrow throughout the entire operation.

Pearl noticed Lorna as she was cleaning the respirator. She pulled loose from George's embrace, walked to Lorna's side and put her arms around Lorna's shoulders. "Thank you for saving our son, Lorna. Kate told us how much you did with so little. If you weren't there, Tom might have bled to death. I believe the good Lord placed you on board the boat today. I love you like a daughter."

As they held each other, the women let their tears flow, while George stood by helplessly and cried alone. Finally they regained their composure, and the trio linked arms and left the ECU.

Tom's life was now in the hands of his Maker. All they could do was pray.

As the trio of the Doctors Fitch and Nurse Hayden left the ER, they found the hallway was crowded with an orderly and silent line of people.

Word of Tom's accident spread in a hurry. George and Pearl were well known and respected throughout the islands. These were their patients, friends and neighbors who were standing in line and waiting to donate blood for their son.

Nearly overcome with emotion, as fresh tears ran down their cheeks, Pearl and George shook hands and spoke with each waiting donor. It took them several minutes to reach the front desk.

Very tired and emotionally drained, Lorna kissed both doctors on the cheek while she assured them again that Tom would come through this ordeal with flying colors.

When Lorna came outside, Jock was seated on the hood of his roadster. He looked worn and held a can of diet soda in his right hand. Lorna thought, *"Jock looks as exhausted as I feel."*

"Are you ready to go home?" he asked. "How bad was it?"

"Doctor Peters did his best to save Tom's arm, but he was finally forced to give up and remove it just above Tom's elbow. It was a long procedure, nearly five hours, and I'm worn out."

"It's time for you to get some sleep," Jock said. "I'll take you home. The Fitch house will be a madhouse with friends and neighbors calling to help. I saw the line inside – it's a sign of the peoples' love for their doctors."

Suddenly Lorna felt like she could cry again, but her tear ducts must be dry and she found she couldn't. Instead, she sighed, put her arms around Jock and said, "Take me home."

Inside the hospital, Harriette glanced up from the paperwork she was preparing for yet another blood donor and saw the two doctors.

She asked, "Isn't the response for Tom wonderful? We turned away at least as many donors as we have now, but asked them to return tomorrow. They all want to help your son."

"Please thank each for us," Pearl said.

As George handed Pearl his already damp handkerchief, he added, "I'll come in tomorrow to thank them in person. Thank you, also, Harriette for your courtesy. I appreciate all the staff who worked so hard for our son."

"It was a long and difficult operation," Harriette said. "Go home and get some sleep. We'll look after Tom for you. Don't worry."

Through her tears, Pearl said, "We know you will. Thank you again. Call us if there's any change in his condition."

"He's in good hands," Harriette said. "Sleep well."

As they walked out the door, Pearl stopped, put her hand to her mouth and said, "Oh dear, I didn't think to notify Tim of his brother's accident. Should we phone at this hour?"

"Tim won't mind," George said. "They're three hours behind us, so it's not late in Obidos. He should be told of Tom's condition. When we get home, I'll phone."

Chapter 18

After he dropped Pearl at the hospital, David drove to the police station. He knew his supervisor would want to hear his report first hand. Other than a Category-Four hurricane, a shark attack in Bermuda was the worst possible catastrophe.

The entire facilities of all government offices would be placed on alert. Every resource would be available to the person or department assigned to deal with the emergency. Since the seven missing person cases were being handled by David's office, he knew he would be the supervisor of the team formed to destroy the menace.

To no one's surprise, David's supervisor, Chief of Detectives Jim Marshall was seated in David's chair. He was leaning backward with his feet atop of David's desk and appeared to be asleep.

The files from David's bottom drawer were strewn over the desktop. One was balanced precariously on Jim's lap. It was about ready to slip off and fall to the floor.

Politely, David cleared his throat rather loudly, and Jim jerked awake. Somehow he managed to catch the file before it fell. Jim seemed embarrassed to be discovered taking a short nap.

David knew Jim had worked late last night on a burglary case. When the shark attack was reported, he was probably called from a sound sleep. David didn't deny his boss the chance to grab forty winks.

At times of crisis, all the detectives caught sleep whenever and wherever they could.

As he thought, *"I doubt if I'll see my own bed for many a day,"* David said, "Good morning, Sir. I see you're reviewing the files. I believe we have our answer."

Jim yawned and asked, "What did the witnesses have to say, David?"

When Jim used his first name, David was relieved Jim hadn't found fault with his recent report. He also knew everything was all right. "They saw a great white shark, approximately twenty feet in length that attacked on the surface of a small lagoon. Tom Fitch, Doctor Fitch's son was the victim. When the shark accidentally beached itself in shallow water, Tom managed to escape. The witnesses claim he put a knife into the left eye of the beast."

"That's quite a heroic feat with your arm in a shark's mouth," Jim said. "How is Tom?"

"He's as well as can be expected. At last report, his father and Doctor Peters were operating in an attempt to save his arm. I doubt they'll be successful. I'm no doctor, but Tom's arm was severely damaged."

"I hope they manage somehow," Jim said. "In the meantime, we have work to do. How do you think the shark attack will play out in the local newspapers and on TV?"

David shook his head. "The paper will probably give it front page coverage. A reporter from the TV station was the first to arrive. They filmed close-ups of the blood on the deck etcetera. With their past record, they'll play the tape every hour. It won't reflect favorably on us or the islands."

Jim frowned and said, "I was afraid of that reaction. I know you did your best to keep the event low-key, David. But now the shark's here. We have to do our best to kill the beast before the story takes on a life of its own."

"I agree," Jim said. "I want to set up a task force to kill this pest and use all of the facilities of the harbor police and, if necessary, the military. Perhaps the Navy can supply us with the proper equipment to help find this monster and destroy it. I don't see the task as being easy. It may take days, perhaps even weeks."

"I speak for the Governor when I ask you to make it a matter of days at the most," Jim said. "We must prevent any further attacks. If we lose the tourist trade, it will be a dismal season for our residents."

In spite of feeling fatigued, David said, "I'll do my best." Then a sudden thought occurred to him. "I just remembered. When he hears the news, Doctor Fitch's other son, Tim, may return from Brazil to assist his brother. If so, I'll ask him to join our task force. He recently led a successful rescue of Tom in the jungles of Brazil. I can always use a man with brains."

"By all means, bring him on board," Jim said. "We'll need all the help we can muster. I've read through the files and agree with your recommendations. I'll get out of your way and let you get to the task at hand. Good luck."

Then he paused as if he thought of something else. "If you encounter any difficulties with any government office vis-à-vis them granting you access to anything, my door is always open. In addition, you'll receive the full backing of the Governor's office. Feel free to call on me at any hour of the day."

"Thanks for your confidence in my abilities," David said.

Jim smiled and patted David's back in encouragement before he walked out the door. "Again, good luck, David. Keep me informed of any developments. Goodnight."

Chapter 19

At long last, Catherine's replacement arrived. Jackie Ronspiez was a pert lady from the great state of Texas. Although she was small in stature, she was large in ambition. Jackie was seventy-eight years young, but looked no older than sixty-five. With her grey hair pinned back into a bun, Jackie appeared every inch a dedicated schoolteacher.

In fact, she was much more – she was a missionary for the Catholic Church. Several years ago, her husband, Louis passed on, and Jackie soon found retired life in the little town of Rockport, Texas was too dull.

When Catherine asked how Jackie came to apply, she said, "When I read in my church bulletin about a search for a replacement schoolteacher in a small town in the jungle of Brazil, I knew it was my calling."

Jackie arrived earlier than Catherine and Tim were prepared for, but she didn't say anything after she discovered the couple was living together without the aid of a marriage certificate. However, Catherine knew Jackie didn't approve too highly of their arrangement.

To avoid further damage to their image in her eyes, Tim moved to a cot in the schoolhouse until the transition was complete.

Tim wasn't too happy with the situation. *"So far, I've spent three restless nights alone on a thin mattress. It isn't the same as sleeping with Catherine."*

They also avoided displays of affection when Jackie was present. *"It appears she and Catherine are joined at the hip. I couldn't steal a kiss if my life depended on it."*

When the phone rang, Tim was seated on the veranda and stewing in his own juices. Catherine answered and then called to him. Without a word, she handed him the phone.

Tim thought, *"I don't like the look on her face."*

The booming voice of his father came through clear and crisp. "Tim, I have some bad news. Tom was injured in an accident yesterday."

Tim asked, "How is he?" *"For dad to phone, it must be serious."*

George's answer was shocking. "I'm afraid Tom lost part of his left arm below the elbow."

With concern in his voice and a lump in his throat, Tim asked, "How did it happen?"

"While he was scuba diving with Kate and Bryan, Tom was attacked by a shark. The youngsters are fine, but they witnessed the assault and are still in a state of shock."

Tim couldn't believe his ears. "God, Dad, I'm sorry."

As she watched the expression on Tim's face and wondered what the bad news would bring, Catherine hovered nearby.

George continued with his bad news. "My friend, Doctor Peters operated on your brother. He did his best to save the arm, but it was impossible. Can you come home to help your mother and me through this time of crisis? For the next few months, Tom will need all the faith and love we can give him."

"Certainly, Dad; I'll phone and make reservations for us both immediately. I'll call you and give you our schedule. How is mom taking all of this?"

"She was in the OR, ready to assist," George said. "Your mother is marvelous."

"Watch over her and Kate for me, Dad. We'll be there as soon as humanly possible. Take care of yourself too."

When George hung up the phone, Tim turned to Catherine, who asked, "What happened to Tom?"

Tim relayed the news and then asked, "How soon can you leave?"

"Is tomorrow too soon? Jackie knows more about teaching than I do, and she's met the children. It's time for me to move on. I'll pack my things tonight and we'll worry about the house later. Phone for reservations, and I'll radio Jose to fly up as soon as we know when we can get a plane out. Okay?"

"Never ask me again why I love you," Tim said. "I'll get busy. Tell Jose to stand by and be ready to fly up here at any hour. If need be, I'll pay him double."

Catherine shook her head and said, "When Jose hears the reason, he won't charge you a dime. He's your friend and partner, remember?"

"Sometimes it's necessary to kick your future husband in the buttocks to get his brain engaged," Tim said. "I apologize. I'm just a little shook up over Tom."

As he picked up the phone, Tim's thoughts were running wild. *"If I'm lucky, we'll stay overnight in Belem. Being a four day virgin has given me some strange ideas. I only have one more night alone on my awful cot."*

Word spread fast in Obidos. Their schoolteacher was leaving and it was doubtful she would return. The children ran to Catherine's house to discover if the rumors were true. Many tears were shed when they learned she was indeed departing for good. Little Carlos appeared to be a lost soul. He refused to release his hold on Tim's leg.

Tim was successful in reserving first class accommodations to Bermuda for the day after tomorrow, with a two hour layover in Miami. Jose would arrive at noon tomorrow to take them to Belem, where they would stay overnight in the Best Western hotel.

With a smile on his face, Tim thought, *"My fantasy is coming true."*

Carlos' uncle finally persuaded the youngster to release his grip on Tim's leg. When Tim assured his young friend he could walk to the helicopter with him and Miss Catherine the next day, Carlos beamed at the prospect. Tim knew it would be difficult to say goodbye to his little shadow.

Finally the children and their parents departed and Tim and Catherine were alone. When they finished packing, Catherine had filled six suitcases and several boxes with possessions, while Tim added two more of his own. Tim thought, *"When we arrive in Bermuda with more suitcases, I'll never hear the end of it."*

As they sat and drank a glass of wine in the late evening, a sudden idea came to Tim's mind. He asked, "Why not give the house to Jackie? How much is the place worth?"

"I don't know," Catherine replied. "Three years ago, I paid twelve thousand dollars. The property includes the schoolhouse and the playground. The gift of the house should make Jackie very happy."

Then she laughed at the thought of their profit on the oil. "Giving Jackie the house is a great idea. Lord knows we don't need any more money than you made with Jose."

As he thought back on the previous weekend, Tim remembered when he and Jose flew to Belem to close the deal with Fernando's company. The entire procedure took less than two hours. They each received a check in the amount of three hundred and seventy-five thousand dollars.

As they were ready to depart, Fernando took Tim aside to thank him for making the deal. "You should know I was authorized to go as high as one million dollars for your property. We believe this will prove to be the biggest oil strike in Brazilian history. You were also correct about my promotion chances. I'm now the head of my department with a substantial raise in pay. I can't thank you enough."

Tim shook Fernando's hand and with a wry smile he said, "Good for you, my friend. My fiancée told me I should ask for a cool one million. I should have listened. To tell the truth, Jose and I are happy with our profit. We wish you well. I hope all your wells are filled with oil."

As Jose walked up and overheard the last of the conversation, he added, "I second the motion."

Tim smiled and said, "Our Jose - always a man of few words."

With another large cigar stuck in the side of his mouth, Jose looked very content. For once, he wore a plain, light yellow shirt. When Tim noticed Jose's folded check sticking out of his shirt pocket, he tapped it and said, "Better watch where you put the check, Jose. Juanita will expect it with no gravy or taco stains."

As his thoughts returned to the present, Tim said, "We can afford to give the property to Jackie's church as a donation and it'll look good on our tax return. Who knows, perhaps I can erase one of my black marks Saint Peter has entered in my record."

Catherine jumped up from her seat and said. "Let's go tell Jackie the good news,"

The next day, it seemed the entire town was on hand to help carry their bags and boxes. On the way to the landing pad, Tim carried Carlos on his shoulder.

Catherine warned Jose in advance about the amount of luggage, so today he was piloting the Big Bad Bird. As Tim watched the helo approach the landing area, it reminded him of their adventure a few months ago.

When the bags and boxes were finally all stacked inside the rear compartment, it was time to say goodbye. It took nearly a half hour for Catherine to shake hands with the men and kiss the women and children.

Jackie assured Catherine she would maintain the fine record

of achievement Catherine had accomplished. "I plan to double the enrollment of children in my classes. God go with you and your fiancé."

As Tim stood and watched Catherine say her goodbyes, Miguel walked up and gave Tim a small wooden statue of a Saint he had carved from a root. "I call this the Patron Saint of Friendship," Miguel said. "I hope some day to see you again, but if not, we'll always remain friends. God bless you, Mister Tim."

"Thank you, Miguel. All we can ask for is to have good friends in our lives." Then Tim shook Miguel's hand again and climbed into the front of the aircraft with Jose. Catherine rode in the rear with the many bags and boxes.

As Jose lifted off for Belem, everyone waved goodbye. Tim knew before they reached their final destination, Catherine would require a complete box of Kleenex. His eyes were also a bit damp. Tim didn't think Jose saw him wipe them on his sleeve, but when he glanced at the pilot, Jose smiled.

Jose set the aircraft down at the airport and then drove Tim and Catherine to their hotel in his jeep. Somehow he managed to stack all the luggage and boxes inside and still fit the three of them into the interior. As he wedged his body behind the wheel, Jose said, "You're my guests for supper tonight."

They showered, changed clothes and met Jose in the hotel dining room. To their surprise, Frank Moses was seated at the table. Frank rose from his chair to shake Tim's hand and receive a kiss on his cheek from Catherine.

He said, "Good evening, you two."

"What a surprise," Catherine said. "Where did you come from, Frank? Jose never said a word."

"Yeah, Frank," Tim added. "The last time I saw you together, you were telling Jose he was number one with the wrong digit. What caused you to kiss and make up?"

Frank frowned for a moment and then chuckled at the memory. "Okay funny man. Jose is a good guy. He upset me when he messed up our fishing, but he apologized and we're now good buddies. Jose might even let me in on his next oil venture."

"Now I see the light," Tim said and laughed. "You always were the slick one, Frank."

When Jose started to light up another foul cigar, Tim knew the evening would be better without a cloud of smoke hanging over their heads, so he stared at Jose and shook his head slightly. Jose put the unlit stogie back into his pocket and Tim smiled his thanks.

Then Tim turned to Frank and asked, "So, to what do we owe the pleasure of your company, Frank?"

"Jose told me about your brother. I wanted to tell you how sorry I am to hear of Tom's misfortune. When you see Tom, tell him I said to hang in there. I really like your brother. He's a stand up guy."

"I'll give Tom your message. Thanks for taking the time to see us off. We appreciate it."

"Jose tells me your brother lost his arm to a shark," Frank said. Then he asked, "Do you have any idea what type?"

Tim shook his head. "My father didn't say, but not too many years ago, a great white attacked and killed another friend's wife. This could be the same one. Since the time I mentioned, there haven't been any other reported shark attacks."

With intensity showing in his voice, Frank asked, "What are your plans concerning this predator?"

In response, Tim shrugged to say he didn't know. "The government of Bermuda will probably organize a large scale hunt for the man killer. But I don't know how successful they'll be. As for myself, I would love to get revenge on the monster that destroyed my brother's arm. How I'd go about it is another matter. Why do you ask?"

"If it comes down to blowing this creature up, give me a call," Frank said. "I've thought a lot about how to deal with something as big as a great white, and in such a foreign environment as the ocean. If you need my assistance, I'll come running."

Then Frank's facial expression became stern. He added, "I'm serious. If you can use my help in any way, I'll be there the next day."

Tim thanked him with a smile. "I'll remember your offer."

The remainder of the evening was a wonderful affair. The meal was delicious and the company very cordial. Throughout the evening, Jose continued his loud laughter, but by this time everyone was accustomed to Jose's outbursts. They knew the chance that they would see each other in the next year or two was remote, but no one made mention of the fact.

When the evening ended, they parted as if they would see each other the next evening for another delightful meal. As she kissed Jose and Frank and brushed away a tear, Catherine thought, *"This is the way true friends part; they retain their memories of days gone by and refer to them over the years. Between true friends, there is no need for tears or final goodbyes."*

The next day, late in the evening, Tim and Catherine arrived in Bermuda tired and weary. It had been a very long day.

Their plane from Belem departed a half hour late and on the flight to Miami, the flight crew was unable to make up the time. In order to make their connection, they were forced to run between terminals and drag their carry-on bags. They arrived at their gate out of breath and perspiring, only to discover their flight to Miami was also delayed.

The evening before was everything Tim dreamed it would be. After four days and nights of forced separation, he and Kate were starved for love. As a result, they didn't get much sleep. The next morning Tim was cranky. Kate was also in a blue mood, so she didn't put up with his nonsense for long.

Finally, after what seemed forever, the plane landed at Kindley Airfield. Tim knew they couldn't let their bad day spoil their homecoming, so he leaned over and kissed Catherine on the cheek. "I'm sorry for my behavior this morning. Let's make up."

Catherine put her hand on his cheek. "You're right and I also apologize. While I was thinking of 'my' children back in Obidos, I was blue. I want your mother and father to love me. Please forgive me. I'm just an old grouch. "

She leaned over and kissed him on the lips, and Tim thought, *"Everything's fine."*

When they deplaned they found George waiting, but Pearl or Kate were nowhere in sight. Tim hoped their absence didn't mean more bad news.

When they met just outside the terminal, Tim patted his father on the back, indicated Catherine with a nod and said, "Catherine, this is my father, George. Dad, this is your new daughter-in-law-to-be, Catherine."

As she hugged George and kissed him on the cheek, George actually blushed. Tim thought, *"That's the first time I saw that kind of reaction from dad. He must like her."*

"You're as lovely as Tim said," George said. "I'm sorry my wife couldn't be here to greet you, but Pearl is at Tom's side. He's doing well, but she wanted to be with him. Likewise, Kate refuses to leave Tom's room. It has been a rough two days."

Tears ran down George's cheeks and he made no attempt to wipe them away. As Catherine searched for more Kleenex in her purse, Tim handed his handkerchief to George while he wiped his own tears away with his shirt sleeve.

They gathered their luggage from the carousel and Tim hired a taxi to carry the boxes and bags. It reminded him of another happier time not so long ago. As he stood and waited at the curb, George seemed lost in thought and made no comment.

When Tim gave the address to the taxi driver and asked him to follow them to the Fitch residence, the cabbie recognized George.

He said, "This trip is on me. Not too long ago, Doc Fitch took care of my boy when he broke his arm and wouldn't take any pay. This way I can repay his kindness. I'll follow you to your home."

"Thank you," Tim said. It was necessary to use his sleeve again. George had kept his handkerchief.

Catherine heard the driver's comments and said, "Your father must be well-liked. That was very nice of the driver."

Tim nodded and said, "Everyone on the islands knows mom and dad. They must have delivered three quarters of the children born here in the last forty years. Yes, it is kind, but I'm sorry to say I don't know his name."

George walked up and said, "It's Paul Thomas. He has four children at home. I don't know how Paul manages on the amount he makes as a taxi driver. He's a proud man. What did he tell you?"

"The taxi fare is on him in repayment for your services to his son," Tim said. "It would insult him if we attempt to pay for the trip. Just tell Paul thank you."

"It's a nice gesture on Paul's part," George said.

During the trip, George was uncharacteristically quiet. Tim allowed the peace of the warm Bermuda evening air to wash over him while Catherine sat beside George in the front seat and held George's hand in hers.

Paul's taxi followed closely behind. When they arrived at the Fitch home, Paul helped carry the luggage onto the front porch and then refused Tim's attempt to tip him. In return for his kindness, Paul would only accept the thanks of all three.

As Paul drove off with a wave and a small touch to his horn, Catherine thought, *"Paul is a class act. Maybe someday we'll be able to repay him."*

"Just set the luggage inside the door," George said. "I know you're anxious to see your brother, Tim. Let's take time for a cold drink. Then we'll go to the hospital to see the rest of the family."

Then he frowned momentarily and added, "For the past two

days, Kate hasn't left Tom's side except to eat. She asked Tom to take her and Bryan scuba diving. Now, she blames herself for his injuries."

"What a terrible burden for a young lady to carry in her heart," Catherine said. "Kate needs love and understanding. I've looked forward to meeting her for so long. I hope my being here won't upset her."

"I doubt it," George said. "Kate's too determined to be distraught with herself. You must speak to her, Tim. Last night she was calling for you in her sleep. She's missed you, but tried not to let it show. She'll be happy to see you both."

"Excuse me while I use the bathroom," Tim said.

Catherine asked, "Can I take a few minutes to freshen up?"

"Sure, Honey."

George seemed content to sit in his favorite chair and stare into space.

The ride to the hospital was short and George remained in his silent mood. After he parked in his reserved spot next to the Emergency Room entrance, George led them slowly through the doors and down the hall to the Critical Care Unit.

Pearl was holding Tom's remaining hand in hers and was half-dozing in a chair alongside the bed where Tom lay, apparently asleep.

Curled into a ball in another chair, Kate was fast asleep. Tim walked to his mother's side, bent down and kissed her cheek. Pearl was startled. She looked up to see Tim for the first time since they entered the room. She cried out, "Tim, thank God you're here. Poor Tom's been asking for you all day. He's in and out of consciousness. Right now he's asleep."

Tim stepped aside so Catherine could move to his side. Then he said, "Mom, this is Catherine."

"Oh, my dear," Pearl said and attempted to straighten her hair with her fingers. "I'm sorry; I must look a fright. Come here and let me kiss you. What a way to meet my new daughter-in-law."

Catherine moved to Pearl's side, bent and kissed her cheek. Tim searched unsuccessfully for his handkerchief and then saw his father use it to wipe his own eyes. When Tim used his sleeve again, he noticed it had become very damp.

"It's wonderful to finally meet you, Mrs. Fitch," Catherine said. "Tim spoke of you so many times I feel I know you very well."

"Please call me Pearl. When he was last here, Tim did nothing but sing your praises. Now I know why. You're as lovely as he said. Welcome to Bermuda. I only wish it were under happier circumstances."

Their voices roused Kate from her slumber. At first she appeared bewildered at her surroundings. But when she saw her father standing by her grandmother, Kate jumped to her feet, ran to Tim and practically threw herself into his arms.

She hugged him tight and cried out, "Dad, you're finally here. I missed you so much."

She kissed him on the cheek again and then turned to look for Catherine. "Hello, Catherine," she said. "I've wanted to meet you for months. I'm Kate, your namesake. May I kiss you?"

Without waiting for permission, Kate ran to Catherine's side, hugged her, kissed her cheek and said, "You're even prettier than dad said. Are you here to stay? I hope so."

The sudden increase in noise aroused Tom from his induced slumber. His eyes fluttered open and he reached up for Tim's hand. When Tim felt Tom take his hand, he turned to see his twin smile up at him with tears in his eyes.

"Hello, big brother," Tom whispered so low Tim could barely hear. "Welcome home."

Tim squeezed Tom's hand and said, "It's good to see you, little brother. Hang in there Tom. I'm back and everything is okay."

Tom didn't say anything else, but his grip increased in strength and Tim knew his brother heard his words. As Tom slipped back into slumber, Tim said, "Let him sleep. Let's go into the lounge to talk."

Stubbornly, Kate said, "I want to stay with Uncle Tom."

"Tom will be fine by himself for a few minutes," Pearl said. "The nurse will come in while we spend some time as a family. Tom won't mind."

When the floor nurse saw them emerge from Tom's room, she went inside to sit by his side.

In the lounge, Tim bought everyone cold cans of soda and cups of very bitter and overdone coffee for him and Catherine.

After they made small talk for several minutes, Tim said, "Catherine and I are fresh. All we've done today is sit. We can look after Tom during the night while you three get some sleep. I'll drive you home and then come back with the VW."

Pearl came to Tim's assistance. "You look too tired to drive, George. Tim can take us home and we'll get some rest. I'm worn out and see my two companions are about to fall down."

She turned to their new guests. "Thank you both for coming home so quickly. Catherine, I apologize again for my appearance."

Then Pearl said to Kate and her husband, "Let's go children. Yes, I mean you, George."

Tim stayed behind long enough to kiss Catherine and thank her for her understanding. "You made a good impression with my parents and Kate. I'll be back in a jiffy."

Catherine turned and walked into Tom's room, where the nurse smiled up at her. "I'll sit with him for awhile. I know you have other duties."

The nurse thanks Catherine and walked out the door. Catherine checked Tom and found he was still asleep, so she took Pearl's chair and held his hand in hers. To her surprise, Tom squeezed her hand. When she looked again, he was still asleep. *"I wonder if he knows I'm here. I hope so."*

It was after ten p.m. when Tim drove his father's VW back to the hospital. On the way, he stopped at an all night diner to fill a container Pearl gave him with coffee.

Tim asked the waitress, "Can you fill my thermos with decaf?"

She returned shortly with the full container, but when Tom attempted to pay, she refused his money. "The coffee is on the house. You're Doc Fitch's son, aren't you? How is your brother? We're all concerned about Tom. Your father sends a lot of customers this way and helped the owner when he experienced a problem with the sanitation inspector. Would you like some donuts to go with the coffee?"

Tim said, "Thanks for the coffee, but I'll pass on the pastry."

He pulled away from the curb and proceeded on toward the hospital. When he was two blocks from the entrance, in his rear view mirror Tim noticed a blue light flashing. *"What now? I'm sure I wasn't speeding. What do the police want with me?"*

He pulled to the curb and awaited the arrival of the policeman. To Tim's surprise, Inspector David Smythe exited the police van and walked quickly to the side of the VW. "Good evening, Tim. I'm sorry to frighten you with the flashing light, but I need to speak to you. Is this a good time, or should I contact you tomorrow?"

Tim stuck his hand out the window and said, "Good evening, David. Tonight is as good as any. My fiancée and I are babysitting Tom while my parents and daughter get some well-deserved rest. What can I do for the police force?"

David shook Tim's hand and said, "Welcome home. I was appointed the action officer for the task force to hunt down and kill the shark that attacked Tom. Now, I'd like to enlist your aid."

Tim was surprised. "How can I be of service? I don't know a thing about sharks."

"Perhaps not, but you think fast on your feet. I heard of your adventure in Brazil and I need people like you on board. I don't have an inkling of how to find this beast, let alone kill it. I hoped you and I might brainstorm this problem. Between us, perhaps we can discover a way."

"I'll be glad to help any way I can," Tim said. "I want this shark dead. It took my bother's arm off and I owe it payback.

"But you have the wrong person. There's a friend of mine

in Brazil who has volunteered to help. Frank Moses is an explosives expert with some ideas on the subject of how to find and kill the shark. If you think Frank can help, I'll phone and ask him to join the party."

"Mister Moses sounds like my kind of man," David said. "The more brains we have at work on this case the better. Go ahead, phone and tell your friend we'll pay his way here and give him a decent wage to go along with it."

Tim shook his head. "He's not in it for the money. Frank helped me rescue Tom in the jungle and they're good friends. If money was offered, Frank would be insulted."

David frowned at his gaff. "Once more, I've stuck my foot in my mouth. I apologize for my comments. Who is this man? Do I know him?"

"Apology accepted, although none was needed," Tim said. "No, you don't. His name is Frank Moses and he claims to come from Brazil. Other than that and his outstanding knowledge of explosives, I know nothing more."

"Your recommendation is all I need," David said. "How soon will Mister Moses arrive?"

"I'll phone first thing in the morning. Based on the flights between Brazil and Bermuda, Frank could be here within two to three days, maybe sooner.

"Until tomorrow then," David said. "If Tom wakes up, tell him I asked about him and I'm praying for his speedy recovery. God bless you all."

"Thank you, David. You're a true friend."

As David returned to his van, Tim pulled back onto the deserted street and drove to the hospital. After he parked the VW in George's reserved spot, he walked through the doors of the hospital.

When Tim passed the front desk, he suddenly remembered he didn't get any cups at the diner. He asked the nurse on duty, Mary Mahoney, if she had any.

"We always have some," Mary said.

She found them in a cabinet behind the counter and gave him several. Tim thanked her with a smile, walked into the ICU and down the hall to Tom's room.

Chapter 20

Deep in the waters off Bermuda, their quarry was experiencing pain and in trouble. After escaping from the shallow bay, the great white thrashed through the water as it attempted to rid its body of the object in its left eye. The eye was dead and gone. Now, the shark was half blind.

In a frenzy of anger and pain, the monster scraped its useless eye socket against the side of the sunken tug boat. At last it was successful. As bloody liquid ran from the wound, the knife dislodged and fell into the depths of the ocean. The salt water stung, but soon it would help heal the damage.

Hunger pangs drove the shark onward and it kept moving. But now, its vision was reduced by half and its depth perception was gone. When it attacked a small school of fish, most escaped the shark's poor one-eyed attempt to chase them down. As the failures grew, so did its hunger. The great white must have food or it would die.

Suddenly, the shark's luck changed and a large manatee floated into its limited vision. The large, ungainly mammal was no match, even against a one-eyed shark. The food filled the shark's stomach for the time being, but the future foretold of slim pickings. Unless it could find a new source of easily acquired food, the great white knew its days were numbered

Then, even with a mind as small as it possessed, the shark remembered the sweet taste of those slow-moving fish that were so easy to catch. Perhaps the outlook wasn't so dismal after all – it all depended on where it searched for food.

Chapter 21

When Tim returned to his parents' home at eight a.m., he found his parents awake and dressed, but Kate was still asleep.

Pearl said, "Let her get some rest, Tim. Kate is more emotionally fragile than we. Witnessing the attack on Tom will remain in her mind for years to come. Sleep is the best medicine I can prescribe."

"I'll drive to the hospital," George said. "You stay here and I'll bring Catherine home while your mother takes over."

"Stay and make your phone call," Pearl added. "You look worn out."

Tim figured the time difference between Bermuda and Brazil equated to either one or two hours, but from the sound of Frank's voice, the time may have been earlier there. Frank might have been asleep when Tim phoned, but after he heard who his caller was, Frank came wide awake.

"Good morning, Frank. This is Tim, your old 'go with me into the jungle and shoot off fireworks while the crocs hide nearby' friend."

Following a yawn, Frank asked, "Howdy, how's Tom doing?"

"He's better. Catherine and I sat with him last night. Tom never woke up, but somehow he knows we're here."

Although Tim couldn't see, Frank shook his head in anger at the shark. "God, it's a shame he lost his arm. I hope you've called me to help you kill this great white."

Tim said, "For a man who was just awakened from a sound sleep, you're very perceptive. Yes, I need your help and advice, Frank. Can you fly to Bermuda?"

"Just as fast as I can pack my bag," Frank replied. "I'll be there as soon as possible. I'll phone from the airport before I take off to give you my flight number. Look for me shortly."

"Thank you," Tim said. *"I'm about to choke up again. It's been an emotional twenty-four hours."*

Without another word, Frank hung up.

Tim thought, *"I can picture Frank throwing clothes into a suitcase as soon as he gets out of bed. When Frank sets his mind to something, look out world."*

True to his word, George returned within twenty minutes with Catherine already asleep in the front seat. Tim went out and carried her into his bedroom. *"Normally, I wouldn't think of sharing a woman's bed in my parents' home. But these are difficult times and we have to make the best of things. If they object, Catherine can sleep with Kate from now on. Today, she's in my bed."*

That evening, Frank phoned from the airport hotel. "I'm on American flight thirty-seven. My plane leaves at 0630 hours in the morning and arrives in Bermuda at five-thirty p.m."

"I'll be there to meet you," Tim said.

When Frank walked down the ramp, he looked tired. His clothing was mussed, but he was ready to go.

Tim shook Frank's hand and said, "I reserved a room at the Royal Palms hotel for the duration. I wish you could stay at my parent's place, but it's full to the brim. The hotel is only a ten minute ride from our home. When we get to the hotel, I'll rent a suitable car."

"Fine, Tim, but I can handle the rental by myself. Drop me off, let me sleep tonight and I'll be ready to go tomorrow morning. I have some preliminary plans I want to discus."

Tim said, "Always the busy bee, aren't you Buddy? When did you last sleep?"

"Don't worry about me," Frank replied. "I'll get a good night's rest and then we'll go after this bad boy shark. With you and me on its case, it might as well swim up on the beach and die. This shark is gonna croak anyway, I guarantee it."

Later, when Tim thought about it, he realized Frank's plan was brilliant. The day after Frank's arrival in Bermuda, he was awake early and ready to get on with the job. Tim arrived with David shortly after seven a.m. and introduced the two men, who took an instant liking to each other. Then the three of them sat down to read through David's case files.

In addition to Tom's attack, Tim was amazed to discover there were five other cases that concerned missing men or women. He looked at David inquisitively. "I had no idea there were so many incidents that involved a shark, David."

David brushed back his hair, sighed and said, "Although we suspected a shark all along, there was nothing to link any of the attacks except for Jock's wife, Leroy Jones and his girlfriend, Sherry. Now we know better. A killer shark has been on the prowl in our waters every spring for over seven years. It terrifies me. It's a wonder we haven't lost more swimmers or divers."

"We need to kill this rogue quickly and very publicly," Frank said. "I have a plan."

Tim nodded in agreement and said. "Let's hear it."

"From what I've read, this shark is a man eater," Frank began. "It likes to follow a boat and wait for someone to jump in the water to skin or scuba dive. Then the beast picks them off, one at a time. Either that or it wrecks the boat and then kills them. The marine biologist was right on target with his report. It's a shame no one listened."

He paused to take a breath and then continued, "But back to our shark. It appears the divers' air tanks pose no problem. None have been found, so either the shark's teeth puncture them and they sink to the bottom of the ocean, or there's some other unknown explanation. My plan is basically simple. We find some plastic explosives and blow this dude up."

In amazement, David asked, "Is that all of your plan?"

"No," Frank said and chuckled at David's intensity. "It's just as simply as I can state the way I would about killing this shark. I know how, but we'll need a long list of technical equipment and supplies. How are we fixed for plastic explosives?"

David said, "We can get whatever you need."

"I hope so," Frank replied. Then he asked, "Got a pencil and paper?

Without waiting for a reply, he said, "I need ten electronic detonators, a dozen receivers and two senders with the same wave length, a small Zodiac, (a stiff rubber raft), with a twelve-horsepower electric motor and six fragmentation grenades.

"If we have access to the Navy, I want to borrow a portable sonar unit and an operator for the duration. The sonar will save us untold hours and days of searching blindly.

"And most importantly, we'll need a dozen sides of beef for bait. I also hope the hospital will give us several pints of whole blood."

David looked up from his note pad in admiration. "Is that all? Is there anything else?"

Frank tapped his head as if he just remembered something. "Oh, yeah, sufficient manpower to do the job and a large seagoing tug or a boat of equal size that's equipped with a boom and power winch."

"Wow, Frank!" Tim said. "You've been busy making plans. Can we find everything, David?"

"My supervisor assures me we have the complete cooperation of all government and military assets on the islands. He also informed me, if I need to, I can invoke the power of the Governor's office. I see no problem in securing all Frank's playthings."

"Great," Frank said. "Let's get busy and round up these items.

The sooner we kill this dude, the better off everyone will be. I imagine the tourist trade has already slacked off. There's no need to make it worse."

Within two days, all the required supplies were on board a large seagoing boat named "The Sea Hunter".

David noted the name on the bow and said. "The boat appears to be quite appropriately named for the chore at hand,"

Petty Officer Lynn Gallagher came aboard with a portable sonar unit and reported to David. "I have two other sailors to help rig the sonar equipment inside and underneath the ship."

By three p.m., everyone was aboard and the equipment was stowed. Ably assisted by Frank and Tim; David, held his first task force meeting.

"Let me introduce you," David said. "Captain Roger Davis is our skipper. The members of his three man crew are William Donavon, Hank Spalding and Charley Turner.

"For those of you who may not know me, I'm Inspector David Smythe from the Bermudian Police Department. I am the project officer for the task force to which you have been assigned. For the duration of our journey, please call me David.

"I'm accompanied by two policemen, Bill Ford and Wesley Adams. You might think of them as two American presidents."

There was an appreciative sound of laughter. David let it die and then he continued, "Our Navy contingent is headed by Chief Petty Officer Lynn Gallagher. Seamen Stanley Higgins and Larry Ziegler will assist her.

"You all know Tim Fitch, the brother of Tom Fitch, who was the latest victim of our quarry. I hope you will get to know each other and work together well."

Before David could begin his initial comments, young Bryan Jessop walked up the gangplank. He carried a long leather case usually associated with a big game rifle and a smaller overnight case.

David turned to Bryan and asked. "And to what do we owe the pleasure of your company? Were you invited aboard?"

"No, you know I wasn't," Bryan said. "I wasn't a lot of help when Tom was hurt, but I'm damn sure going to come along to help kill this sucker. You'll have to lock me up to keep me away."

Tim pushed off from the rail he was leaning against and said, "It appears we have another member of our task force, David. Bryan appears determined to accompany us, and I suggest we can use all the help we can get. He's seen the beast, so he can tell us if we've found the right shark. I vote we take him along."

"I second the motion," Frank said.

David stared Bryan in the eye and asked, "Bryan, if I ask you to do something, no matter how difficult or strange it might be, will you obey my orders instantly?"

"I'll do anything you say, anytime you want," Bryan said. "Please let me stay on board."

"You gave the answer I hoped for," David said. "If you have your parent's approval, I'll allow you to come with us."

From the dock, Bob Jessop said, "He has my permission, Inspector. If I was his age, I would do the same. Good luck and God bless you all."

David stuck his hand out to Bryan and said, "Welcome aboard, Bryan."

After Bryan's interruption, David continued his briefing. "I haven't thought of an appropriate name for our task force, but I'm open to suggestions. Our mission is to find and destroy a man-eating great white shark. Our quarry is at least twenty feet in length and may be responsible for as many as seven deaths and one maiming here in Bermuda.

"And don't forget, this shark would just as soon eat you as look at you. When you're on deck, I want safety lines installed and used at all times.

"Sharks are not my forte, but Tim has imported a friend from

Brazil to assist us. He is also no shark expert, but he has a plan to destroy the beast."

David waved Frank to the front of the group and said, "This is Frank Moses."

There was a small amount of applause, but Frank quieted the group by raising his hands. "As David said, I'm no shark expert, but I know how to use explosives. My plan is simple; we'll find the shark and blow it up. But our task won't be as easy as I stated. We'll need luck on our side and hard work from you all.

"There'll be danger in the chase, so if anyone here doesn't feel like they're able to work with explosives or deal with a man-eater of a shark, I understand. If you wish to leave, stand up and walk down the gangplank. No one will believe you're a coward. You probably have more sense than any of those who remain behind."

General laughter followed Frank's last statement, but no one moved toward the gangplank. Frank smiled at the group and said, "Thank you for remaining aboard. Okay, I'll give you a quick rundown on my plan. Our first chore is to find this shark and discover how intelligent it is. From what I've read, the beast is very smart.

"One thing to our advantage is the fact Tom Fitch may have blinded the shark's left eye, which also might have destroyed the shark's peripheral vision and depth perception. In other words, the shark is unable to focus on its prey. With any luck, it'll starve to death. But our greatest fear is the shark may decide to eat nothing but humans. Is everyone with me so far?"

The group answered with a ragged, "Yes, Sir."

Then Frank said, "We have several boxes of plastic explosives aboard. Unless you hear differently from me, no one handles them except yours truly. Do you understand?"

Again, they replied, "Yes, Sir."

Frank pointed to Lynn and said, "First, with the help of the Navy, we find this monster. Sharks are creatures of habit. They always return to areas that have previously provided them with food. That's where the Navy comes in. We'll run sonar grid searches over a wide area where this beast previously attacked."

He paused to take a deep breath. "Okay, we find the shark. Then what? We entice it into eating a 'human', which actually will be a side of beef with air tanks attached. They'll be filled with explosives and wired to an electronic detonator."

Frank held up a device. "This detonator will be wired to a receiver unit with the same frequency. Again, no one touches this but me. This is the key to our success. Damage it, and we're out of business. I learned of redundancy in the Army, so I have two devices on board.

"Hopefully, we entice the shark to attack the dummy. When it eats the bait, I'll blow the sucker out of the water. Then we go home heroes. See, I told you my plan was simple."

Tim raised his hand and when Frank indicated him, he said. "All joking aside, your ideas do sound simple. What happens if something goes wrong?"

After carefully removing a fragmentation grenade from its packing case, Frank held it aloft. "If I can't detonate the explosives, I'll resort to one of these."

The grenade resembled a metal pineapple with a wire clip that held down a spring activated handle.

"These are lethal weapons of war," Frank said. "They are nothing to fool around with. You might have seen John Wayne throwing similar grenades in 'The Sands of Iwo Jima' and thought he was cool. If I accidentally pulled this pin, the resulting explosion would kill us all in ten seconds.

"You may have heard the expression, 'you can run, but you can't hide'. That applies to these babies. Don't think I'm being melodramatic. I'm serious."

David continued to stare at Frank in admiration as he thought,

"Whoever this Frank Moses is, he's accustomed to giving orders and being obeyed. I'm glad Tim invited him to this picnic."

"Okay, let's get to work," Frank concluded. "Each of you must learn to do the jobs of everyone else on board. We might have to search in shifts for days, so you need to know this boat inside and out."

He pointed toward the stern, where a small rubber raft was stored. "One other 'off limits' item is the Zodiac. If we have to resort to the fragmentation grenades, we'll use the small boat.

"Unless there are questions, let's get to it."

There were none, but everyone knew later there would be many. The hunt had begun.

Chapter 22

Four nautical miles south/southwest of Hamilton Harbor, Bermuda, Petty Officer Lynn Gallagher calmly said, "We have a confirmed contact."

Over the engine noise, David shouted, "Another contact, Frank."

The task force was now named "Shark Killers". It was a very logical name, since that was exactly what they planned to do – at least once.

Today was the fifth day of grid searches. So far, the crew had suffered through five false sightings, four of which were smaller sharks. The last was a small killer whale, and for a while it appeared they had found their quarry. After they trailed the image for an hour, when the whale breeched, everyone was disappointed.

Now the report of a large "blip" on the sonar screen had begun to wear on their nerves. As with the wolf in the fable, no one believed this sighting was the real thing.

As Frank entered the main cabin, he asked, "Where is it, Lynn?"

She turned in her swivel chair and pointed to the scope. "If this is our shark, it's on a steady course to the west at a depth of seventy-five feet. Whatever it is, it's big and appears to be following us. The target is approximately one quarter of a mile off the stern, bearing ten degrees to port."

"What do you think, Frank?" David asked. "How do we know if this is our quarry?"

"We don't, but I'll prepare a dummy," Frank said. "With a pint of fresh blood poured on the beef and the air tanks strapped on, that should entice our friend down below to take a look at what's on the menu."

David referred to the fact the cold storage locker on the boat had malfunctioned when he said, "Go to it; we have plenty of rotten meat."

The remaining seven sides of beef were very rank. It took an individual with a strong stomach to carry the large chunks of meat from the locker to the deck. It was Bryan's turn to haul the putrid cargo. When he reached Frank's side, Bryan's face was nearly green.

Frank looked at Bryan closely and thought, *"The kid's not a complainer. He does everything anyone asks of him. I'm glad we brought him along."*

He held his nose as long as he could and said, "Thanks, Bryan."

Hank helped Frank wire the meat onto a large hook that was attached to a thin steel cable. When they were satisfied it would require a mighty strike to remove the bait, Frank turned to the chore of attaching the false air tanks.

He used more thin steel cables and hooked the tanks around the foul smelling meat. When they were secure, Frank installed an electronic detonator and receiver unit atop one tank. Then, after inspecting his work twice, he said, "It's ready to go."

Frank signaled William, the operator of the power wench, and told him to raise the dummy until the beef hung over the water, two feet from the side of the ship. Then Frank punched a small hole in the top of a bottle of blood and poured half the contents over the carcass. The dark red liquid ran slowly down the side of the meat and a steady stream of droplets fell into the water.

Frank jammed the half-empty bottle upside down into a crevice in the side of beef and watched as the blood continued to drip slowly from the neck of the bottle.

"Dead slow," he shouted, and Roger slowed the boat appreciably. There was now only a very small wake. Frank turned to Lynn and asked, "Is the shark still there, Lynn?"

She nodded and said, "It's in the same position."

"Lower away, William," Frank called. Then he watched the steel cable play out from the large wheel as the dummy diver sank deeper into the water. "Stop it at fifty feet," he ordered.

When the cable jerked to a halt, Frank looked over the rail to see that a trail of blood had spread out behind the dummy. He turned to Bryan and said, "If this doesn't do the trick, nothing will. Now we wait."

Frank walked back to the wheelhouse, picked up the electronic sending unit and asked, "Where is the shark, Lynn?"

"Our friend is slowly moving toward the bait. It's at sixty-five feet and rising."

Then Frank noticed the steel cable that was trailing backward, away from the ship and did some fast calculations in his mind. *"If the current and speed of the ship remain constant, the bait will rise slowly to approximately thirty-five feet and will be the same distance from the ship. That's too close for safety."*

He shouted, "Let out another fifty feet of cable."

At first, the bait sank a few feet. Then the current lifted the carcass higher in the water and carried it further away from the stern. Frank thought, *"That's better."*

The he turned to the captain and said, "Bring your speed up two or three knots, Skipper. I want the bait to rise even higher. I'm not sure how deep the receiver can be and still acquire my signal."

The boat lurched forward slowly and the cable played out in a longer arc. Then the drum stopped turning and William shouted, "At one hundred feet."

"Our target is at forty-five feet and its speed is increasing," Lynn said. "It probably smells the blood. If it isn't our shark, it's one hell of a big fish."

As David looked over her shoulder at the sonar image, he agreed. "I believe this is our shark, Frank."

"The bait is steady at thirty-six feet," Lynn added.

Frank smiled evilly and said, "Thanks Lynn. Keep up the reports. Let me know when it strikes."

As Lynn watched the image of the approaching shadow, she thought, "*Whatever is going to happen, it won't be long now.*"

Chapter 23

Forty-five feet below the boat, the great white swam in a steady course toward what its senses said was food. Several minutes ago, the shark's sensory system informed it of a blood trail in the water.

The hunter was slowly starving. Its daily intake of food was down by fifty percent from the amount required for it to remain in prime condition. Lack of substance had already affected its physical ability, but the missing left eye was its greatest deterrent. The hunter was desperate for a kill.

The smell of blood was stronger now. The great white was on the trail of whatever was leaking this delicious nectar. When it sensed the target was less than one hundred feet away, the shark increased its speed to attack mode and slipped slightly to the left so it could see its prey with its good eye.

Sunlight reflected from the steel tanks that surrounded the beast's prey. The shark's tiny brain recognized this fish as one similar to many it had killed previously.

In past attacks, the shark's jaws were so strong they easily crushed the tanks. The first time this happened, the sudden burst of compressed air frightened the beast. But as it gradually became accustomed to the noise and air bubbles, they no longer bothered the predator.

After it reached the proper depth, the beast attacked.

Aboard the boat, Lynn saw the attack begin. She shouted, "The target's rising quickly from port. It's going after the bait. Be ready."

Although there was absolutely nothing to see, (the bait was too deep and the water too blue), everyone aboard clung to their life lines and watched the water to the rear of the ship.

Frank scanned the water and watched the steel cable that was dragging the bait. In anticipation of Lynn's signal, he flipped up the safety cover of the sending device. With his thumb poised above the button, he waited for Lynn's command to detonate the explosives.

With its poor eyesight, the shark's attack struck near the top of the air tank where the receiving device was attached and broke the wires that ran to the detonator. Now, the explosives were dead in the water.

The force of the attack loosened the beef, but it didn't dislodge the dummy from the large hook. With its teeth tangled in the steel cables that held the explosives, the shark struggled mightily and nearly ripped the entire package away.

The two air tanks hung just outside its mouth and banged against the shark's jaw. The beast was enraged at the inability to eat its prey and struggled mightily for the bloody meat as the cables wound around the hook.

"It took the bait," Lynn called. "Detonate."

Frank pushed down on the red button. Nothing happened.

He pushed again. There was still no response. *"What's wrong? My equipment can't fail me now."*

The great white fought the cables and hook. In a last ditch effort to rid itself of the entanglement, it began a slow ascent to the surface. The heavy equipment tangled around its fins slowed the monster somewhat, but still it swam steadily upward.

Larry cried out, "There she blows." He was unaware his cry was incorrect, one that was usually reserved for whales. But, nevertheless, his message came through loud and clear.

Sixty feet behind the ship, their quarry broke the surface. When Frank saw the cables and air tanks that were caught in and around the beast's mouth, he was amazed at the shark's strength. *"How can it lift the heavy hook, cables and air tanks as if they are toys?"*

He shouted, "Help me with the Zodiac."

Four men ran to the stern, picked up the small two man craft and lowered it over the side. There Larry climbed into the Zodiac, lowered the electric motor and insured the battery cables were properly connected.

He climbed back aboard and shouted, "It's ready to go."

As he thought, *"I hope the shark remains on the surface long enough for me to use the grenades,"* Frank shouted, "Dead slow, Skipper."

Frank ran to the wheelhouse, removed four grenades from a box and carried them gingerly to the stern, where he felt a presence by his side.

He turned to discover it was Bryan, who said, "Let me handle the Zodiac for you. You can't steer the boat and throw the grenades accurately. Take me along."

Frank knew if he had to make a choice, he would take one of the sailors, but time was short, so he said, "Get in."

Bryan vaulted over the railing easily and landed on the hard floor of the small Zodiac. After he handed Bryan the grenades, Frank watched as Bryan laid them against one side of the craft. Then Frank joined Bryan in the small boat.

Bryan started the electric motor and heard it purr satisfactorily. Frank cast off the line of the Zodiac and they sped off after the shark.

As they moved toward their target, Frank hooked two grenades onto the lapels of his fatigue jacket. His companion pointed to the shark and said, "It appears the shark is making headway."

The words were no sooner out of Bryan's mouth before the beast finally managed to free itself from the hook. With the air tanks and smaller cables still tangled in its teeth, the great white shook its head as if it were an irritated youngster who was told to put up his toys. The tanks banged together and made a loud dinging noise.

"It's a shame C-4 won't go off the way dynamite does," Frank shouted. "Try to get closer before it dives."

As if the great white heard his words, the shark was suddenly gone. It dove underwater and dragged the air tanks with it as if they were toy balloons.

Frank shouted, "Damn it, we're too late."

As Bryan kept the Zodiac headed for the last spot occupied by the beast, Frank scoured the water and searched for the shark's shadow. *"I'm willing to try a grenade from this distance. Maybe the concussion will paralyze the beast and I can get in another grenade. I doubt it. I think we missed our chance."*

In anger he shouted, "Just a few minutes more and we would have bagged it."

Bryan continued to steer the Zodiac in circles nearly a quarter of a mile from the boat. He thought, *"I know Frank doesn't want to give up. I don't either."*

The shark was angry. At a depth of fifty feet, it thrashed in circles and finally freed itself from the entanglement. Their weight sent the cables and tanks to the bottom. In the confusion, the meat was lost and the shark knew its promised meal was gone.

Suddenly its never sleeping sensors noted a familiar noise above – the sound of a small boat motor. The great white turned and swam upward. Perhaps it could still find food.

As Bryan continued to circle, Frank stood and held a fragmentation grenade in each hand. The remaining two were still hooked to his jacket. *"All I want is one more chance at this sucker."*

In the last five minutes, a breeze came up and the waves were steadily growing stronger, so Bryan hooked his jacket to a safety line. Since they had no idea of the location of the shark, he didn't want to be thrown into the water.

Suddenly as it powered upward, the shark struck the boat from underneath. The small craft was thrown into the air. Frank flew upward and outward, and landed thirty feet from the Zodiac. The force of the collision wrenched both fragmentation grenades from his grasp.

Although the small craft landed on its right side, the electric motor of the Zodiac continued to run. The propellers bit through air instead of water and made a high-pitched, humming sound.

As Frank glanced at the Zodiac, he realized Bryan's safety line had kept him safe inside the craft, but the youngster appeared to be unconscious. The Zodiac slowly righted itself, the propellers bit into the water and the small boat moved away from Frank. Bryan's body remained slumped over the wheel. He wasn't moving.

Frank knew two things. There was no hope Bryan could rescue him, and the larger boat was too far away to help. He watched as the monster turned and headed his way. The dorsal fin was aimed directly at him. Frank thought, *"I may be a dead man, but I'll take you with me."*

Calmly, he removed the grenades from his lapel, pulled the pins and held the spring activated clips tightly in his fists. *"I'm ready to die, sucker. I hope you are."*

As Frank waited to meet his foe, he shouted, "Come on, you bastard!"

Almost as if in response to Frank's command, the shark sped on its way toward his next meal. Frank's floatation jacket kept him upright and as the shark approached, he stuck his hands out in front of his body. His last living thought was; *"Eat these, you son of a bitch!"*

The shark struck Frank squarely and sucked Frank's arms and head into its mouth. In his last conscious moment, Frank relaxed his muscles and his hands flew open. The grenades rolled further into the shark's mouth, and spring clips flew from both.

Ten seconds later, with a sharp report, the grenades detonated. From where the two antagonists met in their last death struggle, pieces of the shark and Frank were blown in a huge circle. The explosion blew off the head of the shark. Flying pieces of metal ripped through and shredded its body.

Although the spectators on the boat thought the action seemed to happen in slow motion, it was over in an instant. Some debris landed on the deck and a terrible stench of death filled the air.

Aboard the ship, there was stunned silence.

Once again, the small Zodiac was knocked onto its side by the force of the explosion. The motor sputtered and died. Bryan hung half-in and half-out of the boat, with a spot of blood on his left shoulder. As the spectators watched, the stain slowly grew larger.

After he kicked off his shoes, Larry Ziegler dove into the water, swam quickly to the Zodiac, righted it and crawled aboard. Larry pulled Bryan back into the craft and laid him on the decking. Then he tried the motor, which started immediately.

Larry grabbed the wheel and sped for the boat. He shouted, "It looks like Bryan caught a piece of shrapnel in his shoulder. I don't see any other wounds."

Larry pulled the Zodiac alongside the boat, caught a line from Hank, cut the power to the motor, tied the craft securely in place and then lifted Bryan to a sitting position. Slowly, Bryan came around, his eyes blinked open and he asked, "What happened? Did Frank get the shark?"

"Yes, he did," David said. "Are you all right, Bryan?"

"My shoulder hurts." Bryan felt the wound with his right hand and was visibly shaken to find blood on his hand. His face turned white and it looked as if he might pass out again, so David ordered, "Get him on board."

Hank and William rushed to the rail and helped Larry move Bryan to the larger craft. David greeted Larry with a handshake and a pat on the back. "Thanks for jumping in after our young hero, Larry. I'll see that the Navy is apprised of your actions. I hope you get a medal for your actions."

"Thank you, sir, but it wasn't a big thing. If it was me, I would have wanted someone to help. I like the kid. He showed real courage by going after the shark with Frank."

Bryan sat up on the deck and his color was better.

Lynn Gallagher knelt by Bryan's side and carefully tore his shirt apart to expose the wound in his shoulder. It was a jagged cut approximately three inches long. After she placed a gauze bandage over the wound, Lynn taped it in place. Bryan winced but didn't say anything at first. Then he looked around and asked, "Where's Frank?"

"I'm sorry," David said. "I forgot you didn't see our friend from Brazil give his life to save you and us all. Frank's dead, Bryan. The shark got him, but Frank took the beast with him. It was the bravest thing I've ever seen."

"Damn it," Bryan said. "Frank was a good man."

David couldn't think of a thing else to say except, "Frank's a hero. I'll make sure the world knows of his sacrifice."

Then he said, "There's not much else we can do here. Chief Gallagher, have one of your men throw out a buoy to mark this spot. I want to return to bury Frank properly."

"Yes, sir," Lynn said. She walked to the wheelhouse, found a marker, threw it into the sea and watched as the weight unreeled and sank. The red and white buoy began to bob in the small waves near the spot of Frank's heroics. As tears ran down her face, Lynn stood at attention and saluted Frank.

David and the remainder of the crew followed her lead and presented their own tributes to their fallen comrade.

"Clean up this deck and throw the pieces of the shark into the ocean," David ordered. "If you come across any human remains, let me know and I'll collect them for burial at a future date.

"Captain, will you send a detail to dispose of the rotten beef in the locker? I find no reason for us to return to port with such foul baggage.

"When the work is accomplished, man your mops and brooms to clean the boat. I don't care to return to port looking like a scow from Liverpool."

From the wheelhouse, David called the port authority to report the successful destruction of the killer shark. "We have a wounded man aboard. Have a doctor and an ambulance stand by. Tell the newspapers and television stations I'll have a statement concerning the hero of this voyage."

"Will do," the dispatcher said.

Then David sat down wearily and held his head in his hands for several moments. Finally, he stood up and grabbed a mop to join the cleanup detail.

The day after the successful conclusion of the shark hunt, Bryan was resting comfortably in a hospital bed. The evening before, Doctor Fitch operated on Bryan's shoulder and removed a piece of shrapnel the size of a quarter that was jagged on one edge.

"You should have it made into a good luck ring to remind you of your adventure," George said. "You don't know how lucky you were, Bryan. If the fragment was six inches higher or seven inches to the right, you wouldn't be alive."

Bryan continued to smile at Kate, who was seated by his side. She held Bryan's hand and stared up at him with lovesick, hero worshipping eyes.

"Don't stay too long, Kate," George said. "Bryan needs his rest."

"The shrapnel didn't hit any vital organs, Bryan. Your shoulder will be sore for several days, but you'll be fine. Tomorrow morning I'll release you from the hospital."

Bryan glanced up at George. "Thank you, Doctor Fitch. I missed hearing what David had to say to the press about Frank. Frank's the real hero of this adventure. David says he never saw a braver act in his life."

"Frank probably knew the shark would kill him," George said. "But he wanted to make sure he was its last victim. David told the world of Frank's bravery and the local TV stations carried the interview."

"Did they find Frank's remains?" Bryan asked.

"Only one finger," George said. "They didn't have time to search the entire blast area. It's sad, but Frank wouldn't want you to worry. He did what was necessary."

Kate interrupted them to say, "They plan to return to the spot tomorrow afternoon and have a burial at sea for Frank. If you want to go along, Bryan, I'll tell David."

"You know I do. Have David hold the boat."

As he left, George said, "Remember, Kate, just a few more minutes." He knew she would stay longer than she should. *"Who wouldn't want to remain by the side of their hero boyfriend?"*

This morning, a few doors down the hallway, before he saw Tom, Tim spoke with Doctor Peters. The good doctor deemed Tom's recovery as excellent. "Although there's still a significant amount of pain in his arm, Tom's attitude over his loss is better than expected."

Tim thought he knew his brother's mind. *"Tom's glad to be among the living. It's far better to be minus an arm than lose his life to the shark."*

Without knocking first, Catherine entered the room, smiled at the twins and gave each a kiss. "I see you're rehashing the events of yesterday. I'm on my way to see Bryan. Kate is by his side, worshipping her knight in shining armor, so I can't interrupt them now.

"Tim, your father says to run your daughter off after another fifteen minutes. Bryan needs his rest. Do you realize how lucky he is to be alive?"

Tim nodded. "Yes I do. It was Frank's decision to take Bryan along in the Zodiac. It's amazing there were no other injuries to the spectators. Those fragmentation grenades are nothing to fool with. You should have seen what it did to our friend, the shark."

"No, thank you," Catherine said.

Tim chuckled. "Let's go see Bryan, Babe. You can use some rest, Tom. Mom will be here shortly."

"You two go ahead," Tom said. "I'm going to practice arm wrestling with mother. I need to strengthen the one I have so I can beat you, Tim."

"The day you do is the day I quit the sport. I bet Mom takes you, two out of three."

"We'll see," Tom said.

Tim and Catherine left Tom to his own resources, walked down the hall to Bryan's room; entered unannounced and found Kate kissing her hero. At the sight of her father, Bryan broke their embrace. His face blushed beet red.

"Caught you in the act of rewarding your hero, didn't we?" Tim asked.

Kate didn't blush, but stared defiantly at her father. "Bryan deserves a reward for his actions. I was just giving him my version."

"Lucky Bryan," Tim said. "I hate to break up your reunion, Kate; but your grandfather, my father and Bryan's doctor, who is all of the above, tells me Bryan needs his rest.

"We stopped by to tell you to get well soon, Bryan. Now that we've done so, we're all leaving. Say goodbye to Bryan, Kate, and come with us."

Kate frowned at Tim, but said, "Goodbye, Bryan." Then she leaned over and kissed him again.

Bryan turned a deeper shade of red.

Kate turned from his bed and winked at Tim as she walked out the door.

"Goodbye, Bryan," Tim and Catherine said in unison.

"Get well," Catherine added. Then she winked at Bryan and whispered, "Kate will sneak back in as soon as she thinks her father isn't looking."

In the hallway, Kate joined hands with Tim and Catherine and they walked to the door to the reception room.

Shortly after Bryan's visitors left, a young nurse came in to give him a sleeping pill. As sore as his shoulder was, Bryan still fell asleep quickly. He dreamed he was attending a funeral.

Frank was lying in a beautiful wooden coffin that was surrounded with baskets and wreathes of flowers. A long line of mourners approached the casket to pay their last respects. A majority were dark-skinned natives who carried fishing lines.

Next in line were a black man and woman. He wore a boat

captain's uniform. She was an airline stewardess. Then there was a striking blonde lady who resembled Lorna, only slightly taller than she, with eyes a lighter shade of blue.

The other mourners were a mixture of nationalities.

Each stopped at the casket and patted Frank's folded hands. Then they said the same thing in many different languages.

The strange thing was; Bryan understood everyone as they said, "Thank You" and moved on.

The last mourner was Tom, who was missing part of his left arm.

Chapter 24

After Tim and Catherine left, Tom lay in bed staring at the ceiling. The television was on, but earlier he hit the mute button so he and Tim could talk. Now, as light flickered on the ceiling, Tom was left with his thoughts of the future.

He continued staring at his left arm, which was suspended in an upright position from a sling that in turn was attached to a steel support of his bed frame. What remained of his arm was wrapped in gauze resembling a long stocking. The end was stained slightly by the bloody fluid that continued to seep from his wound.

The loss of part of his arm didn't bother Tom as much as he originally thought it would. When he was lying on the deck of the boat on the way to Hamilton after the attack, he knew there wasn't much chance that he could keep his arm. *"I'm amazed Pete saved as much as he did."*

The second day after the attack, a rehabilitation nurse named Sue came by to visit. She said, "Several different prostheses are available for your use. With practice and patience, you'll be able to complete any task you set your mind to. Thousands of handicapped people throughout the world are leading active, productive lives with artificial arms and legs. There's no reason to believe they can do more than you. It will take several weeks for the stump of your arm to heal."

When Sue saw Tom's reaction to the word, she paused and said, "You'll have to become accustomed to the term. The loss of part of your arm doesn't mean you're any less of a man. If you want a speedy recovery, you must face the fact of your loss."

Tom had some questions. "Won't others think of me as a cripple? How do I deal with their opinion? Won't they be inclined to treat me with more sympathy than a normal person?"

And Sue supplied the answers. "You'll come across people like those you described. My advice is to ignore them. You're only a cripple if you perceive yourself as one. Your frame of mind is the most important thing. If it makes you happy, tell people you're slightly handicapped."

"I see your point," Tom said. "I'll do my best. If I can use an artificial arm and hand the way you describe, I'll manage. Thank you."

Sue's comments put him in a better frame of mind, but still Tom thought, *"For the umpteenth time, I'm having second thoughts. It's time to make a decision. I thought about this for a long time and my mind is finally made up – I'll leave the priesthood. It's a monumental decision, but one I should have made years ago. I feel God has sent me a message. The past few weeks have been full of strife, but mostly of my own making.*

"I don't think God is displeased with me. I'm upset with myself in God's eyes. My recent failures made me believe there's another calling for me somewhere. I'll officiate at the double wedding of Tim and Catherine, and Jock and Lorna, but what I'll do afterward, I don't know yet.

"Mom and dad won't understand. Neither will Tim and my other friends."

"They'll probably think I'm crazy," Tom said aloud.

The door opened and Pearl came in. She walked quickly to the edge of Tom's bed and kissed him on the cheek. "Did you say something, Tom?"

"Mom looks more rested today. The last several days have been difficult for her. I'm glad to see her. She's just the one I need to talk to."

"No, Mom, I was talking to myself."

She asked, "How are you today?"

"I'm feeling much better. I told Tim I would arm wrestle with you today, so I could beat him when I get out of here. He said you would take me two times out of three."

Pearl laughed and said, "As good as I feel, I probably could. It is good hear you joke again. I'm glad you've responded to your accident in such a positive manner."

"A young nurse was here to tell me about the available artificial arms," Tom said. "She says I'll be able to function as well as before I lost my arm."

Tom saw his mother's reaction to his statement, smiled and said, "You might as well get used to saying 'lost your arm' instead of 'accident' Mother."

Delicately, Pearl changed the subject. "How long do you have to stay in the hospital? When can we take you home?"

Tom continued to smile. "Now there's a first – a doctor asking a patient when he can go home."

"You are in a feisty mood today," Pearl said. "Good for you."

Silently, Pearl said a prayer of thanks for Tom's reaction to his "accident". *"It will be some time before I can refer to his accident as 'losing his arm'. Some things are more difficult as a mother than as a doctor. Today, I'm a mother."*

Chapter 25

When the phone rang in the Becker household, Jock's mother, Gerda was watching two small, brown and grey sparrows pecking hungrily at an ear of corn she hung from a branch yesterday.

Gerda ran to the phone, picked it up and answered before her butler, Geoff could. It was a game they played.

When Gerda first began dating her husband of forty-four years, Geoff was here. He was the only butler Gerda could remember serving the Becker family. He appeared younger than his true age, so Gerda had no idea how old Geoff really was. Through the seasons, he was always there to assist her and Dieter.

Geoff never took a sick day, but every year just after the Christmas holidays; he would depart on his annual two week vacation, destination unknown.

When Gerda thought about it, she realized she didn't know very much about her manservant. It was curious, but she was so busy with charity work that she seldom was able to answer her own phone. Therefore, when she was in residence, Gerda and Geoff played their little game.

"Mrs. Becker here," she said in German.

To her immense surprise, Gerda found her son, Jocquin on the other end. "Hello, Mother," Jock said. "How are you? Did father tell you of my engagement?"

"Yes, he did, you naughty boy. Why didn't you phone me directly with the good news? Your father is in a dither as he attempts to arrange our passage to Bermuda in June. Have you and your fiancée set the date yet?"

"I'm afraid the wedding is on hold for a while," Jock said.

He heard his mother's intake of breath and knew she would milk him for every detail. It wasn't long in coming, as Gerda asked in quick succession; "What's wrong? Did your young American girl get cold feet? Or did you jilt her? Tell me everything."

"It's nothing of the sort Mother. One of our friends, Tom, the priest who will serve at our wedding, was attacked by a shark and severely injured. Until Tom recovers, Lorna and I decided to postpone our marriage vows."

"Oh my," his mother said. "Was Tom seriously injured?"

"He lost most of his left arm. The doctors say Tom is recovering nicely and his physical health appears to be fine. It's his mental aspect we're worried about."

"I am sorry," Gerda said. "I understand your feelings. Your father and I agree with your postponement. Keep us informed and we'll adjust our travel plans until later in the year. How long will you have to delay the nuptials?"

"We still hope to make Lorna a June bride. We might be joined in a double wedding ceremony by Tom's twin brother, Tim and his fiancée, Catherine. If Tom recovers quickly enough, we plan to be married on June thirtieth."

"I'll pray for Tom," Gerda said. "Give him our love and give Lorna a kiss for me. I would love to receive a picture of her."

"There'll be a package of photographs on its way by the end of the week," Jock promised. "Thanks for reminding me."

"That's what mothers are for," Gerda said and smiled a secret smile. "Your father gave me the good news of your resolve to give up alcohol. I'm very pleased. God bless Lorna for making you see the light. I can't wait to meet her."

Jock smiled at his mother's response. "I'll tell her what you said Mother. Tell father hello and let Geoff know I said he's slowing down in his old age. Goodbye and God bless. I love you."

After she hung up, Gerda said aloud, "Ach Gott'. It was so good to speak with him again."

Chapter 26

T hree weeks after his "accident", Tom was released from the hospital. Since he was unable to attend Frank's memorial service, Tim told him it was a wonderful affair. "There were so many people wanting to pay their respects to our dead hero it took a small flotilla of boats to carry them all. Leroy Jones' mother was there, as were Sherry Lee's sisters. Jock went along to lay a wreath of his own, not only for Frank, but also for Lori."

Tim paused to recall recent events. *"I believe Jock has finally bid his first wife goodbye. In a few short days, his new life with Lorna will begin. It's time to let go of ghosts from the past. I know Lori would understand."*

Then he continued briefing Tom. "The governor of Bermuda was there to give Frank a heart-rending tribute. I know it would have embarrassed him.

"I called Red, Frank's partner, and told him of Frank's demise. Red wasn't able to attend the funeral, but he sent a floral arrangement. As far as Red knows, Frank didn't leave any relatives behind in Brazil.

"David was there, along with all the members of Task Force Shark Killers. Dad released Bryan from the hospital with his left arm in a sling, and he was with his friends on the Sea Hunter for the memorial service."

Tom asked, "Was it nice?"

Tim frowned. "Yeah, except for one bad incident that upset a lot of people. The local TV station sent a helicopter to cover the affair and the downdraft from the blades blew the floral arrangements all over the ocean."

"I wish I could have been there," Tom said.

With only a few days left in June, Lorna, Catherine and the other ladies were busy planning the double wedding.

Since they knew Jock's parents were coming tomorrow, he and Lorna nervously awaited their arrival.

Kate had begun to forgive herself for Tom's accident. Everyone continued to tell her she was not to blame for the shark attack. They claimed it was just bad luck or fate that stepped into their lives.

"*We may have managed to get through Kate's stubborn self-blame,*" Tim thought. "*She seems happier the last few days. Helping plan the weddings is certainly a contributing factor.*"

Tom told everyone, "I feel strong enough to perform the wedding vows and the mass. Father Bartholomy will assist me."

Then Tom thought of his decision. "*I'm ready for the services, but I don't know if my family and friends are prepared for my announcement that I'm about to give up the priesthood. I'll soon know.*"

Across town, it was time for a confession from Jock. Although Lorna didn't know, Jock was aware she had looked through his personal papers. One of his deposit slips was out of place and there were other subtle changes. Jock was a creature of habit and knew when any of his things were not where they belonged. "*I don't mind if Lorna looked through the desk. There's nothing there I wouldn't share with her. I'm ashamed I haven't told her the truth about my financial status. Lorna has a right to know the man she intends to marry.*"

He turned to face Lorna and thought, "*Truth time.*"

"Lorna my dear, I have a confession to make."

Lorna laughed. "My, you sound as if I should be a priest. Have you been running around with some other woman behind my back? So, you aren't always out on the golf links every other day. Now the truth comes out."

At her attempt to joke, Jock looked so shocked that Lorna actually thought he believed she was serious. Quickly, she went to him, sat on his lap, kissed him tenderly and said, "I was only joking, lover. Tell me your story. I'll listen."

"You know how you joked about coming to Bermuda to find a rich husband?"

Lorna smiled. "Who was joking? I was serious, but now I don't care. I've found my Prince Charming. I'm sitting on his lap."

"Thank you," Jock said. "Actually, while you were finding your Prince Charming, you also found your rich man."

Lorna leaned back and laughed again. "Now you're going to tell me you're secretly a millionaire with a mansion in Germany."

"To be truthful, yes," Jock said. "I am rich – at least I will be shortly. My family owns a great number of businesses in Germany. Have you heard of Becker Hotels?"

Lorna appeared to be shocked at the news. "No, I haven't. Are you serious?"

"Yes, I am. What about Becker Steel?"

Lorna moved from Jock's lap, stood up and repeated, "No."

A smile began to form on Jock's face. "Those two are our biggest companies. My father has diversified into several other businesses in Germany and France. If you don't know by now, you will soon marry the only son of a multi-millionaire. I'm the heir apparent to my father's fortune.

"I shudder to think of the total amount of filthy money I'll inherit, not to mention, yes, you guessed it; a true mansion with more than forty rooms. Now do you believe me?"

Lorna crossed her arms in front of her breasts, hugged herself and thought, *"I knew Jock might be wealthy or rich, but this is far beyond that. Jock is filthy rich. What do I do now?"*

She didn't know what to say. "Why didn't you tell me earlier?"

Jock's demeanor changed to a serious mode, but he still held a smile on his face as he said, "I didn't want to scare you away. I love you and wanted you to love me. Now I know you do; there's no question. Don't be angry."

Questions rolled out of Lorna's mouth like marbles from a Mason jar. "Have you told your father about our engagement? Is your mother still living? Does she know about us?"

Jock's smile grew larger. "Yes to all your questions. Two days ago I spoke with my mother. My parents plan to fly here to attend our wedding. Mother sends her love and thanks you for saving her only son from drinking himself to death. You two will get along fabulously."

Lorna seemed to shudder. "I hope your parents don't believe I'm a gold digger. Did you tell them I knew nothing about your money? What a confession to spring on me."

"I told my parents you had no idea of our wealth."

She looked relieved. "Thank you. What do we do now?"

Now Jock laughed. "We fall into bed and make mad passionate love. You always said you wanted to marry a rich man. Let me show you how a millionaire makes love to the woman he loves and wants by his side for the remainder of his life."

Lorna continued to smile. "That's not exactly the answer to my question, but I do like your style."

Jock bent, picked Lorna up in his arms and carried her to their bed.

Later, while they lay in the darkness speaking of their future together, Jock answered Lorna's latest question. "I want to return to Germany and work with my father until he retires. Then I'll take over operation of the entire corporation. Would you mind being the wife of a corporate magnate?"

"I could become accustomed to it," Lorna said. "I can't believe this is all true. It's like a fairy tale and I'm Cinderella."

Chapter 27

With the household a madhouse of activity, George hid in the den, out of the line of fire. To his dismay, the telephone rang constantly.

Friends and neighbors phoned to ask if they could help, and caterers called with questions about the food, placement of chairs, etcetera.

Soon, Pearl grew weary of answering the phone, so she assigned her husband the unwanted chore. George just hung up after answering a call from the florist concerning the number of boutonnières required for the service.

Of course, when George didn't have the answer, he was forced to break into the women's gab session to ask Pearl for the answer. *"Why does Pearl have me answering the phone when I have to ask her for every detail? It makes no sense."*

Although George seldom swore, even to himself, he was tired of the constant interruptions. Then the phone rang again, and he couldn't help himself. *"There goes the damned phone again. I can't concentrate on my crossword puzzle. At this rate, I'll never finish one."*

Nearly at the end of his patience, George practically snarled into the receiver, "Fitch Residence, Doctor Fitch speaking."

A woman's soft voice asked, "Is Kate there?"

"She's with the ladies who are planning the weddings. Hold on a minute and I'll get her."

Before the caller could reply, George laid the phone down and walked quickly to where the ladies were gabbing. *"I have no idea who the caller is, but Kate can answer her own phone calls."*

When George came in the door to interrupt their meeting, again, Pearl was upset. "Now what is it, George?"

He said, "Kate, you have a caller." Quickly, he turned around and beat a hasty retreat before Pearl could add anything. Then George was hit with sudden inspiration and made up his mind. *"I'll go play golf."*

Kate trailed into the den behind her grandfather, picked up the receiver and spoke into the mouthpiece. "This is Kate Fitch. How may I help you?"

"Kate, this is Judy Boyer. Do you remember me on the plane from Fort Worth to Charleston? Did I interrupt something important? I can call back later."

"Yes, of course I remember you, Judy. It's nice to hear your voice again. Are you calling from Fort Worth? You sound as if you're right next door."

"Actually, I'm a few miles away. I finally found time to take the vacation we discussed. I'm staying at the Royal Palms hotel in Hamilton. I remembered your name, found your card and thought I would call to say hello."

"I'm glad you did, Judy. It's hectic here. We're planning a double wedding. My father and a very good friend will be married to their fiancées on the thirtieth of June. All the women of the household are here preparing everything. As usual, the men are out playing golf."

"Where else would they be?" Judy asked. "Don't let me keep you from anything. I'm taking three weeks to rest and relax. While I'm here, I hoped we might get together for lunch one day. I have a million things to tell you, but I know you're busy. When would be a good time?"

Thinking quickly, Kate asked, "How would you like to attend

a Bermudian wedding on Saturday? I'm one of the flower girls. When the ceremony is over, we can meet at the reception. Please say you'll come."

"I would love to," Judy said. "Yes, if I'm not an extra burden, I'll attend. Give me the details."

After returning to the gathering in the kitchen, Kate announced, "I've invited another guest. A friend from Fort Worth just called. She's here on vacation and would love to see a Bermudian wedding."

Pearl smiled and said, "Fine; the more guests, the merrier the party will be."

Kate explained who Judy was and told them of her husband's death.

Catherine said, "I'm glad Judy got away on vacation, Kate. It'll do her a world of good. I'm anxious to meet your new friend."

"She's your age. You two should get along fabulously. You'll like her too, Lorna."

Lorna patted Kate's hand. "I know we will, Honey."

Since they knew there was still much to be accomplished, they returned to the wedding plans. Then the phone rang again, several times. As Pearl ran to answer the kitchen extension, she asked, "Where's George?"

After completing the call, Pearl went into the den in search of her husband. Instead she found a large note:

"I've gone to play golf with the other men. Love U, Me."

With a frustrated look on her face, Pearl carried the portable phone into the kitchen and said, "It figures."

Dieter and Gerda arrived two days prior to the ceremony, and met Lorna for the first time. Although Lorna was nervous about their initial meeting, Dieter and Gerda's acceptance of her was immediate and loving.

"We can't thank you enough for our son's change of character," Dieter said.

"I love you as my daughter," Gerda added. "Thanks to you, Jocquin is a new man."

At a rehearsal dinner held the evening before the weddings, everyone met and got acquainted. Since Lorna's mother and father were deceased and she was their only child, there was no one from her family to attend. But Lorna didn't mind. *"My new family and friends are all I need."*

As George prepared to give a toast to the soon to be newlyweds, he said, "We welcome Dieter and Gerda to Bermuda. Would you like to go first, Dieter?""

Dieter raised his glass high and proclaimed, "May they be blessed with many children." Everyone laughed.

The small church was packed to capacity with friends and relatives. Lorna and Catherine wore identical white gowns with long trailing trains while holding bridal bouquets of pink and white carnations.

As they awaited their respective bride at the front of the church, Tim and Jock stood nervously, moving from one foot to the other. Their antics brought chuckles from the assembled audience. After the service, Tom announced, "I'd like to introduce Mister and Mrs. Tim Fitch, and Mister and Mrs. Jocquin Becker. You may kiss your bride, gentlemen."

At the reception held at the Castle Harbor Country Club, Tim thought there was at least one huge platter of every type of food imaginable.

He said, "It's too bad Jose isn't here."

Catherine agreed. "He would have a ball."

When Judy and Kate met at the reception as planned, they hugged and kissed each other's cheeks. Then Judy spoke first. "Wasn't it a beautiful wedding, Kate, or should I say they were beautiful weddings?"

"You look lovely, Judy. You seem more alive and happy. What happened since we parted?"

"For one thing, I won my suit against Hambone. He settled out of court for twenty-seven million dollars. I wanted to continue with the trial, but my lawyer advised me to take the money."

Kate patted Judy's hand and said, "Congratulations, what are your plans?"

"I'll open my own chapter of Mothers Against Drunk Drivers," Judy said. "If we can get the drunks off the street, perhaps more children will grow up with a father."

Kate asked, "When will you begin?"

"As soon as I return to Fort Worth – but first, I need to find a director for my chapter. It's not an easy task. The job requires a strong person."

Judy glanced at her watch, took a minute to calculate and said, "But that decision is still twelve days, seven hours and twenty minutes away. For now, I plan to have a good time in Bermuda."

"Good for you," Kate said. "Come with me and I'll introduce you to my family. I love living in Bermuda. I believe I'll stay here forever."

After introducing Judy to everyone at the party, Kate noticed Tom sitting off to one side. She took her guest to meet her uncle and said, "Judy, this is my Uncle Tom, the priest who performed the weddings."

"Tom, this is Judy Boyer from Fort Worth. She's another Texan like you."

"I didn't know you were from Texas," Judy said. "I thought you lived here."

"Many years ago I graduated from TCU," Tom said. "So I still consider myself a part-time Texan. Once you've lived in the state, it's difficult to let go of the mystique."

"I know exactly what you mean," Judy said. "It's as if you're part of something so big you can't explain it; like a fellowship of men and women. It's hard to put into words or explain to someone who hasn't experienced Texas."

Tom toasted Judy with a glass of water. "Well spoken, fellow Texan. I'm pleased to make your acquaintance."

Kate said, "Not too long ago, Uncle Tom lost part of his arm to a shark."

Judy smiled and said, "I hadn't noticed."

Tom returned her smile. "You're the first person who hasn't asked me how it felt when the shark took it off. Thank you."

Judy's smile changed to a look of concern. "I saw the news report of your friend who killed the shark. It took an extreme amount of courage to do what he did."

Seemingly lost in thought, Tom said, "Yes, it did."

As she and Kate walked away, Judy glanced back at Tom. *"He's very handsome, almost as good-looking as Kate's father."*

Then the resemblance struck her. "Is your father a twin, Kate?"

"Oh, I'm sorry. I thought you knew Uncle Tom and dad are twins. I apologize."

"They aren't alike in build, are they?"

"No; and from what my grandmother says, they never were, but I love them both."

"I can see why," Judy said.

Strange thoughts caught Judy unaware. *"For some reason, I'm drawn to this strange one-armed priest. What a silly notion. Priests can't marry, can they? Why did I think of that?"*

While shaking her head at her crazy thoughts, she took a glass of white wine from a tray offered by a waiter. *"Maybe it will clear my head of such ideas. You are really something, Judy."*

The day after the double wedding, Tim and Catherine departed on their honeymoon trip. They would tour Texas for a month and end their trip in Fort Worth.

"My partners believe it's time for me to return to work," Tim said. "If I want part of the profits, I should do some of the work."

After flying into Houston and renting a car, Catherine and Tim toured the space center and other attractions. When they attended a baseball game in the Texas-sized Astrodome, Catherine laughed at the message board in center field and said, "I love it."

Leaving Houston behind, they drove on to Rockport, Texas, one of the best fishing villages in Texas, where they stayed for three days catching redfish in Copano Bay.

After Catherine landed the biggest fish of the weekend, she asked, "What's next?"

"Big Bend country," Tim said. "You'll love the Davis Mountains. Then we'll take a raft trip down the Colorado River."

With "that" look in her eyes, Catherine asked, "When will we have time to rest?"

Tim smiled at her statement and said, "Every night."

After stopping in Fredricksburg to tour the home of Lady Bird and Lyndon Baines Johnson, they motored on to Austin and a private tour of the state capitol. While tipping her new Stetson to the crowd, Catherine said, "I love Sixth Street."

"It's a honky-tonking place," Tim replied. "They have an arts and crafts show tomorrow and Sunday. You can pick up some gifts for mom and dad."

Although they spent their days having fun, their evenings were dedicated to a plan Catherine told Tim of many months previously; making love on a variety of beds throughout Texas.

One night in Waco, Catherine noticed a small inverted scar on the cheek of Tim's right buttock. She poked him in his dimple and asked, "What's this?"

"I knew some day you'd find it. It's my last reminder of the Viet Nam War. Actually that's what got me out of that God-forsaken place."

Catherine patted him again in the same place. "I don't understand."

"Do that one more time and I'll never get to the end of the story."

"Promises. Promises."

"If you must know, it isn't a dimple. It's a bullet hole."

"You were shot in your butt?"

Tim grinned and said, "I know what you're thinking. How did I get shot in the rear? Was I running away?"

"Well, were you?"

"You're damned right I was," Tim said. "My helicopter was shot down and this wound was my third purple heart. When you're hit three times you automatically get sent home. I'm lucky. The doctor who removed the bullet said it came from a very small caliber weapon. I'm glad it wasn't an AK-47 or bigger, or I might not have my family jewels."

"Thank goodness," Catherine said.

"Anyway, I caught this bullet as I was running to be picked up by a rescue copter. Small or not, it hurt like the devil. "After checking myself over, I knew I was okay. In the hospital, when I discovered I was going home because of this little scar, I wanted to shake the hand of the guy who shot me."

As Tim ended his story, he asked, "When it comes to my family jewels, would you care for a demonstration of my prowess?"

Catherine smiled coyly and said, "I thought you would never ask."

Chapter 28

Jock and Lorna delayed their honeymoon for two days to take Gerda and Dieter sightseeing. "What are your immediate plans?" Gerda asked.

"I'll list my house for lease with a local reality company," Jock said.

Dieter interrupted his son, smiled at Lorna and said, "The Becker family believes in never selling, always buying."

Lorna asked, "But what about the lovely furniture?"

"In Germany, you'll find a mansion filled with four centuries of fine furnishings," Jock said. "Leave everything behind except your personal belongings."

"I can't wait to see my new home. Does it come with a map to find the nearest bathroom?"

Gerda laughed. "I'll show you around."

When they arrived in Germany, Dieter surprised the happy couple. "Take a month's honeymoon and tour Europe as our wedding present. Then you can get to work, Jocquin."

Gerda patted Lorna's hand and promised, "I'll introduce you to the aristocracy of Germany, Lorna."

"I hope I'm up to the challenge."

Sensing her trepidation, Jock said, "You'll do fine."

With Lorna and Catherine gone, the Fitch residence was lonely.

"I feel like I'm rattling around inside a large empty space," Pearl thought. *"Kate's still here, but she's busy with her school chums. I do miss Lorna and Catherine.*

"Today, Kate's with her friend, Judy. They're shopping downtown in the morning and sightseeing later. Judy rented a taxi for the entire afternoon. By now, Kate knows the islands well enough to be a tour guide."

"Tom spends his days resting and gaining strength while he exercises daily to insure he remains in top condition. Each morning, Monday through Friday, a physical therapist comes by the house to assist."

Pearl's thoughts strayed to something she had noticed.

"Tom hasn't worn his reversed collar lately. He seems to prefer shorts and T-shirts. I wonder why."

Two days after Jock and Lorna left for Germany, Tom decided to tell his parents that he planned to leave the priesthood. He waited until Kate left the house to meet her friend, Judy. Then Tom walked into the living room where George was reading the newspaper and preparing for his daily battle with the crossword puzzle.

Across the room, Pearl was knitting. It was a hobby she had put aside for the weddings. Now she hoped to make baby clothes for any future grandchildren.

"Mom, Dad, I have something to tell you," Tom said. "I hope it won't upset you. I have prayed to God and made peace with Him and myself over this decision. I intend to leave the priesthood."

Both parents were stunned by Tom's announcement. Pearl was the first to recover her composure. "Does this have anything to do with the accident?"

"Not really; my life has been a long string of misfortunes. I intend to search for another way to serve the Lord. I doubt you'll understand my decision, but I do hope you'll support me in what I choose to do."

George asked, "Are you sure this is what you want?"

"Yes, I am. I need another challenge."

"We won't question your decision," George said. "We wish you the best."

"We'll support you any way we can," Pearl added as she thought, "*I'm relieved. Over the years Tom has confided in me and said he was experiencing second thoughts. I know he's questioned his abilities. Perhaps now he'll find a vocation he can excel in. All I want for Tom is his peace of mind.*"

"I'll inform the bishop of my decision in the morning," Tom said.

He knew there wasn't a thing more anyone could say, so Tom left his parents to think about his announcement.

George turned to his puzzle again, but his heart wasn't in it. After she dropped several stitches, Pearl put her knitting aside, reached over to take George's hand in hers and joined him in a silent prayer for their son.

In Hamilton, Kate and Judy were enjoying another day together. When they finished shopping and buying souvenirs for Judy's family and grandchild, they decided to eat lunch at the Buckaroo. "This is the neatest little café in the islands," Kate said.

Judy agreed. "The food is delicious."

"I can't get over you being a grandmother at thirty-six, Judy. You don't look old enough. I always think of grandmas as elderly ladies, like mine. You could get married again and have more children."

"That thought has occurred to me," Judy said. "Do you believe it's terrible of me to think about another man when it's only been a year since John was killed?"

"No, I don't. John would want you to go on with your life. You're too young to turn into an old maid and much too pretty not to attract another man. Do you have anyone in mind?"

"Lord no, Kate. I'm just toying with the idea. If I marry again, it will have to be a special man. John was the love of my life. We met as sophomores in high school and were never apart."

"I know how you feel," Kate said. "I really like Bryan. Although we only met a few months ago, I can see myself married to him. Not right away, but sometime in the future."

"Bryan is a handsome devil, just like your father and his brother."

"Dad's taken and Tom's a priest, so either one is out of the question."

Judy blushed and said, "I was only commenting on how handsome they are. I don't have designs on either."

"Great," Kate said. "After all her time in the jungles of Brazil, Catherine's pretty good with a blow gun. She wouldn't give up my father without a fight."

Judy laughed. "You're a crazy young woman. Let's find my taxi."

When they walked outside, the weather had turned cooler and there was a slight chill in the air.

"Must be a Blue Norther out of Texas," Kate said. "Would you mind if we stopped by my house to pick up a wrap? These convertibles are notoriously windy and I don't want to catch a summer cold. There's too much swimming to do."

Judy asked, "Can I borrow a sweater?"

"Of course - our place is not far out of the way. The taxi driver will take us wherever you want to go."

As the taxi approached the house, Kate saw Tom sitting in a chair on the front porch. He waved as they walked up the sidewalk. "Good afternoon, ladies; are you out for a drive?"

"Yes, we are, Uncle Tom. You do remember Judy, don't you? We stopped by for a sweater."

She turned to Judy and asked, "Why don't you stay and talk to Tom while I run inside, Judy? I'll be right back."

Judy walked over to Tom and stuck out her hand. "It's nice to see you again, Tom. Are you enjoying the chilly weather?"

When Tom took her hand in his, Judy felt a warm feeling in her breast and wondered, *"What's going on?"*

"I'm staying out of my parents' hair," Tom said. "I just gave them some bad news."

A sudden idea hit Judy. She said, "If you'd like to get away for a while, come with us. We're touring the islands and you probably know some out-of-the-way places to visit. The taxi is rented for the afternoon and there's room for us all. Come along and relax. You look like the weight of the world is on your shoulders."

"Perhaps you're right," Tom said. "Okay, I will. I know some secret places."

Judy smiled. "Wonderful."

As Kate returned from the house, she wore one sweater over her shoulders and carried another. She handed the extra one to Judy and said, "Here you are."

"If you'll wait a minute, I'll get a jacket and ride along with you," Tom said.

Kate asked, "What happened while I was gone?"

Through a smile, Judy replied, "Tom appeared to be upset. He said he gave your grandparents some bad news, so I suggested he join us to get away for a few hours. I have no idea what he's talking about. Maybe he'll tell you later."

As Tom rejoined them, he said, "I'm ready." His half-empty left sleeve blew in the wind and flapped against his side. "I'll have to remember to pin my arm up."

He reached across his body, tucked the sleeve into his belt and said, "There, that's better. Let's go."

The driver asked, "Where to?"

"What's your name?" Tom asked.

"Harry," he replied.

"Take us to Somerset Village by Middle Road, Harry. Stop by the world's smallest draw bridge."

"Yes, sir," Harry said and put the car in gear. Then he smiled at the girls in his rear view mirror. "It's too bad the weather has cooled down, but it's still a lovely day for a drive."

"Yes, it is," Tom said.

Fifteen minutes later, Harry pulled up next to the bridge and parked. "Here we are."

"I thought you said this was a draw bridge, Uncle Tom. It's very small and I don't see any towers."

"There are none. Look in the middle. See the long, narrow piece of wood at the top of the rise in the road?"

Judy asked, "What's it for?"

"A sailboat's coming. I'll let you see for yourself."

As the boat approached the bridge, the pilot pulled to the side of the canal. A crewmember jumped out, ran to the road, and lowered two guard rails; one on each side. Then he turned and removed the piece of wood Tom had previously pointed out.

After placing the board to one side, the sailor waited until the spar of the boat approached and then he guided it through the small opening. Once it was clear, he replaced the board, quickly raised the barriers and waved two cars through from the opposite direction.

"What a unique idea," Judy said.

"Think of the money the government saves by not having to keep a watchman on duty," Tom said.

"Boats have the right of way," Harry said. "Here comes another."

"See, I told you I knew some secret places," Tom said. "Have you seen the bridge before, Kate?"

"No, I haven't."

Judy asked, "What's next?"

"On to Somerset Village, Harry," Tom said.

Ten minutes later, they arrived at their destination and Tom said, "Park in the shade and wait for us, Harry. I'll take the ladies to Scaur Hill Fort and Heydon Trust Chapel. If I know women, they'll probably want to do some shopping."

He handed Harry a five pound bill and said, "Take a break, Harry and have a coke at Jimmie's."

After two hours of sightseeing and shopping, Tom led Kate and Judy to Jimmie's for a cup of English tea. They sat down, and Kate asked, "What sort of bad news did you give grandma and grandpa, Uncle Tom?"

"I might as well let you know. I'm sure your grandmother expects me to. Don't be shocked, but I've decided to quit the priesthood."

Regardless of what Tom asked, Kate <u>was</u> shocked, but she recovered her surprise and asked, "Why? I love your sermons. What will you do now?"

"I'm not sure," Tom said. Then he turned to Judy. "I'm sorry to burden you with our family problems. If I've offended you in any way, Judy, I apologize."

Judy had also been surprised at Tom's comments, but she smiled to ease his discomfort and said, "There's no apology necessary, Tom. But I am surprised at your decision. Haven't you been a priest for some time? Why the sudden decision to chuck it all?"

Tom frowned for a moment, but then he returned her smile. "Actually, this isn't spur-of-the moment on my part. For many years, I've experienced second thoughts about my vocation and had my share of problems, mostly due to my own, poorly-timed actions. The others have appeared as a sign from God to indicate He is displeased with me.

"Again, I apologize. This is a private matter and I've burdened you two ladies when you came on this drive to have fun. Let's pretend I didn't say anything. Okay?"

"If that's what you want, Uncle Tom," Kate said. "I only want you to be happy. If giving up your vows is your path to happiness, I'm pleased for you."

Judy changed the subject and said, "This is delicious tea."

Tom smiled his thanks.

That evening, Judy thought she was behaving like a giddy young school girl. *"Instead of thirty-six, I act like I'm eighteen again. Why am I so pleased to hear Tom's decision to leave the priesthood? And the big question; why do I find him so attractive?"*

She knew that answer; after a year of forced separation from a man's love, Judy was lonely.

Her thoughts were full of remembrances. *"When you're in love and leading a wonderful life filled with the everyday and every night pleasures of marriage, including sex, it's an earth-shattering experience to have it ripped from you in a moment's notice. Even Kate recognizes I'm too young to go through life as a widow."*

Judy still loved John and always would. But John wasn't here to fulfill her needs. *"And I have needs."*

She and John enjoyed their sex life. Since their son left home, their lovemaking became even more enjoyable. Then in a heartbeat, it was gone. *"I'm not seriously looking for a replacement for John. No one can replace him in my heart."*

But still, Judy felt the urge to scream at the unfairness of it all.

In the past year, she received subtle, (and some not so hidden), hints from other men, both single and married, to let her know they were available for a "quickie" or an affair.

"I wonder what or who those jerks thought I was."

Judy spurned their advances and stayed true to John's memory. But now, along came a priest, of all people. *"I couldn't believe how my heart jumped when we were introduced. When I shook Tom's hand today, I had to fight to keep from blushing. For a priest, Tom's very handsome."*

And now, Tom told her he was giving up the priesthood to search for another vocation to serve God in a different way. *"And heaven help me, I'm thrilled by his decision."*

Frightened of her feelings, she silently asked for the second or third time today, *"What's with you girl? Is Tom aware of how I feel? I doubt it. The last thing on his mind is a woman."*

Ten days of her vacation remained and then Judy must find a director for her chapter of MADD. Just the thought of having to interview a group of people for the position was tiring. She attempted to put it out of her mind.

But then, an interesting thought occurred. *"Didn't Tom say he was looking for a new vocation to help people? What could be better than assisting women and children who are left behind when a drunk driver kills their husband or father? Wouldn't an ex-priest be just the man for the job?"*

The longer Judy thought of the possible solution to both her problems, the more interesting she found the proposition.

"Is it my interest in Tom as a man that makes me think of giving him the job?" She asked aloud. Then she thought, *"Or is it because he's well-suited for the work? First, I need to know if he's interested. Why would Tom pull up roots and move to Fort Worth just to please me? Will he be intrigued by the offer? How should I go about it?"*

She felt heated and was troubled by her thoughts, so Judy took a long hot shower, followed by a cold one. She soon felt better, and after slipping into her nightgown, she studied her reflection in the mirror and thought, *"I'm still a desirable woman."*

"Would Tom think so?" she asked her reflection and then cried out, "Stop it, you'll drive yourself crazy."

It was a very restless night. Judy took a sleeping pill and went to bed, only to find her dreams filled with images of Tom making love to her.

The next morning, Judy had a thought. Somewhere in her past, she remembered reading the sage advice; "If you want to know all about a man, ask his mother".

So, in a round-about way, she did. Two days after their taxi ride with Tom, Judy and Kate were drinking coffee at a restaurant on the lower level of the Palms Hotel. Judy invited her guest for breakfast and "a question and answer" period. Now she asked, "What do you think Tom would say if I offered him the job as director of my MADD chapter?"

Kate shook her head slightly. "I don't know. Why don't you ask him yourself?"

"I just met the man," Judy said. "He's your uncle. You know him better than I."

"Not as well as his mother," Kate said. "She's the one you need to talk to."

Judy asked, "Would she be willing to ask Tom for me?"

"Probably, or she could set up a time and a place for you to meet with Uncle Tom. This seems to be a sudden choice on your part. Why did you pick Uncle Tom?"

"I thought as an ex-priest with a background of consoling people, Tom would make an excellent director. Since he's looking for a 'new direction', this seems like a proper choice."

Kate smiled and remarked, "And he's also handsome. Are you sure there's no ulterior motive?"

Although Judy attempted not to, she blushed and Kate noticed. "Yes," Judy said. "Tom's handsome and that's a plus for the job. Women tend to listen to a good-looking man, but that's not the main reason. I believe Tom would do a good job."

Kate continued to smile as if she could read Judy's mind. Then she said, "If you say so. I'll talk to my grandmother. If she thinks Uncle Tom will be interested, I'll get back to you."

With her heart beating a little faster after they spoke of Tom, Judy said, "Thanks, Kate."

Later in the evening, while Tom helped George do the dishes, Kate told Pearl about Judy's proposal. Kate reached the end of her story and asked, "What do you think, Grandma? Would Uncle Tom be interested?"

"The job sounds perfect for him," Pearl said. "I can only ask. I understand Judy's reluctance to speak to Tom directly. She's a very intelligent lady."

"I like her," Kate said. "And I believe Uncle Tom would do a wonderful job. Thanks, Grandma."

When they were finished with their chores, the men walked into the living room, where George settled down for his nightly battle with the crossword puzzle. *"Tonight just might be the night."*

Tom sat down and began to read another section of the newspaper. Then Pearl asked, "Could I trouble you for a minute, Tom?"

"You're never a bother, Mother. What's on your mind tonight? Do you need a partner for Bridge?"

"No, it's a different matter. I was presented with a proposition for you by Mrs. Boyer. Judy wants to know if you'd be interested in becoming the director of her new chapter of MADD."

"What a surprise," Tom said. "I had no idea Judy might believe I was qualified. It would be a different way to serve the Lord. I wonder what's involved."

Pearl replied, "Judy believes you have the experience for the job. If you take the position, you'll have to move to Fort Worth. What do you think?"

"I'm not sure," Tom said.

Kate interrupted their conversation. "I can phone Judy. You could meet with her for lunch to discuss the job."

"That is an interesting idea," Tom said. "Give me a few hours to think it over. With Tim and Catherine living there, Fort Worth would be nice."

Pearl asked, "Why don't you sleep on it? If you'd like to know more, I'm sure Judy will be happy to discuss the idea."

"Good advice, Mother. If you speak to Judy tonight, Kate, thank her for her offer."

During the evening, Tom thought long and hard about Judy's proposal. *"Maybe fate and God have combined to give me another chance. It's not just coincidence that Judy came to Bermuda at this exact moment in my life. There has to be a higher force at work. This may the sign I've been searching for."*

Before Tom could make a decision, he felt he needed to find out what was involved. *"Can a one armed ex-priest fill the position?"*

In six months, his stump, *(the word still took some getting used to),* would be healed sufficiently to allow Tom to be fitted for an artificial arm. *"With practice, the physical therapist tells me I can do anything I could do with my natural arm."*

If so, there was no reason he should turn down the job because of his handicap. The longer Tom thought about it, the more he liked the idea. In the morning, he asked Kate for Judy's number.

Judy answered on the second ring, and Tom said, "Mrs. Boyer, this is Tom Fitch. Kate tells me you would like to discuss the possibility of my becoming your MADD director."

"Don't be so formal, Tom. Please call me Judy. Yes, I'd like your opinion. Are you interested?"

"Yes, but before I make a commitment, I'd like to know what my duties would be. Can we meet for lunch today?"

Judy smiled secretly at her success. "Certainly; I'll be happy to tell you what I envision the job to be. I believe you're uniquely qualified to help the type of people we'll deal with. But I'll wait until we meet to discuss my feelings. Would noon at the Palms restaurant be agreeable?"

Tom was smiling too. "I'll meet you there. Thanks for the offer."

"Kate gave me your thanks last night," Judy said. "I'll see you at lunch. Come with an open mind."

"I will," Tom said. When he heard Judy hang up her phone, Tom did the same and thought, *"I'm glad I phoned."*

Just the idea of being needed made him happy. If the nuts and bolts of the job weren't too difficult for a temporarily one-armed man, Tom knew he would accept her offer. *"I'm looking forward to lunch."*

Across town, Judy was ecstatic. *"I must hurry. It'll take hours to choose the right dress for lunch."*

Chapter 29

After Tom agreed to take the job as director of Judy's new MADD chapter, when her vacation was over, he and Judy flew together to Fort Worth. Until he could find an apartment, Tom would stay in Tim's empty house.

Tom enjoyed his new duties and discovered after years of dealing only with other men, (the priests ran the churches - women were tolerated), it was a strange but exhilarating experience to take orders from a woman and work closely with many others. The chapter has gained fame for its work and is now a model to emulate. Both Judy and Tom are very proud of their achievements.

For a while, Judy was able to keep her feelings for Tom hidden in her heart. However, as they worked closely together, their mutual admiration for each other grew. Finally, late one evening, she said, "I can't hold it inside any longer, Tom. Like it or not, I'm in love with you."

"I definitely like it," Tom said. "Until you said those magic words, I assumed I was the only one who felt that way. I love you too."

That night, Tom and Judy became lovers. Shortly thereafter they were engaged and six months later they married. Tom said, "I wanted to wait until I became more accustomed to my new arm."

In order to receive the new digital arm, Tom was required to undergo additional surgery, which enabled his muscles and tendons to be moved and properly aligned to activate the sensors.

While continuing to grow more proficient with his artificial arm every day, Tom says, "I'm very pleased."

When it came time to slip the ring on Judy's finger, Tom used his artificial hand. Just before her thirty-ninth birthday, Judy delivered twin girls. She named them Carol and Carla. The babies are well and growing like weeds.

At the conclusion of their honeymoon, Tim and Catherine returned home. To the joy of Ken and Bill, Tim rejoined the construction company.

Periodically, Tim finds time to play a round of golf with his brother. Tom has slowly adjusted to his new arm very well, but has yet to beat Tim in arm wrestling.

For six months, Tim and Catherine attempted to conceive a child. When they were unsuccessful, they went to a doctor for tests and advice. He told them there was nothing physically wrong with either of them. "You may be tense or trying too hard. Relax and let nature take its course."

They followed his advice, but nothing happened. Frustrated, Tim remembered his vow to help the orphans of Brazil with a portion of his income from the oil property. After three months of red tape, the happy couple welcomed little Carlos into their home as their adopted son. There was never a happier child.

When Carlos saw Tim and Catherine arrive in Obidos to bring him home to Fort Worth, he danced in circles. Now the happy couple helps others adopt their own orphans. The adoption program is a huge success.

When Tim and Catherine returned to Brazil, Jose, Miguel and Red met them at the airport. Jose stays busy flying his latest modern helicopter on charters. Juanita has almost completed furnishing their new home. After Jose loaned his friend enough money to begin a fishing guide service, Miguel has made money hand over fist. Plans are being made to open a small business loan office to help many others.

The oil strike in the jungle proved to be as big as Fernando estimated. The revenue the two partners receive yearly from their venture continues to allow both to finance more dreams.

Red took control of the demolition business, but said it isn't the same without Frank. He plans to sell the company and return to South Dakota to take up cattle ranching.

The murder of Daniel Steel remains a mystery. The file was recently marked "Cold Case". It will be reviewed annually for any new leads. The outlook is dim.

Jackie Ronspiez has done wonders with the children's schooling. Her classes have grown to twice the size as when Catherine was the teacher.

Miss Lela is still going strong. At the age of ninety-two, she continues to manage the hotel and cooks the meals. Tim and Catherine promised to return for her ninety-fifth birthday party. Lela assures them she plans to live to be at least one hundred.

As sometimes happens when there is a child in the home, Catherine finally became pregnant. To their joy and surprise, she delivered twin boys two years and a day after Judy's girls were born.

After choosing Charles and Christopher for his brothers' names, Carlos enjoys helping raise his younger brothers.

The homes of both Fitch twins are full of children and love.

Lorna and Jock returned to Germany with his parents. After enjoying a month's honeymoon spent touring throughout Europe, they returned to Dusseldorf. A year later, Dieter retired, and Jock took his place as President of the corporation.

Within a year, Lorna became pregnant and delivered a healthy blond baby boy they named Frank.

While helping Gerda in her charity work, Lorna has become fluent in German and French. Renowned for her work with handicapped children, Lorna is pregnant again. This time, she hopes for a girl she will name Kate.

Chapter 30

At home in Bermuda, George joined Pearl in the fully retired category. With Jock gone, there isn't as much business in the emergency clinic. Now he lets younger Doctors work the long and late hours. To everyone's amazement, (especially Pearl's), George has become very proficient at solving crossword puzzles. He framed the first he completed and now displays it proudly.

Two years after the successful climax of Task Force Shark Killers, Inspector David Smythe married CPO Lynn Gallagher. So far, they remain childless. Lynn must serve two more years before she is eligible to retire. When Jim Marshall retired, David was made Chief of Detectives. He remains very busy with the Bermudian Police Force.

After two years of bouncing back and forth between Virginia and Bermuda, the Jessops sold their home in Virginia and now reside year round in Bermuda. When his schooling allows, Bryan returns home to visit. He is in his senior year at Virginia State University.

Citing the influence of her two grandparents, Kate is studying to become a Doctor. Although she is enrolled in her junior year at the

University of Texas, during spring and winter breaks, she and Bryan meet in Bermuda. They e-mail or phone one another every day.

So far, Texas has won both football games they played against Virginia. Bryan informed his girlfriend this year was Virginia's time to shine. Their football team is rated as number one in the nation.

Kate smiles knowingly and says, "Just wait and see."

Grandma Pearl works day and night knitting clothes for her four new grandchildren. Carlos is too big for her products, so she tends to go overboard buying things for her oldest grandson. To his credit, George never complains and has been known to accompany Pearl on some of her shopping forays.

Now Pearl believes within two or three years, she'll be knitting for their first great-grandchild. This morning she received the same phone call Tim and Catherine did. Kate called to say she and Bryan were engaged and plan to marry at the completion of his senior year.

"My poor fingers," Pearl sighed.

That evening, George noticed two interesting articles in the evening newspaper:

> Hollywood, CA, UPI--The music industry is mourning the loss of one of its own.
>
> Popular Rap and Punk Artist "Hambone" was killed last night in a single car accident.
>
> Police say Hambone was traveling at a high rate of speed when he crashed into a concrete overpass pillar on I-5. The vehicle exploded on impact and before help could arrive, the driver burned to death.
>
> Preliminary tests revealed the rapper was under the influence of alcohol or drugs. He was not wearing a seat belt.
>
> Funeral arrangements will be announced shortly.

Hamilton, Bermuda, AP--The government of Bermuda awarded two divers with a finder's fee of twenty-five thousand dollars each for their recovery of ancient treasure from a wreck located several miles off the Bermudan coast.

During a diving expedition last month, local cab driver Paul Thomas and his son Robert discovered four gold bars. Complying with the local law, they turned the treasure over to Bermudian authorities.

The estimated value of the recovered items is one million dollars.

See picture and further article on pageA-12.

The end.

Having just finshed Karl Boyd's *The Lost Priest,* may we suggest another of his books by BluewaterPress LLC? If you really liked this book, we believe you would enjoy his very thought-provoking *From China With Love.* You should also check out his website, KarlBoyd.com for this other titles. Additionally, here are a few other titles from the BluewaterPress catalog.

From China With Love
by Karl Boyd

If China is to survive, it must have more land for its millions of citizens. The Chairman tasks his ministers to formulate a ten-year plan to conquer all of Mexico, the U. S. A., and Canada, thereby turning the territory into "New China" while avoiding a horrific third world war.

Within twelve months, the strategy is finalized and the multi-pronged invasion of North America begins quietly. The devilishly clever operation is totally unobserved by the American public, their military and/or politicians, and their neighbors to the north and south.

As with all of Karl Boyd's novels, the ending is unexpected and decidedly different. You'll be tempted to turn to that last page, but please don't until you get there naturally. Why spoil a wonderful novel?

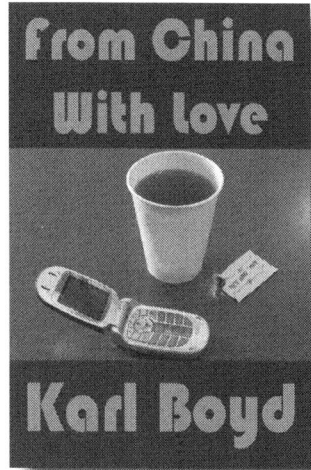

You may order online at www.bluewaterpress.com/china or by mail:

BluewaterPress LLC
52 Tuscan Way Ste 202-309
Saint Augustine FL 32092

Name: _____

Address: _____

City, State, Zip: _____

Phone number: _____

Email Address: _____

(All information kept in the strictest confidence)

Please send me Karl Boyd's *From China With Love*. Cost is $17.95 per copy. Shipping & handling is $3.95 per book for one copy, $6.95 for up to seven of any titles, and $1.15 per book for any combination of more than seven.

Number of books _____ x $17.95 = _____

Shipping and handling = _____

FL residents, please add sales tax for county of residence = _____

Total remitted = _____

We gladly accept payment of your choice: check, money order, or credit card.

Papa's Problem by Patrick Kendrick

Papa's Problem

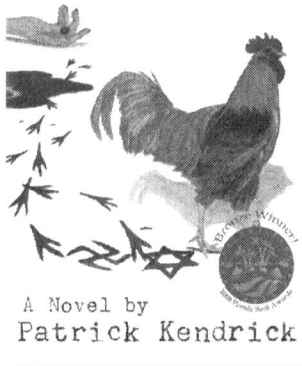

In depression era Key West, Ernest "Papa" Hemingway becomes embroiled in a plot that involves illegal gambling and smuggling refugees when he finds himself the suspect in the murder of a Cuban prostitute. Working with the mysterious former Scotland Yard inspector, Emmet MacWain, they must delve into the dark side of this sunny paradise and find the answers that may help save hundreds of innocent lives as well as their own.

"Rarely have I been so riveted as I have been with Patrick Kendrick's story of Key West, Ernest Hemingway, Cuba, murder, and the plight of the Eastern European Jews who sought refuge in Cuba. Kendrick writes like the love child of Elmore Leonard and Barbara Taylor Bradford."

- Parker Ladd-former host *The Palm Beach Author Series*.

A Novel by
Patrick Kendrick

You may order online at www.bluewaterpress.com/papasproblem or by mail:

BluewaterPress LLC
52 Tuscan Way Ste 202-309
Saint Augustine FL 32092

Name: _____

Address: _____

City, State, Zip: _____

Phone number: _____

Email Address: _____

(All information kept in the strictest confidence)

Please send me Patrick Kendrick's *Papa's Problem*. Cost is $16.95 per copy. Shipping & handling is $3.95 per book for one copy, $6.95 for up to seven of any titles, and $1.15 per book for any combination of more than seven.

Number of books _____ x $16.95 = _____

Shipping and handling = _____

FL residents, please add sales tax for county of residence = _____

Total remitted = _____

We gladly accept payment of your choice: check, money order, or credit card.

Switch-Pitchers by Norman German

The 1952 Lake Charles Lunkers are entrenched in fourth place in the Gulf Coast League when left- and right-handed Cuban pitchers—twins smuggled to Key West by Ernest Hemingway—arrive in May.

Trying to arbitrate between the twins, who have a Major-League sibling rivalry, is Bobby, a quiet southpaw with a tragic past. In the last game of the season, his arm in excruciating pain, Bobby sees something in the grandstands that alters the course of the game, the season, and his life.

From the comic opening to Bobby's shocking resolution to his problems, readers will be laughing and crying at this realistic portrayal of racial tension and healing during the Jackie Robinson era in baseball.

You may order online at www.bluewaterpress.com/pitchers or by mail:

BluewaterPress LLC
52 Tuscan Way Ste 202-309
Saint Augustine FL 32092

Name: _____

Address: _____

City, State, Zip: _____

Phone number: _____

Email Address: _____

(All information kept in the strictest confidence)

Please send me Norman German's *Switch-Pitchers*. Cost is $16.95 per copy. Shipping & handling is $3.95 per book for one copy, $6.95 for up to seven of any titles, and $1.15 per book for any combination of more than seven.

Number of books _____ x $16.95 = _____

Shipping and handling = _____

FL residents, please add sales tax for county of residence = _____

Total remitted = _____

We gladly accept payment of your choice: check, money order, or credit card.

Morgan 41 by M. Randolph Mason

M. RANDOLPH MASON

MORGAN 41

M. Henry Lee's wife of 30 years is accidentally shot by a policeman in a botched bank robbery. He drags himself into the rent-a-captain trade to escape his despair. "Captain Mikey" is an empty vessel begging to be filled.

Lori is not normal. In an act of self-preservation, and fleeing from an attempted date-rape, this hyper-vigilant young woman takes refuge in the night on Tattoo, a Morgan 41 Out Island Sloop - a sailing yacht.

Captain Mikey arrives to take his hired captain position on Tattoo. Discovering the battered young woman, Captain Mikey assumes responsibility for her safety. Neither one has a plan for the rest of their life.

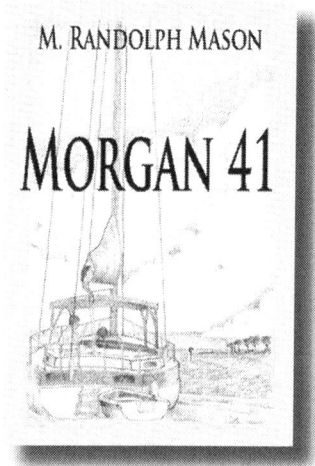

You may order online at www.bluewaterpress.com/morgan or by mail:

BluewaterPress LLC
52 Tuscan Way Ste 202-309
Saint Augustine FL 32092

Name: _____

Address: _____

City, State, Zip: _____

Phone number: _____

Email Address: _____

(All information kept in the strictest confidence)

Please send me M. Randolph Mason's *Morgan 41*. Cost is $16.95 per copy. Shipping & handling is $3.95 per book for one copy, $6.95 for up to seven of any titles, and $1.15 per book for any combination of more than seven.

Number of books _____ x $16.95 = _____

Shipping and handling = _____

FL residents, please add sales tax for county of residence = _____

Total remitted = _____

We gladly accept payment of your choice: check, money order, or credit card.

Hard Days in Paradise
by William Hallstead

Elrod "Rod" Montgomery (please don't call him Elrod), a Philadelphia private investigator, received a call from a Florida Public Defender. Apparently, his ex-partner, Stanley McKance, who had disappeared with all $20,000 of the partnership's money two years previously, was alive and well in a South Florida jail--charged with murder. Irene Hutchins, Esq. called to enlist the aid of Stan's old "buddy."

So, who murdered Daniel Bauer? Rod from Philly attempts to acclimate to sunny South Florida as one discovery leads to another.

This cleverly written detective story is generously spiced with humor and engaging characters. It is an entertaining page turner that will leave you wanting more.

You may order online at www.bluewaterpress.com/paradise or by mail:

BluewaterPress LLC
52 Tuscan Way Ste 202-309
Saint Augustine FL 32092

Name: _____

Address: _____

City, State, Zip: _____

Phone number: _____

Email Address: _____

(All information kept in the strictest confidence)

Please send me William Hallstead's *Hard Days in Paradise*. Cost is $15.95 per copy. Shipping & handling is $3.95 per book for one copy, $6.95 for up to seven of any titles, and $1.15 per book for any combination of more than seven.

Number of books _____ x $15.95 = _____

Shipping and handling = _____

FL residents, please add sales tax for county of residence = _____

Total remitted = _____

We gladly accept payment of your choice: check, money order, or credit card.

Made in the USA
Charleston, SC
03 October 2010